Cupido Sacra

R P Baker

authorHOUSE®

AuthorHouse™
1663 Liberty Drive
Bloomington, IN 47403
www.authorhouse.com
Phone: 1-800-839-8640

First published by AuthorHouse 5/25/2011

ISBN: 978-1-4567-8287-0 (sc)
ISBN: 978-1-4567-8288-7 (e)

Printed in the United States of America

In loving memory of Fred Baker and Gibson Paterson.
Two men who inspire me, I wish I had known you longer.

PART I

Prologue

"Where's the portal?" The young trainee looked frightened. He had never been in war before.

"It's about a mile north from here. I have beings protecting it."

"A mile! We'll never make it that far." The young warrior, who was called Jago, was beginning to realise he could die today.

They both had to duck down quickly as they heard a loud explosion. It was chaos all around them. The Fifth Realm was at war. The many beings that were kept under control by Gathnok were now fighting back. Now that he was missing and Cupido Sacra was gone, the Fifth Realm was being turned into turmoil. Only a few renegade warriors were left, but now they knew the only way they could survive was to retreat.

Marvie looked back at the five innocents he was trying to save. As a blood relative and trainee of Gathnok, many of the beings of the Fifth Realm had turned to him for help.

"I have beings through the portal waiting to help. I just need you and the others to make it through."

"But, Marvie, there must be a thousand beings between

here and there. We won't outrun them." Jago kept his back close to the wall and hoped that they remained hidden.

"Let me worry about that. When I give the signal you just get these beings and make sure you run!" Marvie's eyes were comforting, as he always seemed so calm and together. The young trainee could see his uncle's legacy within him.

Marvie stepped out from behind the decaying wall, where he witnessed utter destruction. Many creatures were battling as the cries of death filled the air. He knew he didn't have long before the mishmash of creatures stopped fighting one another and began fighting him. Marvie twirled his staff round at a deadly speed so that it spun and whistled in the wind. Some creatures stopped and noticed. However, Marvie couldn't get distracted. He closed his eyes and continued to mutter some magical words. A baby dragon, which was rather close to Marvie, began to walk closer to him, but the twirling of Marvie's staff created such a force that the dragon struggled against the wind.

Jago looked round and saw what was going on. He was seconds away from plucking the courage to go help him, when suddenly the ground in front of him erupted. It formed a mound shape that began to mould itself into a large tunnel. Jago peered inside and saw that the newly created tunnel stretched beyond his eye line. Jago was rather taken aback by this impressive display of sorcery from Marvie.

"Go now! It will take you to the portal!" Marvie shouted urgently.

"But…" Jago watched as Marvie knelt down, weakened from the strong spell.

Marvie turned round in desperation. His only concern was protecting the people of the Fifth Realm. "Go now!"

Jago didn't wait as he ushered everyone into the tunnel. He led from behind and forced them to keep up a pace. They ran so hard they couldn't feel their legs until they saw the glowing portal in the distance. There was suddenly a literal light at the end of the tunnel. The other beings didn't hesitate, and he stood and made sure they all safely walked through. Jago looked back. He could see no sign of Marvie, so Jago jumped through the portal after saying a prayer to the Elders.

Marvie was feeling so weak. He stopped and winced. Still kneeling and panting, he knew he had to summon the energy to carry on; he was too close to getting out. He took one deep breath before flying up and hitting the approaching dragon on the nose. Then he spurred his legs to run back into the mouth of the tunnel – at least there he'd be safer from attack. Once in the tunnel he let himself sit back and relax whilst he tried to gather up some energy. The problem was that he hadn't finished his training with Gathnok, and some larger spells were proving to be very difficult. He was about to get up and begin his slow walk to the portal, when without warning flames shot through the tunnel wall. Marvie jumped as he narrowly escaped the blaze, but the flames still managed to singe his hair. He was on his feet again before he knew it and was running now towards the portal. Flickers of fire shot through the wall every few seconds, each time only inches behind the running wizard. Marvie was feeling the drain of casting demanding spells, and the muscles in his legs began to betray him. He knew he had lost stride as he looked to the right in time to see flame flicker through and hit him. The ball of flame struck him hard as he was thrown onto the tunnel floor.

"Who are you?"
Chapter One

The sound of the hammer against solid wood filled the room. The judge had reached his verdict. His hollow, empty eyes seemed to stare at the four prisoners. The prisoners before him stood side by side in front of the judge. They were held together by a linking chain around their wrists, and their faces were covered with black hoods because it was forbidden to see inside the Great Ruling Chambers. The chambers were situated in the south of Sahihriar. It was a place of great importance and respect, and there were many rules dating back aeons that must be obeyed. Sahihriar was the central planet or the Common Realm as some called it. It was the planet in which most creatures lived out their lives. However, Sahihriar held portals to five other realms. These realms were different in their own way, and only the Elders themselves knew everything about them. It was their mysteries that led most beings to stay on Sahihriar, and few dared stray and settle in the other realms. Back in the Great Chambers, each of the prisoners felt confused by the verdict they had just heard. They knew that the day was coming, and even though each had a reason for their crime, they also had justification for the way they were. They certainly did not expect this decision. The Grand Courtroom was empty apart from two fairies acting as witnesses and two footmen to control the prisoners. In front on a high stand stood the judge. On either side of the prisoners, the two footmen loomed, masked in shadow. The fairies flew and glistened on either side of the judge.

The prisoners' fate was sealed. The skinny skeleton judge rose from his seat and looked at the prisoners. He had never given such a sentence before and wondered why the High Council decided to give such an odd order. However looking at the crimes of the prisoners, he was fully aware that none of this was of the norm. After waiting a few moments, the judge left the room in an eerie and silent motion. Before the four prisoners were able to think about what had just happened, the two guards began pushing them out of the room, using long spear-headed staves. They were too overwhelmed to argue or hesitate, so they each began to walk as they were being prodded along.

They left the smaller courtroom and proceeded into a large hall. The walls were lined with wood, and the top of the ceiling had thousands of tiny stars shining from the painted ceiling sky. Some of the prisoners moved awkwardly as the mask made it difficult to see. Other creatures within the hall turned to stare at them. Most worked in the grand building and were used to the sight of prisoners amongst them. The great hall had rich marbled stone flooring, and the prisoners could feel the difference under their feet. This was the only real indication of where they were being led. They were led out of the large hall through a door on the left. Well, they assumed it was left, but they had been very much disoriented during their short walk. This door led to a small, dark, damp tunnel. The prisoners could feel the change in air as the moisture seeped through the masks and into their nostrils. One of the prisoners coughed but was soon hit hard in the side by the length of the spear. The prisoner wanted to cry out in pain but wasn't foolish enough. He wasn't going to give the guards any excuse to inflict more pain. They stumbled on for a minute or so, and the prisoners found themselves occasionally grazing against the moist stone walls. The guards were showing no consideration as they led them through the narrow passage. The passage soon took them to a large rustic iron door. The prisoners were forced to stop with a bump as the guards warned of nothing. Soon the metallic sound of bolts and locks could be heard. The door clanked, and the sound echoed around the tunnel. It creaked eerily as it slowly opened. The prisoners were pushed out into a smelly, dirty back alley ridden with filth and rubbish. They began to wonder what smell was worse – the dampness of the tunnel or the alley. The two guards were mostly shrouded in shadow, but they were small and round in stature. Once all the prisoners had been led out onto the street, one of the guards spoke in a husky voice.

"Ere's yer bags, you freaks!" With this, two large satchels were flung out into the street, hitting one of the prisoners. They seemed to weigh an awful amount, as the force of impact made the prisoner stiffen with pain. The other bag landed on the cobbled back alley street with a sharp thud.

"Remember to take it to the Council of the North. We'll also be checking numerous places along your path as they will inform us of your progress. If you use up the supply, then you can go to certain storage facilities around the northern border. If you try to escape or do anything funny, you'll be hunted down and killed." As the guard spoke, he was removing the chains that bound them together.

The prisoners heard sniggering as they felt themselves being moved against a wall. The guards laughed until the sound was lost as they closed the door with a thud. One of the prisoners was about to question what he just heard, but as the door had closed, he thought it was worthless. All four were left standing in a damp side alley with the heavy rain spitting from the sky. The wind was warm and comforting though. The full moon alongside the second half moon beamed an orange glow across the sky.

Silence fell upon all four prisoners. None of them knew what to say. They pondered their sentence in disbelief. This was unexpected to say the least. The way the law worked, they could have been set free or sentenced to death. This was the first time any of them had heard of such a punishment. As the silence grew, so did the tension. All of the prisoners began to use their free hands to lift off the blackened masks that covered them. One prisoner took a deep breath and then regretted it as the alley air was far from fresh. He tried his best to let his eyes recover as the little light from the early evening stars helped illuminate the alley he was in. He was standing in between two stone buildings. The starlight showed the middle of the alley whilst the two side walls were in shadow. They were similarly sized buildings with thatched roofs that narrowly stuck out on the overhead of the alley. The alley was lined with rotten fish and meat that lay against the wall he was leaning against. A couple of old wooden boxes stood on the opposite end to him. However, if it wasn't for the broken box on the floor in front of him, he wouldn't have been able to see clearly enough to make out what the other objects were. As he peered around, he noticed a few drops of water come from the thatched roof above. It was raining hard, and he found it refreshing, as the masks were hot and uncomfortable. He looked into the shadows beside him and opposite him. He tried to see, but all he could make out was the faint outline of their shape. A tension began to grow as quiet remained. Were they all waiting for someone else to speak first? After a moment's hesitation, he broke the silence.

"I'm . . . I'm confused. We're meant to walk the whole of Sahihriar and take this stuff to the Council of the North and tell them about . . ."

He seemed to be having difficulty with the next part. He looked at the two satchels with a worried, uneasy expression. One lay directly in front of him at his feet. However, he couldn't see the other one. They were brown with large straps and brass buckles. He was sure he had heard two thuds when they left the chamber.

"Essence, sweetie!" The voice spoke from the shadow opposite him. He peered into the shadow, and he could make out a smallish round shape.

He continued to peer until eventually the figure stepped into the light. He was wearing a thick blonde wig that flowed to his shoulders. His lips were a shimmering ruby red in colour. He wore a long pink dress made of a thin, light fabric that gently glided a few inches above the ground. His face had been powdered with red blusher that was applied to his cheeks. His bright blue mascara surrounded his eyes. The prisoner was taken aback by his appearance. He had seen many an elf in his lifetime, both male and female, yet he had never seen anything like this. The silence grew again, as did the tension. He was aware he should answer the elf but was unsure how.

"So, does anyone even know what this Essence substance is?" He peered round to try and direct the question to everyone, as the sight of his elven travelling companion had startled him somewhat. He thought it might seem clearer that he was trying to include the others if he too stepped into the light as he spoke.

The elf smiled as he saw whom he had just spoken to. The dwarf was of average height and was thin in build. He had a look of innocence to his face, with a pale complexion and a small brown beard. He wore dark rich clothing which seemed to have been dirtied and worn over time, making his appearance common and shabby. The few stray hairs that stood on his head were grey and tangled. The stain-ridden clothes made him seem foul and distasteful.

They both waited and let their eyes wander up to the alley where the two shadowed prisoners stood. The elf was beginning to find it very intimidating that he didn't know who they were.

"The judge said something about it being a new fuel substance," the elf responded. He had a high-pitched feminine voice, which made it hard to tell if he was putting it on.

"Well, I for one am not going to touch any!" The dwarf gave an extremely prolonged stare of disgust at the bag. It seemed the reality of the situation had yet to sink in.

The two bags were very large – almost the height of the dwarf. The bags were marked with the word "Essence" printed on them in big letters. It seemed odd that something so trivial was such a punishment, thought the elf.

The dwarf looked at the other two in shadow for a while to see if either would speak, but nothing came of this. He did want to see them though, as they seemed almost creepy lurking among the shadows. So he decided to turn back to his cross-dressed companion.

"So what's your name?" The dwarf tried to sound friendly yet casual, but it was hard as he wasn't sure what he was talking to exactly. Sahihriar was home to a vast variety of creatures and mystical beings, in many differing shapes and sizes, but the dwarf had never seen anything as peculiar as the person standing in front of him.

"Oh sorry, sweetie, my name's Trickle." Trickle gave a

cute little smile. The masculine features of her elf-like face destroyed any real potential for beauty.

"I'm Flick," Flick nodded as a sign of greeting.

"So . . ."

It had become very awkward indeed. What do you say to a complete stranger meeting for the first time in an alley after a prison sentence? Flick was trying to break the ice, he wanted it to be relaxed, he wanted to meet the others and find out the reason for Trickle's attire.

"So, are you a performer?" Flick's eyes widened as he noticed Trickle's expression sadden. He couldn't believe his own stupidity at asking such an inappropriate question.

Trickle felt a twinge of pain. She hated people not realising her situation on their own. Why did she have to continue to explain herself? Despite the annoyance, she took a deep breath and tried to stay calm. He was just interested, and he did kind of have a right to know if they were to travel together. She just wished she didn't have to.

"Oh, um . . . no. I have a firm belief I am a she-elf, and I don't know how you're gonna' deal with that, but I didn't choose this and neither did you, so I don't care what you think of it. Just keep your opinions to yourself!"

Trickle bit her lip to avoid saying any more. She didn't want to sound so defensive, and in her mind it was a lot less hostile. She had said it so many times now that it had become routine, and a tiresome irritation. She thought she ought to move on before she accidentally offended Flick or anyone else listening. The thought of travelling with criminals made her uneasy. Her "crime" was due to discrimination against her appearance, and there was no real justification to call it a crime. The idea that she had no clue what these people had done made her nervous.

"Oh, I didn't mean to offend…" Flick's voice trailed off.

His mouth talking before his brain could think had caused him many problems over the years.

"It's alright," Trickle attempted a smile, but it didn't really convince Flick that there was no harm done. "So what breed of dwarf are you?"

"I'm a Surthan breed," Flick replied.

A cough from the shadow on the right announced someone's presence. Just then one of the other prisoners took a stride into the light. He was tall with grey hair that was long, and he looked rather smart. His beard covered his whole chest and nearly touched the tip of his belly. He had a long blue velvet coat that stretched down to his feet. He had a tiny nose on which his thin glasses lay. His bright blue eyes shone through the spectacles like a headlamp in fog. His wrinkles gave his face more definition and wisdom. He looked old, weary, and tired, but he also gave the feeling of warmth. He held in his right hand a long piece of wood stained a forest green. His stance made him look impressive and bold. Flick and Trickle had to look up in awe.

"Umm . . . hi…" Trickle waved and then realised how stupid she looked. "This is Flick, and I'm Trickle."

Flick just stood in awe, not even managing the feeble nod he had given Trickle.

"Greetings!" The wizard's voice was old and full of wisdom. Flick and Trickle looked very impressed but said nothing.

"I look forward to properly getting to know you all. My name is EggWiff."

"Thanks," Flick muttered.

Trickle began to peer round the side of EggWiff towards the last remaining mystery within the group. She slowly walked past EggWiff, and Flick watched her go to speak to the criminal. As Trickle brushed past, EggWiff shot out his arm and grabbed Trickle's hand. She spun round with a confused look and saw his magnificent blue eyes staring into hers.

"They told me to give you this." EggWiff's eyes looked different, his lips quivered, and his voice was low. He threw a parchment scroll into the hands of Trickle.

Trickle didn't say anything. Instead she pulled away the tattered string and rolled out the parchment. It was a fresh scroll, the ink smelled new, and it showed no sign of discolouring. Trickle rolled it down to see the first words written it big letters at the top.

ATTENTION TO ALL PRISONERS TRAVELLING WITH EGGWIFF

Trickle saw this and then waved Flick over. She contemplated gesturing towards the shadows but whatever it was could just read it later. Once Flick was by Trickle's side, they continued to read.

ATTENTION TO ALL PRISONERS TRAVELLING WITH EGGWIFF

WARNING: THE WIZARD YOU ARE TRAVELLING WITH IS VERY DANGEROUS. HE HAS A UNIQUE CONDITION WHERE HE IS PRONE TO DRASTIC CHANGES IN PERSONALITY AND BEHAVIOUR. THE HIGH COUNCIL WILL OVERLOOK ANY UNFORTUNATE EVENT IF YOU WISH TO DEFEND YOURSELVES.

Trickle and Flick looked up alarmed at EggWiff. He stood and did nothing.

"Do you know what this says, EggWiff?"

EggWiff nodded.

"And is it true?" Trickle was finding it hard to find any truth in this. He looked so old and frail. How could he harm anyone or anything?

"I do have a condition. It is known as SplitrianPersonosa. My body made two minds to handle the magic. I am two beings as one, although I swear to you that I won't harm you." EggWiff sounded sincere and genuine.

Flick glanced at Trickle. She wasn't his usual choice of friends, but he wanted some reassurance that he wasn't in some surreal nightmare. Trickle gave a smile to make Flick aware of how blatant his uncertainty was.

"Right, EggWiff, we'll try and remember that!" Trickle seemed to accept it as she smiled comfortingly at the wizard. So far her punishment was nothing like she had expected. Even the people didn't fit her preconception of the typical prisoner. She wasn't sure yet whether that was a good sign or bad. EggWiff smiled to say thank you as wrinkles creased the end of his mouth.

"EggWiff, what was your crime?" Flick asked. Trickle could see the compassion, but Flick was still a little on edge. Trickle couldn't help but give Flick a disgruntled look for staying with the subject.

"Well, I…"

EggWiff was interrupted by a loud yelp from the shadows behind him. Flick and Trickle also looked as the last prisoner had stepped out into the light. Trickle gave a little gasp, and Flick jumped. EggWiff, however, just stood and watched curiously.

A white skeleton was now standing in the centre of the alley. He was looking up at the sky, and his pure white bones glistened as the light reflected from him. The skeleton, however, was cowering as tiny drops of rain fell onto him. The group peered, seeing the flash of chalky white bone. He seemed to be purposely hiding. as if he was edging towards the light and then backing away again. Either way, he seemed confused and frightened.

"Are you okay?" Trickle sat up and edged towards the shadowy end of the ally with caution.

"Fine," The skeleton said, hiding most of himself within the shadow.

"I know this punishment seems a little weird, but we'll get through it. Don't worry." Trickle eased slowly towards the shadow; she felt a slight sense of fear but continued nonetheless.

Flick's face suddenly fell with disbelief. He looked around as if hoping someone would jump out and pretend it was just a game. Unfortunately, he knew only too well that it wasn't. Trickle, who had stopped still, looked back to see Flick's reaction. She ignored his undisguised expression of surprise. She glanced at EggWiff, who seemed to have a face ridden with curiosity. She also was intrigued and decided to continue to focus on the frightened skeleton.

"It's just that things make me get upset, and I cry a lot and feel down over simple things." The Skeleton's speech had become distorted as if he was struggling to say the words. Afterwards, you could hear him absorbing some more air as it howled through his empty body. He continued to dive back and forth from the light and shadow.

"Umm, sure. But you're not sad now, right?" Trickle looked back at EggWiff. He seemed wise and powerful, but up to this point he had been pretty useless.

Trickle turned back to the skeleton. He was still jumping back and forth and huddling from the rain. He seemed in a bad way.

"Hey, sweetie, it's okay. Seems like we've all got stuff to deal with. Besides, trust me, you don't want to see how easily I get upset or annoyed if I can't find my lipstick!" Flick was silently hoping that her comment was a misguided joke.

Trickle had gotten closer to the skeleton. She was now able to look into his deep black sockets. Her green eyes were comforting, but not nearly as striking as EggWiff's. "It will be okay, I promise. What's your name?"

"M – Morbid" His jaw moved up and down; it seemed weird hearing sound so clearly from such a rigid motion.

Trickle looked back slightly concerned, and Flick's eyes widened. Morbid took a peek and began to huddle back in the shadows. EggWiff just stood and watched as if he was fascinated by the skeleton. Morbid seemed so scary and dominating, yet he was acting like an insecure child.

"Well I'm… "

"I heard you introduce yourselves before, Trickle." Morbid stayed in the shadows.

"Oh that's good, sweetie." With this Trickle took a few steps back and looked at the others.

The group stood in the alleyway for a further few minutes of silence looking at each other and taking in each other's oddities and such. They wanted to say something, but now they knew each other's names it just seemed tense again.

"So where shall we begin? It'll be even darker soon, and I vote we set up camp or find somewhere to stay before it gets too late." Flick was looking up at the stars.

He sounded commanding and level-headed even after his poor reactions towards the others. However, he didn't like the quiet and was hoping this would spark some kind of conversation or movement.

"There is a village only a few miles from here. We should rest there and decide our best course of action tomorrow." EggWiff peered at the smaller companions and then back at the skeleton.

"Umm, okay, sure, well, you lead the way!" Trickle

smiled and then stopped as she looked at the Essence. "Wait! Who's going to carry these?"

"We'll just have to take turns, I guess. Change every five minutes? Ten?" Flick didn't seem too confident when it came to addressing the group, which was odd as he had just broken the silence before. Was he putting it on?

"Ten minutes shall do." EggWiff nodded a reassuring smile. The smile then spread to Trickle as she saw the first sign of compassion in EggWiff.

EggWiff went and picked up the satchel and couldn't resist a quick peek inside. The Essence looked like large pieces of grey rock that glistened slightly in the light. It wasn't anything impressive. Even though the satchel was heavy, EggWiff managed to carry it with ease by the long handle in one hand whilst holding his staff in another. Flick walked over and found the other satchel that was initially by his feet. He heaved as he picked it up but then pretended it was fine. He managed to slide the handle over his shoulder and instantly felt the weight. As they walked, Trickle stopped and waited for Morbid. He lingered for a while and seemed to bend down and pick up a rag from the alley floor. At first Trickle couldn't understand what he was doing, but soon it was draped over him like a robe with a large hood. The robe looked stained and dirty and had clearly been worn away over time. Once the hood was up, Morbid began slowly coming from the shadows and walked towards and then past Trickle. He didn't say anything but hung his head low and followed the others. Trickle stopped and looked at all three of them walking off into the distance. Once she had heard the deep sounding judge tell them their punishment, she had the feeling of pure worry. Never had she been so scared. She stood letting the relief wash over her, and she began to clop her heels on the cobbled street as she followed them.

EggWiff led at the front followed by Flick, Morbid, and then Trickle. They had been walking for around twenty minutes when suddenly he paused as if he realised something all of a sudden. He froze dead still in the middle of the path.

"What's up, EggWiff?" Flick asked.

Flick moved cautiously to see if anything was wrong up ahead, but all seemed clear. Just then a green smoke appeared around EggWiff. It only lasted for a second, but it was noticeable. The whole group stood back curiously. EggWiff stood perfectly still. They now stood together staring at EggWiff.

"Eww! What is that stench?" Flick was holding his nose.

"It smells awful." Trickle began to cough slightly; the smell was unreal. EggWiff was still lifeless.

"It smells of…" Flick began to sniff. He knew what the smell was but couldn't quite put his finger on it.

"Egg . . . It smells of rotten egg."

Morbid didn't seem too affected by the smell. Trickle wondered if that was because he was a skeleton, or maybe being dead meant you smelt really bad things all the time.

"Great! So it wasn't just a name!" Flick shouted. Trickle nudged him to shut him up as EggWiff still hadn't moved.

Flick sighed heavily. He looked at Morbid and Trickle who were staring back at him. They both motioned to EggWiff, gesturing Flick to talk to him. Flick gave a disgruntled look at them both and then took a step forward. Thankfully, the stench was fading.

"EggWiff, what just happened?" Flick spoke with an unclear tone as he edged around EggWiff to get a better view of EggWiff's face.

EggWiff turned his head at the sight of this small creature. His eyes were creased in a confused expression.

"What the blooming' heck 'ave I gotten myself into?" EggWiff's voice was lively, and he had more energy. EggWiff looked back at Trickle and Morbid, which was instantly a bad idea. "Whoa! Cor blimey! I know I am meant to be wise and understanding, but this is absurd! Can anyone explain why I am travelling with a circus?" EggWiff looked around awaiting a response.

Trickle's head hung low with shame. Morbid began to whimper softly and turned away. Flick realised that the personality change the scroll warned of had happened, and he walked up to EggWiff slowly with a stern expression and then leaned in close to his ear.

"He warned us about you. So say what you want, do what you want, because it doesn't matter. Get in my way and I will hurt you." Flick whispered, but it still lingered with bitterness.

He leaned out and walked on down the path as if nothing had happened. EggWiff looked startled and rather taken back at such a small creature confronting him. Trickle edged past him keeping her head low, and Morbid sniffled as he walked past. EggWiff paused before following on behind reluctantly.

Trickle didn't like the new EggWiff, How dare he insult them like that? She no longer cared what he went through or had been through. If this was the person she had to travel with, then suddenly her punishment seemed like what it was – a punishment. She looked back at Morbid who was whimpering behind her. She wanted to help but what could she say?

They were walking along a grassy path in the rain. It made the ground soft, but it was bearable. Fields lined either side and stretched for miles. On the far right they could see the darkened outlines of some forest. Flick didn't like the dark fields. They seemed scary and so vast. He still wasn't used to seeing a skeleton appear from the corner of his eye either. Flick was still so annoyed with EggWiff. Perhaps he had been a little harsh, but he didn't like his arrogance. Plus, if he had to put up with that smell every few minutes, he was going to go insane.

They walked in a new pattern after that. Flick led with Trickle at the front, and Morbid became distant once he had cried and remained lingering in the middle. EggWiff was left slumped at the back. Nothing much had been said until . . .

"Hey, any of you guys got a drink? You know one to get me juices flowing." EggWiff beamed a smile maybe to encourage the others.

The group stopped, and Flick looked back annoyed. Flick opened his mouth and stepped forward to have words with him once again, but then Trickle walked up and placed a hand on Flick's arm. She smiled at Flick and then walked up to EggWiff. She pulled out from her bag a tall thin bottle with an orange water substance in it and then slowly, almost cowardly . . .

"You can have this." She gave a little misguided smile and then walked on back by Flick.

Trickle was still annoyed at EggWiff, but she had forced herself to calm down somewhat. She couldn't help remember the nice wise man she first met. If this was a "condition", then it wasn't fair to blame him. It was that, and also the fact she didn't want Flick to be getting into a fight anytime soon. He seemed so angry.

EggWiff smiled briefly but then tore the bottle cap off and took a swig of the drink. Flick leaned in and whispered something in Trickle's ear about "alcoholic". Morbid looked up at the two new friends and looked back at the wizard, who was now already staggering and singing a lively tune to himself. As he wondered along the path, it became obvious that he was a light drinker. Morbid was feeling left out. He didn't mind it so much though. Over the years it had grown comforting; not belonging made him feel free.

They walked on for about an hour. The warm breeze began to feel sticky under their clothes. The weight of their punishment began to take toll as they all took turns in carrying the Essence. Eventually they managed to get to the village. The lights looked inviting as the whole village glowed. It was so small that it couldn't really be called a village. Only ten houses on each side lined the path. It was nice as the houses matched, and it looked pleasant. Flick was glad of some light and other people. He felt very aware who and what he had been travelling with for the last hour or so.

EggWiff, with his bottle now long finished, pined for a quick trip to the inn. They all agreed on this, as they thought they deserved a rest. Luckily, just before they arrived, EggWiff managed to revert to his normal personality. The stench hit them just before the smoke. The group had to wait outside and wave off the air before entering. As they did so, Morbid dropped his travelling cloak on the floor outside. Trickle now understood why it was so dirty. The inn was a small building with a thatched roof. The smoke flowed out into the ever darkening starry night and drifted swiftly through the air. The old pub sign looked torn and worn and hung eerily from the hinges above. It read "Rock-a-Hula's Fecki & Baby". From the doorstep you could hear the faint music seeping through the door. They took a deep breath and then took a step inside.

They were confronted by warmth that seemed to overcome their bodies. They had got rather wet whilst walking in the rain, so it was a welcome change to be dry. The inn was a busy place, full of all sorts of mystical folk. They stepped in the doorway casting a strange shadow silhouette on the stone floor. Silence fell in the room with a thud as every single eye in the room turned to stare at them. It wasn't so much what they were as such, more how strange it was to come across them all travelling together; it seemed like an odd group of companions. Trickle's bizarre appearance was enough to draw attention. Flick knew that if EggWiff were to turn back into his drunken form, then his reaction to the inn would be much more enthusiastic. Instead he stood still, tall, and proud. The group had already decided they much preferred the wise EggWiff; the other one was just an annoyance.

The inn with its stone floor and low-hung wooden ceilings looked so cosy. To the left of the main door were four or five tables with chairs dotted around. This small area was slightly raised, as two steps lead down to what seemed like another drinking area. However, these seats looked more comfortable and less formal. A roaring fire stood on the back wall. In the back left hand corner stood a curved bar with a barbarian woman who was cradling a baby behind the counter. The door opened out with the right wall coming off it, so it was a rather small establishment.

They took a few uneasy steps forward, and after the initial shock the inn began to come alive with banter once again. Trickle didn't seem too affected by the extra attention and seemed rather pleased. They all sat down at a table and sighed, as they were finally able to release their grasp of the Essence.

"Wow! I knew I was attractive, but that was amazing." Trickle smiled cheekily to herself and whipped out some lipstick.

Silence fell upon the group. They were unsure what their next course of action should be, and they were still in shock and bewilderment at the day's events. The silence was interrupted by a strange chattering sound. It was harsh and grinding and was bellowing out over through the inn. They stared round for a while and noticed attention had been redirected at their table. The group stared at Morbid, who was hiding his face behind his skinny pale fingers. Flick gave a troubled look at EggWiff, who in return gave a blank expression.

"I – I don't mean to cry. It's just being stared at like

that. It reminded me of when I was…" Morbid's speech faded into further chattering that seemed to get louder and louder.

"Oh, you were crying? For a second there I thought you swallowed an electric eel," Trickle giggled to herself. She looked around and noticed Flick was looking at her harshly. She stopped immediately.

People began to stare. Even the fairies at the bar began to dance in the air closer towards them. EggWiff sat uneasily. Usually wizards of such a high order wouldn't be seen dead in such a lower-class establishment. Trickle looked back at the bar and leaned in closer towards Flick.

"Flick, sweetie, shouldn't you go to the bar and tell them about the Essence?" Trickle gave a little wink and sat back straight.

Flick welcomed the chance to relieve himself of the insanity that had taken over his life. He hauled the bag of Essence and began to drag it across the inn floor. As he did so, he muttered under his breath something about toilets and humming. Flick walked over to the bar. Fecki the barbarian had long brown hair and hazel eyes. Flick couldn't help but think this inn wasn't very "rocking" or "hulla-ing". Fecki and her baby stood behind the bar serving the few regulars. She seemed uncomfortable at Flick's approach, and before he could get to her, she moved into the back room. Flick thought it odd to see a timid barbarian but thought he'd sit at the bar and wait.

However, Flick didn't know that the prisoners had just given Fecki the information she had been awaiting for many months. Still cradling her baby, Fecki prepared her journey to tell the others of her news.

Trickle sat and looked around smiling at anybody who still stared. She was about to make conversation with EggWiff, when she found herself shrouded in a green mist.

The stench hit the table like an apple falling from a tree. Trickle gasped as the smell invaded her nostrils again. Flick shook his head and hurried away, whilst Morbid continued to grind his jaw as if nothing had happened. As Trickle screwed up her face, she was painfully aware of what just happened and what was about to happen.

"Whoa! An inn! This is bloody brilliant! Anyone up for a drink?" EggWiff's voice bellowed throughout the inn and dominated the entire area. Two dwarves at a nearby table got up and walked away after giving an expression of disgust. Flick stopped and looked back and felt like crying. Trickle was bad enough, and Morbid's chattering was almost becoming unbearable, but the last thing he needed was to have a drunken phoney wizard as well. He figured he'd play it safe and stay at the bar. Trickle sat uncomfortably noticing people rapidly leaving their side.

"Yes, yes, we are, sweetie, but you have to shut up!" Trickle pulled EggWiff's cloak to make him sit down as he was beginning to stand up. He already seemed drunk.

"And who are you to tell me what to do?" EggWiff stared at Trickle smugly.

Trickle smiled. She was so small in comparison to the tall grand wizard, even given the fact EggWiff was now slumped on his chair. She leaned in a little so he would hear her.

"I'm the one wearing high-heeled boots, who just got them dirtied, who is tired. So if you don't want to see my boots and get a drink, I suggest you shut up, okay?" Trickle didn't waver from his eye. She just smiled and sat back.

"Okay, small thing, I promise I am sorry." EggWiff sat up straight and looked round the table. However, his eyes saw Morbid. EggWiff now couldn't restrain himself from shouting and decided to stand up and bellow, "What the hell is up with this old bag of bones? He didn't just realise he was dead, did he?" EggWiff found this remark hysterical and roared with laughter. More people began to leave the inn.

This scene was very different from the one that was taking place on the eastern side of Sahihriar. Deep underground, the air felt fresh as the dampness made it moist. This didn't matter to the inhabitants of this underground lair. The cave was impressively large and had ritualistic symbols painted among the red stone walls. The concrete floor always had a thin layer of water, making it slippery and damp. Candles lit the hollowed-out area dimly. They were on high candle stands and lined the circular side walls of the cave.

Forty-nine pigs sat in their blackened robes, each facing their holy leader. No one flinched; each was solid and lifeless, gripped to every word their master said. Their snouts pointed upwards, and their beady eyes stared. Their pale pink skin looked eerie with only the soft candlelight to show against it. The air could move freely around them, and still their master fixated them. That's because they were the elite. They were the ultimate holy warriors who were trained for nothing else but their faith. The master was a large pig, standing at a podium at the front of the other pigs. Surprisingly, the cave was rather inviting considering it was a cave. The Holy Master was waving his hands about enthusiastically as he was pacing back and forth. He wasn't saying anything yet. He sometimes just liked to warm up.

The Holy Master hated talking to the elite, as they were so cold and ruthless. I mean, he wasn't against doing what had to be done; everything was worth it for the Essence. But his strength came from his faith while theirs came from a lack of compassion. He prayed every night to the Elders that he would never become like that. He heaved a deep sigh and then began his sermon.

"Holy pigs, welcome to this heavenly day. Let me

hear ya' praise it." The Master's voice was deep and full of enthusiasm.

The pigs oinked all at the same time. Their faces still remained lifeless, still empty.

"My brethren, I have heard news of travellers who carry the holy Essence. They are travelling to the Council of the North. They will be weak and defenceless. Remember, my children, once we have the Essence, only then can we truly be cured of our sins."

The Master's arm waved as if he was conducting an orchestra. His robes were purple, and the material reflected the soft candlelight that shone out from around them.

A hoof was raised to head height among the seated pigs. The Holy Master stopped and nodded his permission.

"Why not just continue to attack the storage facilities along the border?" The pig's voice was raspy and sore.

"The travellers are weaker, and we have lost many to the triplets that guard those facilities." The Holy Master went silent for a moment thinking of his fallen brethren. He suddenly snapped out and continued with passion. "Besides, the Elders have spoken."

The Holy Master wanted nothing more than to stop the innocent bloodshed, but he didn't dare defy the Elders.

"So it is my conclusion, my holy brothers and sisters, that we must kill these travellers and gain access to the holy Essence!"

With this, a mighty roar of oinks spread across the crowd. They stamped their feet and raised their hooves to their Holy Master. They applauded their master. They applauded the plan. They applauded the death.

However, the Holy Master didn't applaud. Instead, he just hid his guilt.

"Yes, I slept fine..."

Chapter Two

A Sacred Past

    The burning embers lit the village with a glow of destruction. Fires had consumed the wooden houses. Faint screams could be heard as they tried to call out for help, but the chaos of the flames drowned out the noise until it became lost. There was one being, however, who was too focused to become dismayed by his surroundings. He was a young soon-to-be apprentice named Gathnok. He had only just turned twenty and was soon to begin his destiny. His white common clothes had been smothered by the black remains of the fire-burnt village, turning them a smoky grey. The heat was intense, and his body dripped with sweat as he managed to wipe his brow, trying desperately to peer through the smoke-filled streets. He witnessed buildings tied to his childhood memories being burnt down, becoming tombs for his friends. He just hoped he wasn't too late to save his own family.

Trying not to inhale too much, he took a deep breath and began sprinting towards his home. His eyes darted around, as he didn't want to be caught by the invaders. He had heard stories of the Darkmagi but never dreamt they would descend on his remote village, so far from the world of magic. They were sinister, evil beings that legend said stole the very soul of Sahihriar and drained the magical life force of the land. His heart seemed to stop as he was about to turn the corner which would reveal if his home was still standing. He struggled to see for a moment, but he was relieved when he saw that the *small wooden building had survived the blaze. However, the buildings to the right were on fire, and soon it would sweep through. He burst through the small wooden door and began calling for his sister. His eyes darted round the room before catching a pair of feet sticking out from the back end of the table. Gathnok's eyes swelled as he began to tremble. He slowly crept round and gasped at what he saw. Two figures lying side by side were his sister and her husband; their eyes were glazed open, lifeless and without colour. Their lips were blue, and their faces were pale. It was as if the blood had been sucked from them. The young apprentice's legs began to feel lifeless as he stumbled to the floor. Tears began to stream as he struggled to breathe. He now had nothing left in the world.*

He was quickly brought crashing back to reality by the sound of a loud wailing from the adjoining room. His eyes widened as he realised there was still hope. He leapt to his feet and went into the next room. He stopped when he saw a hooded figure standing over the small cradle in the centre of the room. The Darkmage was smothered in its black clothing which revealed nothing about its identity. It turned slowly towards Gathnok but showed no signs of reaction. It simply raised its hands over the child. Gathnok was terrified but knew he had to do something. Without logic he instinctively took two strides forward and tried to grab the Darkmage by the face. In doing so he found himself reaching into the hood and touching its bare flesh. The hooded being turned as Gathnok withdrew his arm. The Darkmage unexpectedly began to gasp and its body began to shake. Gradually a small beam of light began to shine from its face showing small signs of features. Its eyes glowed red as it began to gasp; if Gathnok didn't know better, it would seem as though the Darkmage was terrified. Gathnok's heart pounded as he thought he could feel a strange sensation pulsate through him. The being's eyes looked on curiously at Gathnok before he heard it mumble something.

"The Heart?"

Gathnok had no time to reply before the Darkmage glowed one final flash of light and crumbled into nothing. The young man stepped back in shock and fear, as he had no idea what had just happened. Feeling the intense heat hitting him again, Gathnok took the baby and ran out of the wooden house. The smoke was blinding, but luckily he knew the village better than anywhere else. Within minutes he was out of the village with the baby, terrified and lost.

* * *

Gathnok had travelled for two nights and three days to reach his destination. He was exhausted by the ordeal and felt far away enough from his threatened home, but he still did not dare to sleep. Instead he lay awake and never let his eyes stray from the infant at his side. He didn't have any food, so he strayed into a nearby wood to feed the baby rich berries or juices from any fruits he could find. Thankfully, the magical bloodline between the baby and him had made caring for baby Marvie easier. His body ached, and his eyes felt heavy. Marvie was suspended in front of him, held in a carrier by some torn clothing. The young apprentice was close to lying down to rest when in the distance he saw what he thought to be a small puff of smoke. He squinted and hoped it wasn't hunger playing tricks, as it spurred his legs to keep moving. A smile grew on his face as he began to see the faint outline of the small cottage appear gradually on the horizon. Gathnok stumbled further towards the house with baby Marvie resting peacefully in front of him. He eventually made it towards the wooden door. He could barely keep his eyes open as he forced his last bit of energy to knock on the door. However, he was too drained even to wait for an answer as he collapsed onto the floor.

The door swung open and there stood a very old frail-looking man. He had long silver hair, but it was tangled and patchy. He was slim, and his face looked tired and worn, as if he was constantly restless. His hand rested on an engraved stick. He wore a large grey satchel that draped over his body. He looked very humble. The old man looked down and saw Gathnok collapsed with baby Marvie resting comfortably on top of him. Amazingly, Marvie didn't stir from the sudden fall. The old man walked out and with surprising ease managed to pick up baby Marvie.

"So it has begun," he said, as he felt despair wash over him.

* * *

Gathnok opened his eyes wearily to find himself lying on a comfortable bed. His head felt groggy, but he was rested. The smell of soup hit his nostrils, and the hunger of his stomach rumbled. He was in a small cottage which seemed completely open. The bed was nestled into a corner with a large bench next to it. A small stove and other units were on the wall facing him, and the old man was standing busily in front of them. Gathnok sat up slightly. He was instantly relieved to see the small cradle sat on the floor against the wall across from him. He could make out the sleeping Marvie. Hearing his sigh of relief, the old man turned and beamed a smile at Gathnok whilst holding a large bowl of soup.

"Feeling better?" The old man sounded old and wise just with these simple words.

"Yes, thank you, sir." Gathnok bowed his head with respect.

"Enough formalities. I've not been an Ancient for years, young one." He chuckled as he handed Gathnok the soup.

"You're one of the most powerful beings known to Sahihriar, Saban." Gathnok looked at this man with much admiration.

Saban thought about these words and merely shrugged them off. Power or glory didn't seem that important to him.

"*Now, tell me what brings you here, child.*" Saban sat on the edge of the bed.

Gathnok stopped drinking the soup and stared into Saban's almost white eyes.

"*They came and destroyed everything. The village is gone. I tried to get to her in time, but I could only save Marvie.*" Gathnok's eyes began to prick with emotion as he recalled the events.

"*I'm sure you did all you could.*" Saban gave a reassuring smile.

"*We were told to seek you out if we ever needed anything. It was the Darkmagi.*"

"*Hmm… And how did you escape?*" Saban asked curiously.

"*Something happened. I reached out to stop them and – I don't know – he just kind of disappeared.*"

"*Disappeared?*"

"*Yeah, like crumbled into a heap. Oh, and he said something. He called me the Heart.*" Gathnok looked at him nervously. What did it all mean?

"*Ah, I thought as much!*" Saban nodded knowingly.

"*You thought? What did you think?*" Gathnok felt apprehensive.

"*There is a prophecy from long ago. The prophecy tells that a great evil will rise and threaten the balance of Sahihriar, and when it does, spirits will be awakened to fight them back, as only they will ensure Sahihriar survives.*"

"*Spirits?*"

"*Five in total, each with their own unique elemental ability. The one to lead them will contain the Spirit of the Heart.*" Saban looked at Gathnok. He told the story well, but Gathnok refused to believe he was meant to lead anything.

"*I've not been trained. I'm barely a man. I can't lead*

warriors!" *Gathnok sat back and curled up slightly. He wasn't ready for any of this.*

"I'm sorry this happened so soon. I wish you had more time to prepare, but truth is you would never have been fully prepared. It's up to you to find the other's child and begin your journey."

"Where? To do what?"

"There is only one way the Darkmagi can be stopped. With every attack they steal more magic from Sahihriar and become more powerful. Only the combined power of the Ancients can stop them."

"So they must fight them."

"They cannot. The Ancients are keepers of magic. They cannot directly intervene. They are bound by the rules of the Elders. There is a jewel that was forged when a lost star fell to Sahihriar many years ago. Only it can hold all the power of the Ancients and be used to fight against them."

"So I have to find some random jewel?" *Gathnok asked.*

Saban chuckled again. He enjoyed the innocence of Gathnok.

"Cupido Sacra is no random jewel. Once imbued, it'll be the most precious thing on Sahihriar. But before you find it, you must find the other Spirits." *Saban walked towards a small drawer as he spoke.*

"I really hope that's a map." *Gathnok was interested to think how he was meant to stumble across four mystic warriors and then a sacred jewel.*

"No, but it will act as one." *Saban held out his hand, and in it sat a small wooden object.*

At first Gathnok thought it was a locket as it had a hinged door on the front with a tiny carved drawing of five small twirls, which Gathnok figured represented the five Spirits. Once opened, the wooden needle began spinning and moved directly towards Gathnok. *The compass, once fixated, began to shimmer and glow softly.*

"Take it – it's yours." *Saban held it out further as a timid, yet intrigued Gathnok picked up the compass.*

"It's warm!" *Gathnok could feel the heat against his hands.*

"Yes, the shimmering compass will react whenever you are closest to the thing you are searching for. It will help you to find the other Spirits first."

"But they could still be anywhere in Sahihriar."

"Yes, but they should be close together. They'd be placed together even though they don't know why. The sooner you find them and awaken them as spirits, the easier your task shall be."

Gathnok paused for a moment. It was a pretty heavy conversation, and he was trying to assimilate all the information. He had to find four Elemental Warriors, then search for a missing jewel, seek out the great Ancients, and then use the jewel to fight them all. But then if he didn't, magic would be stolen from Sahihriar, and no one could predict what destruction that could cause. He took a deep breath and looked over at Marvie.

"I shall ensure his safety. If you believe anything, believe that." *Saban's voice was reassuring and as a former Ancient, Gathnok didn't doubt his claim for a second.*

Gathnok smiled, when all of a sudden he felt his fingers became warm as the compass began to glow again.

"What's it doing now?" *Gathnok suddenly felt very uneasy.*

Saban's eyes widened as he looked at the compass. He sat up and immediately hobbled to the door. Gathnok followed.

"You must go. It's a warning. The Darkmagi are nearby. They will never be far behind you!"

"But, I…"

Saban was pushing Gathnok from the house. "Go. I have given you all I can. If all hope is lost, then contact Death. He'll see you on the right path. The baby will be safe."

Saban quickly shut the door, and Gathnok was left alone with the shimmering compass in hand. He opened it and found the needles pointing north-west, so that's the direction he began to sprint in without being left time to collect his thoughts.

Ten minutes later Saban sat by the cradle; he knew that they were coming. Soon enough, the door slammed open and in marched three hooded Darkmagi. Saban didn't even get up.

"Give us the child." Its voice was harsh and deep.

"You are too late. The prophecy has already begun." Saban couldn't help but smile. "We won't let it come to pass. We won't allow you to destroy Sahihriar."

The Darkmage stood still but spoke with compassion.

"And you believe stealing Magic will stop it. You are fools meddling with things you don't understand."

The Darkmage looked at Saban and then at the baby. Without hesitating, the Darkmage took a step forward. Saban quickly placed his hand on baby Marvie and he immediately began to glow. He glowed so bright that it soon became blinding and forced the Darkmagi to stop in their tracks. Soon the flash became unbearable, and they couldn't see anything. Then suddenly the light dimmed and soon disappeared. Saban and Marvie had disappeared completely.

* * *

"You know, sweeties, this hard ground does nothing for my back." Trickle looked down at the hard muddy ground; her face wore an expression of discomfort.

"Yeah, and my bones are kind of frozen." Morbid sat huddled against the tree, rubbing himself to try and keep himself warm.

"Well, if you guys hadn't got us chucked out, then

maybe sleeping outside wouldn't have been much of an issue." Flick's tone was tinged with anger. He started to lay out his sleeping bag across the clearing floor.

They sat in a small forest clearing, bordered with trees. It was rather large and spread for a few meters on either side. The grassy floor felt cold in the midnight breeze. The breeze brought a piercing chill, but the sky was now clear as the rain had stopped. This allowed the stars to provide adequate light. Flick didn't like it. He had been so relieved to get out of the dark, he did not appreciate the fact he was now back in it.

"I simply agree. The fact was that neither of you two had the self-control to contain your behaviour. "EggWiff spoke with importance and was looking down on the others.

Trickle's and Morbid's mouths hung open as they stared at EggWiff in shock.

"You were the one that got us chucked out!" Flick was getting increasingly annoyed.

"No, I was not. A wizard can keep still and focused for hours upon end at a time," EggWiff replied in a poor defence.

Flick could see that another argument was imminent and decided to leave things as they were. He crawled into his sleeping bag and pulled the cover over him. The sounds of the midnight air and the forest made him uneasy. He still didn't trust them, and he swore to himself he'd be the last one awake, purely for his own safety. Morbid leaned against a tree and almost instantly was lost in the world of dreams. However, no one could tell, as he had no eyelids to give any indication if they were closed or not.

Trickle and EggWiff remained awake. They sat on the log side by side with their blankets wrapped over their heads to obtain as much warmth as possible. They both sat in silence for a while. It had been a long day for the both of them, and their lives had taken a dramatic turn. They both took in where they were and what had happened to them that day. Trickle let the breeze wave through her blonde wig. She was secretly hoping EggWiff wouldn't "turn" whilst they were sitting together. She wasn't sure if she could withstand the smell, and she wasn't fond of the other EggWiff – at least not yet, anyway. After a while Trickle decided to break the silence.

"I know it wasn't entirely your fault that we got chucked out of the inn." She looked up at EggWiff and gave a small smile.

He stared for a few minutes longer and turned to look down at his friend. "Thank you."

His face had so much depth to it. It was amazing to think that this man could even be aware of alcohol, let alone be dependent on it.

"Umm, EggWiff, I've got to be honest with you. I was sort of mean to you before." Trickle looked sheepishly at EggWiff, who was looking back confused. "Well, not you. I mean the other you."

EggWiff nodded in realisation. He shuffled his body slightly to get more comfortable on the log beneath him. "Most people are, Trickle. Most people are."

"It must be hard, not having any control sometimes." Trickle wasn't sure how far she should be pushing this, but she also wanted to show she cared.

"When you're as old as I am, little one, you realise that the hardest thing in this world to have is control."

Trickle was taken aback by his wisdom. He actually seemed very much like a real wizard.

The wind decided to give a mighty burst of chill through their bodies. "It's freezing out here. Wouldn't you agree?"

"Yeah, pity we couldn't find any more blankets. I guess

we'll have to make do though. We are meant to be criminals after all," Trickle joked.

"Criminal or not, I shall not allow us to freeze. May I ask you to step back, little fellow?"

Trickle stepped back curiously. EggWiff stood up and began to chant some words. His hands waved level in front of him over a piece of grass beneath him. His eyes turned a blood red as firing swirls of red energy surrounded him. First it was slow, but gradually it got faster and faster until Trickle nearly felt herself go hurtling backwards. He chanted some mystic words and then flung his arms at the ground beneath him. The spiralling red energy thrust through his arms and hurtled towards the ground. A blinding flash of light appeared all over the clearing that seemed only to last for a fraction of a second. When Trickle opened her eyes, she could see a blazing fire before her giving off a warming glow, but even better – heat. Trickle's mouth flew open with a baffled expression. EggWiff sat back down and stared back at Trickle. He noticed her expression.

"What?" EggWiff still looked at Trickle.

"Where the Elders did that come from?" Trickle was now staring between the fire and EggWiff. Never had she seen magic before, and never would she have expected EggWiff to be a real wizard.

"I am a wizard, am I not?" EggWiff smiled to himself. He didn't abuse his magic, but he couldn't help feel good when someone was impressed by it.

"I guess so, sweetie." Trickle let herself smile. The thought of having an actual wizard would help no end; their punishment would be a piece of cake now.

Trickle looked around at the others. She saw Morbid's white silhouette against the tree and Flick's body lying on the blankets where they had left him. Trickle was amazed the spell hadn't awoken them.

Trickle and EggWiff fell into silence as they sat by the fire. Although Trickle's mood had been heightened by the discovery of EggWiff's magic, she couldn't get her mind off the situation she was in. Yesterday she was sure she was going to be killed for her crime; she wasn't completely over the fact she was still alive.

"What is the Council of the North?" Trickle asked, feeling a little embarrassed she didn't know. Elves were mostly found on the south of Sahihriar and before her crime she hadn't gone far beyond the Elven City.

"The Council of the North control most of Sahihriar. They decide what rules and laws are to be upheld and what businesses and trade can be allowed," EggWiff replied.

"What do you think they want with the Essence?" Trickle asked, not seeing any use in lumps of grey rock.

"I don't know, but I'm sure it shall have some use. Most things do," EggWiff replied with a smile.

Trickle smiled back as another silence swept in. She didn't want it to last as she was enjoying getting to know EggWiff.

"So, how did you learn magic?" Trickle was also hoping this question might lead to what crime EggWiff had committed.

"I learnt magic when I was practising with the H.O.M." EggWiff looked down to see Trickle's blank expression. "High Order of Magic – a school that trains warriors from all over Sahihriar. I was lucky enough to be accepted, and I had the best few years of my life there. Well, that was well until…" EggWiff fell silent, his head hung low as his face fell with it.

"Until…"

EggWiff took a deep breath as he slowly took off his glasses and got a small piece of cloth from his pocket. He wiped them delicately and placed them back.

"Ever had everything you wanted – the one thing you had been searching for your whole life – and then have it taken away, through no fault of your own?" EggWiff's face looked so weary and sad. His eyes were intense with emotion; it was clear this was an emotional subject.

"I wish I could say I have, sweetie, but look at me! No one accepts who I am. No one can stare me in the eye. I can't even be myself, let alone have everything I wanted."

EggWiff looked at Trickle. For the first time he could see what was behind the lipstick. She suddenly had so much depth to her that EggWiff admired. Trickle smiled back. She was glad to have finally found someone she could talk to, someone who understood what it was like to be someone you don't want to be.

"Well, I was learning with the High Order of Magic. Everything I ever dreamt became mine. That's before *he* became too much – the other me. When he first started emerging, I could hide it. But soon the other me couldn't handle the magic. He tried to control it, but . . . Well, let's just say because of it I got banished by the council and sentenced to community service." EggWiff's voice, although husky, quivered; it was obvious he was holding back the tears.

Trickle sat listening. Her life had been so consumed by her own pain that she never really thought of anyone else's. Trickle stared into the flaming blaze, thinking of her life and how she got to where she was. The conversation was meant to distract her from her life, not make her question it more. She yawned as the day's events hit her lungs.

"Well, I must rest. No doubt we'll have a long day ahead of us tomorrow." With that, EggWiff stood up and brushed his blue cloak down. He smiled and nodded to Trickle and went off to the far end where his blanket lay. EggWiff was used to sleeping on a hard surface, so this didn't trouble him as much as the fact that his blanket was too small so that his feet were forced out into the midnight air.

Trickle was about to go and try to sleep, when out from the shadows appeared a tall figure.

"Jeez, EggWiff you scared me." Trickle stared at him. He seemed different from how he was a few moments before. He was just staring at her as if she was the most precious thing in the world. "You good, sweetie? What's wrong?"

EggWiff stood in the darkness for a while. He stopped his staring and broke into a smile. "Nothing is wrong at all, little one." He looked down and let a tear roll down his cheek as he spoke. "It's important that, you know, you are one of the greatest females I have ever met both inside and out"

Trickle was rather stunned by this. She could tell from the sincerity of his tone and the look of admiration on his face that he was being genuine. However she found it odd as she hardly knew him. All she could manage was to beam a smile as words seemed to escape her. EggWiff didn't seem to wait for a reply as he turned after one prolonged stare and walked off back to sleep.

Trickle rolled her blanket out on the grassy floor beside the log and the other side of the fire. She smiled to herself. She wondered what she would be doing if she was free, if she would ever have spoken to someone with as much depth as EggWiff. Most of her friends were shallow, and Trickle never really felt like she belonged. However, she never really cared much. She was used to being alone. She tossed and turned, the cool breeze making her shudder. She was exhausted, yet her mind was racing, so she figured she would just lay awake until morning came.

After a couple of hours, they were all asleep. Trickle slept awkwardly on the log next to the burnt-out fire. The midnight moon gave a yellow glow out onto the clearing.

It made for a peculiar view to see such different beings scattered across the small forest clearing.

Morbid, who was propped up against a tree, could feel his vision returning to him as he slowly began to wake. At first his vision blurred the darkness with a green haze, but soon it returned to normal. Without realising it, he took a step forward in his awakening daze. His chalky white legs buckled as he lost his balance. It took him a while to gain awareness as to where he was and why he was sleeping upright. Still dazed, he stumbled forward and fell to the ground with a thud, His bones scattered off in a few direction with the impact; thankfully, as Morbid was dead, he felt no pain. Instead he lay there with the midnight air weaving around his stilled body, the cool breeze gently touching his bare bones. He waited for a second; although the ground was moist, the thud may have been loud enough to wake the others.

He hoisted his head up off the floor and peered into the darkness. He could make out three lumps of shadow scattered across the clearing, each differing in size. From the gentle rise and fall of their bodies he figured none had woken. He slowly began to reassemble himself as quietly as possible. (This task was made much easier by the fact one of his arms had remained attached.) After a minute or so he was standing again. He was going to go straight back to sleep, but the thought of what had awoken him came upon him, stopping him from his usual habits of sleeping for months if need be. He wondered if his new environment and companions had something to do with it, but still he couldn't shake away a feeling of danger. So Morbid began to listen intently. The wind whistled in the air, the leaves swayed, and the bushes bustled. He began to wonder again if it was just the day's events that had caused the odd occurrences, when he heard a mumbled whisper coming from just inside the forest boundary. Morbid began to investigate, creeping slowly towards the muttering. The darkness surrounded him, and the air had become thick with fear and mystery. Most people would have been scared or even wary of this, but as Morbid was dead and didn't have much respect for being undead, he didn't mind. As he got to the closest tree of the forest border, he looked between the branches to see who was talking. Now the voices could be heard a lot more clearly. He saw three shadowy figures huddled close, talking in low deep voices. The wind howled through Morbid's hollow head as he strained to listen. The three shadows were of similar build to EggWiff's. Even though it was strained, he could manage to make out a lot of the conversation.

"So, he is with that band of freaks! Doesn't seem like a fitting punishment, though." The far right shadow's voice was deep and seemed to be tainted with disgust.

"Well, it isn't, is it? Not after what he did, don't you agree, master?" The far left turned to face the tallest middle shadow. Both voices were deep and monotone, almost weak and depressed.

"You ignorant fool, you have no idea of the type of pain he will feel, and when I have the jewel, he shall feel pain that has never even been comprehended. He will want to die within seconds, but unfortunately death is too merciful for that pathetic pile of filth."

The middle figure's voice sent a cold chill down Morbid's spine. The anger, the pain, and the hatred that came just from the pitch of his voice made Morbid fear. He was afraid for the first time in his afterlife, and the scariest part was that he couldn't explain why. Startled by this sudden wave of emotion, he lost concentration and stepped back into the rustled leaves. The sound shot through the trees and was clear and loud to the three shadowed beings. For a second the world stopped. Morbid knew what he had done. The shadows immediately shifted to him. The shadow's pain was now on him, and he could feel nothing but fear.

Morbid was frozen. His mind was telling him to run, he willed his bones to turn, and he tried to force his jaw open in a scream to awake the others, yet he was paralysed. The two shadows on either side hustled towards him without making a sound, as if their feet merely hovered towards him. As the two shadows loomed eerily towards him, he saw that no matter how and where they moved, no light shone on them. They were like living black holes reaching from the darkness. Two rough slimy claws grabbed either arm and threw him at the feet of the darkest creature. For the second time in the last thirty minutes, Morbid found himself lying on a moist grassy floor. However, this time no bones broke free. Morbid stayed looking down, trapped by his own fear. He wanted to see the face of his enemy, he wanted to show bravery, but all he could do was to lie helplessly waiting. The leaves brushed against Morbid's vacant, emotionless face. All he could do was to pray that the feeling of fear pulsating through his body would end. His body was now flowing with freezing air. The two creatures lingered at the back of Morbid, whilst the tallest towered above him. Silence lingered for a while and then was broken by the shrill, sadistic voice.

"You, what do you think you were doing?"

Morbid didn't move; he didn't respond. The fear was now agonising as he struggled to hold it in.

"You dare not answer me, filth?"

Morbid felt himself struggle, as he was determined he wasn't going to tell him anything. He may have been feeling fear, but death didn't scare him. He wanted to cry. All his energy was spent resisting the stranger's power.

The shadow waved his left arm over Morbid. Green pulsating energy appeared and slammed down onto him. His chalky white body became smothered by the mystic energy as he then began to slowly be lifted into an upright position. He was held up, floating in front of the shadow. No matter where the shadows stood, no light would reveal their faces.

"Now, what do you know?"

The shadow was playing with Morbid, treating him like some rag doll hung up for amusement.

"You want . . . you want to kill one of us for . . . for what they did." Morbid was not talking of his own accord as he told every ounce of himself to stop, to not care, to just end it all. But the power was too strong. His presence was too strong. He couldn't believe magic was working on him. To the dead magic is just a memory. Whoever this being was, he was certainly extremely powerful.

"Master, he knows too much! He could ruin everything. If he finds out about Cupido Sacra then…"

The most dominating shadow stopped walking around Morbid and turned his head and looked at the other shadow. He moved his head slowly, and the sheer intensity of the movement forced the smaller shadow being to shut up as it cowardly moved back.

"I shall deal with him accordingly!" The shadow moved behind Morbid, who was still paralysed in mid-motion, "Don't fear me! Don't fear anything, because soon, soon nothing will matter, soon all your fear will be all you are." Morbid's vision became covered by darkness. He felt himself slowly letting go, as that was all he could do.

* * *

The sun spread across the clearing offering an early awakening. It was warm, and it made it clear how moist the damp grass was beneath them. Flick twitched uneasily underneath his cotton sheet. The light rays shone directly on him, and it was obvious he wasn't ready to be awake.

Trickle yawned and sat up. Her hair was frayed, and her make-up looked blotchy. She peered round and saw EggWiff begin to stand up in his lush, rich robes. She smiled as she remembered the comfort he had given the night before. She stood up and began to brush off crumbs of dirt from her bright pink dress. She walked across to the log where she had sat the night before. On the way she passed an already awake Morbid.

"Oh, morning, Morbid! Sleep well, honey?"

Morbid walked uneasily towards the same log and looked at Trickle.

"Yes, I slept fine . . ."

* * *

The fields were littered with pigs – miles and miles of pigs – each ready at command, each with their guns, each with their weapons, and each with the thirst to kill. The forty-nine elite pigs stood staring at the vast army. It was their job to train and impose order amongst them. The wind weaved among them, brushing gently past. None of them moved; none of them blinked; they were statues standing to rest. They were all waiting. The discipline, the control was unnerving. They were waiting to hear the words of the one that controlled them all, the words of the great and grand Holy Master. He wasn't to be seen and he wasn't to be heard. He was in the headquarters as the morning sun was heating his tent. He was pacing and he was psyching himself up for his speech, which in his eyes was more of a performance than anything. He needed to get the Essence: it was promised, it was owed, and it was needed.

Whilst in mid-pace, a small crackling sound began to emerge from behind him. At first he thought it was the rustle of the early morning leaves outside, but then it grew louder. He swung round immediately to see a small blue light darting in front of him. The light then separated, two lights darted faster than the eye could see, and then it multiplied again, and then again. Soon they were separating by the seconds – tens, then hundreds of tiny blue lights swirled creating a blinding light. The Holy Master stepped back, mouth wide with fear. He lurched into the corner and then fell to his knees and closed his eyes, overridden by fear. The tent glowed blue as the sound of swirls, crackled liked thunder. The Holy Master tensed his whole body, closed his eyes, and wanted to escape inside himself. Almost as soon as it began, the glowing stopped, the crackling ceased, and everything was returned to normal. The Holy Master relaxed, slowly lifted his head, and nervously got to his feet.

"I have changed the plan." A voice from the shadows spoke with a dark, tormented tone.

The pig gasped and fell to his knees.

"Elder, I didn't see you. What an honour it is to be graced with your presence." The Holy Master looked scared as he bowed his head low beneath the shadowed figure.

"Shut up! You will stand down your pigs. I have chosen a new leader – one that shall lead him into darkness, one that shall lead you towards your dung." The shadowed voice seemed revolted by the Holy Master – seem revolted by the world and all that stood in it. He did enjoy, however, the pig's misguided belief that he was an Elder and the power it gave him.

"I – I don't understand, sire. Who is our new leader? How will he destroy them?" The Holy Master looked up into the lost face of the shadow above him.

"You shall wait. All will be clear. All will soon suffer my wrath, suffer the death that was placed upon me."

"I understand. And then we shall get the Essence?" The

Holy Master was secretly disappointed that they wouldn't have the Essence sooner. This was the chance, as the travellers were weak.

"You shall get it when I see it fit, but know that without me you have no chance in ever gaining your Essence. But first he'll kill them all for me – painfully, slowly, and happily."

The Holy Master's eyes swelled at the thought of such slaughter, although he was quick to hide his pain. The shadow laughed. A deep disturbing tone filled the tent, and as it faded, so did he, back into the darkness.

"And you would be . . ."

Chapter Three

The four unique creatures continued their punishment. Flick, who seemed to have taken a leadership role, began to lead them down a hilly path. It had been decided that they should try to reach the northern border by travelling along the paths to the east. The clear paths and open areas meant less risk of attack from Mugglers or Thifnesses and any other menacing creatures.

Mugglers were ghost-like creatures that waited in the shadows. They would float out, steal whatever you were carrying, and be gone before you noticed. Only the most mystical of warriors were able to stop them, however. They can only be stopped by magic, and considering EggWiff's mood shifts were so unpredictable, they were not willing to take the chance. No Muggler had ever been killed, and not much was known about them, only that they were most commonly known near the western routes of Sahihriar.

Thifnesses, however, are mole-like creatures that burrow under the ground and creep beneath your feet. They're said to hold unique mystic powers, but many dismiss it as rumour. Once beneath you, they shoot from the ground to steal your possessions and dive back down, similar to a dolphin in the sea. Thifnesses are rare, and their existence is shrouded in rumour and lost thoughts.

Trickle's heels clapped along the road as she struggled to put on makeup in the haste to keep up. If it weren't for the odd click of his bone, it would be hard to tell if Morbid was with them. He didn't speak, he didn't breathe, and he hadn't cried in weeks. The group felt relieved about this, but even so it had made him distant. EggWiff kept turning about four times a day; neither seemed to accept that the other alter ego had been present, but the group quickly learnt to make sure that they had some form of alcohol with them when the more offensive EggWiff surfaced.

Flick was still bitter after EggWiff punched his nose one time. They had a row over stealing a drink. It turns out that drunken EggWiff had some violent tendencies. They had been together close to a month. EggWiff and Trickle had become close friends, often staying up late swapping stories. Trickle had been teaching EggWiff some mind techniques to try and control his condition. It wasn't working, but EggWiff appreciated the gesture. Flick, even though he had taken the leader role, seemed to stay within himself and didn't seem to make much effort in socializing. Maybe he felt it was easier to stay clear-headed if he did so. It was hard to tell how Morbid was acting; no one had really interacted with a skeleton before, and even then Morbid still was "different". The only time he really spoke or made himself known was when he was deciding what path to take. Somehow Morbid had become the navigator, and it was he who decided on the eastern border route towards the north. The group couldn't help feeling uneasy around Morbid, and EggWiff had taken a huge dislike to him.

They were all tired, muscles pounding, bones weak, make-up running. The still-heavy satchels were more like chains of their crime than anything – so much so that Flick did once wonder if the Essence had a more symbolic meaning. Eventually the night sky drew in again. The sky was cast in deep purple with clouds being replaced by the stars. Even EggWiff's noble and wise face looked strained. They were heading to the forest to set up camp for the night. EggWiff and Trickle were walking side by side at the front whilst Flick and Morbid walked behind them.

They were on a path which very gradually crept upwards, and either side of them was nothing but open fields. Trickle preferred being able to see, as it made her feel safer. Her feet were sore with blisters, and she was about to complain when EggWiff suddenly stopped. He raised his hand to the group, signalling them to stop.

"What is it?" Flick peered out onto the horizon.

Silence fell upon the group. Trickle's heart began to pound. She looked intently around and then out towards the horizon line. EggWiff was peering as his eyes narrowed, yet nothing seemed to appear.

"Sweetie, nothing is out there."

Suddenly a loud groan could be heard from just beyond the horizon. The group initially jumped but then peered, awaiting to see what was coming. Ten large trolls began to appear over the grassy horizon. The footsteps of the large creatures began to shuffle the dirt that stood beneath them. The trolls were grey and wore red sheaths around their waist. Their arms bulged with muscle, and their bellies were rounded. They wore spiked armour, and their faces were flat as the noses were small and crooked. Their eyes were a red-lit flame. The trolls were carrying swords and shields; they were armed for a fight.

"What are they?" Trickle stood back. The trolls were tall and slightly larger than EggWiff.

"They are bandit trolls, deadly and ruthless." EggWiff narrowed his eyes at the oncoming enemy.

EggWiff's mind raced. His first thought was to protect the group. He stepped forward and twirled his staff. The trolls were only meters away now, walking hastily towards them. EggWiff looked majestic in his robe. The others naturally moved in behind him. The trolls didn't seem to hasten or respond to anything. Instead they lifelessly continued to slump towards them.

"EggWiff, trolls are immune to magic!" Morbid's bony fingers pointed to the trolls as he spoke.

The trolls said nothing; they just loomed in closer and closer. The sheen of their blades was visible now they were so close. Luckily, EggWiff already knew this and had prepared another spell, although as always he wasn't sure of the strength of his magic.

"Yes, Morbid, but luckily we are not!"

"Shouldn't we run?" Flick was already somewhat edging backwards.

"And what if they run too?" Morbid's deep blackened sockets stared into Flick's innocent eyes. Flick shuddered but chose not to respond.

EggWiff continued to twirl his ivory stained staff in front of him. His beard was fluttered by the force, and yet the trolls didn't flinch. They continued to advance step by step. Each time the weight of the feet slammed the ground, the group could feel a small quake in the earth beneath them. The trolls were extremely strong.

Over the sound of crushing feet and the twirling staff, Flick heard the mystical words from EggWiff's mouth.

"Protecteria!" EggWiff's voice had power once again. He

tingled as he felt the surge of magic through him. He was connected to the earth.

Up from the ground around them a blue flame appeared. It swirled a rich and lighter blue. It let out no heat and encased them in a sphere of what EggWiff hoped would be protection. However, the trolls still moved towards them as if nothing had happened.

"Umm, EggWiff, it's very pretty, but what does it do exactly?"

"Watch, little one" EggWiff gave the impression he was very confident, but even he doubted the reliability of the blue flame. He stood tall and proud and peered through the haze of the flame at the oncoming trolls. His mind raced with potential spells that could continue to help, but none of them seemed appropriate. This spell was all they had.

The ten trolls stopped in front of the blue flame. They stood side by side and circled around the group. The trolls squinted at the blue flame for a second before they raised their swords in unison. They waited a further moment. Flick looked up and could see the sharp edges through the blue flame. He closed his eyes. The trolls then swung the blades down heavily upon the four prisoners.

The flame swirled as the blades tried to penetrate the magical seal around them.

"Impressive, EggWiff!" Morbid chattered. It was the first time anyone other than Trickle had witnessed EggWiff's magical abilities.

"Wow, Morbid, that's three times you've spoken in the last five minutes. It's nice to know you're back." Flick's sarcasm was on top form.

"EggWiff, will this thing last? What's, like, the main plan here?" Trickle was looking at the trolls cringing at their constant attempts to break the barrier above them.

"I have no idea on either matter, Trickle!"

Trickle's hopeful smile had quickly faded. The relief of them being safe was now turning into shock as they realized that they were trapped.

"You know, we should just have run. It would have made more sense." Flick sat on the ground. There was little else he could do.

"If you're going to use logic, then you can just go away, Flick!" Trickle was getting upset. Each new slam made the blue flame weaken, and she could see the concern on EggWiff's face.

"If I could go away, we wouldn't have a problem!" Flick was once again wishing he wasn't in this situation and thoughts of hating pixies came flooding back.

"What did I just finish saying about logic?!" Trickle had already turned her back on Flick.

The steel cut through the blue flame, but only by inches. The magic was fading fast and none of them could do anything.

"EggWiff!" Trickle's voice was filled with worry as she had nothing but fear.

"There is nothing I can do. I'm sorry I failed you all!" EggWiff closed his eyes and awaited his fate.

After one crashing blow, the blue flame dissolved around them. Trickle closed her eyes and huddled on the floor. Morbid was secretly pleased that he was so easily fulfilling the dark master's wishes. Flick squinted up at the flaming eyes of the trolls.

"Urgggggggghhh!" The trolls groaned as they began to slash the blades down onto the four defenceless prisoners.

A blade cut through a gut . . .

Flick opened his eyes and thought he was dead as his arms instinctively shot out to cradle his belly, but his belly was fine and he felt no pain. He looked at the group. They were all fine too. Flick peered down at two trolls who lay dead on the ground at his feet, and with a startled expression he looked up.

A small dwarf was having a sword battle with one of the trolls. She wore a chest plate made of green steel that was woven round her bosom. The underlying torso was plated with brown and silver armour. Her hair was tinted green. She wore a green metal padded skirt that flowed to above her knees with brown leggings underneath. Flick recognized what she was instantly. The dwarf was battling the trolls at lightning speed. Her sword slashed and swung. On her back was a green wooden crossbow with a sachet of arrows. She was a valiant fighter.

She ducked down beneath the swing of the troll, and seeing its chest, she kicked out with her leg and swung up in the air. Rotating completely she held out the sword and slashed off the troll's head. Another troll moved swiftly in behind her. Without looking, she just twirled her sword and plunged it back killing the second troll instantly. She smiled, which surprised Trickle. The others too were looking on in amazement. She then looked over at the group.

"Duck!" Her voice seemed soft, which was surprising. It seemed to conflict with the anger and violence they were witnessing.

The group stopped for a moment, puzzled by what she said. It wasn't until the dwarf grabbed her bow and arrow and aimed it at them that they thought best to heed the advice. An arrow followed shortly right over their heads and into the forehead of one of the trolls. Some of the other trolls had vanished, and only one was foolish enough to remain.

The troll was only meters away from her. It stopped and then started to assess its tiny foe. They lingered. The heat of battle was coursing through the dwarf's veins. The dwarf stared at the troll. Flick couldn't help notice her sly smile. Even though she was clearly a warrior, she was also very beautiful. The troll dropped its shield and sword and began to charge towards the warrior dwarf. She quickly dropped her sword and did nothing but close her eyes.

The group looked confused. Was she sacrificing herself? Was this it?

The instant the troll got close enough, however, the warrior dwarf dived to the ground, swung her leg out, and sent the troll hurtling in the air a few feet in front of the group. After giving a very painful groan, the troll remained still on the ground.

The warrior stopped and peered at the four huddled prisoners. Trickle's mouth was open as the violence and grace of this person amazed her. The dwarf walked towards them, her sword in her hand. Her expression was stolid and gave no sign of her intention.

"Wow, thanks! I mean…" Trickle began to say.

The warrior dwarf twirled her sword and rested it upon Trickle's neck. The steel edge began to cut lightly into her neck. EggWiff stood up instantly and pointed the tip of his staff into the dwarf's chest.

EggWiff slowly leaned in. "I believe you are not immune to magic." His piercing blue eyes glared with power.

"I wouldn't be so sure." The dwarf withdrew her blade and stood back from the group, looking at each one individually. She noticed the satchel of Essence on the floor and shook her head with despair. "Looks like you're the bunch then." She looked at their blank expressions. The dwarf stood as if everything was now explained. It was a very surreal scene as they stood amongst the dead trolls scattered around them.

"And you would be?" Morbid asked in his creepy monotone way.

"She's an Amazon dwarf, the worst kind. I say you destroy her now, EggWiff!" Flick spoke with a bitter tone.

He had been impressed at how well she fought, but he despised Amazons.

The group looked at Flick and then back at the new figure with confused expressions.

"Well, southern filth, unfortunately I'm not that easy to get rid of. I've been sent to watch you. Make sure you do your punishment and don't deviate. It's my job to ensure you reach the Council of the North." She spoke as if they were nothing. Trickle had already decided not to like her.

"So you're like a guard, a bodyguard" Trickle seemed happier with this change in power.

"If you go out of line, I have permission to kill you."

Trickle leaned in to EggWiff and whispered, "Not a bodyguard then."

She turned to address the new character. "So do you have a name? Are we allowed to call you by your name?" Trickle looked confused, but she didn't want her neck sliced.

"My name is Saria" Her face remained stern and cold.

Flick's eyes stared at Saria. For him, the punishment had just got so much worse.

"Well I'm…" Trickle threw out her hand with her newly painted pink nails.

"I know your names already. I know everything about you, Trickle." Saria's voice was bitter, and she looked disgusted.

"I'm Dead"

Chapter Four

They began to walk slightly off the path and down towards a small covering of trees. They preferred to sleep in clearings, as it provided safety and closure. The group didn't say a word to Saria as she walked ahead. She acted as if danger was round every corner, whilst the group just casually walked on. When they had finally found the entrance to the clearing, Saria insisted she go and scout it out first. After ten minutes of impatient waiting, Saria returned and nodded. They managed to get inside. It was a small square shape that made it seem cosy. Only the faint light of stars turned the darkness to shadow.

"So, sweetie, we set up camp . . ."

"Silence, little one!" EggWiff threw his arm across Trickle and leaned forward protectively like a mother over a child. Trickle and Flick stopped still and listened. All seemed normal; all seemed still.

"Not again." Flick's mumbling had gone unnoticed.

Saria swung back and immediately looked back at

EggWiff. "What is it?" Her thin fringe flicked just over her eyes.

"I don't know. I just sense some form of danger." EggWiff began to stride forward staff raised and ready.

Saria drew her blade and was peering amongst the shadow; both of them were surveying everything around the group.

Normally Trickle would have felt scared, but instead she smiled and glanced at Flick. There was something comforting having two powerful beings protecting you. However, she still pulled a face behind Saria's back.

After a second Flick turned and whispered, "You okay Morbid?" No reply came, and as he turned to look, Morbid had gone.

"Umm, where the heck is Morbid?" Flick asked, huddling closer to EggWiff, fear now taking over.

Saria looked back and sighed when she couldn't see Morbid. "It's my job to make sure you stay together. EggWiff, can you protect these two?" She spoke as if Flick and Trickle were nothing but mere possessions.

Trickle and Flick awaited his response; Trickle was actually wondering if he'd defend them. Whilst waiting, her nose caught a sniff of horrible egg-like stench as she noticed a green mist began to emerge around them. She looked back at Flick as they both cringed, knowing that EggWiff had turned again.

Saria began to cough as the wind carried the smell towards her.

"Okay, he so gets the award for bad timing!" Flick yelled now attaching himself to Trickle.

"What just happened?" Saria was walking back towards the group. She looked confused.

Flick and Trickle smiled sideways at each other as they

couldn't help be somewhat pleased that Saria had no idea what she had gotten herself into.

"Saria, meet Wiff-Egg, He's EggWiff's other side." Trickle sounded rather cheerful as she looked across at the still smiling Flick. EggWiff stepped back in confusion.

"What the bloomin' hell is going on?" EggWiff demanded. He peered back at the group and caught sight of Saria. "Who the heck is that? I thought the circus group was full?" EggWiff's voice rasped, and his mannerisms were again loose and giddy.

Saria turned enraged and drew her blade instantly. Trickle ran up and stood in front her.

"It's not his fault! He has a condition. He just needs a drink and he'll be fine. Please don't kill him!"

Saria looked into Trickle's eyes; she was very confused as to what to make of her. She was different and seemed odd. The fact she showed compassion for the others made Saria feel uneasy. However, loyalty was something she admired, and Trickle seemed to have a lot of it.

"I will go find Morbid. When we return, I want him to be calm and you to have some answers." Saria placed her sword into its scabbard and walked off into the borders of the clearing.

"That woman has serious anger issues."

"You've got that right!" Trickle sighed as she took out the half-full bottle of gin from her handbag and handed it to EggWiff. His eyes lit up as he started to drink immediately. Trickle had learnt that thanks weren't to be expected.

"You think we're alright out here?" Flick asked.

"I hope so. Saria will probably deal with anything dangerous." Trickle was trying to convince herself more than Flick.

"Guess we set up camp then." Flick slid the blanket

and bag off his back and let it slump onto the moist grassy ground.

Trickle was about to discuss the safety of collecting fire wood when the clearing flashed with a blue light. Flick looked at Trickle's face which confirmed he wasn't imagining anything. Again the clearing flashed. All three of them looked around, but the clearing looked still and lifeless.

"Saria!" Trickle called out. She was about to call again when she saw.

Out from the far end of the clearing, three tiny blue glowing lights appeared. They hovered eerily towards them, darting from side to side abruptly. It was hard to make out if they were hostile. At first Flick thought they were fairies, but these were too large, bright, and rounded to be the glow of a small fairy. The clearing was lit up by the glow of the floating orbs. Flick, Trickle, and EggWiff all turned to run, but they seemed to be entranced by the lights, as if all thoughts were meaningless. Trickle tried to scream out for Saria, but her mind was being taken over by the orbs. Just watching them glide towards her was hypnotic. The lights continued to dart in front of them. They came so close to the three travellers that their eyes glowed, and the wrinkles in EggWiff's face were visible. As the lights swayed in front of them, so did their bodies, as if they had lost all control.

Then within the space of a second, all three lights flew back at head level, each floating in front of one of the three travellers. Flick, Trickle, and EggWiff didn't move, they didn't flinch, and they just stood transfixed to the point where they stood. Then the lights pulsated forwards, and each light flew inside one of the three. Flick, Trickle, and EggWiff stood in the forest clearing. For a few moments there was nothing. It was as if the lights were never there, just a mere figment of imagination. If it wasn't for the fact that none of them could move and none of them could feel, then they might have questioned what had happened. Instead all three collapsed on the forest-clearing floor with a thud, not knowing the dangers they were in. Morbid and Saria were still missing from sight.

The rest of the stars took their places in the sky, and the world turned to darkness as they continued to lay there helpless, until EggWiff opened his eyes and twitched uneasily. He yawned and got to his feet, still dazed and disoriented. He looked down at Trickle and Flick lying on the ground. EggWiff peered over the clearing: all was silent and still. He bent down and picked up the bottle of gin he had dropped. Using the sleeve of his robes, he brushed down the moisture from his clothes and face and then walked up to Trickle. Using his staff, he began to nudge Trickle gently in the hope she would awaken. She soon did so, followed by Flick. They were all soon standing, dazed and unsure.

"Darn it, I just redid my make-up!" Trickle moaned whilst looking into her small mirror.

Flick rolled his eyes and looked at EggWiff who seemed to be drinking the remainder of his drink.

"Oh, great! I am stuck with you two! I swear I am never humming anywhere again." Flick seemed tired, agitated, and annoyed.

"Where did old hollow head get to?" EggWiff shouted as if the others were deaf.

Trickle and Flick looked around and then at each other.

"That's a good point. I don't think he was here before. I can't remember." Flick was holding his pounding head.

"Yeah and, umm, that new one – was she with us?" Trickle's head also pounded with pain.

"Oh, I really don't like her!" Flick said with bitter realization.

"Shouldn't we look for them? I mean, we're not allowed to stray too far from each other remember?" Trickle asked.

"I suppose me and you will go. EggWiff can look after the blankets." Flick didn't bother waiting for EggWiff's opinion and began walking towards the forest.

"I think the new one is pretty, don't you?" Trickle couldn't help wonder about the possibility of some romantic interest between the two dwarves.

"She's an Amazon. That's gross, Trickle!" Flick couldn't have liked Saria even if he wanted to – not that he wanted to, or so he kept saying to himself anyway.

They were just out of sight when EggWiff cried out in immense pain. Flick and Trickle both spun fast and sprinted back down, though Trickle found this hard to do in her high heels. EggWiff was huddled in a corner, his back against a thick tree. He was cuddling himself and rocking back and forth. His eyes didn't move, as if he was looking at nothing. He was muttering to himself. It wasn't until Trickle bent down close that she could make out what he was saying.

"He has been tainted, lost by the hands choking him. He will lead us to darkness, lead us to peril." EggWiff continued to mutter this constantly.

"Well, this can't be good!" Trickle said.

"It's us, of course. It isn't good. What the hell was in that gin?" Flick was annoyed and tired.

"Nothing. It's the one you got from the last inn we went to. It could be part of his illness" Trickle was still sitting by EggWiff. He seemed so lost and scared. Trickle was placing a comforting hand on his arm.

"The courts would have told us if this was his illness. We need that new one – what is her name?"

"Sarah, Sasha – something stupid. Either way, we can't just leave EggWiff!" Trickle's eyes were beginning to swell up as she hated to see her friend in so much distress. "Do you understand him? Do you know what this means?" Trickle got up and stood back next too Flick. She looked concerned and confused as her eyes began to fill with pools of water.

"Please don't start, Trickle. I really can't have you having a mental breakdown right now!"

Flick began pacing back and forth, EggWiff continued muttering, and Trickle burst into tears, letting her mascara run down her cheeks.

"I'm alone, aren't I? I'm always alone. No one ever comes near me. They see something new and different, and they get scared, they cower. Still makes me alone though. So lost is my soul, so bitter is my hatred." Trickle fell to her knees and continued to mutter.

Flick knelt beside her. "Trickle look at me! We need to find Sasha. Come on!"

Trickle said nothing. She began to rock and cuddle herself as her eyes became lost and only small blue tears came from them.

"Sasha!" Flick began frantically calling out. "Morbid!"

He stared at his two companions. The clearing seemed darker and scarier, the air was thick, and the light was dim. The fear was now overwhelming. His heart pounded so much he could almost hear its echo amongst the midnight air. Morbid was gone, his two friends had been turned into nothing more than zombies, and Sasha was gone also. Whenever he thought of her, he just kept thinking of how beautiful she was. He shook the feeling off. He was under some curse, and he knew that he had little time himself.

Meanwhile Morbid sat in the bush, watching as Flick and Trickle ran back to EggWiff's aid. He watched as Trickle fell down and watched as Flick fell to his knees. He knew the time was near when they would soon all be helpless. He was well hidden amongst the trees, and he was sure Saria wouldn't find him. If Morbid had skin, he would have been smiling smugly to himself.

Saria walked around in the forest looking for Morbid. This job was far too important to her to allow him to aimlessly wonder off. She hacked at the bushes as she went past, hoping to ward off any unwanted attention. She had actually wandered further than she had intended, but EggWiff was there to protect the others – if he was feeling better, that is.

Her mind wandered as her eyes were used to looking for the chalky white of Morbid's body. EggWiff seemed to be a good wizard when he wanted to be, and Trickle at least had loyalty. However, she didn't care for the Surthan breed. She hated the divide of her species and especially those who felt above their station. She disliked Flick, and she was annoyed he occupied her thoughts so much. Meanwhile, she continued to search for Morbid, refusing to go back without him.

Flick knelt in front of Trickle and began to shake her "Trickle! Come on! Snap out of it!"

Trickle continued to mutter, her eyes lost, not once even registering Flick was there. Flick went to shake her again, but his arms didn't connect with Trickle's body, as Trickle had vanished from sight. Flick shuffled back. Trickle was gone. Flick looked around for EggWiff, but he too had vanished. Flick was all alone. Everyone had gone. He had nothing. Flick huddled to the floor and swayed, trying to comfort himself.

Morbid watched all three of them as they sat as huddles of shadows, none talking to each other. All three were at the clearing, but none of them really there. The faint sounds of Trickle's and EggWiff's muttering could be heard. Other than that, all was silent. Morbid knew this was his chance. Morbid knew they were all defenceless. He also knew he had completed his mission. He had to send the signal that would trigger one of them being kidnapped and used for the Shadow Master's plan. Morbid raised his hand and was just about to trigger it all, when he noticed something strange about EggWiff. The shadow that covered him had become tainted with green.

"Morbid, what are you doing?" Saria asked appearing behind Morbid.

EggWiff gasped heavily. It was if he had been allowed to breathe for the first time in minutes. He panted as his vision slowly came back to him. He didn't even mind the fact that he was inhaling the foul stench. As he lay, he saw a small blue light appear from him, and slowly fade into nothing. His thoughts were muddled, out of place, and confused. Once his lungs were full and his sight returned, he stood up. Now for the first time he could hear a faint muttering sound from the shadows a few feet away from him. He bent down, picked up his staff, and slowly crept towards the sound. As he got closer, he noticed that the muttering was coming from Trickle. She was cowering and hugging herself. EggWiff sprinted the few paces towards his friend and knelt by her side. She was muttering something about being a "freak" and how unfair life was. EggWiff chose to ignore it; it wasn't important as he only cared about helping his friend. He placed a comforting hand on Trickle's arm as he flicked through his mind, searching through the endless spells he'd learnt. It didn't help. He didn't know what had caused it.

He decided on a basic reverse spell. He was good at them, and he had little else to go on. EggWiff still felt somewhat drained from the protection spell earlier, but he was willing to try anything for Trickle. He stood high next to Trickle, who remained still as a statue. He pointed his staff at the small creature and tapped her head gently with the tip. The spell was a matter of concentration, so no words were used. The spell showed no energy, no light, and no sign of its presence. EggWiff waited. His magic was hit or miss on the best occasions, and he couldn't bear it if his magic hurt anyone – again.

Trickle suddenly gasped. Her lungs were tight, and she fell to the floor breathing in as much air as possible. Her vision was blurred, but she saw a small blue light float above her and then vanish. She lay still as the moist grass pricked her whiskers. Her thoughts began to become clearer as the world was coming back to her. She got to her feet and looked round. She was still frightened. She shrieked at her first sight of EggWiff. His appearance was dominating, and it was still dark.

"Jeez, EggWiff, you frightened me! What's going on? What's happening?" Trickle held her head as she tried to keep balance.

"I don't know, young one, but you seemed to be under some form of spell, as does young Flick!"

"Spell? By who? You?" Trickle looked very confused.

"No, not me. Some entity. But it's Flick we need to worry about now." EggWiff gestured to Flick.

"Better not have put a spell on me!" Trickle was half smiling as she playfully hit EggWiff's arm.

Trickle looked back at where EggWiff was gesturing. It was only now that she noticed Flick a few yards away. He too was huddled on his knees, and she could make out the odd cries of her name. She walked towards him hastily. She was no longer scared, as concern had overcome her emotions. Flick was still under the influence of the spell. He kept calling out, looking past the others.

"Flick, sweetie, I'm here. Look, it's all better now." Trickle spoke in a slow comforting tone. Flick carried on. Trickle was invisible to him. "What has happened to him?

I wasn't like that, was I?" Trickle spoke fast to EggWiff; she seemed worried and scared.

"No, you were slightly different. You were muttering something else. Either way, I am hoping the same spell will reverse it."

EggWiff was eyeing up Flick, as if to see if he could tell what was really wrong. EggWiff wasn't sure he had enough energy, but as it was a relatively simple spell, he hoped he would succeed. Trickle looked at EggWiff, and then a thought occurred to her.

"Where's Morbid? Did you save him yet?" Trickle was peering across the clearing to see if she could catch a glance of the white skeleton.

"No, I haven't seen or heard of him. We should concentrate on Flick before worrying about it though. Stand back, please." EggWiff stood forward and again tapped his staff. His confidence was better this time around, but his hand still trembled slightly. They both waited. The leaves on the trees made a faint rustling in the darkness, but that was all the sound that could be heard. Flick stopped calling and with a sudden gasp fell to the floor panting. Trickle jumped at the sudden sign of motion. As Flick was trembling for breath back into his lungs, EggWiff and Trickle noticed a small blue light coming from Flick as it too slowly vanished into the darkness.

After a few minutes they were all back on their feet fully aware, and all seemed unharmed.

"You better now, sweetie?" Trickle asked, beaming at Flick.

"Yeah, I think so. What happened? Why did we go like that?" Flick was keen for an answer.

"EggWiff put a spell on us!" Trickle exclaimed jokingly.

Flick's mouth grew wide with shock as he looked at EggWiff. EggWiff gave a stern look at the playful Trickle.

"As I have already stated to young Trickle, I was not the one who cursed you. It seems we became infected. A mystical energy of some kind took hold of our conscience." EggWiff was once again wise and powerful, his voice calm. No emotion wavered and no fear remained.

"Okay, you're aware you just said infected, right? Because that sounds creepy. I mean when you say infected . . . By what exactly? Who would do that?" Trickle had a look of disgust, and it seemed she kept trying to check her clothes for a sign of insect or bug.

"Well, shouldn't we leave before it comes back? I still don't feel completely myself." Flick's voice quivered with fear as he folded his arms in comfort.

"Yeah, the sooner we find Morbid, the better" Trickle began to wander cautiously around the clearing. Her heels would occasionally sink into soft bits of ground. After much travelling, dirt had nearly completely immersed the once-pink shoes.

"What do you mean, we've lost Morbid? Why is it I get left with the weirdest people on the planet?" Flick was greeted by a stern look from EggWiff. As usual, his whining had gone ignored.

"Is it possible he could be infected? Maybe he wandered off and doesn't know where he is?" Trickle began to seem genuinely concerned. "I mean, it is dark now."

"And Sasha – Saria – didn't she go look for him?" Flick was still hazy, as he felt like his mind had just been squashed. Flick was conflicted by the hatred he had for Amazons and the warm feeling he felt every time he thought of Saria.

The skies had begun to cloud over, and the clearing was only dimly lit now. EggWiff stood resting on his staff pondering. They did need to get Morbid back. For some reason EggWiff could sense it was important, as if there was something special about it all.

EggWiff was about to suggest that they quickly go in search of the others, when Saria and Morbid's chalky outline could be seen coming out of the forest border.

"Morbid!" Trickle's voice boomed throughout the clearing as she noticed his silhouette appear from the forest boundaries.

"Are you two well?" EggWiff asked.

"Of course. Morbid apparently got hit by a light thingy and wandered off!" Now back with the others, Saria put her sword away.

"How did you un-curse him then? Because EggWiff has been putting spells on everyone." Trickle was pleased to see Flick smile at her playful comments. It was sometimes nice to relax the uptight EggWiff.

"I'm dead"

The group stared at Morbid. It was a very random yet obvious statement for him to make. They all awaited an explanation.

"You cannot infect what isn't there," Morbid continued after much delay.

Everyone seemed to make some sound to acknowledge their understanding. EggWiff had a flash of Morbid appear into his head. It was scented with cold and fear, as if it was a flashback from the spell. It dazed him, but after a few moments it had gone.

"You alright, EggWiff?" Trickle could see his eyes wince in pain.

"Fine, thank you." He smiled and spoke as if the situation had merely been a small distraction.

"We won't be fine if we let those things come back. Look, we're all back, so let's just get out of here; there must be another clearing nearby." Saria stood with the group awaiting them to move on command.

"Sure, sweetie, I guess we can now." Trickle looked back at EggWiff for his sign of approval. EggWiff still felt uneasy. The more he thought of Morbid, the more troubled he became. He couldn't leave this unsaid. Something was wrong. His thoughts were dazed, but he knew that something wasn't right. The rest of the group was looking at EggWiff as he seemed completely lost in thought.

"Oh, great. Well, I'm going to move on now anyway." Flick began to walk as Trickle and Morbid followed behind. EggWiff was left confused and surrounded by a green tainted smoke and that smell. He had turned once more.

Later on that night, the group had set up camp in a nearby clearing. There was nothing like being taken over mystically to tire someone out. Trickle, Morbid, and EggWiff were fast asleep, leaving only Saria and Flick awake.

"You should sleep. We have to travel far if you wish to reach the eastern border tomorrow." Saria wasn't speaking from concern.

"Telling me what to do now?" Flick looked at Saria, as he couldn't help but stare into her eyes every time they spoke.

"I am your guardian for this trip."

"And you're also Amazon. Look how that worked out." Flick's heart pounded. It was easier to hate her.

"Yes, and as a Surthan you would have a problem with that wouldn't you?"

"Yeah, can't imagine why the third-rate breed would have a problem." Flick was getting annoyed; Amazons always looked down on his kind.

"Well I didn't make it how it is, did I? Look I'll do my job, and you do your sentence, and then maybe I won't have to kill you." Saria was up on her feet.

Flick stood up and leant in close to Saria's face. Although angry, he couldn't help feel excited as he felt her warm breath on his lips.

"Trust an Amazon to settle everything with death." Flick's voice was bitter as he stared into her eyes, showing no sign of the affection he felt.

As he walked away, all he could think about was how close he was to her. If only he knew that Saria, for the first time in her life, felt something for a Surthan breed.

* * *

"You should have told me!" Morbid spoke into the shadow void.

"I should have told you? When did you become so important as to tell me what I should and should not tell. You're nothing but a toy to me." The voice was rasping and ridden with pain.

Morbid stood lifeless and still. He dare not question his new master further.

"You let them escape the forest of lost souls? I could have had him in my grasp right now. I could be squeezing the power out of him right this second, yet you continue to fail me!"

"The situation is complicated, but now I am aware of the full situation, my task will be easier!" Morbid's voice was eerily monotone.

"They know of their plan, and you're not to intervene. You just make sure they are where I need them to be."

Morbid said nothing as he bowed his head in shame kneeling before the shadowed figure. The trees masked them completely. Even the stars themselves cowered behind clouds. Now Morbid knew his name, it made the being that much less frightening. It made him seem more human.

"Return to them. Make sure they keep heading north

towards the Black Sea. When I strike, I will decide if you're worth sparing." The shadowed figured voice was twisted. Enraged by hate, he had the darkest of souls known.

* * *

A Sacred Past

After travelling for a few days, sleeping on leaves and living off berries and fruit from the nearby woodland, Gathnok arrived at a small village. The compass had glowed slightly brighter, and it was getting warmer in his hands. He could tell that he was now at the right place. It gave odd comfort as the village wasn't too dissimilar to his own. The village must have had ten streets in total that seemed to each be lined with small houses combined by the large row of thatch roofing. Gathnok smiled at passers-by and tried to keep the shimmering compass hidden as best he could. He walked the streets and followed the needle as it led him down another street. Once he reached the end, where he now seemed to be at the edge of the village, the needle pointed to a largish-looking building which stood on its own. A sign stood fixed in the small front garden, lined by a tiny fence. "The Mucker's Inn" was clearly the place to be in this village.

Seeing as the compass stayed fixated, Gathnok hoped that one of the Elemental Spirits was inside. He opened the door and was greeted by noise and heavy banter. It was a big place, and no one acknowledged his arrival. The place was all on one level with three supporting pillars spaced out. The bar rested on the left-hand wall with people sitting by it. Tables littered the rest of the floor space. Gathnok began walking around slowly, occasionally glancing down at the compass. The needle would move slightly, but had yet to point at anyone specifically. So as not to draw attention, he was shielding the glow in his hands as he held on tight against the warmth. Gathnok jumped as a shot of heat was suddenly emitted from the compass. He stopped and looked down. The needle was fixed in place. He followed it's arrow to a nearby table. Sitting down were two beings. One was male with short thick black hair, another was a woman with long flowing black hair. They had dark complexions and both shared the same deep brown eyes. Gathnok noticed a similarity in their looks. They were also well dressed, as the lady wore a soft-flowing red dress that appeared to delicately fit her trim body. The male wore a light under-tunic and a dark fitted blazer; both seemed a fair bit older than Gathnok.

"Hi . . ." Gathnok had walked up to the table but wasn't entirely sure how to approach the subject.

"May we help you?" The man had a deep voice, and although his words were polite, his manner seemed annoyed.

"My name is Gathnok. I need to speak with you." He was nervous and rather intimidated.

The man looked over at his companion. "Just me?"

Gathnok looked down and noticed that the shimmering compass was no longer fixed and instead the wooden needle kept switching between the man and the woman he sat with.

"Or both of you, apparently." Gathnok gave a nervous smile.

"What do you have in your hand?" the man asked.

Gathnok was going to try and hide it, but he soon figured that the shimmering compass was the only real proof he had of anything. He raised his hand and opened it out as it rested on the table. The compass shimmered, but it wasn't enough to draw attention to itself.

"Why does it point to us like that? Who are you?" The female sat back and stared at Gathnok with concern.

"I promise I wish you no harm. I'm meant to find you both, to help you."

"Help us with what?" the man interrupted.

"I know this sounds crazy, but you must believe me. You two are both spirits who need to be awakened. I'm one too. We have to find a jewel and stop the Darkmagi before they take all magic." Gathnok was aware, even when he was speaking, that it wasn't coming out in the right way.

"The Darkmage? What do you know of them?" They both looked concerned at one another.

"They burnt down my home, village, and family, and I know they won't stop until they have stolen all magic – unless we stop them." Gathnok looked at them both with complete resolution.

"A similar thing happened to our own home a year ago. I wish you well, Gathnok, but we are not spirits."

"If you weren't, then the shimmering compass wouldn't have found you."

"I'm sorry. Let's go." The man stood up and placed a hand on the woman's shoulder. Gathnok panicked as he couldn't allow them to leave.

"No, please!" Gathnok placed his hand on the man's arm. Just as he did so, for a single moment all three of them were connected by touch. In that moment Gathnok felt a similar rush, like when he destroyed that Darkmage. He hoped he wasn't about to crumble the two new spirits, but something felt different this time. This sensation felt pure and strong like some powerful potent energy rising up within him. His mind flashed as he felt strong and sure. It was a feeling so hard to describe, but it was very real. Gathnok broke away and stopped feeling a little faint.

"What was that?" the man asked.

"I think we just partly awakened," Gathnok replied.

"Partly?" the woman asked further.

"There are two others. We'll be strongest when we're all together. I'm the Heart."

"What are we?"

"I don't know. We're Elemental Spirits, so something tied with one of them, I'm guessing."

"Forlax, I did see great pools of water just now. That sensation, I…" The woman looked dazed and confused.

"I saw great burning flames." Forlax looked more controlled than his companion.

"Excellent. So you'll come with me, Forlax?" Gathnok wanted to confirm his name.

"He is Forlax, and I am Wispar." Wispar almost extended her arm to shake his but was wary of touching Gathnok. Instead she gave a polite nod.

"We need time to discuss this," Forlax said sternly.

"Oh, sure. I'll give you both an hour." Gathnok was thrown by the request, but it was actually rather sensible.

Magic can be deceitful, and as overpowering as that awakening had been, it was also rather terrifying. Gathnok picked up the shimmering compass and placed it back into his pocket. Now they had been found, the compass didn't shimmer any more.

Gathnok was walking the narrow streets of the small village. It felt strange to be walking along the stoned streets again, seeing houses which mirrored the style of his own village. This village, however, was dark and foreign to Gathnok, and the cool chill of the breeze made his flesh shudder. He thought about baby Marvie. He trusted Saban's pledge to protect him, but he worried for the future of Sahihriar. If the Darkmagi were to capture all magic, then Sahihriar would surely perish.

The streets were dimly lit by torches that were spaced across the street on the outside of small buildings. He was clearing his head after the day's events and giving Forlax and Wispar time to think. He found himself yawning as he stretched his body out. He hadn't taken another step when suddenly he felt a strange warmth coming from his pocket. He reached in and felt that the shimmering compass was sparking and getting warmer. He remembered the words of Saban, and he instantly knew that this was a warning. There were Darkmagi very close by.

He stopped as his heart began to race and peered out amongst the streets, but all seemed still. His mind raced to thoughts of destruction and despair for the village, but he couldn't let these thoughts distract him. The most logical thing would be to go and get Forlax and Wispar for help, for now he wasn't alone.

He was about to dart back when suddenly he heard a scream come from a nearby street. He didn't have time to get help as he burst into stride towards the sound of the shrill scream. He turned left as his legs pounded the cobbled floor, his eyes constantly peering into the dimly lit streets. He turned a final corner and stopped dead as he saw the most beautiful woman he'd ever seen. She was standing in the middle of a narrow path with four large hooded Darkmagi standing around her. One was on the ground and was beginning to stumble to his feet. She had long blonde flowing hair and a perfect oval face. Her skin was slightly pale, but her soft big red lips complemented it well. Awakening was nothing compared to what he felt looking at her. He was surprised, however, that she did not look helpless but looked strong as her stance was fixed and her arms raised to fight.

"Which one of you wants to try next?" She spoke with confidence.

"You cannot fight us all!" The hooded being stepped in closer whilst the others mimicked his movements.

"No, but I can!" Gathnok took a step forward and smiled a sly smile. He wasn't sure why he was coming across as confident as he was petrified inside. He just hoped that all he needed was to touch each one in order to stop them and have faith in the Ancients' prophecy.

The woman looked up and saw Gathnok standing further away. She had never seen him before, but there was something attractive about his green eyes hidden slightly by the fringe of his unkempt dark hair. The Darkmagi did nothing. The two behind her moved in closer whilst the two facing her turned and headed towards Gathnok; the fight was on. One Darkmage leapt towards the woman from behind. She was ready though and simply swung her elbow back into its face. It connected with a sharp blow, causing him to retreat. She spun on her heel trying to anticipate the next attack from the second hooded assailant, but she was met by a kick to her torso before she could react. She stumbled backwards but soon regained her poise. She clearly was not as delicate as she seemed.

Meanwhile Gathnok was coping with his own pair of attackers. He managed to dive under a hefty punch from one of them but was knocked sideways by a forceful punch from the other. He needed to bide his time as he watched their movements. They were pretty much covered by their hoods. Even their hands were shielded by clothes. The only place to make contact was through the hoods. It was rather menacing, as it almost seemed as though they didn't have faces, as they were lost in darkness from the fabric shielding. Taking a deep breath, he knew he had to act. He lunged one of his legs forward as if to kick the right one. He moved his hands low and arched his body to block. Gathnok didn't waste a moment and quickly launched his hand inside the hood. He felt his hand touch against the rough skin of the Darkmage, and as he did, he felt the similar sensation go through him as the Darkmage stumbled back. Gathnok watched as the other Darkmage stopped and noticed that his ally had begun to glow before he too crumbled into nothing before them. The remaining Darkmage stood back startled.

Gathnok waited, but instead of attacking, the being turned and ran towards the shadows. He knew it wouldn't be wise to let him escape, but he had to help the warrior lady. He ran towards her, as she had both of her enemies now in front of her. The mysterious woman was again tall and poised as her eyes darted between the two. Gathnok didn't wait for them to choose and grabbed one of them by the arm from behind. Working this to her advantage, she jumped into the air and did a flying kick which quickly hit, throwing the second one back. Gathnok had spun his one round by the arm and shot his arm into the hood and again touched the exposed flesh. Not even waiting, he spun round and swung his arm again through the second disorientated Darkmage. Soon both had flashed and crumbled, leaving Gathnok standing with the power still tingling through his body. It was an impressive display of skill that seemed to come from instinct. He was very shocked where this ability had come from. He looked up to see her startled, yet smiling.

"That was . . . How did you do that?" she asked. Even her voice was soft.

"Oh, that was nothing." Gathnok was lying through his teeth, but he couldn't help but portray a cheeky confidence when around her.

"Well, it was impressive." Her smile grew wider as her eyes sparkled.

"Thank you." Gathnok's smiled lingered as he struggled to think of something more to say.

"You're not from here, are you?"

"Not really. I'll be gone tonight."

"Oh, that's a shame." She looked down at the ground. She was fascinated by this new stranger.

Gathnok gave a small laugh. "Why?"

"You seem like a handy person to have around."

"Then maybe you should follow me," he said with a cheeky grin. He was enjoying the banter.

"You also seem like a dangerous person to have around," she said with another cheeky smile.

Gathnok beamed back a smile. "Well, if you get into trouble, I'll look out for you!"

"My own guardian? Lucky me!" She met his eyes now and smiled a playful smile.

They stayed lingering in that moment of shared smiles before

Gathnok shuffled uneasily. He nodded as a sign of respect before turning and walking away.

"Wait! What is your name?" she called.

"Gathnok!" He tuned as he spoke but continued to walk backwards. He didn't wait for a reply and had soon turned a corner.

Gathnok ran back to the inn and walked briskly towards Forlax and Wispar's table. He was clutching the compass in case it indicated any more Darkmagi. They looked up at him and seemed startled. He'd promised them an hour, but it had only been twenty minutes.

"Gathnok, we . . ."

"Darkmagi were here. I stopped them, but if you're coming, we must leave now!" Gathnok had hushed his tone, but his sense of urgency remained.

Forlax and Wispar's eyes widened as they looked at each other. They stood up and quickly followed Gathnok out. Gathnok wasn't short for his age, but the height and stature of Forlax and Wispar were intimidating. They stood by the gate and Gathnok turned to face them.

"I'm sorry I can't wait. Are you coming?" Gathnok was clearly agitated.

"I don't know. It's a lot to just come and . . ." Wispar clearly was still confused. They had just started making a life for themselves in the village.

"I know, and I'm sorry. I didn't ask for this. But we have to move on before they come back."

Forlax was about to speak, when suddenly they were all interrupted by shouting from down the street. They all turned, and Gathnok's heart jumped a beat when he saw it was the beautiful woman from the alley. She was running right towards him. Gathnok smiled and went to take a step forward to greet her, when suddenly Forlax beamed a great smile and ran towards her. Gathnok stood stunned. He watched as he approached her and they embraced. She also smiled to greet him and they stopped and stood talking. Wispar looked at Gathnok and noticed his confused expression.

"That is Lainla. She and Forlax have been friends since childhood."

"Friends?" Gathnok couldn't help see more affection from how they looked at one another.

"Forlax has always wanted more, but Lainla, she's more cautious. I think she's scared of ruining the bond they already share. Why, do you know her?" Wispar looked curiously at Gathnok.

"She was attacked by the Darkmagi. I helped her." Gathnok didn't take his eyes of them both as he spoke.

Wispar laughed upon noticing his fixed stare. "Don't worry; you're not the first kid to be enchanted by her."

Gathnok gave an uncomfortable look and broke his gaze. He wasn't about to argue as she was indeed beautiful. Soon enough, Forlax and Lainla walked back over to them.

"If we go, we're taking Lainla with us." Forlax seemed protective.

"If that's all right . . ." Lainla gave a dismayed look at Forlax's lack of tact and smiled at Gathnok.

"Oh, sure. You've proven you can take care of yourself. So does that mean you're all coming?" Gathnok gave a hopeful smile towards Lainla.

"Indeed," Forlax nodded, but the smile between Lainla and Gathnok hadn't gone unnoticed.

"Where to now then?" Wispar asked.

"To find the other Spirits." Gathnok took out the shimmering compass and held it up. Somehow it knew what Gathnok needed, and the needles began to spin.

Acknowledging its direction, they all began to walk out of the village to begin the journey. They walked for what seemed like a few hours. The sun had begun to fade, and the craziness of the day's events had hit them all hard. Wispar yawned, which triggered Gathnok to do the same.

"Maybe we should rest for the night?" Lainla commented after watching them both.

"Do we have time?" Forlax asked.

"They'll definitely catch us if we're too tired to walk. We'll sleep in forest areas where they won't find us." Wispar seemed to be rather sensible with her suggestion.

The path they were walking on seemed rather isolated, and thick tall trees lined either side of the path. Wispar was right: they did need rest, and the darkened forest would be the best place. They left the path and soon began walking into the woods. The tree rooftops blocked out most of the moonlight, but it was just light enough to see. Gathnok was finally relieved to have some company and he felt he could relax a little.

"What about here?" They had come to a small open area that seemed well enough away from the main path.

"Sure," Gathnok agreed.

"I'll get wood for the fire," Forlax nodded and began to walk away.

"I'll help." Wispar welcomed the chance to properly chat to her brother away from the others. Lainla and Gathnok were left standing in the enclosed circle.

"So you know Forlax then?" Gathnok felt a little intimidated.

"Yes, we're . . . close," Lainla said, not letting her gaze leave his.

"Is that why you came with us?" Gathnok asked, recalling their conversation from the alley.

"Of course. What other reason would I have?" Lainla gave a friendly smile, but it left Gathnok confused.

"Yeah, you're right, I guess."

Lainla smiled and then went and began to clear out the centre for the fire. As she did so, Gathnok couldn't help wonder how Lainla even knew Forlax was with them before she followed him. He knew he shouldn't, but he couldn't help feel some connection between them. Meanwhile, Forlax and Wispar were collecting dry branches and twigs for the fire.

"Do you think we made the right choice?" Wispar asked. She was younger than her brother and knew he was rather hot-headed and reserved. He'd only really open up with just the two of them there.

"The Darkmagi took a lot from us. This way, we can fight back," Forlax replied, as he continued to pick up small twigs.

"And you're sure that's all? Lainla has nothing to do with it?" Wispar wanted to sound casual but she was worried about him.

"You know how I feel about Li." Forlax beamed a smile as he thought about her.

"And what about Gathnok?" Wispar remembered the look on his face outside the inn.

"What about him?" Forlax asked innocently.

"Nothing . . . never mind"

After a while they had made a fire and had managed to clear patches on the floor for them to rest. They were so tired they didn't care that they were sleeping on dirt. It wasn't long before all four of them were fast asleep. Whilst they slept, Gathnok wasn't aware that the shimmering compass was burning brighter and getting warmer, warning them that the Darkmagi were nearby. They weren't aware that lurking in the shadows one of the hooded figures hid with someone else.

"Why would you show me this?" the Darkmage whispered, as he was confused.

He was standing next to Death himself, a skeleton draped in a black cloak, He stood menacingly in the shadows with his pointed reaper in his hand.

"To aid the prophecy. But remember, don't kill them yet. Learn of their plan first." With these words Death vanished from sight, leaving the Darkmage to watch over the Spirits.

"Choices . . ."

Chapter Five

The warriors known as Freeyers all sat in the old carpenter's factory in the Fifth Realm. It hadn't been used in years, and all that remained of its former purpose were a few piles of wood and the odd chair or table. The dirtied windows and broken lights meant it was pitch black inside. The outside wall was formed of rotten wood. The old industrial buildings were the only reminder of the peaceful times before the "great change".

Although the Freeyers were skilled warriors, there were only a handful of them left. It was now night time in the Fifth Realm, and even these elite warriors dare not tread the streets at night. They were waiting and hiding. All of the Fifth Realm's hope lay in this abandoned factory. If they were caught, then the Fifth Realm may never be saved. The legend says that the once-great healer Gathnok ruled over the Fifth Realm and held great power. The day of darkness came, and Gathnok never returned. However, that was many years ago and is now just considered to be a myth used to create false hope.

Minso's father had often told him stories of Marvie and how they had escaped together. After Marvie was gone, his father felt he had to come back and do what he could to honour the great wizard. He began to train warriors in secret ready for them to travel the realms and Sahihriar, initially to seek help. However, Minso's father gradually heard rumours that Marvie was still very much alive.

Fecki ran from in between the buildings outside. She had left her baby, as she couldn't risk being caught. It was deadly to be outside and if any of the patrolling dragons and ogres caught sight of her, all could be lost. She was rather excited by her discovery and was now so close. She pictured Minso's face when she told him. It would be worth it to see him smile. For now though, she would have to stay focused. She was the only female Freeyer warrior left, and she didn't want to be the last. The rain fell down hard, which was a helpful distraction to the wondering creatures. She saw the old worn factory. Letting her heart pound in her chest, she ran out across the exposed alley and knocked on the old door.

Minso ran over to the door and pressed his ear to it. The other warriors all got ready in case.

"Elders, betrayal." Fecki spoke the password. Since the abandonment of Marvie, all Freeyers believed the Elders had betrayed them by not helping.

"Fecki?" Minso swung open the door, as he wasn't expecting to hear her voice. Minso was greeted by a beaming Fecki. She looked tired, admittedly, but still naturally beautiful. She was ushered inside quickly. Minso smiled as he saw his old companion. However, he was a little surprised; she wasn't supposed to report back for another month.

"I have news." Fecki had a twinkle in her eye, and she spoke in a hushed whisper.

Minso didn't say anything back. He knew that Fecki wouldn't tease him, yet he didn't dare believe it.

"It's what we've been waiting for."

* * *

The group woke up the next morning. The sun shone out bright across Sahihriar. It was a warm day with the sky casting a pale blue. They had been walking for half a day. The morning was pleasant as Trickle and EggWiff walked and chatted about silly things. Flick and Saria somehow managed to end up walking side by side, but after last night's disagreement, neither of them seemed to want speak to the other. Morbid, however, had taken the front and seemed to be leading the way. The others followed aimlessly all morning, lost in conversation or in their own thoughts.

Flick felt uneasy. He wanted to apologise for the night before. He was so desperate to see the person underneath the warrior. However, every time he glanced at her, she was walking sternly with her head faced forward. He would occasionally attempt the odd smile, but that seemed to go unnoticed too. He couldn't for the life of him begin to understand why he cared so much, but he did.

As the morning turned to afternoon the group began to feel hungry. It was usually the decision to stop for lunch that broke the silences. Trickle was just about to comment on the lack of food rations when EggWiff disengaged from the conversation, stopped, and looked around confused.

"If this is something bad, then I'm just not walking with you anymore," Trickle moaned.

"No, little one, it's just that we're going the wrong way!" EggWiff continued to survey the land around him.

The rest of the group had stopped also to listen to whatever the trouble was with EggWiff.

"Morbid, are you sure this is the right way?" EggWiff's distrust in Morbid was growing more and more. The painful flashes of Morbid in the forest weren't helping.

Morbid nodded.

"But we are travelling north. The eastern border is that way." EggWiff gestured the direction with the tip of his staff.

Morbid stared blankly. It was sinister the way his skeleton sockets just glared. Trickle often felt uncomfortable by him. Flick was looking at Saria, as she seemed rather annoyed at the situation.

"Morbid is the navigator, and if he feels this is right, then we will follow it." Saria's voice was cold and commanding.

"Well, EggWiff doesn't agree." Trickle glared at Saria. Her dislike for her destroyed any fear of her.

"I didn't ask you to speak!" Saria took one step forward towards Trickle.

"Good, because I don't need you to!" Trickle too took a step forward.

Flick ran in front of Saria.

"Look, if Saria and Morbid say this is the right way, then it is! Just leave it alone and trust them, Trickle." Flick pleaded with his eyes to let Trickle back down.

Trickle glared at Flick. She couldn't believe he was defending Saria. Well, actually she could. It was obvious how he felt for her.

"Fine!"

The group went back to walking. EggWiff and Trickle began to talk about how clear it was they were going the wrong way and how stupid Flick was. Morbid continued to walk at the front, and Saria and Flick were back side by side.

"Do you really trust me?" Saria said softly. Her head was slightly low, yet her gorgeous eyes were staying at Flick.

"Yeah, I do." Flick nervously looked up at Saria and smiled. To his amazement, she gave a quick smile back.

The afternoon soon turned to evening, and still they hadn't come across the eastern border. They still had a satchel full of Essence, so they weren't worried. However, Trickle found it hard not to point out how they must have been going in the wrong direction, and if they only listened to EggWiff they wouldn't be lost.

They were each setting out where to sleep. After much debate, Flick plucked up the courage to go speak to Saria. She was trying to find a soft piece of dirt to rest on. The clearing was overcast with trees, so the ground was laden with mud and leaves. They hadn't had time to find a clearing they actually liked.

"Here, you can use this." Flick shyly handed over a blanket.

Saria looked shocked; at first she didn't know what to think. Why a Surthan breed was being so nice to her was baffling. She wanted to dislike Flick, but she couldn't help feel some form of warmth to him.

"Don't you need it?" she said with a smile.

"No. Actually, it's one I swapped with Trickle so she can bathe before me." Saria gave Flick a confused look. "She really likes to be clean."

Saria tried to hide her smile. She shouldn't let her emotions control her – not when she knew what her mission was.

"Thank you."

Over on the other side of the clearing, Trickle and EggWiff sat talking as they so often did.

"I knew we were going the wrong way." Trickle was overly preparing her muddy patch beneath her.

"Trickle, we are prisoners, and Saria's wishes should be obeyed." EggWiff was lying down on the ground. "The only thing I worry about is that we're very close to the border of the Black Sea"

"I've never really seen the Black Sea. Is it pretty?" Trickle was now carefully brushing the dirt away from her small patch of land where she was to sleep.

"Yes and no. It is one of the most deadly things in Sahihriar. It has taken countless lives. You see, the Black Sea isn't merely an ocean. It is a vacuum of darkness. When any living being or conscience touches the sea, it becomes lost forever." EggWiff spoke calm and casually.

"So that's a 'no' on the pretty thing, then?" Trickle's face screwed up in disgust at the thought of the ocean.

Flashes of a white figure flashed into EggWiff's mind. Fear and terror overcame him. He held his head sharply. Something was missing. Something still seemed awkward, but whenever he tried to reach it, all he received was searing pain.

"What's wrong? Are you having another one of your headaches?" Trickle gave EggWiff a concerned touch on the arm.

"It's getting better. The pain is fading." EggWiff tried to ignore the pain.

"Want to try some mind techniques again? It might help you relax."

"I appreciate the offer, little one. However, I believe that rest will be best for me for now. I bid you goodnight."

With this, EggWiff turned over and rested. Trickle was a little taken back; it was unusual for EggWiff to just dismiss her like that. However, she assumed he was in pain and felt sympathetic. Trickle knew that it was too early for her to sleep. Besides, she was absolutely starving and couldn't possibly rest yet. She got up and walked over by Morbid.

"What are you making, sweetie?"

"Nigglewart boil!" Morbid didn't look at Trickle. Instead he remained transfixed on the green murky liquid substance that bubbled within a small black cauldron above the fire. His voice had no warmth to it. As much as Trickle tried, she couldn't help but feel some form of dislike towards Morbid.

"Oh well, let me know when you are done. I can't wait!" Trickle formed a smile before returning to her patch of dirt. She looked over to see Flick and Saria chatting. She was still cross about what he did earlier, but she also couldn't help childishly getting excited by the potential of a romance. Soon the food was ready. They all ate alone and in silence, and as soon as they were finished, they all decided to go to sleep and awaken early in the morning.

Trickle awoke with a stir. The ground she was resting on was uneven, and seeing as she sacrificed one of her blankets so she could bath before Flick, she felt far from comfortable. She looked up at the stars, as it was something she used to do it a lot before her crime. She would often think of the stars as her friends, as a form of guidance. She sat for a while and pondered how she came to be here. She smiled as she realised how worth it, it all still was.

Two Months Earlier

The parade spread across the city like plague. The music thundered for miles as the cheers and laughter of the on-looking crowd was almost deafening. It was the day of celebration. The parade was run by the governing power of elves. Everyone was celebrating the liberation, the concept that they were free.

Elves were once creatures of slavery and abuse. They were treated as worthless beings, and it wasn't till the great battle of Himbawai that the abuse ended. The parade was to celebrate the independence and free thinking among the species.

That's just what everyone wanted to believe. Trickle knew differently. She knew how she was "nicely" asked not to take part. Apparently, a confused freak would offend. It made her sad, it made her sick, but more than anything else, it made her determined to march. Trickle spent the next week preparing, as she was going to make sure everyone at the parade saw her. She knew she could be killed for it, but she didn't care. At least she would go out believing in herself.

She waited by the gate awaiting her chance. The parade had sequences. Between each one was a gap of around a minute. When the next gap came, Trickle was going to make herself known. Her heart was pounding. She knew she was going to pay for this, but she couldn't help it.

She took a deep breath, closed her eyes, and ran out screaming wildly in her sequinned glittery dress. She was dressed up in the best, richest make-up she could afford.

"I am someone! I am someone! I am someone!"

The only problem was that no one was noticing. They were too busy cheering and laughing to notice one oddly dressed elf. Trickle peered around. Somehow she must be heard! She was determined that this discrimination wouldn't continue. She began to walk forward because she was now wedged between the parading elves in front and behind her. She frantically looked around. Every time she called out, she was drowned out by the cheering of the crowd.

But then she saw it. Up on the highest parade was an old elf talking into a long stick of bamboo; this magnified his voice so everyone could hear. Trickle smiled as she knew what she had to do. She forced her way through swarms of elves until she was at the bottom of the main cart. She paused for a moment and looked down at her outfit.

"Ugh! I knew I should have worn the skirt with a slit in it," Trickle muttered as she leaped up on the wooden frame.

People began to gasp as finally she was visible amongst the crowed. Trickle stood up straight on the wooden frame and peered out. Everyone had stopped and stared at the odd elf. Trickle didn't care though. She smiled a sly smile with a glint in her eye. Trickle quickly pushed off the older elf and gripped the end of the bamboo shaft. She took a deep breath and screamed once more.

"I am someone! I am someone! I am someone!"

The guards were out almost immediately. They were dragging her back. Trickle kicked and screamed with everything she had. She loved the freedom and sense of power. She wanted them to pay. She was liberated. One month later, Trickle was in court . . .

* * *

Trickle soon found herself softly drifting to sleep until she heard a sound. Faint footsteps could be heard further up the path. She lay still for a while wondering if it was one of the others. She had completely lost track of time in the distilled darkness. She contemplated waking EggWiff, but he had needed his sleep since his headaches. She raised her head again and waited. She heard it again. She looked up over across the muddy clearing. The footsteps were just on the other side of some nearby trees. Trickle couldn't remember if that's where the path was or not.

Even though it was pitch black, she decided to get up and investigate further. She thought about waking Saria. If this was a dangerous creature, then her skills would be useful. However, Trickle's pride was too great to ask anyone for help and, besides, she was only going to take a quick peek.

She could definitely hear footsteps coming along the path. She hid behind a small bush, as she didn't think it was anything dangerous, but curiosity got the better of her. She waited with anticipation. Her mind raced with different thoughts as she waited in the cold night air. Her heart pounded as she peered through the leaves. She could now see a shadowed outline walking along a dirt path. The footsteps were rather loud as the creature bustled along. Trickle sighed as the shadow didn't appear to be sinister at all.

She smiled to herself about her imagination and was just about to turn back when she felt an icy brittle cold hand come behind her and cover her mouth. She tried to scream, but it was reduced to a murmur, as she began to struggle violently. She kicked her heels, but her attacker was holding her from behind. She frantically squirmed, but then another being was holding her down. Her eyes wandered frantically, but all she could see was shadows. Despite her frantic struggling, they managed to hoist her into a sack. Fear overcame her, she was dazed and shaken, she couldn't think what to do, and her mind was racing over all the creatures that would kidnap someone, especially a male she-elf. She barely had time to breathe in the darkened enclosed sack when she felt it being hoisted in the air. She continued to kick and scream, screaming for EggWiff, screaming for Saria. She couldn't see or hear anything. She had never been so afraid in her whole life.

EggWiff was having the same nightmare; the white silhouette still haunted him. In his dream the white figure was talking with a shadowed figure. Both were evil, but it was the black shadowed figure that forced the fear of death into EggWiff. The dream was always the same. The two figures would talk in shadow. EggWiff would be standing, watching them from afar; the figures were oblivious to his presence. He could never hear what they were saying. It was as if he was a ghost watching in on a secret moment. After a few moments, the black shadowed figure would vanish and the white silhouette would walk away into the distance. When EggWiff would turn, he would see Morbid standing only inches from him, and all that Morbid would do was touch EggWiff's head with his small white skeleton fingers and whisper the words, "See without pain, and do what must be done."

This is when EggWiff would wake up in confusion and fear, and always with a teary face. The dream often felt so symbolic and always left EggWiff feeling confused. It was also the reason for his increasing distrust in Morbid.

However, this time it was different, when EggWiff turned, he didn't see Morbid. Instead he saw Trickle. She was crying into her hands. EggWiff found this strange and took a step closer. As he did so, Trickle looked up at him with tear-ridden eyes. Then in a sudden harsh shock screamed the words, "Help me!"

EggWiff was thrown from the realm of dreams back into harsh reality. EggWiff's eyes shot open as he sat bold upright in an instant. He didn't need to look down and see Trickle wasn't there. He knew she was in trouble. He didn't have time to wake Saria. Trickle needed him now. He stood to his feet and began to sprint furiously. His long legs gave him a good stride. Although old and an occasional alcoholic, it was clear EggWiff was very fit indeed.

Two shadowed figures dragged a sack along behind them up the path.

"That wasn't much fun. She gave up way too easily!"

"Don't celebrate yet! You know this is only part one of the plan." The two shadows stopped. Up ahead on the hill a blackened shadowed silhouette stood.

"Master! We have her, master!" Both shadows knelt, still firmly grasping the sack.

Trickle listened intently. She was pleased the sack had stopped being dragged for a moment.

"I am not your master. Now I strongly advice you let my friend go, and there shall be no further trouble." EggWiff stepped out of the shadows into clear view. The two shadows stepped back with fear.

The two blackened shadows moved their heads and looked at each other. They were so lifeless and blank. EggWiff narrowed his eyes trying to see them as they sometimes blurred with the shadows around them.

"You may be powerful, but our master will smite you. After what you did to him, you deserve to burn!"

The shadows' voices now had confidence. They threw the sack to the side as if it were rubbish. Trickle landed on her back and cried out in pain. Now on the ground, she tried to claw her way out of the top of the sack, although it was tied firmly on the outside. Trickle could now hear the conversation more easily and listened intently.

"I have never met your master, and he is of no concern to me. All I care about is you returning my friend!"

EggWiff twirled his staff twice through his fingers and then slammed it down into the ground. With this, the wind began to gently flow in the air. EggWiff was ready for battle. The two shadows took stance and suddenly both shouted the word "Fadair!" Two dark purple spheres of energy went hurtling towards EggWiff as the area glowed with a purple mist. EggWiff shouted, "Dispel" and waved his staff through the purple spheres. This caused them to vanish and have no effect on EggWiff. He smiled smugly to himself. No one was going to harm his only friend.

EggWiff shouted "Timeless!" A wave of green energy shot out in a violent burst and went soaring through the air at the shadowed creatures. Before they could call a response, the shadows were hit. The green energy turned into a cage around the two shadows, engulfing them in a green watery substance. They seemed frozen and encased by the green mystic energy. EggWiff waited. He wasn't confident enough in his magic to know how long it would work. Nor did he have enough knowledge about his enemy. He slowly began to creep towards the creatures, as he needed to be certain they were definitely frozen.

EggWiff stood straight in front of them. Even though surrounded by a green glow, they still remained pitch black. They truly were shadowed creatures. They looked much like someone from the Fifth Realm; they had a similar silhouette to EggWiff's.

Just moments before he was about to turn and free Trickle, an arm shot out from the mist and began to strangle EggWiff. EggWiff, who was taken by surprise, gripped the hand desperately as he felt himself being lifted up by the strength of the arm. EggWiff glared at the shadows as his legs dangled. Now penetrated, the spell began to dissolve to nothing. The two creatures stepped out and were free. With the shadowed being's other hand, he pushed it into EggWiff's chest with a hard punch. The force hurtled EggWiff back across the path floor landing with a violent thud. Seizing their chance, the two creatures grabbed the sack and began to run hastily into the forest border.

Although temporarily dazed, EggWiff leapt to his feet and followed. He staggered into the forest as his back was sore from his fall. The trees were thick and plenty. Once in the forest, there was scarcely any light. This made it hard to see obstacles in his path. Twigs and branches and tree stumps would smash into the two creatures as they ran from EggWiff. EggWiff too faced the same problem, and it didn't take long to realise how much this was slowing him down. He began to mutter a spell, and once he had finished, all the leaves, twigs and branches would fall back automatically, giving him a clear path towards the creatures. This gave him a vast advantage as he continued to focus on the brown sack a few feet in front of him. The two shadowed creatures looked back and could see that EggWiff was gaining. The weight of the sack flew behind, and Trickle began to feel a bit sick. Once close enough, EggWiff flung out his staff. It hit the shadowed beings' legs and evidently caused both creatures to buckle in stride and trip. As they fell, the sack went hurtling to the ground and the rope that tied it began to loosen. Trickle fell on her head hard, and she began to feel herself slowly losing consciousness.

EggWiff stood tall over the creatures. They trembled with fear as their faces looked up at EggWiff's. His blue eyes, once innocent, now burned with fury. His face was stern and bold. He didn't move. He was rigid and solid and just stared into the lost creatures' faces.

"What did you want with Trickle?" His voice was deep and he stood tall and commanding over the creatures like a warrior about to slay his enemy. He allowed his staff to hover above one of their chests.

The two creatures looked at each other for an instant and then began to laugh. It was a sickening, shrill laugh that echoed throughout the forest. EggWiff raised his staff in fury and was about to bring it down, when a shining, blinding red light flashed and seared throughout the forest. EggWiff stumbled back covering his eyes. He felt himself lose balance and began to fall backwards, when a creature caught his fall. One creature managed to be holding his legs. Another had twisted his arm behind his back and was holding it there. EggWiff froze with fear and his eyes widened as he listened to the words the creatures was whispering.

"We didn't want *him*, we needed you . . ."

With these words, the two creatures vanished into the shadows. EggWiff went with them.

A Sacred Past

"Are you sure this is right?" Wispar asked. They had strayed from the main path and had since been walking in the forest for about six hours.

"It's not been wrong so far," Gathnok replied.

The trees were thick and tall, and the ground was littered with leaves. The trees had markings on them which seemed important; the markings were on more and more trees the longer they followed the needle.

"These are Amazon markings. We must be near the city," Forlax warned.

"You think the other Spirit is an Amazon?" Wispar asked.

Gathnok shrugged as they continued to walk. Not long after they slowed, they noticed a high wooden fence spread across the horizon. It was made from thick tree trunks, and the top was spiked. They all peered and could see that it wasn't just a fence, but rather a wall, as there were Amazons with bows standing at its top. Amazons were small dwarf beings. They were known for their great strength and courage. Their skills as warriors were often spoken of highly. However, they were beings of principle and would only embark on missions which helped their cause.

"State your intent," one of the Amazons called from the wooden wall.

"We wish you no harm. We simply seek to find someone," Gathnok called.

"Who?"

Gathnok looked at the others. He wasn't really sure how to respond, but he had little choice. At least one of the other spirits was inside the Amazon City.

"Whomever this points to." Gathnok held up the shimmering compass. It glowed brightly, and its pure light amongst the dim *covered forest made it seem enchanting. There was a silence as the Amazon who spoke disappeared behind the wall.*

Soon the wall began to open. It was impressive and a surprise, as the gate matched the rest of the wall. Its two big wooden doors swung outward, sweeping the leaves and dirt as it did. Out walked about ten Amazons. They wore the green colours of the forest, and each brandished a sword and shield. They stepped out towards them. Gathnok was surprised to notice they were followed out by two other people. They were not Amazons. They were tall and didn't wear the colour green. Instead, the male wore a blue tunic and dark trousers whilst the woman wore a red satin top that hung from her petite frame. She also wore dark trousers and had blonde hair. The woman was pretty in a natural sense whilst the man was clearly very well built. He looked as if he'd been chiselled from ice. Gathnok looked down and almost smiled as the heat reached his hand. The needle was spinning between the two as the shimmering compass glowed even brighter.

"Whom do you seek?" the Amazon asked, being cautious of the glowing compass.

"Them." Gathnok pointed at the two strangers. The rest of the group stared at them whilst they both looked very confused.

"Euthan, do you know of these people?" the Amazon called back.

"I do not, Asemai?" Euthan's voice was deep and mirrored his physique.

"No."

"I know you don't know of me, but I wish you no harm. I need to speak with you about the Darkmagi." Gathnok hoped his innocent pleading look still carried some weight.

At the mention of the Darkmagi both their faces fell. The Amazon turned to look at one another to agree to a wordless response, and Gathnok was relieved when he nodded his acceptance. They were all led inside the gate into the Amazon City. However, they remained under guard.

"So, let me guess. He's your brother?" Gathnok asked Asemai as they were being led through.

Asemai gave a weak smile which showed sadness in her eyes.

"No, my brother was killed by the Darkmagi a while ago. He was also Euthan's best friend."

Gathnok felt guilty. He just assumed after Forlax and Wispar that maybe they were related too. The Darkmagi had stolen much from them all.

Euthan and Asemai sat at the table in a large room in the Amazons' main chamber. They had been sitting for a while as Gathnok desperately tried to convince them of their mission. Wispar was very impressed by the sheer scale of the Amazon city – the craftsmanship and care behind every carving, the tall buildings, and the many layers all interwoven around the thousands of trees. It was beautiful as the warrior dwarfs inhabited the peaceful surroundings. The shimmering compass sat at the centre of the table. Forlax was looking annoyed as he sat uneasily.

"I understand your cause, and I wish you well, but we cannot leave until we know the Amazon City is safe."

"But if you don't come, then we may not stop the Darkmagi at all, risking the safety of all Sahihriar – not just this city." Forlax stamped his fist onto the thick, smooth wooden table.

"The compass led us to you. We are the Elemental Spirits." Gathnok tried directing his plea towards Asemai in the hope she'd be more understanding.

"You said there were five of us in total. Which one of you is not a spirit?" Asemai's voice was soft and gentle, almost soothing in tone.

"I am not. My name is Lainla."

"Why do you choose to follow them?"

Lainla had to stop herself from once again looking towards Gathnok. She felt guilty for betraying her heart, but she couldn't help it. Instead she looked at Forlax and forced a small smile.

"Because I trust them."

"Plus, she's a good warrior!" Wispar gave a friendly smile towards her friend.

Gathnok smiled. Both Euthan and Asemai seemed a little surprised by Wispar's statement, just as Gathnok had been back in the alley.

"Well, we cannot allow..."

Euthan's sentence was drowned out by the loud cries and ringing of bells all around the city. People were screaming as they moved hurriedly in every direction. The three strangers looked around confused.

"It's an attack! Looks like the Darkmagi have found you." Asemai was now standing and moved towards the door. Euthan was behind her.

"Let us help! We can stop them." Gathnok now stood. As bad as the attack was, it may be a chance to show them their potential.

"Your choice."

They stepped out to see Amazons all preparing, many with shields and swords running towards the main gate at which they had been greeted. Gathnok stood and looked out over towards the gate. They stood up high on one of the wooden tree-top pathways so he could easily see. Amazons had lined up behind the great gate ready for battle, whilst others stood high on the wooden platforms above the gate ready with bows. Although raised, Gathnok and the others struggled to see past the wall.

"Well, this isn't good." Wispar looked round worried.

"We must help them fight." Forlax took a step forward.

"No. We should fight for them. It's the only way they'll see." Gathnok also moved forward. "Will you help?"

Lainla was taken aback by Gathnok's sudden shift of focus.

"No. There are too many, and this isn't her cause. You'll be safer up here." Forlax almost glared at Gathnok for risking her life.

"Forlax, I love that you love me, but I can help, and I shall." She placed a comforting hand on his arm, which sent a rush of warmth through his body. Forlax couldn't help but be entranced by her.

They rushed down towards the main gate where Euthan and Asemai were already preparing the Amazons.

"Wait!"

"We must protect this city," Euthan began in protest.

"Don't send them out there. Let us deal with this as spirits." Gathnok hoped he was doing the right thing.

"We've never fought as spirits before, Gathnok. Besides there are thirty Darkmagi out there."

"Oh, thirty…" Gathnok's eyes widened. He figured that maybe eight would be out there at the most.

Seeing his sudden change in confidence, Wispar stepped forward.

"It doesn't matter. We were meant to do this. It was destiny." Wispar stared deep into Euthan's eyes as she refused to let go of his gaze.

"We'll go out first, and in five minutes the Amazons will open the doors and attack." Euthan nodded to ensure the Amazons understood.

"Let's hope that's all we'll need then!"

They each stood in a line in front of the large wooden doors.

"Take each other's hands!" Gathnok was beginning to feel natural in his role and to have more belief in his ability.

"Why?" Asemai looked concerned.

"To awaken," Wispar replied.

They each began to take the hand of the person next to them. Euthan took Asemai's to his right and began to reach out the other hand for Lainla's.

"This wasn't meant for me." She smiled as she spoke.

At first Euthan looked confused, but then he was suddenly overcome by a strange sensation. Somehow the Spirits instinctively knew what to do. They each began to move whilst holding hands and formed a circle. The power was made stronger when they were all connected to one another. Then when the moment felt right, they each let their fingers part and began to raise their hands high above them. Euthan looked across and all five Spirits began to shimmer like the compass that had been shown to him. He felt a comforting feeling run through him. It was powerful, but it felt natural, and in that moment Euthan felt as though he had awoken to his true destiny. Lainla watched as the mystical power swirled above and around them before settling and slowly fading. They didn't have time to discuss anything before the giant wooden doors swung open and revealed the large huddle of hooded beings in front of them. They stood still and silent. Gathnok peered round and almost jumped at the sound of the wooden door closing behind him. Seeing as they weren't throwing themselves into battle, Gathnok thought he might try something new.

"*Why do you come here?*" *Gathnok called out as they were still some distance away.*

"*We're told you have the power to defeat us. This cannot be allowed to continue.*" *The voice came from a hooded figure. It was deep and authoritative.*

"*We wouldn't need to fight if you stopped what you are doing!*"

"If we don't protect magic, then you cannot destroy it." The hooded figures didn't waver as they spoke.

The six of them all looked at each other confused.

"You're stealing magic. You kill for your cause. I've heard the prophecy. It's us who are stopping you."

"The prophecy is vague in parts, but the ending is very clear. Five warriors will destroy Sahihriar."

"Then we are not that five. It is you who kill for your cause."

"The death is regrettable but unavoidable. We must keep magic safe – from you."

"Stop killing, and we both can walk away."

"We can make no such sacrifice."

"Then fight!" Gathnok braced himself for battle as the others did the same.

The Darkmagi began to run towards them. Instantly the Spirits had to react. Surprisingly, it was Asemai who was first to react as a shot of wind came hurtling in towards three of the Darkmagi, throwing them back on the ground. Gathnok watched as three shots of water erupted from the ground, throwing the Darkmagi up in the air. Gathnok was so distracted by what was going on around him that he didn't notice one of them only seconds from him. His mind went blank as he saw the Darkmage coming closer. The dark hood seemed empty and vast, and for the first time since the beginning Gathnok felt completely overwhelmed. He jumped as the Darkmage was suddenly swept to one side by a large branch of a tree which appeared almost alive. Gathnok looked over at Euthan who merely nodded.

The battle looked magnificent as all the elements were being used to battle the startled Darkmagi. Fire circles were used to trap some of them. Others were being punched away by the trees that seemed to dance around them. Water was being sprayed all over the Darkmagi, whilst little swirls of air threw them off *balance. Any Darkmagi that got through were met by Lainla, who continued to prove her skills as a warrior. It wasn't easy though, as already the Spirits looked tired. So far Gathnok had just stood there.*

"If you can destroy them, I think you had better start now!" Wispar called whilst jets of water sprayed from her hands.

Gathnok was snapped back to reality as he realised his place in all this.

"Get them together," Gathnok called.

Impressively, the team worked well in unison. Their individual attacks ceased, and soon a circle of flames trapped them all. The flame circle got smaller, forcing them to step back in closer. When they were pretty close, Euthan knelt down and touched Sahihriar. The others watched as thick tree vines appeared and quickly wrapped themselves around the Darkmagi, forcing them all to be huddled together and tied. Taking this to be his cue, Gathnok took stride and went towards them. The flaming shield had been dimmed, which allowed him to walk through. Now they were captive, the Darkmagi just sat still and almost lifeless. He went up to them and didn't say a word. He almost felt guilty that he had to destroy them, but they had never shown remorse and their justification was based on lies. Gathnok began touching each of the Darkmagi through the hood. It was still a chilling sensation. He sped up the process as he walked around. The vine grew tighter as fewer of them remained. The others watched on with curiosity. It was a strange sight. Gathnok's skill was a gentle yet lethal one. Soon enough all of them were destroyed. Gathnok felt weak from using up so much energy and stumbled back slightly.

"Are you alright?" Lainla asked, seeing him stagger slightly.

"I will be."

"Well that was intense," Asemai noted.

"We seem very powerful," Forlax commented.

"But only when we're a team." Gathnok looked at Euthan and Asemai. He hoped the battle had proved their worth.

"So it would seem. We'll all rest here tonight, and tomorrow we shall join you." Euthan turned with Asemai and headed back towards the gate.

"Good, because I doubt getting Cupido Sacra to the Ancients will be easy."

As they disappeared into the gate, they didn't know that one of the Darkmagi had remained in hiding. Although concealed by his cloak it was smiling as it had learnt their plan. Once again it was joined by Death.

"Now you know their plan," Death said in his raspy voice.

"I still don't know why you help us." The Darkmage was uncomfortable with the thought of Death helping them. He was very mysterious.

"I'm here to help the prophecy."

"Which version? The one where he destroys Sahihriar. Or the one where he saves it?"

"The correct one." With this, Death nodded his white chalky skeleton head and disappeared from the Darkmage's side once more, leaving the Darkmage even more confused than he was before.

"I'm Sorry . . .
But Who Are You Again?"

Chapter Six

"Quick! You gotta wake up, sweetie. It's important!"

"Huh?"

"Flick! Get up!" Trickle was frantically poking Flick's arm.

Flick opened his eyes slowly. "Arrghhhhhhhh!" Flick moved his head back. Trickle had her face with its smeared make-up extremely close to Flick's.

"Flick, it's just me." Trickle eased back; his yelling had made her jump.

"Don't do that, Trickle! What time is it?" Flick noticed that it was still dark.

"Flick, something has happened." Flick had never seen Trickle's face so serious before.

"Saria?"

Trickle's mouth fell open, and to Flick's shock she whacked his arm.

"No, not Saria! EggWiff!"

"Ouch!" Flick sighed as he sat up. "What about EggWiff?"

"EggWiff's been kidnapped!"

"What do you mean kidnapped?" Flick was mumbling. His eyes were still heavy as he forced himself to fully wake up.

"Look, go wake up Morbid and Saria. I've packed all the things, and I'll tell you as we get moving, okay?"

"Go where? It's the dead of night." Flick was really confused.

"Just do it, Flick!" Trickle got up and walked away, leaving Flick with his orders.

It wasn't long before they were all awake. Saria had been furious no one had awoken her. Flick kept protesting he was asleep or else he would have done so. Morbid didn't seem that bothered; he just listened intently whilst smothered in his travelling robes. They were all sitting in the clearing listening to Trickle.

"I mean, I couldn't see or hear much because I was in the sack, but there were two of them, and they used magic and were really strong." Trickle couldn't focus, as she was too worried about EggWiff.

"You didn't fight them?" Saria asked bluntly.

"They had magic and were strong." Trickle was annoyed by her lack of common sense.

Trickle noticed as Saria looked sideways; it was clear she had little respect for Trickle.

"Well, we have no idea who these shadow people are, what they want with EggWiff, or where they've taken EggWiff," Flick declared, trying to avoid further confrontation.

"So we have to do something."

"Do we?" Morbid stared blankly at Trickle.

"What? Of course we do! We can't leave him!" Trickle

was looking desperately at the three of them; she was angered by their lack of compassion.

"Trickle, we have no idea what EggWiff's crime was, or who or what these creatures are. I don't want to risk my life for him."

"Well, doesn't that just sum you up, Flick?" Trickle's blood was boiling.

"That's not fair, Trickle. And may I remind you that we are prisoners on a sentence. You have no choice in the matter. We can report him missing once we get to the eastern border. Then it can be dealt with properly." Saria stood up finalising the discussion.

"You don't seriously think we should just keep going like normal? He needs our help!" Trickle screamed.

"We can't help him. We can't do anything for him. Besides, it is no great loss. All he did was switch and drink." Morbid stood still and let his hollow vacant expression stare into Trickles face.

"What! This coming from Mister 'I'm dead but haven't got over it'!" Trickles voice was enraged.

"At least I know what I am; you're nothing but a pathetic he-elf, in a pink dress!"

Trickle stared at Morbid stunned. The hurt and hate on her face was clear. Morbid had overstepped his mark. She paused for a second before lunging towards Morbid. She frantically grabbed his bones and tried shaking them. Although this was pretty pathetic, she didn't care. She wanted to smash something.

Saria pulled Trickle off whilst Flick stood in front of Morbid. Saria drew her sword and glared at Trickle.

"You either do as I say or you will die!"

Trickle wasn't stupid. As angry as she was, she knew she couldn't help EggWiff if she were dead. She stepped back and loosened her stance. Morbid stepped back also.

A silence fell upon them as the tension began to turn from violent to uneasy.

Flick looked over at Saria. "What now?"

"Seeing as we're awake, we'll head towards the eastern border and try to make up for lost time." Saria nodded at Flick and then walked on, Flick, Morbid, and Trickle followed.

They walked as the sun lit up Sahihriar in an orange haze. They didn't speak as they all seemed lost in their own perception of the night before.

Trickle felt ill. With every step she took, she felt guiltier and guiltier about EggWiff. He would never just abandon her like this. But what more could she do?

"You made the right choice back there." Flick wondered how much comfort his words would really give.

Saria looked at him. She admired him so much. If only he knew the conflict she had. Should she listen to the warrior or the woman? She managed a weak smile.

"I hope so."

After walking a further few minutes, Saria suddenly stopped and drew her sword. No one else needed to ask why, as they could see a blinding light shining from the pathway. It was pure white, and it was warm but not hot. The others stepped back in fear and confusion; however, Saria stood still and focused. The light was only a few feet in front of them, and they couldn't understand where the light was coming from or what was causing it. The light made them squint, as it was beginning to be harder to see. Eventually the light completely faded though, and in its place was a beautiful fairy.

She was a fairy unlike any other fairy they had ever seen. She was as tall as a wizard and had beauty that shone from her. Instantly the group felt safe and protected. They were all stunned in amazement. Saria lowered her sword and smiled.

The fairy had long blonde silky hair, with deep hazel eyes and a smile to warm the coldest of hearts. Her wings glowed a pastel blue and fluttered delicately. She wore a white satin dress that shimmered in the light.

Trickle looked at Flick, whose mouth had become permanently open, whereas Morbid just stood still. The fairy just hovered in front of them.

"Who are you?" Saria's voice wasn't harsh or demanding, more inquisitive and soft.

Trickle thought she could see the fairy give Saria an off glance. She couldn't help be pleased that Saria was getting an odd look for once.

"I am Lainla, Spirit of Magic." Lainla smiled. They all felt entranced by her. Even Morbid felt his bones tingle. This is when Flick and Morbid began to slowly come back to reality. Flick's face looked confused, and Morbid's vacant expression revealed nothing.

"Please don't take this the wrong way, but what do you want?" Saria still had her sword in her hand. She wasn't going to allow herself be fooled.

"I know of your friend EggWiff and what happened. I've been sent by the Elders to give you a message." Lainla showed compassion when speaking of EggWiff. Trickle felt relieved.

"Is he okay? Who took him?"

"He is safe for now, but the Elders have sent me to tell you that it's crucial you get him back."

"Why's that?" Flick was only beginning to comprehend the situation.

"Because if you don't, Sahihriar is doomed." Lainla's face was serious but not cold.

"I'm sorry – what?!" That was the last thing Trickle expected Lainla to say.

"It's very complicated. Simply put, you all have a role to

play in this journey. There is a reason for everything, and all will be made clear. For now you must travel across the Black Sea and begin your search. It's the only way to save your friend."

"Search for what?" It was Morbid who spoke this time.

"The mystical jewel known as Cupido Sacra. Only with it destroyed can you save Sahihriar!" Lainla fluttered to and fro. Trickle loved her hair.

"I'm sorry, but who are you again?" Flick was clearly slightly distressed.

"I am Lainla, Spirit of Ma…"

"Yeah, I know that. But you can't just appear from thin air and tell us to go save Sahihriar. We have no idea who you are, and besides, we can't. We have a sentence to fulfil, don't we Saria?"

"Not anymore," Saria replied, much to Flicks amazement.

"What?"

"We'll do as she says. We can still tell people about Essence as we search. The Council can wait."

"But…" Flick was looking at Saria with a baffled expression.

"I'm not discussing it any further, Flick." Saria glared at him; her decision was final.

Saria smiled and nodded at Lainla. It was as if they had reached some hidden understanding. Flick hung his head low whilst Trickle grew a smile. Finally they were saving EggWiff.

"No, wait! This is ridiculous. You can't be seriously considering this!" Flick said, refusing to let the subject go.

"Flick, I've already said . . ." Saria tried to interrupt.

"No! Come on! We're not warriors, Saria. We're not spirits or magical or anything. Look at us!" Flick was now screaming, and it was now clear that the events had taken their toll.

"Flick, sweetie, it'll be okay." Trickle went to place a comforting hand on Flick.

"No, it won't. You're in a dress, Morbid doesn't speak and is known to cry, and I'm not anything special. We're not meant to save Sahihriar. We can't begin to do this!" Flick stared at them all before his eyes welled. He turned, ashamed, and trudged off along the path.

He was so frustrated he didn't know what to do. It was awkward enough trying to travel with them, but to be told they had to save Sahihriar was too much. How could anyone expect him, them even, to do that? He was a Surthan breed, the lowest of low.

The group stood in silence for a while. Saria felt anxious and wanted to go speak to Flick, but before she could do so, Trickle sighed and had begun to walk off after him. Morbid, Saria, and Lainla were left standing in the path.

"She'll get him back. Don't worry," Morbid said in his eerie tone.

Trickle walked for a few minutes and found Flick sitting on a log by the side of the path. The morning sun had now taken its place in the sky, providing comforting warmth.

"You okay, hun?" Trickle said, sitting down next to Flick.

"No. I know you're worried about EggWiff. I do understand that, Trickle, but some floating fairy can't just turn up and tell us to do this. We just can't." Flick was sat with his head in his hands.

"Listen, Flick. I'm not stupid. I know we're not warriors or powerful in any way. Heck, I'm not even 'normal' apparently. But I do know that I'm not worthless." Trickle spoke softly but there was power in her words.

"Worthy enough to save Sahihriar?" Flick replied.

"Worthy enough to try. Listen, I don't know what will happen tomorrow or the next day, but I'll deal with that when it comes. All I know is today I need to help EggWiff." Trickle stood up, and after brushing dirt from her dress, she held out her hand to Flick.

"So you gonna try and help us?" Trickle grew a smile as Flick took her hand.

Soon enough Trickle and Flick appeared on the horizon and re-joined the three strangers. It was awkward as they all stood in silence. Trickle was sure she had heard them talking as she walked back. She hoped they hadn't been talking badly about Flick. Lainla smiled a comforting smile whilst Trickle gave a reassuring nod. Flick just stood sheepishly and couldn't look anyone in the eye.

"Once you reach the other side of the Black Sea, I shall speak to you again. For now, follow my dragon. He shall take you. Please be safe, and I wish you well." With these words there was another blinding flash of light, and Lainla was gone from sight.

They all stared around. It was as if they were waiting for something. They knew that something should happen. This was confirmed by an ear-piercing screech from high above. All four of them covered their ears as their eyes darted up to the sky. High above the clouds was a small shadowed outline of an enormous bird-like creature.

The shadow grew larger as it began to hurtle down towards the ground. Saria began to run first. Flick and Trickle also began to run once they realised what Saria was doing. They needed to be out of the shadow of the dragon so they wouldn't be hit by the mammoth beast. They all waited in anticipation until the winged beast landed. The ground quaked as it crashed into the land beneath it. It was the largest dragon ever known. Its wings stretched out to the width of the tallest trees. Its body was lined with soft red scales that shimmered in the beaming sun. The force of the wings flapping made all four of them fall back onto the ground.

"Ouch!" Trickle looked over at everyone else. They seemed unsteady but unharmed.

All their mouths were open in awe. The dragon's body was enormous and intimidating, being a darker shade on top, and its spine was lined with little horns that gradually got smaller along its spine. Its head was enormous, and it had huge bulging red slits for eyes. As it had landed, the dragon knocked over many trees either side of the path. Its tail was incredibly thick and thinned out into a webbed leaf shape. The whole landing lasted less than a second. The whole event was loud and dominating as the Dragon now stood proudly in front of the four. They all got back on their feet and walked up close to it.

Its breath was nauseating and made the surrounding air smell rank. Its breath was so powerful it felt more like a gentle wind. The dragon's claws were long and dug into the path floor. It slithered its long tail from side to side and turned its head towards the group. All four of them began to huddle as it slowly put its face only inches away from their own. Saria, of course, showed no sign of fear. Trickle could feel her heart pounding. Flick smiled; he liked the thought of having a pet dragon. Morbid stood tall in front of the beast. The dragon stared into Morbid's hollow eyes. Trickle and Flicked looked at them; neither moved nor made a sound. It was as if they were frozen in each other's stare, and it was hard to tell what Morbid was doing, as he was hidden in his stain-ridden travelling robe.

"Lainla said we must follow her dragon. It wants us to climb on its back." Morbid then walked to the side of the enormous creature and began to scale up the side, using the tip of the wing as foothold. Once on top, he stood and held on to one of the small horns.

"You can talk to it?" Trickle asked, whilst pulling Flick back to his feet. Morbid looked quite impressive as he stood tall on such a valiant creature.

Morbid nodded. Saria finally put her sword away. Considering her height compared to the dragon, she easily managed to climb on the beast. Amazons appeared to be very agile.

"Guess we're off to save Sahihriar!" Flick moaned.

Trickle and Flick crept to the side of the dragon. Because of their height they had to be helped up by Morbid and Saria. It took longer to help Trickle, as her skirt severely limited the movement of her legs. After five minutes, when they were all firmly rested in between or next to a horn, Morbid signalled for its take off.

The dragon's wings began to flutter, and its legs bent lower into the ground. The scaly body began to move slowly. The sensation was strange, and they all gripped tighter onto one of the horns on the dragon's back. With a mighty push off, the dragon soared into the air and began to flap its wings. Flick found it immense fun, Trickle felt sick, and again Morbid showed no sign of emotion. Flick was behind Saria. Her green hair bounced with the wind. The wings made Trickle's wig flow too, but it didn't create the same feelings for Flick. Flick could hardly breathe, and the wind howled as it circled Morbid's hollow body.

They began to soar high above the clouds. The view was phenomenal, as they could see the very tip of the Mountains of Paradise. Trickle for the first time felt free and alive, although her thoughts were stuck upon EggWiff. The only warming thought was that she was going to do something about it. They flew for ten minutes until Trickle saw something ahead. The land stopped and turned into a

Black Sea that spread out into the furthest horizon. It was murky, and its depth was impossible to judge. At first Trickle wondered what it was. It was as if a black sheet had been laid over the land.

Trickle remembered her conversation with EggWiff, and a shuddering chill made her feel uneasy and tense. "Yes and no. It is one of the deadliest things in Sahihriar. It has taken countless lives. You see, the Black Sea isn't merely an ocean; it is a vacuum of darkness. When any living being or conscience touches the sea, it becomes lost forever."

Trickle thought it was better to warn the others. "Hey guys, we're above the Black Sea. Whatever falls into it instantly dies. Morbid, make sure the dragon is careful!" Trickle shouted as loud as she could.

Flick looked confused. Saria was looking at the sea with a curious expression. Trickle managed to see Morbid nod, or at least she hoped she did. It was strange for Morbid. It wouldn't have been that long ago that he might have willingly lunged into the Black Sea. However, Morbid sent the message to the dragon to slow down.

Sure enough, a few seconds later the dragon slowed down, the force changed from howling wind to calming breeze, and Trickle became more relaxed. Trickle patted the scaled floor and smiled.

"Thanks, sweetie. That's better!"

Trickle jumped with fright as the dragon let out a mighty screech. The dragon began to swoop to the side and bent down lower. No longer was it graceful; its movements had become hard and jerky.

"Saria, what's wrong with it?" Trickle gripped tight as the dragon began to twist violently and shake. With the depths of the Black Sea beneath them, Trickle began to get seriously scared.

"Nothing's wrong with him, Trickle. Look to your left."

Trickle could only just make out Flick's voice from behind her.

For the first time she really looked to the left, and she gasped at the sight. There were hundreds of Mithworks. Trickle couldn't believe she had been so distracted by the Black Sea that she hadn't noticed them sooner.

Mithworks are bird creatures but have no magical connections. Their wings are made of the strongest feathers, and great warriors coil their shields with them. Trickle had never seen a real Mithwork. She didn't mind, as in old elf law it was said to be early death to see one. But now she wasn't just seeing one, she was seeing hundreds. All the Mithworks began to swoop under, over, and to the sides of the dragon. Giant black Mithworks scattered throughout the sky. The dragon was trying to weave amongst them, but they soon surrounded all sides. They were above, below, and to the left and the right. The dragon was stuck in the middle.

After Morbid saw this, he knew what was to happen. He told the dragon to stop and hover. The dragon stopped so that it was hovering. The sound of flapping wings could be heard, along with the roar of the waves beneath.

"This is a magnificent day, my brethren, a truly wonderful day! Today we have fought back! Today we have won the Holy Grail of Sahihriar, and we have got the Essence!"

Trickle, Flick, Saria, and Morbid looked up. Rising from a Mithwork beneath them was a pig, a pig wearing bright purple ceremonial robes. He was looking at all the other Mithworks. Flick peered amongst them, and on the top of each Mithwork were small pigs, each wearing black. There were about ten on each. With the mention of Essence, they all roared!

"So, do we just attract psycho evil people?" Trickle cringed with fear.

"What's so special about the Essence?" Flick was now

standing, as was Morbid. Trickle seemed to just cling to the horn.

"I don't know. Not really caring much either!" Saria had reached for her bow and was aiming her first arrow.

"Look around you, Amazon. We could destroy you before you even make your first hit!" The Holy Master was yelling from only a few meters away.

Saria glared. She was annoyed but wasn't stupid. They could easily be defeated. The first rule of an Amazon is to stay alive. She sighed as she lowered her bow.

"Not if you want your holy Essence!" Trickle smirked, as she was hanging the satchel loosely over the edge of the dragon.

The Holy Master's heart jumped. Nothing was more important to him than the holy Essence. Nothing made any sense otherwise. However, the Elder had spoken to him. His faith had to go beyond the Essence, no matter how much it was killing him.

"Are you ready, my brothers?" The general pig called to all Mithworks.

All four of them looked confused, and Trickle's smirk died. For some reason the threat of losing the Essence didn't seem to matter.

The pigs began to mumble, as clearly they too were confused.

"For the faith!" The Holy Master's voice quivered, but it was firm – firm enough to stop the murmuring. All the pigs began to rustle, and then they all stood at a stance, with a staff in one hand. In unison, all of the pigs pointed the staffs at the centre of the dragon.

"Saria, why didn't that work?" Flick yelled.

"I have no idea. Just try to hold on tight" Saria tried to sound comforting, but she too was frightened.

"Fire, my brothers! Bring back the promised world!" These were the words that signalled the attack.

The dragon roared with pain as shock waves of energy came pulsating towards them. Blue swirls of energy filled the sky and would smash into the dragon's scales. Flick and Trickle held on as the dragon began to toss and turn in pain. The dragon screeched, but this only encouraged the pigs. Their oinks and cheers echoed across the sky.

The dragon was hit in the face, and this caused it to go spinning a full rotation to the side. Flick clung to the horn to compensate and held on with bated breath. Morbid, being the tallest and lightest, found it easy to stay grounded. Saria too managed to flip her leg up just in time. They all had to keep their heads low and pray the energy waves would continue to miss them. Trickle froze, as she wasn't prepared for such a sudden movement. She tried to hold on to the Essence and hoist her leg up, but her skirt made it impossible. In a sudden moment of shock, she lost all grip, thought, and emotion.

She began to fall from the dragon's side, only to be gripped by a pure chalky-white hand. She looked up. She was dangling, and her hand gripped his frail fingers. Her eyes were ridden with fear. She dangled, and still the dragon tilted. The Holy Master ceased the firing as the skies turned silent. Flick and Saria were helpless to watch.

"Don't let go, sweetie. Please don't let go! I don't want to die! I can't. I need to help EggWiff. I'm sorry about before, okay. You just need to…"

Morbid flung away Trickle's hand.

Flick's heart stopped as she fell further and further. They could hardly see her before she hit the Black Sea with a thud. Flick watched as she struggled amongst the waves before slowly being submersed.

121

"Say Goodbye,
Not Goodnight . . ."

Chapter Seven

A Sacred Past

They travelled along the path, and all seemed pretty quiet. There had been little said between the travellers. Gathnok often walked with Wispar, as Forlax was normally with Lainla. Euthan and Asemai stayed side by side. They didn't speak much, but there was a natural feel to the group, and the silence was not awkward. They had just turned a corner, and the path that lay in front of them was lined with open fields. It was a fresh, clear day, and the heat was close. Gathnok was about to complain, when he heard something. The others heard it too as they each slowed down.

"It's coming from over there." Lainla pointed to the right side of the path where a small side path seemed to have been created.

The sounds were peculiar, like a sort of grunting. They could also hear soft whimpering as if someone was in trouble. They walked along the small side path, and almost instantly *they saw the cause of the sounds. Five pigs were all gathered round a small cage. It was hard to see, but they caught glimpses of what seemed to be a small imp. The cage was extremely small and cramped, even for an imp.*

"State your business here," Gathnok demanded.

Suddenly the five pigs stopped and were soon standing in front of them, each brandishing a spear. They were dressed in ceremonial robes. The Spirits were aware they didn't have time for such a minor distraction, but they weren't about to let a being be caged up, especially a childlike imp. Imps are said to be greedy little creatures. However, they are peaceful and will always barter for something rather than steal it. The imp was huddled in the extremely cramped cage. He looked dirty and tired. His head hung low, and he barely seemed conscious.

"This is not your concern, stranger." The pig's voice was deep and authoritative.

"We're making it our concern. What is his crime." Forlax stepped slightly forward. His stance was challenging.

"He . . . erm . . . stole something from us." The pig kept his eyes fixed on Forlax, but his voice wavered slightly; it was clear they were lying.

Not much was known about pigs amongst the common people. They had appeared about a hundred years ago. They avoided most populated areas and seemed very segregated. There had been whispers that they are extremely religious and were preparing to restore their lost faith.

"What?"

"Huh?" The pig looked confused.

"What did he steal?" Forlax repeated.

"Nothing that concerns you." The pig shuffled uneasily in his stance. The others stood poised behind him.

"We disagree. Release him!" It was Asemai who spoke this time.

The pigs said nothing, but instead all raised their spears and pointed them at each of the Sprits.

"You have no weapons. You're not in a position to tell us what to do." The pig's snout curved into a confident grin.

Gathnok stepped forward to challenge these words, but Asemai looked at him and smiled. "We've got this."

Gathnok noticed Asemai was referring to Euthan. She took a deep breath and waved her hands to the right. As she did so, a large powerful gust of wind swept up around the pigs. It caught them off guard as each of them let go of their weapons which were carried off in the wind. During this confusion Euthan had crouched down low and placed his hand on the ground. Wispar noticed a sly smile from the usually stern Euthan as everyone watched the pigs. Whilst they struggled against the wind, large thick tree roots shot from the ground. They quickly began to curve themselves around the legs of the pigs. They seemed scared and confused as they struggled to free themselves. Soon the wind died down and the pigs were stood in front of them, trapped and without weapons. Wispar took the opportunity and walked over to the small cage.

The imp looked nervous, as it had managed to witness some of the spectacle. The cage was only locked by a small rod pushed through the opening latch. She quickly removed it and opened the cage. The imp looked up; he had enchanting purple eyes. She placed her hands in and gently took him out. He was about three feet tall and had the face of a child. His body was weak, and he kept opening and closing his eyes.

"Wow, you're really pretty!"

Wispar was taken aback by the compliment as the small imp passed out in her arms. She walked back over to the others where Gathnok was chatting to the pigs.

"Give him back to us. You have no purpose for him," the pig yelled, as it struggled against the vines.

"He is not yours to own."

The Spirits and Lainla began walking away. There was little more they needed to hear, and they weren't about to kill for the sake of it.

"He is dangerous! You don't understand. I will kill you all for this!" The pig's threats seemed desperate and empty as they continued to walk on.

They walked for an hour whilst the Imp rested comfortably in the arms of Wispar. They wanted to stop somewhere out of plain sight and give themselves enough distance from the pigs. It wasn't so much that they were worried about the pigs, but it was further confrontation they could do without. They soon came to a small archway into a small enclosure of trees. It was covered but rays of light still streamed through between the branches. They were even more surprised to see a small pool of water at its centre. Lainla thought it was rather beautiful. Wispar placed the imp on the ground as the others looked on. He continued to lay on the soft grassy floor inches from the pool, oblivious to the world.

"Should we wake him?" Gathnok asked.

"He looks so peaceful though." Wispar looked down affectionately.

"The pigs said he may be dangerous." Forlax erred on the side of caution.

"Yes, he looks terrifying." Asemai's sarcasm gained a few smiles.

"Wake him. I'm sure we'll handle it if he's dangerous." Lainla agreed that he didn't look dangerous but wanted to show support for the reserved Forlax. She knew him well and believed in his kindness and loyalty.

Wispar waved her arms over the pool. A small bubble of water floated up and danced in the air. They watched as it hovered over the body of the imp. She looked over to Gathnok who nodded for her to continue. She clicked her fingers and *watched as the water exploded on top of him. He immediately opened his eyes and began to splutter.*

The imp looked interesting. His dirtied hair was short and scruffy. He wore a green blazer which slightly exposed his chest. His trousers were brown and made from thick fabric tied by a rope around his waist. He sat up and rubbed his eyes for a moment before stopping. He peered up, and his mouth fell in awe. Standing all around him were what looked like six magnificent warriors.

"Wow!"

"Are you okay?" Wispar held out her hand to help him up.

"I will be." The imp got his feet and rushed to the side of the pool. He began sipping the water and washed down his face. The others looked on curiously.

"What is your name, child?" Euthan spoke this time.

"Kip."

"Greetings, Kip. I am Lainla, and these are the Elemental Spirits, Gathnok, Wispar, Forlax, Asemai, and Euthan."

Kip stopped and looked at Wispar. "Hi, Wispar" He felt as though he should acknowledge the warrior that saved him.

"We're running out of time." Forlax was speaking to the others and ignoring Kip.

"Kip, is there somewhere you wish us to take you? To your family maybe?"

"I don't have any family, not since they were killed by the pigs." Kip carried on sipping and didn't seem too saddened by the question.

The Spirits took a step back and began facing each other as if they were having a secret meeting.

"So what shall we do with him?" Gathnok asked.

"Take him with us?" Asemai looked for the reaction.

"We can't take him with us. It's too dangerous!" Forlax already didn't like him.

"Well, if we leave him he could die," Lainla noted.

"He's so small and cute!" Wispar added.

"I don't think smallness and cuteness is going to keep him alive," Forlax argued.

"Well, I don't know. It's worked well for me so far."

Lainla gave a small smile at the playful Gathnok, which didn't go unnoticed by Forlax.

"How can we ensure his safety?"

"I will. He'll be my responsibility." Wispar looked over at Kip with a sense of warmth.

The others felt no reason to argue, as the burden had been taken from them.

"Very well." Gathnok finalised the decision.

They decided to stay in the shelter, as they figured they could all do with some rest. They also didn't want to overwhelm Kip. Wispar decided to sit and explain to him who they were and all about the quest they were on. He seemed to be taking it rather well. Meanwhile, Gathnok sat on a small log collecting his thoughts.

"Are you okay?" Lainla appeared behind him with a smile.

She knew she shouldn't keep talking to him every chance she could, but she couldn't help herself. She had watched him with excitement, and she liked how she felt in his company.

"I'm tired." Gathnok rubbed his eyes. So much had changed in such a small time.

"Oh, sorry." Lainla got up to leave.

"No, I meant just emotionally tired. I've had a long day. But, yeah, I feel better now all the Spirits are together," Gathnok said with a smile.

"And Kip . . ." Lainla said, looking back as Wispar looked overly dramatic in her explanation of everything.

"Yeah, poor kid."

"We will stay the night here?" Lainla asked, looking

around. It was only midday, and she didn't think Gathnok would want to waste the time.

"No, we'll stay here for a few hours and also clean up, but then we should get moving. I don't know how far the tomb is," Gathnok replied.

Forlax was sitting by himself. He was looking over at Lainla and Gathnok and had noticed the familiarity the two now shared. He worried that he might be losing her. He was distracted from his thoughtful gaze when Euthan and Asemai approached him. They looked over at the pair.

"How long have they been together?" Asemai asked.

"What?" Forlax responded in a stern tone.

"Gathnok and Lainla. They are a couple, right?" Asemai said with a confused expression. She had just assumed from the way they acted with each other.

"No, they're not. Excuse me." Forlax got up and brushed past Euthan as he walked towards Gathnok and Lainla.

They were laughing about something when he appeared but quickly stopped.

"Everything okay?" Lainla said, greeting him with a worried smile.

"Can we talk . . . alone?" Forlax asked, glancing at Gathnok.

"Oh, yeah, I should go wash anyway." Gathnok smiled at Lainla and gave a polite nod to Forlax before walking away.

Euthan was rather intimidating in his size and build, but Forlax was intimidating as he didn't give much away with his expressions.

"What's up?" Lainla said, shifting herself to face him more.

"Why did you come here?" Forlax asked.

"You know why." Lainla gave a confused expression.

"You said it was to be with Wispar and me." Forlax wasn't

sure how far he wished to push the subject; he was worried he wouldn't like what he might hear as a reply.

"That's true," Lainla said slowly, looking into his eyes.

"What about Gathnok?" Forlax continued.

"Is that what this is about?" Lainla sighed and gave a smile.

"Well, you seem rather close to him, considering we barely know him." Forlax didn't like how easily she dismissed his worry.

"Forlax, he just had his family and home destroyed. He's grieving. Remember how you were when you lost your parents? He's dealing with that and all of this on top of it. I'm just trying to be there for him." Lainla was speaking fast but took Forlax's hand in comfort. "I didn't mean to hurt you," she finished.

Forlax shuffled uneasily on the log. He thought about how he and Wispar had dealt with the loss of their parents after the Darkmagi attacked.

"You're right. I'm sorry." Forlax gave a weary sigh and smiled at Lainla and enjoyed the touch of her soft hand in his.

They stayed there for another few hours. Each took time washing in the small pool of water, and they even managed to find berries from the nearby bushes. They felt revived and fed and were ready to begin following the compass. They ended up walking through most of the night, as they felt less wary of an attack in the dark.

The stars and moons made it peaceful, and from their earlier rest they weren't that tired. Wispar enjoyed chatting to Kip and getting to know him. Forlax remained pretty much to himself, and Lainla often walked between him and Gathnok. Asemai and Euthan trailed at the back. They rested for a little while before continuing on the next morning. They were walking on main paths lately, but they soon found themselves wondering off again into the woodland.

"So we're looking for a jewel?" Kip asked, as they walked along the path.

"Yes, Cupido Sacra. It'll hold the power of the Ancients so we can use it to stop the Darkmagi." Wispar had been over this more than once with the young Kip.

"And that glowing thing will help us find it?" Kip watched as Gathnok lead the way ahead.

"That glowing thing is the shimmering compass!" Wispar smiled at Kip's innocence.

"Oh," Kip said.

They were now walking in forestry once again. However, instead of tall trees, this place was smothered in greenery. It had old stone ruins dotted around which were covered in vines. The lush greenery was beautiful and vibrant in colours. Soon Gathnok stopped and held up his hand. The compass was glowing bright, and Gathnok could feel the warmth. Looking at the needle, it was pointing to one of the derelict ruins. It didn't look like anything in particular. It was like a wall that was just standing on its own. It was made of big old stone that had clearly been weathered in time.

"Are you sure?" Lainla asked.

"The compass is." Gathnok also looked a little surprised.

"Maybe there is a door somewhere?" Forlax inquired.

They all began to walk around the large stone building. It looked like a perfectly normal derelict wall. There was no building or openings to speak of.

"Maybe this time the compass was wrong," Asemai suggested.

Kip giggled slightly; they all seemed crazy to be walking around a half-broken wall.

"I hope not. We're kind of lost without it." Gathnok went up to the wall and held the compass up to it. It glowed, and the light hit the wall. As it glowed, he noticed that the wall began to shimmer as the light hit it.

"Guys!" He called everyone over.

He held the shimmering compass up along the wall to show the others.

"Do you think it's a doorway?"

"I don't know," Gathnok shrugged.

"Should we go through?" Forlax asked.

"I guess." Gathnok looked at the shimmering wall; there was something disconcerting about walking through a wall.

"What if it's a trap?" Wispar suggested.

"True . . . true . . ."

"Maybe we should test it?" Euthan said.

"Yes, but with what?" Lainla asked.

"Oh, my Elders! You're meant to be spirits, for crying out loud!" Kip rolled his eyes and nudged past them.

Before any of them could process what was happening, Kip had disappeared through the wall. There was a moment where they all stood still and a little shocked before Kip's head popped backed out.

"Come on then!" Kip yelled, before disappearing back behind the wall.

Lainla and Gathnok shared a smile before they all walked into the wall to face what was next to come.

* * *

The mystical window showed Trickle falling into the Black Sea. EggWiff stared in sheer horror to see his only remaining friend struggle against the life-taking waves. EggWiff's prison was a small magically-charged cage, which was invulnerable to magic. His mind raced with emotion, pain, anger, loss, and suffering. He wanted nothing more than to break free and destroy his captors and bring ruthless pain on Morbid. He saw how carelessly he had flung Trickle off, as if she meant nothing. Now he was going to make sure that Morbid would not just suffer but would feel the complete wrath of his magic. His training to controlling his emotions was gone. His gentle nature had been consumed by hatred, and he would avenge his little friend's death.

"You see now? Nothing can stop our master. No one can stop him from wreaking his revenge. You may think you're in pain now, but this is just the beginning."

The shadowed creature was standing next to the mystical window that was replaying Trickle's death like a constant reminder. The other shadowed creature remained silent and stood eerily in the corner.

"I had no issue with your master. I don't even know who your master is. But you have started something which I swear will end your life." EggWiff spoke calmly with a chilling intensity in his voice. His eyes were firm, and although huddled within the cramped cage, he still looked dominant.

"You should be used to that by now." EggWiff watched as the darkest and most dominant shadowed creature came up from the stairs.

The room was made of stone and was circular in its shape. It was a large room with a small stand in the centre on which were placed a number of magical items. EggWiff's cage was suspended from the ceiling. Only a few windows were spread evenly across from EggWiff. He figured they were high up in a tower, as he could only see the blue sky from outside. To the right of EggWiff was a small dark opening on the floor, which also gave the indication they were up high.

"Who are you? Why have you brought me here?" EggWiff's voice was still enraged as he roared at the shadowed creature.

"You're angry? Tell me how is it you get to kill the one I loved and be so angry?" The voice was calm but had so much pain still hidden within it. EggWiff fought back the fear.

"I have killed no one! I have never come across your kind before. You have mistaken me, and because of it I now must avenge my friend's life." EggWiff was talking fast, his voice angered; he wasn't going to be afraid any more.

"You're very convincing, but I remember I saw you there. Your lies are useless here, and in turn you will die the most painful death." The shadowed master was now standing in front of the cage. Even though he was so close in the sun lit room, he was still shadowed.

"Then do it! End me. If you're so powerful, then destroy me where I lie." EggWiff stared into the blank surface of his face. He knew he wouldn't kill him; if that were his real intention, then he would have been killed long before now. He was merely trying to find the reason for his survival.

"Don't think I won't kill you. The reason you're still here is because I need your help with Cupido Sacra. The draining of your magic will cause a much more painful death than any I could have thought of, and believe me, I have thought of a lot."

EggWiff's expression changed at the mention of the jewel. He hadn't heard anyone mention it in years. Not only had this creature helped cause Trickle's death, but he was now searching for his old master's jewel. His mind began to ache. He dreamt about Morbid and the shadowed being. He knew about them talking and that Trickle was in danger. Although EggWiff possessed great power, he never had the ability to see the future, so how did he come to obtain this knowledge?

"What is your concern with Cupido Sacra? Who are you?" EggWiff knew many creatures from the Fifth Realm, but never had he come across a shadowed creature such as this. Nor had he heard of one.

"You honestly don't know who I am yet, do you?" The creature bellowed with laughter as he moved back from the cage. As he laughed, a small light appeared over his face, and for a second a face peered back at EggWiff.

"Gathnok!" EggWiff was paralysed with shock. "It's a lie. Gathnok was banished after . . . after . . ." Realization swept over EggWiff. Gathnok thought that EggWiff killed his lost love. It was him, but how? It didn't make any sense. Gathnok was a being of good, not hatred. Why was he now in shadow? So many questions filled his mind, but all he could do was stare at his lost relative in disbelief.

"After you killed the woman I love."

EggWiff lost himself in thoughts and emotion. He didn't kill anyone. He couldn't – he didn't have the ability. He loved his uncle and his wife. He had no reason to cause such pain. Suddenly he stopped and broke down in floods of tears. His stance weakened as his face streamed. His aging face lost all life and he kept praying to god it wasn't true.

"You remember now, don't you, Marvie? How you came to my house, took your blade, and stuck it in her as if she was nothing." Gathnok was pacing back and forth, enjoying seeing the pain he was causing.

"It wasn't me." He held his head up and looked through his tear-ridden eyes. "It wasn't me." But even EggWiff didn't have enough faith in his sanity to believe what he was saying.

* * *

The dragon was now flying slowly. The fact the dragon was full of pigs didn't make the situation any better. Flick sat without saying a word. He didn't care that twenty spears were poised and ready to lunge if he so much breathed wrongly. Trickle was gone. It wasn't so much that he was close to Trickle, but he couldn't help but feel a small amount of fondness towards the creature. Everything was going through his mind. So much had changed since the night before. EggWiff had been taken to goodness knows where, Trickle was now gone from the world, and Morbid – well, Morbid had betrayed them all. Flick wanted nothing more than to leap up and take revenge. Instead he sat silently. He wasn't sure if they would kill him anyway, but he sure wasn't going to give them a reason to try.

Instead he sat looking out on the Black Sea. The waters looked like a giant pit of oozing black tar. Saria said and did nothing. She looked blood-lustful and angry. Her arms had been chained down, and her weapons had been stripped from her. She was scowling at her captors, but even she could do nothing. The wind gently grazed Flick's face as his mind remained lost in thought. Only a few Mithworks flew with them now, one at the back and one at the front whilst another two flew by the sides. Morbid flew to the side. His body was still lifeless, and his empty hollow sockets stared straight ahead without moving an inch. Saria could feel nothing but revulsion towards her former prisoner. The Holy Master stood tall and proud at the front of the leading Mithwork. They flew for about another hour, but it seemed much longer to Flick. If it wasn't for the fact the sun was at its highest point, he would be questioning the time of the day.

After a short time, the Holy Master waved his arms frantically and shouted something. Flick strained to hear what it was, but the wind consumed his words. Flick paused for a moment. Everything seemed normal, until he began to see that the guards had moved a little away from him and started to hold on tight to the horns of the dragon beast. Taking this to be an example, Flick cowered down lower to the beast and grasped the scaly skin as best he could. Moments after he had done so, the dragon tipped itself down towards the ground and began heading towards the sea. A sheer panic consumed Flick as his mind raced with the thoughts of death. He was half expecting to be killed, but he never imagined the pigs would sacrifice themselves too. He did only what he could and closed his eyes and tensed himself ready to be consumed by the life-taking ocean beneath them. His mind flashed with images of times long forgotten.

<u>Two Months Earlier</u>

Flick was desperate for the bathroom. He had wanted to go for hours, but no lavatory could be seen. He would have willingly gone in a bush or tree or anything, but as luck so happened, he had stumbled into a desert. The desert mostly had tiny fairies and Sandorians. Sandorians feed off sand, and they're spoilt, greedy creatures who hate noise. Flick had been walking for what seemed like hours and hours. His belly hurt, and he came close to just relieving himself there and then, but then something stopped him. In the far-off horizon he could see a small shack. Flick's smile appeared all over his face. He wanted nothing more than to be able to run, but instead he was being aware of every step. Eventually he got there. The hours of agonising walking were intense, but they had paid off. The shack was wooden and looked frail and worn. The stench came through the door like a wave on the shore. His nostrils were invaded by the foul stench.

"Hello."

Flick jumped and almost had an accident as the voice came behind him. Standing there was a small pixie. She was the size of a child, and her pale blue skin clashed with the rich orange of her short hair.

"What's your name?" The little pixie beamed up at Flick.

"Look, I don't mean to be rude, but I really need to use the toilet, so if you don't mind…"

"I do mind." The pixie just continued to smile, hanging on every word.

Flick was in desperation. He was tempted to punch the pixie in the head, and no one was around, so why shouldn't he? Flick smiled and then quickly threw out his hand. The pixie was small and nimble and swiftly dodged the attack. She giggled as if it were some game.

"Too late now, Dwarf! You're in trouble!" And with that the pixie vanished.

Flick looked around, but the horizons on each side were clear. Nothing but the sand flowing in the wind made any movement. Flick didn't hesitate and swung himself into the hut. Once inside, Flick began to relieve himself in the small bucket. The bloated feeling in his belly decreased. After a few minutes he began to hum a little tune. Only a few seconds after he had finished, the door swung open. Two Sandorians with large knives came behind Flick and dragged him out.

"What is going on?"

The two Sandorians didn't speak. Instead they thrust a piece of paper into Flick's hands.

"By order 229011, no being must make voluntary sound within these borders. We are placing you under arrest."

One month later Flick was in court.

* * *

Flick waited for the impending contact with the Black Sea, but the crash never came. Instead, the dragon wailed a piercing scream as it legs thundered into solid ground beneath them. Without taking a breath, Flick opened his eyes. He could see the Black Sea all around him. The sky was still clear, and he could see the Mithworks in the air circling them like ravaging vultures. Peering down, Flick could see they were on a small island, only slightly bigger than the dragon itself. The Holy Master began to prod Flick in the back with a spear, forcing him off the side of the scaly dragon. They did the same with Saria. As soon as Flick's feet touched the floor, the dragon's wings began to flutter into life as it soared into the air and off into the distance until it couldn't be seen any more. The Holy Master had a spear pointed to Flick's neck whilst five pigs held spears to Saria's throat.

"You will be left here until you either starve or throw yourself into the Black Sea. Either way, your damnation is assured." The Holy Master slowly backed away and onto a Mithwork that had swooped low onto the island. He climbed onto the Mithwork and flew off, leaving Flick and Saria completely alone.

All that was beneath him was sand on his feet, nothing else. Flick slumped onto the sandy floor as he began to process the day so far. He looked over at Saria, who was standing tall and proud, looking out at the Black Sea. Flick peered out as well to see if it would help. Ironically, he thought, the Black Sea was rather beautiful.

* * *

The pigs dropped Morbid off on the shore of the Black Sea. He was told to wait in the nearby cave for their master. Morbid waited in the damp dark cave. His skeleton body stood tall and ridged. Elders forbid anyone should stumble across him, as they would no doubt be consumed with fright. He could sense him coming. The power of darkness drew closer as he felt the same cold chill that he did whenever they were close.

"I have done as you asked, Master. They are separated. Do you now have him?" Morbid spoke into the darkness of the walls.

"You have done well, and killing the meddling freak the

way you did was a nice touch." The voice of Gathnok echoed in the darkness.

"So I am free now. My death is now my own."

Gathnok began to bellow with shuddering laughter. "You're free when I say you're free. For now I have another use for you. Find me Cupido Sacra."

"And that would be?"

The shadows around Morbid began to spiral out of control, swirling, lashing, and smashing into his chalky white bones.

"Don't dare question me! You will find Cupido Sacra and bring it to me, or else the consequences will be beyond your wildest fears." The shadows morphed back into the walls as the shrill hatred of Gathnok's voice fell into the darkness.

* * *

Morbid stood by the fire in the clearing amongst the trees. He remembered it well, as it was the first clearing the group ever slept in the night . . . the night he was supposedly stolen from the world again. The stars shone brightly, as the wind was slowly entwining around the world. His mind was running through with different emotions. He hoped the protection spell would be in place. If Gathnok knew what he was about to do, everything he had worked for would be for nothing. He hoped that the incantation still worked. It was many years since he was taught. Hours went by, as Sahihriar continued to surround him, but Morbid did not move. He was still until he heard the footsteps behind him. He turned to see a skeleton face staring back at him through the black hooded cloak it wore.

Morbid was taken aback at first, as he'd forgotten what it was like to see him again.

"Hello, Death."

"Hello, son. I assume the plan is well?" Death's voice was husky and dry, as if spoken by an old man with his dying breath.

"Gathnok believes I am under his control, and as predicted he has used me to get to the stone." Morbid was relieved to relax; he was tired of living out the charade for so long.

"I'm sorry you had to take your friend's life. I know it's never easy!" The tall hooded skeleton figure's rasping voice was sympathetic. However, it continued with a sense of urgency.

"The prophecy must come to pass. It's for the greater good. I understand, Father." Morbid stood tall and proud. He respected his father so much. He knew what had to be done and because of his legacy, Morbid felt no remorse for his actions against Trickle.

"Gathnok must be allowed Cupido Sacra. You will find the portal to the Nether Realm at the centre of Magmount, as Lainla told you. I shall distract Gathnok long enough and ensure that joke of a wizard stays under his protection! Go my son. Be well."

"What about Flick and Saria?"

"You just do your job. I have everything taken care of. Now go."

Death's voice was always monotone like his son's, although the rasping dryness tainted it with more fear than Morbid's.

Morbid stared into the sockets of his father's eyes. He couldn't shake the feeling that something was missing, that this was all for some higher reason. He nodded and slowly turned his back and walked out of the small forest clearing.

* * *

Flick was annoyed. He hated the fact that he was drawn to Saria. She wasn't right for him. She was an Amazon, and he was a Surthan breed. No one would accept it. Surthan dwarfs were designed to do hard manual labour and little else. They were considered the lowest of the low among their kind. He paused for a moment and realised that none of it mattered. The black waves of death were gliding further in, and he felt that he was dead for sure. His little life seemed dwarfed by the enormity of what he had experienced, and as this thought hit him, Flick broke down in tears unable to handle it any more. Trickle's death, the pigs' ambush, EggWiff's kidnapping – he had done absolutely nothing to deserve any of this. He cried and cried until the tears just stopped coming. Saria did nothing and made no attempt to comfort him. She knew just as well as he did that they were dead. Well, he was anyway. It just made what she had to do easier.

"It's okay, you know. I don't know how or why, but it's going to be alright!" Saria stood in front of Flick.

"And how is that? Because we are going to die?" Flick wiped his face and stood up to face Saria.

Then the strangest thing happened. Saria had a look in her eyes. They were soft and filled with compassion. Flick felt numb and slightly giddy. Suddenly the waves vanished as the butterflies grew. He noticed they were only inches from each other's faces as the moment of high emotion led him to this strange situation. Even though he now felt sick with nerves, Flick leaned in, his heart pounding as Saria couldn't help but do the same. Her warm breath caressed his lips before they touched. Her lips were tender and moist. Saria could feel the hairs of his beard brush softly against her cheek. They held the kiss for a second. However, Flick couldn't see that tears had formed in Saria's eyes. She held on with all she could, wishing she could stay in this moment.

The anguish of what was to come next was written all over her face. Flick couldn't see her face and instead let himself get lost as he felt loved for the first time in his life, comforted and warm. For the first time, he felt worthwhile.

"Wow! That was awesome!" Flick whispered as he pulled away. His eyes remained closed in the lingering passion.

"Yes, it was." Saria tried to smile through her tears.

Saria stepped back from Flick. He looked more handsome than she'd ever seen anyone look. She let her fingers move to the quiver of arrows on her back. She took a deep breath and let her warrior instinct take over. With a single motion she pulled out an arrow and placed it in her bow. The sound of the string forced Flick to open his eyes. His face that was only moments ago filled with a smile and glow now looked terrified and pale.

"Wait! Why?" Flick struggled to mutter the words as he stepped back in shock.

Saria wanted to sound cold, but her voice wavered as she spoke. "Ask Death."

She let go of the arrow and closed her eyes as she heard the impact. Saria had to cover her mouth as she gasped in shock. She stumbled backwards. Fighting back the tears, she began to compose herself. She placed her bow away and knelt by the body and turned it over. She couldn't understand why Gathnok had been so adamant that she kill him. The Black Sea would have done it for sure, but she wasn't willing to take the risk. Besides, she wasn't stupid. She knew something else was going on here. There was too much that didn't make sense, but she was determined to find out. She withdrew her arrow from his gut and wiped the blood clean from it. She stared at it for a moment – such a small object, so trivial, so meaningless – yet it had just taken a life. It had just taken Flick.

Never had Saria looked at a weapon like that. In a

moment of pure rage, Saria flung the arrow in the Black Sea and screamed violently. After a moment she closed her eyes and collected her thoughts. She was a warrior; she could do this. Slowly she knelt back up and walked over to Flick's lifeless body. She knelt down and scooped him up in her arms. His body hung as she cradled him. She stood up and slowly walked over towards the edge of the small island where the waves were hitting the sandy shore. She looked down and kissed Flick on the forehead. She closed her eyes and opened out her arms. Flick's body rolled off into the Black Sea, consumed and lost just as Trickle's had been.

* * *

<u>Two Nights Before</u>

"Morbid, what are you doing?" Saria asked, appearing behind Morbid.

Morbid swung round and lowered his skeleton hand. "I was looking for the others. I got lost"

Saria looked blankly back at him. She had walked for a good long way and didn't like being lied to.

"If you're trying to impress Gathnok, then killing them all isn't the way to do it." She walked across to where Morbid was looking. She saw what looked like EggWiff tapping Trickle on the head.

"Who is Gathnok?" Morbid glared at Saria. Had she too been taken over? Were her reasons intentional?

"Big shadowed being. The one calling all the shots here." Saria continued to peer at the others.

"You work for him too?" Morbid tilted his head in curiosity.

"He told me to tell you the plans have changed. You have to take care of that Trickle, but only once we send them towards the Black Sea. Got it?" Saria was now staring Morbid straight in the eye.

143

"And you . . ."

Saria peered back into the clearing. She watched as Flick was just beginning to get back up onto his feet.

"I have my own mission. Look we'd better go back or they'll worry. Let me do the talking." Saria stood to the side, allowing Morbid to walk past back towards the group. Morbid now knew his target and wasn't going to fail.

* * *

The pigs danced and cheered. Troughs were filled with the finest of ales. The Essence was theirs, and now nothing could stop them. The Essence was placed on the altar, as many pigs queued to pay their respects to it and the Master. What a joy it would be just to watch over it or even touch it. Some were crying with glee, while others were just happy they could finally rest. The holy prophecy announced that the Essence would show them the true path. What could go wrong now?

However, the Holy Master wasn't joining in the celebration. He was tired of being a figure, a leader, an example. He'd led his pigs into battle and followed what he believed to be the Elders' wishes, but it was now all over. Finally he could put his purple robe down and just be another pig. His mission was complete. He was so happy, and what was the best part – for the first time in years he was allowed to be. He lay down flat out on his straw bed and let a tear of glee fall from his eye. It rolled round his snout and dropped on the floor with a small splash.

"Touching!" Gathnok's sinister voice snapped the Holy Master back into reality. Suddenly all that glee and relief was being drained out of him and in turn was being replaced by cold anxiety and fear.

The Holy Master sat up to see Gathnok standing in the

shadowed corners of his tent, not much unlike how he had done only a few weeks before.

"I've done your bidding now, Elder. We're free." The Holy Master tried to sound demanding, clear, and commanding, but the presence of this being – the hatred that oozed from him – just made the Holy Master feel weak.

"Listen! That's the sound of your brothers, your family, and your army blissfully happy. You delivered that to them like the good little pig that you are. They owe you everything, don't they?"

The Holy Master stared into the darkness.

"Ah, but in fact it's me they owe. I gave them the Essence, and I can take it back." Gathnok laughed, a sickening sound.

"You can't! Don't you dare! We did everything. You have your wizard, and we disposed of the others for you." The pig knelt and looked up into the shadow. Although he couldn't be seen, his presence was still very visible. "I beg you, don't do this!"

Gathnok laughed once more. "Look at how pathetic you are! Scrabbling on the floor for your worthless Essence! The truth is I may still need you, so I'd better keep it for insurance sake." His face loomed out of the shadows for only a second before he was gone.

The Holy Master stood up. Suddenly from outside he began to hear oinks of hysteria. He darted out of his tent and looked across at the fields of pigs. No longer were they dancing and drinking. Many were crying, and others were searching, whilst some just sat stunned in silence. The Holy Master peered around at the altar. He could see that the satchel of Essence was missing. Only the Holy Master knew it wasn't missing. It had been taken. He stared out at the despair, the emptiness of his people. The Essence was everything. Words couldn't describe its importance to them – and now it was gone. That's when the moment of realisation came upon him. That's when he knew that the Elder wasn't an elder at all. He didn't feel empty or dead inside; he felt anger – raw primal anger within him. The shadowed master had gone too far, and no longer would he succumb to the shadowed master's will.

The Holy Master walked amongst his lost army and kinsmen. His robe trailed on the floor, but that didn't matter. His snout was held high, and his eyes began to burn with rage. A few pigs knelt at his feet and begged for guidance, but the Holy Master just ignored them. After a minute or so crossing the field, the Holy Master took his stand on the altar, but he was careful not to stand too close to where the almighty Essence had once rested.

"My brothers!" The Holy Master yelled out across the fields, his voice recognizable amongst the pigs. They all stopped and stared at him. The field fell silent, other than the sobs of a few pigs. "It is true that the Essence has gone…"

A few pigs cried out, while others gasped, mortified as hysteria almost broke out once again.

"Too long have we walked alone. Too long did we live in the darkness of our faith. We had the almighty Essence, we knew its warmth and power, and we let it bathe over us. Tomorrow night we shall go into battle, we shall lead ourselves into victory, and we shall take back what is ours. Tomorrow night we shall truly be free!" The Holy Master raised his hands as the pigs cheered for their Holy Master. The Holy Master was only cheering for one thing however – the death of the shadowed creature.

* * *

Saria waited on the sand, as she knew Gathnok would send someone to pick her up. She wasn't really worrying about it though. She was pondering whether to go swim in the Black Sea and end it all. She kept fooling herself that she would then be happy, but killers don't go to the blessed realms.

The sky was turning clear, and although the day was ending, the breeze still remained. It whirled the sand around on the tiny island. Saria was sitting cross-legged and looked out at the waves; she loved the way the ocean forced her to dream. She was casting her thoughts back on the countless battles she had encountered – saving villages, stealing from the rich, even capturing slaves. It all seemed a bit pointless now.

Saria stood up and walked to the edge of the waves. She peered into the black tar of the sea. For some inexplicable reason she kept expecting to see Flick looking back at her, as if he was still in there waiting. She held her arms and raised her leg as if about to place it into the sea below. She knew that with one touch her life would be taken. Who knows what could have happened if a load roar from above hadn't been heard. Saria looked up to see the dragon flying above. It circled once or twice before sweeping down towards the island. However, the dragon was enormous and wouldn't be able to fit on the island – well, not without knocking Saria out of the way or risking its own life. Instead it hovered a few meters above the island. Saria didn't need to look up to see who it was, as she could sense the warmth instantly.

Lainla fluttered gently down from the dragon.

"You ready, Saria?" Lainla looked at the weak, worn-out Amazon before her. It wasn't the ruthless warrior she knew. "Are you okay?" Lainla glided next to Saria, the sand beneath her gently disturbed by the motion of her wings.

"I'm fine. He kissed me, and then I killed him" Saria looked up at Lainla.

Lainla's face softened. She too hated the situation she was in. She didn't realise Saria cared so deeply for Flick. She had sensed some romance when they met back in the forest, but she wouldn't have dreamt that Saria would return his feelings. Lainla knelt down low to the dwarf.

"You did what you had to. He told you how important the mission was."

"The mission? I don't care about the mission." Saria's warrior anger was rising within her.

"I'm sorry you had to do this." Lainla placed her warm glowing hands on Saria's face. "But please have faith that what we're doing is for the right reason." Lainla stared into Saria's face for a moment. She looked into the dwarf's green eyes, reassuring her of the words she had just spoken. Saria forced a fake smile that let Lainla go.

"Is the creepy shadow guy waiting for us then?" Saria stood up and began stretching her legs. They were sore after sitting so long in the same place.

Lainla smiled. "I've been told we're meant to meet him at the tower tomorrow night."

Saria nodded and began to scale the large dragon.

"What's he like then, the shadowed master?" Lainla tried to hide the pain in her voice.

"I thought you knew him?" Saria held her hand down out of habit and pulled it away when she realised how easily Lainla could float up.

"I did, but it was a very long time ago . . ."

That Morning

The group stood in silence for a while. Saria felt anxious and wanted to go speak to Flick, but before she could do so, Trickle sighed and had begun to walk off after him. Morbid, Saria, and Lainla were left standing in the path.

"She'll get him back, don't worry," Morbid said in his eerie tone.

"Good. Your father has sent me a message, Morbid." Lainla was checking that Trickle was well out of earshot.

"I thought Gathnok was in charge?" Saria asked inquisitively.

"He is, but Death is advising him the best he can. Morbid you're to dispose of Trickle in the Black Sea. The pigs shall intervene and are waiting for you. Saria and Flick will be taken to a small island where you can deal with him. I'll come join you once you've finished." It was a strange contrast to see someone so beautiful talk of such ruthless deeds.

"So I should just use the Black Sea too?" Saria pondered.

"No. Gathnok doesn't want to risk it. Make sure his soul is lost beforehand. Morbid, the pigs will take the Essence and you're to start searching for Cupido Sacra. I trust you understand?" Lainla said.

"My father prepared me well." Morbid could hear faint footsteps from far away. "We shall all meet again soon."

They each then stood in silence, as they could see Trickle and Flick appear upon the horizon.

* * *

EggWiff was huddled in his cage. He hadn't switched in weeks, and he'd never ever tried to before. This was different though. He wanted answers, and only one person could give them to him – himself.

"You should have left this between you and me. Taking Trickle means you caused an unfair injustice!" EggWiff wasn't going to allow himself to grieve in a cage. He was going to wait to do it properly as Trickle would have wanted him to.

"Unfair? How dare you speak to me about unfair!" Gathnok moved so his hollow face was staring into EggWiff's.

"For years I protected the Fifth Realm. I sacrificed everything to do good. I made it into a heaven. I taught others. I healed. I did it all. I gave my life to good, and then you come and kill the woman I loved more than anything in this life, and you dare . . . you even begin to think you can talk to me about fair?" Gathnok walked back to the towering arch and peered out, awaiting Death and his two companions.

"I can't excuse what happened, but you've got to know how much I loved her, and you – you're my family. How could you let yourself become this?"

"Because they took me from her. They just intervened because they could. It wasn't enough that she was dead. All the good and pureness I gave, the love and sacrifices in the end meant nothing because they let you take her, and then they stole her body from me! The pain you feel over your friend, that's not even close to how I feel."

"I am so..." EggWiff began to say within his tiny suspended cage.

Instantly Gathnok swung his head. "Don't you dare say sorry to me. You will die, and there is nothing that will change it."

EggWiff began to think back to when he was happy – his sheltered life training at H.O.M. Those years were fantastic. They helped him grieve the tragedy of the Fifth Realm, taught him power and wisdom he only dreamed of – except for that day, that one fatal flaw.

Two Months Earlier

The great teaching hall! Warriors, warlords, warlocks, wizards, and witches had all been trained in the great hall. The room was like sitting inside a tall round pillar. The circular walls were lined with small pillars. In between were painted artist impressions of the five Elders, the ancient guardians of all the realms and Sahihriar. They are the highest of beings, and all at H.O.M. worshipped them.

EggWiff sat at his chair amongst the hundreds of students, each one wise, each one with knowledge and power that could be potentially deadly or beautiful, each one with knowledge enough to change the world at a whim. The message he was about to deliver was one of responsibility. The High Order of Magic was more than a magical institution; it was a legacy. Only the best of the best were taught at H.O.M. EggWiff had earned his place by keeping order in the Fifth Realm after the day the darkness came. EggWiff had a secret though, one he had managed to keep hidden for years, and no one at H.O.M. knew anything about his other side. He memorised mind techniques and spells to hide the alcohol stains and the effects of his attacks.

This day, however, had been intense. Something wasn't right. EggWiff could feel himself losing touch with himself and knew that the other side of him was coming out. No one had noticed the sweat building on his face. He hated himself for being this way. He told himself over and over that he was normal, that he didn't deserve this, but today he couldn't help but know. Instinct told him that today was the day they would all find out. His lip was trembling, his eyes closed shut, trying his best not to scream, not to move, to stay poised like the others. It couldn't work though. He couldn't hold on any longer, and before he knew it, he had let out an almighty scream. His voice echoed across the room, and a green mist of smoke filled the room.

"Cor blimey! This room is big! Must 'ave cost loads!" EggWiff's voice echoed across the room.

The old teacher looked up at EggWiff through his small spectacles, which were similar to those of EggWiff.

"EggWiff, is there something you wish to say?" The old

teacher peered at the wizard; no one had ever dared interrupt a lesson before.

"Yeah! Yeah! Is there an inn around? Because I'm thirsty!" EggWiff began to smile a giddy smile and peered over the vast group of peers who looked at him appalled.

The old teacher moved his arms forward and muttered magical words in rage. The motion lasted not a second, and a purple mist shone through his fingers. It whirled like the wind over the heads of witches and warriors, the students of great skill.

"Whoa! Explorianta!" EggWiff looked puzzled as the words came from nowhere.

The mist cleared, and EggWiff staggered as he peered through the swarm of now standing warriors. They all looked in awe: the teacher had been turned into a chicken! One month later EggWiff was in court.

"Redemption"

Chapter Eight

Fecki watched Minso as he talked to the old wizard. The wizard had grown too old to channel magic, so instead he taught the young apprentice the ancient art of the portal opening. It was a rare gift to conjure portals, but a handful of gifted creatures could. Minso's father had sought out the child shortly after he was born, as he knew of his importance.

The Freeyer warriors were sitting in the old Amazon settlement. It was now overgrown by the forest, but a few buildings remained. Fecki continued to watch as the other warriors prepared Minso's faithful companion, a Mithwork called Emae. Mithworks are bird-like creatures that often are used by warriors. She couldn't help but wish she could go with Minso, but she knew he'd never allow it. This was something she knew he had to do alone. Ever since Fecki's partner died, Minso had really taken care of her. He helped her through her grief and then helped her set up her inn in Sahihriar. She did love the father of her child, but since knowing the compassion provided by Minso, her heart had begun to open again.

She got up and walked over to Minso who was now stroking the beak of Emae.

"Nearly ready then?" Fecki asked, trying her hardest to smile.

"Yes, just waiting for the portal to open. Are you alright?" Minso could sense something was troubling Fecki.

"You will come back, won't you?" Fecki hated sounding weak, but the thought of losing someone else so close to her heart frightened her.

Minso couldn't help but smile. He stopped stroking Emae and turned to Fecki. He continued to smile and placed a comforting hand on her cheek.

"Of course I'm coming back, and I'll have what we need to restore the Fifth Realm. Don't worry yourself, Fecki."

The comfort of his touch suppressed the feeling of uneasiness in her stomach. He was right though. Soon Minso would return, and everything would be as it should.

"We're ready for you now!" The wizard spoke from one of the old tree huts suspended by the roof of trunks above.

Minso turned back to Fecki and gave a boyish wink which was a reminder of his youth. Despite the fact he'd had to grow up very fast, he still had a twinkle in his eye. He then turned and walked away with Emae, ready to fulfil his promise. Fecki watched as she hoped that he knew enough to do what was right and make their home realm safe again.

* * *

EggWiff pondered his past. He hated his curse more than anything. He represented everything he didn't want to be. He'd destroyed his family and his friends, and now he was soon to destroy himself. The weirdest part was that

EggWiff couldn't bring himself to care anymore. He was too tired and old to fight himself.

With those thoughts, he found himself feeling the familiar sensation, and then a green mist appeared throughout the small cage and with it the foul stench.

"How is it that whenever I appear, old stuff-bones has got himself into something stupid?" EggWiff looked through the cage and around the room.

Gathnok stopped and peered at him, the green smoke fading into the air around them.

"So you're him?" Gathnok sounded rather intrigued and began studying the inhabitant of the cage as though it was new.

"Who the bloomin' heck are you? And where did you put your face?" EggWiff wasn't scared. He was too sober to feel much of anything. Instead he just continued to study the room.

"You're so pathetic. Tell me how is it you could take some one's life?" Gathnok stood staring into the cage, and his bitterness overwhelmed him.

EggWiff stopped and took off his glasses. He rubbed them with his cloth and placed them back on the bridge of his nose. He showed no signs of being either EggWiff. Instead he peered into Gathnok's empty face and leaned in very close.

"Because there are things at play here you don't yet understand." EggWiff's eyes were transfixed, and for the first time in years Gathnok felt as if someone was staring him in the eye.

EggWiff smiled a cheeky smile, and then as if nothing had happened, he went back to being the sober alcoholic. His mannerisms and eyes changed. Gathnok stopped and stared as his mind raced. There was an explanation for EggWiff's behaviour and the knowledge he possessed. However, Gathnok refused to believe it.

"What do you mean? What have you got planned?" Gathnok began to be enraged by EggWiff's incompetence.

Gathnok was distracted from his thoughts of EggWiff's potential hidden knowledge as a gust of wind filled the room and his attention was drawn from EggWiff to the new arrival.

"Hello, Gathnok." Death spoke from his black cloak.

* * *

The stillness of the day soon turned to the clouds of night as the splutter of raindrops fell, bringing the darkness with it. The darkness consumed everything. The bridge he was about to cross was lost from sight. The dark quarry formed beneath him, like a bottomless pit of despair.

Morbid was annoyed he had to cross the bridge, but it was the quickest way to Magmount and then the portal of the Nether Realm. He had to make it seem like he was carrying out Gathnok's wishes. Also, getting Cupido Sacra first would mean he could protect it for the right person. He missed the days of his father teaching him the art and skill of soul collecting. That knowledge, though, allowed him to understand the importance of his mission.

As he began to cross the darkened bridge, he knew something wasn't right. Although it was now night time, he thought he could see a small orange glow far off in the distance. If he had eyes he would have squinted. Instead he continued to peer out until he realized the light was getting bigger and bigger. It wasn't long before he could see it was a huge ball of fire travelling across the bridge towards him. The ball of fire then hurtled itself across the bridge travelling at immense speed. It became larger still the more it travelled towards him, destined to collide with Morbid.

Morbid's chattering became loud and harsh as he slumped to the floor transfixed with the fear of a child. Morbid looked down at the thundering pit beneath him. If he were to stay on the bridge, then he were sure to be shattered into a thousand pieces. Once upon a time he would welcome this, but now his mission was too important. He had to ensure Gathnok retrieved the stone and harnessed its power. He watched as the ball hurtled towards him at tremendous pace.

As he looked at his second death, his final becoming, he flashed back to the moment this adventure began. The moment his journey into destiny really began.

<u>Two Months Earlier</u>

"We have another attempt." The white skeleton torso was being wheeled into the medical centre. The rest of the body parts were piled up in a basket behind them. Two nurses were dealing with them.

The nurse wheeled the torso into the large room where the doctor was waiting.

"What do we have?" The voice was low and tainted with an unheard-of accent.

"Un-dead skeleton by the name of Morbid. He has a broken skeletal frame. History of suicide attempts." The nurse was peering at a board with information, Morbid moaned with pain.

"Why aren't I dead? Why am I not gone?" Morbid's detached head was speaking from the top of the pile of bones beneath him.

"We're going to fix you right up, Morbid. It's okay. Your body needs some mending, but you'll be fine." As Morbid peered down, he could see his doctor was a small leprechaun.

"No, I don't want to be fine. Destroy me now. Leave me

157

broken. Please don't re-attach me." Morbid was begging. The slamming of his bare jaw made a chattering sound.

The doctor was wearing green clothes and was standing on a high wheeled stool. He leaned over and was about to speak, when suddenly he stopped in fright. Death had appeared in the corner of the room. Death didn't even look down at Morbid. He didn't have too. Instead he waved his hand over Morbid, leaving his body healed and attached. Death then threw his reaper, which was caught by Morbid as he sat up from the table. The doctor and the nurses didn't have any time to process what was happening before the doctor's eyes widened, and blood spurted from his mouth. His body was flung to the side to reveal the reaper stuck in the leprechaun's back. The two nurses screamed in sheer horror, only to be dead on the floor within seconds. Morbid nodded at his father. Death disappeared from sight and left Morbid with the knowledge that the plan was in motion.

Morbid sat on the bed peering round the room and at the three dead bodies. He began to get bored waiting, so he began to make up lives for the victims. He playfully decided the two female nurses lived together and had both fallen in love with the leprechaun. However, unfortunately he was too in love with his work, so they planned to kill him. Morbid knew his father would have killed them if he could, but Death was forbidden to take souls before their time. Morbid was enjoying this game until two guards stormed in and arrested him for murder. If Morbid could, he would have smiled.

One month later Morbid was in court.

* * *

Morbid looked around. He knew he had to act. The bridge looked rickety and old, the planks worn with time, whilst the yellow weak rope looked frayed and torn. Morbid took one final look at the twirling ball. He bent his skeleton legs and jumped up high in the air. Once in the air, he slammed his feet down hard onto the weakest part of the plank, forcing the bridge to snap under him and detach from the rest of the bridge. Making sure his body faced the right direction, Morbid dug his white fingers into the plank as it swung loose. He felt his body swing hundreds of feet down into the pit as he felt the heat from the fireball pass above his head. His only worry now was that the bridge should stay attached at the top of the ledge. Morbid wished he had eyes to close, and he knew he would soon smack into the side of the wall. He could only hope this wouldn't be the end. He thought it odd how he didn't think of Trickle in what may be his final moments. He had killed before, but somehow killing Trickle was different. It was due to circumstance and not by his own intent. However, this was the curse of being the son of Death.

Morbid's body was slammed into the side of the wall. He felt his bones clatter within his joints. A few chips of white bone broke off and clunked as they fell against the wall beneath him. Everything was pitch black. The fact he was hanging masked the light from the stars. For a moment he pondered whether he had truly died, but the weight of the bridge soon brought him back to reality. He began to climb the planks of the bridge as if they were the rungs of a ladder. The bottomless pit was dark and uninviting. Morbid wondered how far down he was. The falling and slamming had only lasted a few seconds, but that was enough. He needed to be more careful of traps like this in the future. His mission could have been over before it had even begun. Only Morbid and Lainla now knew the true importance of this mission after his father had set it all in motion.

* * *

The Holy Master stood up and faced the thousands of hovering Mithworks and his loyal army.

"My holy brothers, you have been with me this entire journey. We have made sacrifices to receive the holy, the almighty Essence! We have bathed in its glory, my brothers, and we have been purified by the lushness of its all-powerful intention. We have seen the destiny, the future that must prevail. We are about to go into battle, my brethren, so know this. These creatures are sinners against the Holy Essence. They will fall because it has given you the strength to do so. For liberation!"

"For liberation!" the pigs echoed as a chorus.

The Mithworks roared as they thundered into the army beneath them, like diving bombs of destruction as they crashed into the earth, Thousands of them raining death onto the shadowed creatures. The battlefield glowed as spells were cast. Blood was spilled, like thousands of ants fighting over a small scrap of food.

A Sacred Past

"So door number five." Asemai was getting tired of all the different chambers and corridors.

The jewel was just an empty shell, and she struggled to understand why it was so well hidden. The tomb was more like a series of corridors than a protective fortress.

"I hope this is the last!" Wispar also was getting a little fed up.

"I think it's a little sad that you're complaining more than Kip." Forlax was annoyed; he somehow expected more from his sister.

Kip just grinned and stayed close to Wispar. Truth be told, he was rather scared of Forlax but felt safe by Wispar's side. So far he had enjoyed travelling, and the many corridors of the tomb seemed more like fun than an annoyance.

"*You sure you have it in you?*" *Gathnok looked at the already tired Euthan.*

"*I'm sure. Stand back.*"

The doors of the tomb were made from large pieces of stone. As stone is a natural element of Sahihriar, Euthan could control it with his powers. Euthan pressed his hand against the stone door and shut his eyes. They were all beginning to get used to their powers, and Euthan was especially used to opening the tomb doors. After a second the door began to rumble as it slowly began to slide towards the right wall, leaving the opening. They were all relieved to see that it didn't open out to another corridor but instead revealed a large chamber of some kind. It was a large room that actually looked rather beautiful. There were two square pools of water set into the stone floor. The gaps in between made the walkway dry, but the water was only inches deep. It reflected the four small beams of light that appeared from the top of the ceiling. At first it seemed as though the chamber was empty, but as they crept further along the narrow path and their eyes adjusted to the change of light, they noticed that one of the stone walls was set further forward, creating a screen that would only be noticed if you went and properly looked at it. They walked on the pathway between the two pools. There was a trickle of water that appeared from either wall that flowed slightly into the pools. Gathnok couldn't help be impressed by the self-contained system.

"*Don't fall in.*" *Wispar smiled at Kip, who would often look up at her with fascination.*

"*I won't, I promise,*" *Kip replied.*

They walked over to the stone wall, and each began to peer around it. Here would lie the jewel that could contain the purest of magic. It's here that they would find Cupido Sacra.

"*Oh . . .*" *Asemai looked rather disappointed. "It's a bunch of junk!*"

They were staring at a pile of junk. The screen that only

stretched halfway across the chamber was hiding storage of all sorts of old things. Axes and spears were piled together, chests were smothered in dust, and diamonds and other precious stones were covered in cobwebs. However, nothing seemed particularly special.

"I was expecting a great big altar with a shining light or something." Wispar and Asemai kept peering to make out different objects covered by the dirt.

"How tacky would that be!" Forlax rolled his eyes.

"I guess we should start looking," Euthan added.

"If we have to look through all of that, it'll take ages!" Kip now also looked disappointed.

"Sorry, it's one of the burdens of being a spirit, I guess." Wispar was trying to be positive but also looked dismayed.

"What about the shimmering compass? Can't we use that?" Lainla wasn't keen to rummage through dirt either.

Gathnok took out the shimmering compass from his pocket and smiled at Lainla. "When in doubt, use the compass. Good idea!"

He held out the compass towards the pile of rubbish as the others looked on eagerly. Kip was annoyed, as even on tiptoe he couldn't see the needles. Nothing happened for a while, and all of their faces looked concerned.

"Maybe it isn't here."

Just then the shimmering compass began to swirl its colours and shimmer brightly. Gathnok felt the familiar warmth in his hand as he held onto it. The needles began to spin slightly. He walked forward and began to follow the needles, running the compass over the piles of lost valuables. The needles pointed him in front of a wooden chest as the compass glowed even brighter and felt almost hot in his hands.

"I think it's in here."

The chest was set a little way in, but luckily there wasn't too much on top of it. Gathnok began removing the sword and *an old satchel from the top. Once clear, he examined it closely. It didn't look very special at all. It was an ordinary-looking wooden chest with black metal framing. It couldn't have been more average if it tried. Gathnok went to touch it, but it was draped in a thick layer of dust which also made it hard to breathe close to it.*

"Asemai!"

"Oh, yeah, sure, sorry." Asemai waved her finger, and soon a small powerful wind was circling over the chest. Gathnok smiled as the dust peeled of it.

"Padlock!" He hadn't noticed it before.

"Allow me." Forlax walked forward and stood by Gathnok. Gathnok was unsure as to what Forlax would do, until he watched him kneel down by the chest. He took the padlock in his hand and closed his eyes. Gathnok was suitably impressed when he saw the padlock began to glow red and the metal soon began to melt from the heat.

"That should do it!" Forlax stood up and nodded at Gathnok.

The others looked on and were also impressed. Gathnok bent down and gave a short sharp tug on the lid of the chest. The padlock was soft enough that it snapped through the lock. Gathnok and Forlax coughed and waved their hands as dust swept up from inside the chest. After the dust settled, Gathnok peered into the chest. He peeled back a small piece of cloth and looked inside. At first he thought it was empty, but sitting in the bottom corner was what looked like a small brown bag tied at the top by some frayed string. He carefully picked it up and held it in his hands. He smiled as he felt a heavy smooth object, roughly the size of his hand. Untying the string, he placed his hand inside and peeled back the bag. Everyone smiled; resting in his hand was a clear but well-formed jewel. They had found Cupido Sacra.

"Feel anything?" Lainla asked Gathnok.

163

"It's definitely the jewel, but it's empty. It won't be any use until we deliver it to the Ancients." Gathnok placed it back in the bag and stood up.

"Let's get going then."

They had all been on the other side of screening stone wall. They quickly turned and walked out into the large open chamber again. Each of them stopped dead still. On the other side of the two pools stood what looked like fifty Darkmagi. They stood still with their features yet again hidden by their hoods.

"How did we not notice that?" Wispar exclaimed. As she spoke she noticed that Kip was still behind the screen. She glanced over and gave a subtle shake of her head.

Kip looked confused at first but then nodded and took a few steps back. She wanted him to remain hidden and safe. Gathnok stepped forward. He was so tired of fighting these beings and wasn't sure he had enough energy to do it again.

"Give us the jewel, and we shall spare the other Spirits," said the hooded figure.

"I do not wish to harm Sahihriar. I only wish to protect it," Gathnok called back. He couldn't believe they were stealing magic based on some prophecy.

"You cannot fight fate."

"No, but once again we can easily fight you." Gathnok got into a stance as did the others.

The Spirits all got ready for battle. Lainla became poised and at some point had picked up a sword. The Darkmagi stood still and did nothing. Gathnok smirked, knowing that the tomb would soon be a light with the colours and powers of the elements. Soon . . . any moment . . .

"Do I need to say it again?" Gathnok asked as he looked at the others.

"Our powers aren't working!" Asemai tried to channel her power but couldn't. They were powerless again.

"What happened?" Lainla never had powers, but there's no way she could fight all of the Darkmagi.

"I don't know," Forlax responded.

"This is why." The front Darkmage reached down into his pocket and pulled out a purple, swirling sphere.

"Well, at least it's pretty," Asemai noted.

"This orb absorbs your abilities. You're defenceless." For the first time the hooded figure had a hint of twisted emotion.

"Telling us couldn't have been a good idea," Gathnok whispered to Lainla.

"You'd think so, wouldn't you?" Lainla replied with a smile.

The Darkmagi approached them and pointed their swords at each of them.

"Weapons? Not like you guys!" Gathnok asked curiously.

"Shut up, Spirit."

They were led across the middle section of the tomb and made to line up against the wall. Gathnok was forced to hand over Cupido Sacra. They were each tied up and then tied to the wall with their arms bound high and their feet shackled.

They looked on curiously. One Darkmage was holding the orb nearby, and the other was holding Cupido Sacra.

"That jewel is the only hope Sahihriar has." Gathnok looked round for something, anything that could help them.

"Destroying the jewel and ending you will bring Sahihriar hope," the Darkmage said.

Gathnok thought about what the Darkmage had said. If they did intend to kill them, then why hadn't they done it yet – unless the orb also neutralised their power. But even so, that didn't change much. They could easily be stabbed or hacked to death, and without their powers they were pretty much defenceless. That's why the Darkmagi had brought weapons.

Just then each of them tried to hide their smile. They all caught sight of Kip who had begun to creep behind the screen *wall. All of the Darkmagi were focused on the Spirits and Lainla. None of them had any reason to suspect they had adopted Kip. The Darkmage had found a small pedestal to rest the sacred jewel on. It remained clear and lifeless. Without magic the jewel was fragile. Kip crept silently across the stone pathway in between the two pools of water. His heart pounded slightly as he hoped the luck of the imps would help him. He could see the Darkmage holding the orb, but there was a wall of Darkmagi in between. He looked around him, knowing he only had one shot at getting this right. The Darkmage was speaking about prophecy as he seemed to be preparing to destroy the jewel. He knew he had seconds left. Picking up a small pebble he found from a small pile of rubble, Kip took a deep breath and said a quick prayer to the Elders before hurtling the stone at the far side wall. It clicked against the wall, and each hooded figure turned and moved slightly to look. Closing his eyes slightly, Kip ran with all his force. Because of his height and surprising speed, he managed to knock through the wall of Darkmagi with some ease. Seeing the Darkmage holding the orb, he shot forward and leapt in the air. He managed to grab the orb from its hands and land safely with the orb intact, which was indeed rather lucky. He quickly leapt to his feet and held the orb up high. Some of the Darkmagi loomed in close.*

"Stop!" the chief hooded figure called.

The Darkmagi stopped and became rigid once more. Kip was facing the leader who had his sword poised and ready over the jewel.

"You break the orb and I'll smash your jewel," the voice boomed from the dark hooded ring.

Kip looked over at Gathnok for some idea of what to do. He guessed they couldn't afford to lose the jewel, but unless the orb was broken, they couldn't regain their powers. So what good would the jewel be if they were all dead?

Gathnok sighed and looked despaired. "They're only going to smash it anyway"

Kip gave a mischievous smile before he raised up the orb and flung it to the stone floor.

"No!" the hooded leader screamed, as he quickly smashed the jewel with his sword, shattering it into pieces. The purple sphere broke as it hit the ground and the light dimmed.

"Our turn!" Gathnok smirked, as immediately he felt the power rush through him.

The wall they were tied to rumbled slightly, and they shook loose the shackles from the wall thanks to Euthan. Forlax managed to burn through his shackles. The might of Asemai's wind blew off her shackles. Wispar stayed put, but water soon swirled up from the pool like a massive tornado and began to sweep up Darkmagi. Forlax helped Gathnok and then the others, and soon they were all free and united as spirits. Pieces of stone went hurtling towards Darkmagi like deadly giant bullets. Gathnok's hand lunged as it touched the cheeks of Darkmagi who had gotten close. Lainla had already managed to steal a sword and was sparring with two of them. The Darkmagi were becoming wise and knew they stood little chance against the full force of the elements.

"Retreat! We have done what we came to do." The Darkmagi began to run towards the door as they flocked out.

"Should we stop them?" Euthan called, as he could easily do so with his vines.

"No, there will always be more." Gathnok stopped and looked at the others. He looked over and saw the smashed pieces of the jewel. It had formed tiny shards of crystal which would be impossible to put back together.

"So what now?" Wispar asked.

Gathnok looked down at the shimmering compass which wasn't glowing and didn't feel warm.

"Nothing we can do. We've lost all hope. They won."
Gathnok looked at the others and felt completely lost.

Saria and Lainla flew on the great dragon, clutching hard to one of the scales sticking from its back. The dragon swirled and glided, cutting through the night sky. They soared higher as the tall tower appeared first, slowly revealing more, until Lainla and Saria gasped in unison. They looked down on the wave of destruction beneath them. At first Saria couldn't see what was slaughtering the pigs, and then she knew. She felt the suffering and heard the oinks of pain from just meters below. Every time she peered down and saw the blades clash, her mind flashed to Flick's face, the pain in his eyes as she killed him. She closed her eyes and fought back the tears. Now was the time to be strong.

Lainla's blue shimmering dress flew out behind her as she rode the dragon. Her heart was pounding as her wings fluttered and the knot in her stomach grew. She knew that she was about to do the hardest thing in her whole life. Worse still, she still didn't have any idea if she was strong enough to do it. She looked down on the vast bodies of the pigs beneath them. Once upon a time, the sheer thought of such pain would have upset her. Now she was numb to pain and had sadly grown accustomed to it. She wondered what her Amazon friend would think when she found out. She prayed she might forgive her. All of this was bigger than any of their feelings.

They saw the stone window set in the tallest tower. The dragon instinctively knew what to do. It hovered next to the window and lowered one wing so it could get right up close. Using the other wing, it hovered suspended, leaving virtually no gap between the two women and the window. Lainla glided up into the air from the dragon using her wings. Her gracefulness still astounded Saria, but she wasn't into the pretty stuff.

Saria peered into the soft candle-lit room. It actually seemed warm and inviting in comparison to the black night air. Saria was an Amazon first, and everything else came second. She felt strange, a presence, an overwhelming sense of danger or evil. Either way, the air was thick. She stepped inside and before anything else withdrew her blade. Candles lit the circular room. The stone walls grew to a high pointed ceiling. The room had a wooden rail appearing from a hole in the floor that clearly led to the rest of the castle. Hanging from the ceiling near to the wall was a cage. Its iron rustic holdings made it look like a huge birdcage. Saria couldn't help feel some kind of warmth amongst the cold when she saw EggWiff's bright blue eyes beam from the dimly lit shadows.

"Saria? Lainla?" EggWiff was stunned to see her here and know she was alive. "How?" He couldn't form the words, as she looked just as beautiful as he remembered. EggWiff spoke quietly and with confusion.

"I'm sorry, EggWiff, but it's more complicated than you think." Lainla floated above the stone floor. The glow was the same, but this time Lainla did not smile.

"Just wait." Saria didn't know what to say. She felt torn and confused. They didn't seem so bad, Trickle, EggWiff, and Flick, but she had killed many beings in her time, including some who were innocent. She wasn't going to let her emotions trouble her now.

The air in the centre of the room began to become distorted, wispy, and thick. It shimmered, and before anyone could realize what was happening, the black hooded cloak and steel reaper blade had appeared into the room.

Death let his time-decayed fingers peel back his black

hood. His jaw was defined and chiselled. The oval shape of his eye sockets made the resemblance unmistakable.

"Morbid's father is Death?" EggWiff looked confused. This wasn't making any sense. Why would Death, Lainla, Morbid, and Saria be trying to stop them? His mind was running through everything – the lost souls and Trickle being attacked. How did it all fit? Trickle . . . Morbid had killed Trickle. EggWiff sat stunned as he realised that it wasn't just Gathnok. They were all working together.

"You have been working together from the start." EggWiff's voice trailed as the thoughts clouded his mind.

"It's bigger than her. It's bigger than all of us. We didn't mean for *them* to die, but it was necessary." Death raspy voice filled the circular room. Faint oinks of pain could be heard from below.

"Them? Who else have . . ." EggWiff's enchanting blue eyes began to fill with tears. He stared into the eyes of his betrayers. His power surged through him. Anger, rage, hatred – everything he swore not to become took over.

"I had to!" Saria's face had tears rolling down them as she could see the anger in EggWiff. She slumped onto the stone floor.

EggWiff's rage was blind to the pain in her soul. EggWiff huddled in the cage trying to control his rage, waiting for the second he was released to exact revenge on them all.

The steps began to thud. They all looked at the hole in the floor, awaiting the presence of the person who brought them all together. The shadowed ruler walked into sight and stood in front of them all.

Lainla gasped in horror.

"Gathnok!"

The shadowed figure stopped. He slowly turned his head. His face grew lightened as features could be seen. He looked old and roguish and had astonishment in his eyes.

"Lainla . . ."

Gathnok ran to his beloved. He embraced her swiftly as shock overwhelmed him. How he longed for the touch of her skin, the warmth of her smile! He got lost in every fibre of her being as they touched again for the first time in years. Lainla stood still, her eyes watered, and she couldn't stop shaking. They had been apart for a lifetime.

"How, how did this happen?" Gathnok's voice was now soft and gentle as a smile beamed across his face and wouldn't leave.

"Shhhh! It doesn't matter. It's fine now. Everything is fine." Lainla's soft tender lips were pressing gently against his ear as she spoke. "There isn't much time." Lainla forced her mind to focus back to what was important. "I need you to do something for me. I need you to use Cupido Sacra, to use it like you were going to before you found me" She prayed every night for this moment to come and then prayed harder that it wouldn't.

"What? There's no need. We're together now." Gathnok pulled away and stared at Lainla. "We're finally together." Gathnok was holding Lainla's cheeks and kissing her forehead in between smiles.

"No, we can't." Lainla shrugged off Gathnok. "Please, if you love me, you'd do this for me." Lainla stared into the eyes she fell in love with.

Saria stood and watched the tearful reunion. She suddenly felt a wave of anger and betrayal. Lainla was just waiting to get back with Gathnok. She clearly hadn't been working for Gathnok, and now Saria felt used. She had to sacrifice Flick for what was right. All along Lainla was just working for herself. Saria was unable to control her anger as she felt it taking over.

Without hesitation she drew her sword. The long silver blade glinted as she ran over to Lainla's back. She took a breath and sliced the sword through her torso. Saria glared into Gathnok's eyes as Lainla let a small cry of pain. Gathnok flung his hand high and with it forced Saria to hurtle back and hit the stone wall behind her. He peered down into Lainla's eyes. It was as if he was reliving that pain all those years ago.

Gathnok stroked Lainla's hair back from away from her face and caressed her cheek.

"I won't let this happen to you again! I won't!" He smiled a comforting smile as Lainla passed out in his arms.

Saria stood up. She felt justice and anger still pulsating through her.

EggWiff screamed. The pain of Gathnok losing Lainla once again was too much. He stretched out his arms, confused by hatred and love for his family. One thing for certain – he would kill Death and Saria; they had no right to inflict this pain, no justification.

Gathnok's body was swallowed by shadow again. The dark retching pain awoke in all of them as Gathnok's fear-dwelling presence returned. He looked up and peered at them all. "I will kill you all!" His voice was certain, definite. EggWiff couldn't help but know that what he said was true.

Gathnok and Lainla began to be surrounded by the dark blue lights as they whirled faster and faster, until both Gathnok and Lainla were gone from the room. Death, Saria, and EggWiff were left alone in the tower.

Saria sighed, her spine tingling from the force of Gathnok's blow. She hated him more than anything and knew what she had to do. She walked up to EggWiff's cage.

"Saria, what are you doing?" Death spoke as he leaned forward and once again covered his tainted white head with his hood.

"What is right!" Saria flicked her hair back and peered at EggWiff. He was huddled, shaking, and holding himself. His grey hair hung over his head, masking his expression. Saria looked at the cage. The dimly lit room hid many secrets. She looked to the back wall. At first she assumed it was a lever, but it was positioned wrong. She crept closer and saw it was EggWiff's ivory-stained staff.

"EggWiff, could this get you out?" EggWiff stayed the same.

"You wish to release him?" Death stepped close behind Saria. His presence was menacing.

Saria smirked and then slammed the ivory staff into the cage. Sparks flew from the impact; then a dark purple haze appeared and then vanished

Death put his fingers on Saria's shoulder.

"EggWiff!" Both Death and Saria peered in at the broken down EggWiff.

EggWiff without warning kicked open the cage door, throwing Saria back. He threw himself out whilst grabbing his staff. Death stumbled back in shock and went to grab the reaper. EggWiff's eyes were dark. The blue had been taken over by darkness, and the anger in his face was overwhelming. EggWiff peered into the sockets of Death's eyes before muttering a spell. Death tilted his head in curiosity. Two red swirls of energy came hurtling from EggWiff's hands like two powerful jets of water. The red swirls hit Death in the stomach as he screamed in pain. He struggled as they continued to lash into him. Death's pain cried out across Sahihriar. It was deafening. It forced EggWiff and Saria onto the floor, covering their ears. Death's hood was no longer covering his face as his pain jerked his body from side to side. He looked up and stared at EggWiff. As he did so, his skeleton face began to crumble and break of into shards. Chalky white dust began to form as his face and body began to crumble He knelt to the floor and made no sound as his body slumped onto the ground and he decayed into a pile of white chalk.

EggWiff breathed heavily. He had begun to exact his revenge for his two former friends. He turned to Saria. Now it must continue.

* * *

Morbid was walking along the snowy paths of the Iciliks Mountains. These were mountains of ice and cold that lay just before the Fire Mountain. Very few creatures wandered through the Elemental Lands. Dark creatures, powerful creatures that had only been rumoured and whispered of lived within the mountains. Morbid's bare white feet scrunched the snow beneath them.

Morbid felt strange – a weird vibe as if energy was rushing over him. He stopped as his bones began to ache. He felt like he could breathe, but he knew too well he couldn't. He tried not to look into the snowy path beneath him. Then flashes came into his head. He saw his father in the circular tower. He was standing behind Saria. Then he knelt down in horror as he saw his worst nightmare come to pass – his father being murdered by EggWiff. He stood up tall and waited. He knew what the vision triggered. He opened out his arms to have the cloak of death materialize over him and the reaper to appear in his hand. Morbid has inherited his father's destiny. He was now Death. The cloak was thick and dark. It was clean and made of the finest materials. This mystical cloak wouldn't fade or become dirtied over time. It would never leave him and was a symbol. Morbid was no longer just a skeleton but something so much more.

He no longer cared about Gathnok. He didn't care much about anything except the one thing that plagued his mind. From now on all his dreams would be of killing EggWiff.

* * *

EggWiff stood tall in front of Saria. His blue robes and ivory staff made him seem more powerful and dominating. Energy surrounded him as his soul became blackened. However, Saria made no attempt to pick up her blade or hold a weapon. Instead she slowly stood up and closed her eyes. Her thoughts were only on Flick. The sight of his death would haunt her in life and in death. At least she would pay for her sins now.

"Do it." Saria could only whisper the words as she struggled to hold back tears. She would die a warrior's death.

EggWiff raised his staff and held it vertically so that the tip was facing Saria's heart. Saria breathed heavily as she thought about all the people she had killed. Most of them had been guilty, but mistakes had been made. She didn't regret her life, as she had done a lot as good as an Amazon.

EggWiff moved his hand back and thrust his staff forward. Saria tensed up and squirmed as she awaited the staff to pierce her flesh.

It never did.

She opened her eyes and saw EggWiff in front of her, his staff stretched out in front of him, but not into her. It was rammed into the wall to the right of her head. She looked back confused at EggWiff.

"I will never forgive you, but I do need you." EggWiff drew back his staff and turned from Saria and looked to the window. "I will avenge my friend's life. I will kill Gathnok."

"I don't want your forgiveness, and I will never deserve it, but I did care for Flick. If today isn't the day I die, then I will spend every moment in between trying to stop Gathnok."

EggWiff turned his head; his compassion had been destroyed with Trickle and Flick. The best he could do was to give a nod.

The dragon had flown off into the night. EggWiff expected as much. He could feel the connection it had with Lainla. The castle ground had been covered in mist, and it was impossible to see or hear the battle below.

"We'll have to go down through the castle and walk out through the battle, and then we can begin."

Saria withdrew her blade and twirled it around in her hands. "Not a problem."

EggWiff went to the hole in the floor and began to walk down the steps into the heart of the castle. Saria followed shortly behind him.

After EggWiff had used a navigation spell and Saria had taken out the two shadowed twins that had kidnapped EggWiff, they found themselves at the door to the main gate.

"Be careful! I need you alive." EggWiff wasn't talking from concern.

If this were any other situation, then EggWiff would have been dead by her sword. But it wasn't; Flick was still gone, and he had a right to his pain.

They both took a deep breath. Saria kicked the doors open, and they both charged out into the mist. Saria screamed with her blade held high. EggWiff ran with his cloak billowing behind and holding his staff in front of him ready to perform all the defensive spells he could remember. However, the mist had cleared, and the sound of the battlefield was deadly silent. They both stopped and dropped their weapons as their gaze wondered across the whole field of vision. They were on the bridge that crossed the moat. Ahead of them was the battlefield, but the battle was over and the clear victor had won. The field was lined with pigs. Hundreds upon hundreds of pigs were lying dead on the ground. Saria and EggWiff walked amongst them. Some had been killed by their own weapons, and others literally had the life sucked out of them.

They had all died for what they believed in – the Holy Essence. EggWiff couldn't stand to look at the wasted lives. The whole situation was pointless, as Gathnok had let his selfish desires take over everything.

For Saria, however, this was just another battleground. She had been in so many fights that this didn't disturb her much. She was sad, but she knew all too well the sacrifice of faith and belief.

They continued to walk through the bloodshed. Every now and then a pig would oink or stir slowly, but Saria and EggWiff both knew that nothing could be done.

Saria stopped. A sound caught her ear lingering in the wind. It wasn't oinks of pain or the shift of dirt beneath a body moving. This was whimpering, a soft crying. Saria drew her blade and looked back at EggWiff. He too was looking around as if to find the source of the noise. She nodded once at EggWiff and moved in towards the sound. She could see a shield raised up leaning against something, something that was making the shield move. Saria crept round slowly, making her footsteps tread lighter. EggWiff was doing the same round the other side. After a confirming glance from EggWiff, they both jumped behind the shield. Saria thrust her sword in front of the being, and EggWiff did the same with his staff.

The Holy Master sat in his dark purple robes. His snout was pointing down, and his eyes were filled with tears. He was huddled, alone, and terrified. He glanced up at Saria, and the pain in his eyes struck her. She peered round and it was only then that it hit her. He had just watched his warriors, his people being slaughtered.

"They didn't have the strength. They didn't," the Holy Master was muttering, his eyes lost in the pain.

EggWiff sighed as he swung his staff and it hit the Holy Master in the face hard. The pig squealed as it forced his head low into the ground.

"What are you doing?" Saria stepped in between them both. She didn't like what EggWiff had become.

"He helped Gathnok. He caused the fight that killed Trickle. Now he must die!" EggWiff's face was blank of emotion, even rage.

"EggWiff, he is the only one who knows how to contact Gathnok. He can help us!" Saria was thinking quickly. It wasn't that she particularly liked the Holy Master, but she refused to let more people die.

"Who, who is Gathnok?" The pig's voice wavered.

"The big evil shadow one, the guy whose army just destroyed yours!" Saria held out her hand to help the Holy Master up.

"He has a name?"

"Yeah, now we've got to stop them." As Saria spoke, EggWiff just looked on. Only the Elders knew what was going on behind those blue eyes.

"Then I must go with you! I must avenge my brothers! Gathnok will pay!" The Holy Master's voice once again had passion.

"He'll do more than that. He'll die!"

The pig brushed down his Essence-stained cloak, and the three of them stood side by side under the cloudy sky. They all looked to the horizon and thought of the journey ahead of them. It was no longer a job or a punishment. It was revenge. Gathnok had stolen Trickle from EggWiff, Flick from Saria, and faith from the Holy Master. The anger and loss in their hearts meant they weren't going to stop And this time nothing would stop them.

Part II

"Farewell"

Chapter Nine

The field swayed as the wind gently brushed the grain; everything was normal. The sky was blue and clear, the trees stood tall and strong, and everything was how it should be. There were no creatures around, as the nearest village was a good few miles away. Only the farmer would be near, but he often fell fast asleep before noon. Fortunately, the creatures that were about to trespass knew this. In fact, there was very little they didn't know.

The light shone faintly at first. However, the sun was not full in the sky. These rays of light were from something far more powerful. The beam shone brighter onto the lifeless field. The light began to grow wider and glowed so bright that soon nothing could be seen. The farmer, who was a slow Marmoth, didn't even stir as the light beams shone through the dirty windows of the barn. The light began to fade after a few moments. As it did, what it left behind could be seen floating the middle of the field.

"I'm glad that worked!" The light was shaped as a person,

but no features could be seen. They were like the shadow beings, but instead of darkness, they were smothered by light. The grain would gently brush through them.

"Yes, I just hope we made it in time." The second being of light had a slight shade of grey. Their voices were soft but gave no sign of emotion or gender.

"Well, as long as our powers work." The first being was represented by having a light shade of blue.

"Let's see."

The being knelt down until its glowing hand was touching the field. It waited a few seconds before floating back up level with its twin.

"Nothing."

"Patience!" The blue shining being watched the field carefully.

After a few more seconds the ground beneath them began to rumble and quake. The dirt in between the grain began to shudder. Then it began to fall, as in the centre of the field there grew a hole into nothing. Soon the hole spread, and more of the field fell into the abyss. The beings stood still and remained hovering over the expanse. It wasn't long before the whole field had fallen, and the abyss crept to the edge of the barn and was soon to swallow it. The grey-lighted being shimmered a darker grey, and as it did so, the hole stopped expanding, leaving the barn safe at the last moment.

"No need to kill. It should be a last resort."

"Things are different down here. Remember the mission is the only thing of importance."

"Of course, but that doesn't change what we are." The lights had begun to float away from the huge canyon they had created.

"We weren't always Elders." The blue light turned to its

companion, before they both shimmered to carry out their plan.

* * *

"I can't believe it's really you." Lainla could only manage a whisper as Gathnok lowered her slowly onto the bed.

"Believe it. I won't let you go again." Gathnok's darkened hand brushed Lainla's hair.

Lainla winced with pain, as she couldn't control the blood seeping from her wound. "What if I leave you?" Lainla tried to smile but her mouth felt cold. Her whole body felt cold, as her wings couldn't even flutter. She managed to let her fingers stroke Gathnok's cheek. As they did, his blackened face would become visible for a brief moment. She had missed those eyes.

"You won't! I won't let you." Gathnok's voice was soft and comforting. He didn't dare take his eyes away from her. Not after last time. Why was he doomed to repeat the same nightmare? He smiled as he looked at her. Lainla was as every bit as beautiful as the day they had met.

"You can't, not without Cupido Sacra." Lainla managed a weak smile this time, but it was only to hide her despair. She hadn't planned on this happening so soon. She had hoped she would have seen the end. At least there was hope, if only she could get him to use the jewel.

"I will make that Amazon pay." Gathnok's face grew darker as his thoughts turned to rage.

"No!" Lainla winced as the effort to shout reminded her of the wound. "Get the jewel first."

Although his face was smothered in shadow, she could sense his look of confusion. She attempted a smile. "Heal me. Then we can both avenge her." Her eyes were fixed and absolute. She was hoping he wouldn't see through her lies.

The silence grew as Gathnok considered what to do. Lainla had to make him get the jewel.

"Don't let me go again."

Gathnok felt a twinge of guilt. She was right. He couldn't lose her again. He leaned in and let his blackened lips kiss her soft cheek and whispered close in her ear.

"Wait for me."

With this, he vanished from her side. Lainla let her swelling tears fall as she hoped it was enough.

* * *

EggWiff, Saria, and the Holy Master had arrived at the foot of the Iciliks Mountains. EggWiff peered up at the grand mountain. The four Elemental Mountains were said to be the home of the Elemental Spirits, all four holding power like nothing known to Sahihriar, except that of Cupido Sacra. If anything could help them destroy Gathnok, it would be them.

Saria hadn't spoken a word to either EggWiff or the Holy Master. Her mind couldn't shake the image of Flick as he slumped to the floor and that look he gave. She knew she didn't love him; she barely knew him. But in that moment they kissed, she was able to let go. She drowned out the screams of her victims. She had felt special, warm, and wanted – something she knew she'd never feel again, nor did she deserve to feel again.

"This is the place," EggWiff said, as he turned to the others.

"For what?" Saria looked around at the flat bare snow around her.

"We shall say our farewell." EggWiff spoke so absolutely. There was no sign of question or tone to his voice. "You have an hour to prepare." He looked at the Holy Master with such hatred.

"I'm not sure I can." The Holy Master bent his snout low, as he was too afraid to look at EggWiff.

EggWiff took a stride over to him and lunged his staff with force right in front of the frightened pig, which made him jump with fright.

"You can and will," EggWiff whispered as he leaned inches away from the pig's face. He picked up his staff and strode off behind him.

"You will help him," EggWiff said as he passed Saria. He didn't even bother to look at her as he passed.

Saria was going to respond or react, but she knew he had every right to his pain. Besides, fighting him wasn't going to stop Gathnok. She looked down at the snow beneath them, thinking about it. It was a good spot to perform the farewell. The snow was thick, and the ground was level. Only a few bare trees were scattered around, with icicles stemming from the branches instead of leaves. The snow fell, but it wasn't heavy. She knew it would be worse up the mountain. Saria looked back at the still timid Holy Master.

"Let's get started." She stopped herself. She was going to call him by his name, but she suddenly realised that neither she or EggWiff had bothered to ask what it was.

The Holy Master stared at her blankly as he waited for her to finish her sentence.

"What's your name?"

The Holy Master looked surprised and a little baffled. He stood back as the question had caught him off guard. "You wish to call me by my name? After the loss I caused you?"

Saria smiled to mask her sadness. "You didn't make me lose anything. I did that on my own."

The Holy Master looked confused for a moment. "Hail. I'm Hail" His voice began to have a slightly majestic tone again as he overly pronounced the end of his name.

187

Saria nodded her acceptance between the falling drops of snow.

"What is the name of the being we are saying farewell to?" Hail said as he began surveying the land for his task ahead.

"The elf called Trickle and the…" Saria glanced over towards EggWiff. She wasn't sure if he would want Flick included. She cast her mind back to the sadness he had shown when he was in the cage. Plus, even though he died at her hand, Flick deserved a farewell. ". . . and a dwarf named Flick."

* * *

Morbid was lying on the ground as his body jerked. His thin and fragile skeleton hands were gripping his head as his mind ached. He was overwhelmed with the cries and pain of the fallen. All over Sahihriar he could sense souls calling to him for his guidance into the next place. However, Morbid had never been prepared for his new powers and couldn't control all the pain and suffering he felt. It was all too much, and the screams were deafening. As he lay on the ground, all he could feel was pain, grief, and suffering. He had to make it stop. He tried desperately to control his powers as his mind raced. It wasn't enough just to kill EggWiff. There was so much more suffering in addition to his own. He now knew what he needed to do. He had to end it all, all life forever, so he could put an end to death and grief permanently. Fortunately for him, Morbid knew exactly how to do it.

* * *

An hour later, the two circles had been engraved into the snow. Two identical circles now stood side by side. They had been dug deep into the snowy floor, so they were deep and would last. The circles were meant to be a symbolic representation of the Everlasting Spirit. One circle was for Trickle, and the other was for Flick. Hail stood in front of the two circles. EggWiff stood in one with his staff dug into the snow next to it, and Saria stood in the other with her sword dug into the snow.

The snowflakes gently fell onto the snowy blanket of white. EggWiff and Saria knelt with their heads laid low. They both remembered the fallen, saying their own personal farewells. Hail raised his head and stood tall. The world around them was silent. Hail began the prayer of Farewell.

"We will never see their smiles. We will never see their eyes. We will never touch their hands again and feel their warmth. They are lost to us now, kept only by our memories. Please guide our fallen, and protect the ones we loved. Let Trickle and Flick know peace now; let them be free as we bid them farewell. We give our thanks, we say goodbye, so you can be reborn again."

Hail stopped, and all was silent. EggWiff placed his hand inside the circle.

"Farewell, Elf" EggWiff let the tear weave down his wrinkled face before splashing on the snow below.

Saria placed her hand in the circle in front. "Farewell, Dwarf."

EggWiff glanced over. He looked at the anguish on Saria's face, the sadness in her eyes. He began to feel a twinge of humanity. He hated her for killing Flick, and no part of him would ever forgive her, but he was all too aware of the complexity of the situation and couldn't help be aware of the guilt Saria felt.

She was holding back; she didn't have the right to cry at his farewell. She struggled to stop her eyes from swelling. The snow fell softly over them. EggWiff stood up as Hail walked away. Saria looked up at him, the tears building in her eyes. She hoped he wouldn't say anything. It was taking all her strength not to break down, and an off word from EggWiff would be too much. Saria closed her eyes and took a deep breath, preparing for whatever insult she had coming. She opened her eyes to see EggWiff staring at her, but this was different; his piercing blue eyes were soft, and his face wasn't stern. She looked at him confused as a tear rolled down her cheek. EggWiff walked up to her and said nothing. Instead he placed his hand on her shoulder and gave it a comforting squeeze.

They stared at each other through tears for a moment, each connected by their sense of loss. EggWiff nodded and then turned and walked away. Saria almost gasped as her head spun. For the first time he had given her compassion. To Saria this meant she was allowed to let go. She had been given permission to cry. She didn't hold back any longer, as she let her grief take control. She became so overwhelmed that she flung herself into the circle. She rested her head on the snow as she let the tears stream down her face. She cried so hard that she could barely breathe.

"I'm sorry, I'm so sorry . . . please . . . please." Her words became lost as she sobbed for Flick. The Amazon dwarf cried and cried as she collapsed into the snow.

Hail looked on in sympathy, as he was slowly warming to the fearless warrior. He turned away and left her alone with her pain. She cried for a while until she could do nothing else but collapse with exhaustion.

* * *

Morbid stood at the top of the Iciliks Mountain. He peered over the Elemental Lands. The blizzard bellowed around him, yet it was a very small distraction to a skeleton. The cloak of death waved over the skinny skeleton frame it was covering. Morbid could see Magmount clearly, as it was much higher than the Iciliks Mountain and was the tallest of all the Elemental Mountains. The mountain had red flames that swirled all around it. Slightly beyond that and to the right he could see the third of the Elemental Mountains, Earthica. The mount looked like a lush green paradise. It was covered in green trees and growth. He could see the some bird-like creatures flying around it. Their souls were so clear to him. The fourth mountain, Aeria, was virtually invisible until you were at its foot. Many people are said to have gotten lost on the misty mountain. Morbid could sense Aeria anyway; he didn't need to see it. Since becoming Death, he was becoming ever more aware of his powers. He wasn't concerned about his duty as Death. He only planned to search for Cupido Sacra. However, he needed to make sure EggWiff wouldn't get in his way. As Death, he wasn't allowed to take souls before their time, which was his only limitation. Therefore, Morbid knew he would have to get someone else to act out his revenge. Morbid closed his eyes and reached out with his soul. He struggled as his newfound powers overwhelmed him; he wasn't prepared for the intensity of his gifts. He could hear the screams of souls from all over Sahihriar, but he struggled to block them out. Soon they wouldn't matter. He was searching for something else, something far more important to his plan. Suddenly he saw it in his mind's eye. He brought himself back into focus and looked over at the view. He nodded as he took note of where he needed to be, and then as the wind blew, he vanished from the top of the mountain.

The room was dark. Morbid materialised eerily like swift wind. The darkness made it difficult, as he had no eyes to adjust to the light. He glanced round quickly and knew he was in the right place. The dungeon walls were damp. He was relaxed as he stood in the dark dungeon. He knew most of the shadow creatures would have gone when Gathnok had vanished the night before. Morbid loomed forward and saw it huddled on the dungeon floor. He walked over and picked up the large satchel of Essence, and as quickly as he had appeared, he vanished.

* * *

The skeleton judge walked into his chambers. He had had a very stressful day. He had to settle a dispute about a farmer Marmoth claiming vandalism on the part of the Molians for burrowing too far into his field and causing it to collapse. The judge pulled off his black cloak and put it on the back of his door. He switched on the light and turned to face his desk. He looked curious as he noticed a large brown satchel on his table. He walked over to it and noticed a small note beside it. It read, "Shouldn't this be with the High Council of the North?" The judge instantly knew what this meant. The odd sentence he had made a few months before had lingered in his mind, and now he knew the prisoners had abandoned their punishment. Without hesitation, he called in his assistant from outside.

"You called for me?" The assistant was one of the small fairies that had attended the ruling.

"Indeed I did. Send out a message. I need to speak with the Triplet Warriors immediately." The judge knew that by summoning these three, the prisoners were now sentenced to death.

A Sacred Past

They walked along the path in silence. Gathnok felt a little on edge, as he didn't even know if the shimmering compass would warn them of Darkmagi. Not that it mattered much. Without Cupido Sacra, they couldn't do much, so they weren't much of a threat.

"*You were pretty great in there, Kip.*"

"*Oh yeah, definitely.*" *Wispar and Asemai were sitting with the small imp in the centre of the clearing.*

"*Didn't help though, did it? We still lost the jewel.*" *Kip looked sad as he spoke.*

"*But we still have our lives,*" *Forlax commented.*

Kip was surprised by Forlax's comment; he was normally reserved, and so far hadn't shown much warmth towards him. He smiled as he felt slightly better. Gathnok was standing looking out on the fields that he could see from either side of the path. The sun was setting, and the two moons were appearing in the sky.

"*We should rest soon.*" *Gathnok barely looked at them as he spoke, disheartened.*

The other Spirits looked at each other. They weren't sure exactly what they were to do now. With Cupido Sacra gone, they couldn't think of how else they would defeat the Darkmagi.

"*We'll look for a suitable clearing,*" *Euthan replied, as they all continued to walk slowly along the path.*

One moon was almost full whilst the other was a smiling crescent in the sky. They were always at opposite ends of the sky and lit up the world of Sahihriar in a yellow glow at night. Many believed it to be rather beautiful. They walked a little further before they felt a shadow flash over them for just a second. They didn't need to say anything as they each looked at one another confused. Before anyone could speak, it happened again. The moon's glow was blocked for only a second.

"Everyone else is noticing that, right?" Kip asked as he hung onto to Wispar's hand.

"Yes, but what's causing it?" Asemai asked, as they each spread out a little and prepared themselves for an attack.

"A big dragon?"

"I hardly think it'll be a big dragon!" Gathnok said, as he turned to face Kip.

"No, really, there's a big dragon!" Kip said casually, pointing to the sky behind Gathnok.

They all looked and saw a large winged creature coming towards them. Its red slit eyes appeared first on its huge head with razor-sharp teeth. Its wings spread across great widths, as its body was the size of most of the smaller clearings they had stayed in. Its scales glistened, as the large thorns down his spine made for a menacing creature. The dragon hovered above them as they moved in closer. They watched as the large beast peered down at them before opening its mouth and breathing.

"Forlax, be ready." Gathnok realised what it was doing just in time.

Large flames erupted from the dragon's mouth as flames rained down towards the group. Forlax was ready and held up his hands and channelled his spirit energy. He caught the flames just before they hit and used his powers to send them flying back up at the dragon. It screeched as the flames hit its face, before fluttering back and twirling its head. However, it didn't seem to hurt.

"So, plan B!" Gathnok shouted.

"We have a plan B?" Lainla replied.

"Let's hope so, because plan A didn't work!" Forlax stood back, knowing his fire had little effect.

Suddenly the dragon swept down low and stretched out its sharp sword like claws. Kip and Wispar had to dive out of the *way just before they would have been shredded. However, as the dragon soared back up, no one noticed it whip its tail as it smacked Lainla in the leg.*

"Lainla!" Forlax rushed to her side.

"I'm fine." She winced as she held her thigh. Tears fell from her eyes; it was like being smacked by a stone.

The dragon went back up and began hovering again, its wings creating a small wind force as they fluttered. Asemai looked up and peered at the giant beast. The wings, although vast, seemed to be the most delicate thing on the creature. She figured she was the only one to stop it. She stood up and gracefully flicked her hair back. She was strong in stature like her brother but also very glamorous. She creased her nose in frustration and held up her arms as she felt the energy of the Spirit go through her. As she felt the energy release, she screamed as suddenly what seemed like the tail of a tornado spun out of her hands and whirled upwards towards the beast. It began to flap its wings harder at first, but soon the twister spun more violently as the wind howled all around them. The others leapt down on the ground so as not to get swept up by the winds. The dragon soon found himself spinning on the spot, and he struggled to maintain flight. Soon he was upside down, spinning in the eye of the tornado as it continued to spin from Asemai's hands. Asemai looked weakened as with one last push of her energy she let her arms go, and a mighty force of wind shot up and pushed the dragon through the air hurtling back towards the clouds, where it soon disappeared from sight. The others stood up slowly and looked at her with their mouths open.

"That was awesome!" Kip said, as he brushed up the dirt from his fall.

"Yeah, well, it annoyed me." Asemai flicked her hair back behind her ears and smiled.

"Are you all right to walk?" Forlax helped Lainla to her feet as Gathnok looked on concerned.

"Yeah, it'll just hurt for a while," she said, but wore a brave smile.

"Well, that came from nowhere," Euthan said, surprised by the randomness of the attack.

"Dragons are known for their randomness. Just glad we had our spirit powers," Forlax said, as he looked at Asemai.

"Can we rest now?" Kip moaned. He suddenly felt very tired.

"Yeah, the next place we can, we'll stop," Gathnok said, as they continued to walk on.

They soon found a gap in the trees. It wasn't really much of a clearing, but they didn't have time to be fussy. None of them had really spoken much since the attack, and Gathnok was still disheartened. He looked out and thought about his village and his sister – how he'd lost the jewel, and now all of magic would disappear. He was tired of being strong and the leader. He was barely just a man, and the weight of the world had become too much. He let silent tears fall from his eyes as he let his pain consume him. Lainla came up and stood by him, which hadn't been unnoticed by Forlax. Gathnok quickly wiped the tears away with his sleeve.

"It's okay, you know." Lainla touched his arm to comfort him.

"Is it? We've let them win. Without Cupido Sacra we can't stop them. They'll just keep killing until they have it all." Gathnok's lips trembled as he fought back the tears. "How's the leg?"

"It'll be okay, just sore," Lainla replied.

They stood in silence for a while. Lainla was going over everything in her head. It didn't make sense that Saban would just assume they would do everything as planned. Or maybe he did underestimate the cunning of the Darkmagi. But even so, there must be something they could do.

"Saban must have told you what to do if something went wrong?" Lainla asked curiously.

"No, he didn't. We got interrupted by the compass, and he just said to find the Spirits, find Cupido Sacra, and then find the Ancients." Gathnok was trying to recall the conversation with Saban. He had been weak at the time, and it was a lot to process.

"Oh well, maybe you should return to…"

"Wait." Gathnok beamed a smile as he began to remember "He did say something else, just before he closed the door. He said if all hope was lost, I was to…" Gathnok stopped and paused and looked very scared.

"To what?"

"Find Death."

"What?" Lainla said, confused; she hoped she'd heard him wrongly.

Gathnok didn't reply and walked over to the centre of the group.

"I remember something that Saban said," Gathnok said with a twinkle of hope in his eye.

"You just remembered now?" Asemai asked curiously, looking at Lainla and Gathnok.

"Yes. Saban told me that if all hope was lost, we're to summon Death."

The group stared back at him blankly. Kip tugged at Wispar's arm as she lowered her ear.

"He said Death, right?" he whispered, although apparently Kip wasn't good at whispering.

"I know it sounds crazy, but Saban wouldn't have said it without reason." Gathnok realised now he was talking aloud how insane his plan seemed.

"Are you sure about this, Gathnok?" Euthan seemed nervous about the new plan.

"Saban said that we needed to speak with Death if all

hope was lost. Only he can tell us if there is another way to save magic." Gathnok didn't wait any longer and began preparing the small fire that would be needed for the summoning spell. The others looked on.

"But we're going to call on Death itself. We don't know our powers well enough yet to do that."

"If there was another way, Forlax, than we would take it. Trust Gathnok." Lainla touched his arm in a comforting way, but her glance had swayed to gracefully catch the glistening eyes of Gathnok.

"What do you need us to do?" Wispar beamed a smile of support as she spoke.

"We must all channel our magic from Sahihriar, and then through each other, once we have enough energy, I'll channel it into the spell." Gathnok had nearly placed the last few logs on the fire.

"I don't mean to offend here, but are you sure you're ready for such a spell?" Asemai looked round at the others, as it was clear they shared her worry.

Gathnok stopped and looked at the concern on the faces of the four Spirits. Lainla seemed to be the only one showing no signs of worry.

"Look, I know I am the youngest here, and yes, I haven't been wielding magic for long. I'm scared too, but if we don't do this, then the Darkmagi have won. We need another hope." He was trying desperately to plead with them; he knew better than anyone how out of his depth he was. However, he couldn't let magic be lost at any cost. He'd already lost too much.

The Spirits looked at one another. Other than voicing their concerns, there was little they could do. Also, short of abandoning the quest, they knew that Death was the way forward.

"Okay, let's do this then."

Soon a fire was emitting a comforting glow in the middle

of the field lands. It was a small fire but enough to shine light on the five Elemental Spirits. They were spread out in a circle around the warming flames. Each of them knelt down low to the ground and let their palms rest flat against the grass. They were all concentrating, lost in their magic as each one was conjuring power from Sahihriar. Each of their bodies tingled as they felt the immense power coursing through them. It was like a warm sensation that rushed through their bodies. Gathnok, however, was concentrating on conjuring energy, whilst still trying to remember the early lessons of magic he had from home. The words were crucial to the transportation to meet Death. Gathnok was tense. He was barely used to magic as it was. His body hadn't developed, nor had it been trained for such a potent ritual. He clung on though, even though it felt as if his bones were shaking. He knew he had to time the words correctly. Through his squinting eyes he began to see the other four Spirits start to rise slowly in unison. He could see the mystical green energy swirling around them. They looked majestic and powerful. Lainla, who stood watching with Kip, had stepped back and gasped in awe. Never had Lainla seen such a grand display of magic before. Soon Gathnok could see the other Spirits standing fully upright. Their faces were tense as they struggled to contain the natural power of the planet. Gathnok gave the nod, which signalled each of them to thrust the mystical green energy into the centre of the fire. The magic swirled forward at great speed and sparkled marvellously as it combined in the flames. The flames became green and flickered fast and high. The explosion of light all happened in an instant. However, Lainla wasn't staring at the flames or Forlax, but instead stood mesmerised by the power and stance of Gathnok. As the green energy departed through his fingers, Lainla could see his mouth had shouted words with great passion and intensity. However, the noise of the joining magic smothered the words of the spell. The Spirits each took a deep breath and hoped that the young

Gathnok hadn't taken on too much. Euthan was about to speak out, as so far the green fire had done nothing, when suddenly he felt his whole body feel light and faint. He tried to look at the others, but his vision had become blurred as if smoke had come in from nowhere and surrounded him. He felt as though he was being lifted, though he was standing still. Dazed and confused, he began to notice the smog clearing. His head throbbed, but at least he felt whole again. He squinted as he could make out they were surrounded by nothing but light.

"Everyone okay?" Wispar looked round as she seemed to be adjusting to the new surroundings.

"Yeah, I think so. Check out the spell caster. Looks like you got us here, Gathnok," Asemai smiled.

"Yes, but where is here?" Gathnok felt into his pocket and took out the shimmering compass. He opened it whilst peering round to see anything that might hint to where they were.

"Looks like your toy is broken." Forlax smirked as the needles began to spin.

"Your magic won't work here, not in my realm."

The Spirits spun round to see Death standing before them. He was tall and smothered in a big black hooded cloak that shielded most of his white skeleton body. He held in his left hand a tall wooden-staffed reaper, with a steel blade that curved into a deadly point. All of the Spirits felt a sudden chill of fear.

"Are you Death?" Gathnok asked curiously.

"I am." The skeleton's jaw moved in a rigid motion.

The Spirits looked down to see a small baby-like skeleton appear from under Death's cloak. They all gave a curious look.

"That's my son," Death said. His rasp and his shrill voice were chilling.

"Oh, erm, okay . . ." Gathnok said, a little taken aback.

"Why are you here, Spirits?" Death tilted his head slightly and glared.

They couldn't be sure if he intended to be intimidating or just was.

"Darkmagi are taking magic from all of Sahihriar. We needed to find Cupido Sacra and use the power of the Ancients to fuel it so that we can fight them, but the jewel got smashed and now we can't…"

Death put up his skeleton hands to stop this rant. Gathnok quickly did so.

"I know of your mission, Spirits. As Death, I am one of the few beings who are able to travel through time. I know more than most, and I can help you."

"Wait! So you know if we succeed – if the prophecy comes true?" *Forlax asked.*

"I know what is to come, but I cannot tell you." *Death showed no signs of emotion as he spoke.*

"Why?" *Asemai asked.*

"I am bound by the laws of the Elders. I cannot tell you what is to come. I can only tell you what already is."

"The jewel is gone. So what happens now?"

"The jewel you speak of was formed many aeons ago. It was formed by an old master blacksmith who made the jewel when Sahihriar was still governed by kings. He made it from the shards of a cosmic star that fell to Sahihriar and moulded it into a jewel as a gift for the royals. However, the star was rumoured to hold great power once it connected with our own magic. Bandits of that time desperately tried to seek out more of the star so they could impress those with power."

"So there was more than one piece?" *Gathnok interrupted.*

Death had been walking back and forth and he recounted his story. He stopped and tilted his head at the interruption.

"However, the bandits never could find the other pieces, for the blacksmith had hidden the star in a necklace that he had passed down to his son and so it continued through his bloodline."

"So we need to find his bloodline and get the star?"

"If you wish to stop them, yes."

"And that would prove the prophecy correct?" Gathnok asked.

Death sighed.

"Prophecies are tricky things. People don't do well with knowing the future."

"Yeah, well, the Darkmagi have proven that," Asemai said smugly.

Death stopped walking and turned to face Asemai. He pulled down the hood of his cloak and looked at her with his dark menacing sockets. He took a brisk stepped forward and leaned in close to her.

"Why do you believe that your prophecy is any more accurate than theirs?" Death turned and looked at Gathnok and turned his head back again.

"Good luck to you!"

Death's voice was lifeless and void of emotion, but Asemai felt a very chilling sensation. He possessed knowledge of the future, and he had no reason to indicate something that wasn't true. Maybe they were wrong. Gathnok was about to question him further, but they felt the darkness overcome them and the spinning sensation in their heads.

"Well, that just isn't nice." Gathnok felt his head as his vision blurred back into focus. They were back at the clearing, the fire was burning normally, and the others were also getting up.

"What happened?" Lainla said, running over to them.

"He has a son, apparently," Forlax said, walking over.

"Oh, how strange!"

Gathnok casually nodded his agreement and got up to his

feet. *Kip ran and held onto Wispar's arm as they all were now on their feet.*

"So you saw him then?" Lainla was still curious as to what had happened.

"Cupido Sacra was made from a cosmic star, which someone will have in a necklace that we need to find. Oh, and maybe the Darkmagi aren't wrong." Asemai gave a look at Gathnok, who returned her look with worry.

"What?"

"It's nothing." Gathnok hoped Asemai was joking, but there was something in her eyes now. Maybe she believed Death's warning.

"So we find the carrier of the star," Euthan noted.

"Do you think the Darkmagi know it exists?" Wispar asked.

"They do seem to be drawn to power. It's likely," Forlax replied.

"Then we must go and find him before they do." Gathnok looked at the group of warriors.

"How?" Kip asked.

"With this." Gathnok took the shimmering compass from his pocket and revealed that it was glowing again. "Let's begin."

They began to walk out of the clearing under the starlit sky, the light of the two moons beaming down on them. They had now found a new hope.

* * *

Morbid had just appeared back on a path when he stopped. Suddenly, Gathnok had appeared before him in his shadowy form.

"Son of Death, your orders have not changed." Gathnok needed to make sure that Morbid would get Cupido Sacra for him whilst he waited by Lainla's side.

"I am Death now. Your magic has no hold over me,

and my will is my own." Morbid stood and stared into the shadow. Although unable to see him, his soul was very strong.

Gathnok stopped and thought about this. It was important that he learn of Morbid's agenda. "So you no longer seek the jewel?"

"I do seek it, but not for you to use as Lainla wishes. I shall ensure its destruction despite the consequences." Morbid showed no emotion or sign of fear as he spoke. His cloak flew in the air as his reaper glistened from the sun.

"How does Lainla wish me to use it? What consequences do you speak of?" Gathnok seemed rather taken back. Morbid thought Gathnok knew more than he did.

"Your wife hasn't told you yet?" Morbid tilted his head to the side. "Interesting . . ."

"I won't allow your mind games to drive us apart. You're lies won't work, Death." Gathnok sounded sure of what he was saying. However, some doubt had been placed into his mind.

Morbid didn't bother to respond. Instead he shrugged and continued to walk forward and passed Gathnok. He didn't have time to get into something with Gathnok, as he needed to search for the jewel.

"I won't let you destroy it. I need it to heal Lainla." Gathnok turned to face Morbid. If he had to, he would fight him. Gathnok suddenly stopped as he realised something. "You don't know where it is, do you? Or else you would have it by now."

Morbid stopped and turned slowly to look back at Gathnok. "I will know soon."

Morbid continued to walk on. He didn't like to admit it, but neither Lainla nor Death had the chance to tell him the location of Cupido Sacra. He knew he needed help.

Plus, he'd need to act quickly if he were to beat Gathnok to the jewel.

Gathnok didn't have time to waste either and transported away. Luckily for him, he knew exactly where Cupido Sacra was and how to get it, although he knew it wouldn't be easy.

* * *

The sun rose above the cold chill of the Iciliks Mountain. Saria twitched on her snowy bed. She felt numb. The coldness of the falling flakes had rested on her as she slept. She brushed them off groggily as she sat herself up. She looked at the circle surrounding her and remembered the night before. She felt better, less tense. She wondered if training Amazons to suppress their emotions was the right thing to do. She stood herself up and brushed off the snow from her warrior garments. She peered through the falling snow to see where the others were. She peered around until she felt something rest on her shoulder. Saria's instincts kicked in as she flung back her arm and drew her blade in a single rotation. The blade swung inches from the pink-skinned flesh. Hail stood stunned.

"Whoa, Hail! Don't sneak up on an Amazon like that." She breathed a sigh of relief and placed the sword back into its sheath.

Anyone else under attack from a flying sword would normally move, duck, or flinch. However Hail didn't. It was as if he didn't even care.

"Time to go."

Saria could see the hurt on his face. His eyes were empty, as he just seemed so sad. As an Amazon, she wasn't used to seeing the consequences of war. Grief was a new concept to her, one she was struggling to understand.

Hail led Saria to EggWiff, who stood at the foot of the

icy mountain. Saria came up and stood next to the large majestic EggWiff. EggWiff was peering up the icy slope and didn't seem to mind the small flakes that fell across his face. Despite the comfort she had been shown before, Saria didn't expect much to change. They still had their own goals. That didn't include friendship.

"Are we climbing that?" Hail asked. He had a look of fear.

"Or we take the path." EggWiff gestured to the barely visible slope that climbed the side of the mountain.

"Oh, that makes more sense" The relief on Hail's face was clear.

"We're going to see her, aren't we?" Saria was peering up at the mountain.

"Hopefully."

"Think she can help us?" Saria wasn't trying to question EggWiff, but she wasn't in the mood to waste time.

"If Gathnok gets the jewel, we have no other hope."

EggWiff started up the snowy slope. Hail's pig-like feet made it easy as he sunk into the snow. EggWiff's staff dug deep into the snow as his long legs strode with ease. Saria, on the other hand, was left to struggle. Her short height and small dwarf features meant she struggled not to slip on the icy patches. Thankfully, her Amazon strength meant she was able to cope with the extra strain without much hassle.

EggWiff was leading at the front. He barely noticed the blizzard and icy conditions, as he was lost in thought. He was thinking about the last month, how so much had happened in his life. He had befriended someone so special, and now they were lost. Gathnok and Lainla had returned. He was trying to recount everything, make sense of how it got to be so complicated. He was all too aware that Morbid would inherit his father's powers, that he had now become Death. EggWiff felt tired just at the thought of two powerful beings

207

after him. If the Elemental Spirits couldn't help, they'd all be killed. EggWiff stopped as he felt a strange sensation overwhelm him – one he was all too familiar with.

"Oh, no!"

Saria winced as the stench of rotten egg filled her lungs. It was shortly followed by the wisp of green smoke.

"What is that abomination of a stench?" Hail fell into the snow as he struggled with the smell.

"EggWiff!"

"Cor, why is it so cold?" EggWiff was shouting despite not even being aware of Saria or Hail. He brushed his arms to keep warm. "Well, least I'm out of that stupid cage."

Hail leaned in towards Saria. "What's wrong with him?" His pig-like hands were covering his snout.

"Hey! It's Sammy!" EggWiff grew a smile of recognition.

"Saria!" She corrected bluntly.

"Sure, sure. Umm, where is everyone?" EggWiff was now merrily childlike as he looked round for the others.

Saria realised that EggWiff, well this EggWiff at least, had no idea what had happened to Trickle.

"Trickle!" EggWiff was calling to his friend, secretly hoping she might have some drink. He stopped as his eyes finally settled on Hail for the first time. "There's a pig!"

"Yeah, umm, EggWiff, something has happened..." Saria wasn't sure what to say or how to say it.

"Sammy, where are the others?" EggWiff had become stiff, and his childlike face had grown serious and scared, like a child when he loses his mother.

"He doesn't know any more?" Hail said, as he watched this sudden change with curiosity.

"What's going on?" EggWiff's face was staring at Saria.

"They're dead, EggWiff"

"They?" EggWiff nearly fell back into the snow.

"Trickle and Flick."

EggWiff struggled to understand. He knew Trickle. She was always kind to him and gave him drink.

"They can't . . . that's . . . I mean . . ." After a small pause, EggWiff felt inside his large pocket. "I have to give her back her bottle!"

EggWiff pulled out a small empty bottle. It was the same one Trickle had given him months ago. "See?"

Saria looked at the weak EggWiff holding the bottle. In everything that had happened, she had forgotten about EggWiff's condition. "I'm sorry."

"How did this happen?" His eyes were beginning to water.

"Well I – I – I…"

"The shadowed being killed them." Hail spoke majestically and strong. He was beginning to realise this new EggWiff wasn't very threatening. Saria gave him a sideways glance. She didn't expect that.

EggWiff listened at first, and then gave the strange pig a confused expression. He then looked at Saria for an explanation.

"His name is Hail. He's helping us." Saria nodded at Hail and smiled at EggWiff.

"How do we know he's not in league with that Essence-loving preacher pig?"

"He's not," Saria replied coldly, as Hail tried not to flinch at EggWiff's words. Saria did frown, though, as something troubled her. How did EggWiff know about the holy pigs anyway? She shook her head as some snow went in her eyes. She looked up and saw Hail forlorn from his comments.

"He's gone now too."

"We're climbing this thing, then?" EggWiff said as he brushed away some tears from his face.

"Yeah, we're going to see some powerful Spirit for some help," Saria said.

"Oh!" EggWiff was still rather taken aback by everything.

"You never know. There might be an inn at the top." She gave EggWiff half a smile. She was all too aware of the pain he was in.

"We should go then. Let me take the Essence." EggWiff held out his hand and looked and Saria and Hail.

"We no longer have it. A lot has changed now. We have a new purpose."

EggWiff looked at them blankly.

"To defeat Gathnok," Hail said as he walked past EggWiff and continued his ascent up the hill.

"And to stop Morbid," Saria added.

Saria and Hail walked on, leaving EggWiff very confused and lost.

They continued to climb the mountain. The flakes of snow grew bigger and heavier the further up they went. EggWiff had listened to how Gathnok had killed Flick and Trickle and how he had kidnapped him, but how Saria rescued him. Apparently, they recently found Hail wandering lost, so he agreed to travel with them. EggWiff's head pounded. He was so frustrated he couldn't remember. He was angry though, angry about Trickle and Flick. He knew them, but then he didn't. It was as if they belonged to a very realistic dream he had, but he still sensed the loss. He was trying to listen to the story, and for once he wanted to understand and tried his best to ignore the desire for drink. He had so many questions – so much didn't make sense. However, the blizzard was howling amongst them, and it was getting harder to speak. He thought he had better wait till they get to the inn.

They eventually came to a large cavern that spread into

the side of the mountain. It was vast but empty. However, it provided temporary shelter from the blizzard. Inside was a giant frozen lake. The ceiling dripped as frozen icicles fell from the ceiling.

"That's better; we'll rest here for a while and then carry on moving." Saria shrugged off the build-up of snow from her clothes. "You okay, Hail?"

Hail nodded as he brushed off the snow from his snout. EggWiff also brushed off the snow and hoped that his head wouldn't hurt as much, now he didn't have to struggle against the winds.

The cavern had a natural beauty about it. The drops of water which fell from the green stone walls made them glisten in the light. Hail got up and walked to the edge of the lake. He peered through the thick sheet of ice, although he couldn't see anything beneath it.

"Be careful." EggWiff watched as Hail peered into the lake.

Hail turned and crinkled his snout. "Why?"

Just then a large shattering of thunder could be heard as large chunks of frozen ice flew off in different directions.

Saria's eyes widened as she saw the large ice shard hurtle towards EggWiff. EggWiff, who wasn't his usual majestic self, stood still with fear. Saria sighed. After today, no one was ever allowed to ask "Why?" again. She spun her bow into her hands and shot an arrow into the ice shard. The arrow hit just in time, breaking the ice. It shattered as large clumps skidded onto the icy floor and landed at the feet of EggWiff.

Hail very quickly ran behind Saria, being careful not to slip on the ice. Hail had just seen something very frightening from the corner of his eye. Saria, Hail, and EggWiff all stopped and looked up. Sticking out of the lake was a large snake. Its tongue lashed as its beady yellow eyes stared at the three travellers. It had a blue scaly body that began to uncoil and slither from the now broken frozen lake. It screeched a deafening sound. It began to slither faster, until it was charging at full speed at Saria and Hail. Without thinking, she prepared another arrow, took aim, and shot. It soared through the air and pierced its scaly skin.

"I better have not just shot the Spirit," Saria shouted.

"If it helps, I don't think it is," EggWiff shouted back over the sound of the snake screeching again.

"In that case, you guys better get back to safety." Saria then got ready as the snake regained focus and fixed its eyes on Saria.

Hail and EggWiff ran to the entrance of the cavern. Saria drew her blade and waited as her heart raced. She had missed the thrill of the battle. The icy blue snake extended its head forward. It lingered before opening its jaw and lunging towards Saria. With her Amazon instincts, she dived to the right and let her blade slice at the tongue. Blood oozed as the snake coiled back and cried in pain. Saria prepared as the snake stopped wincing. The snake then paused and stared. It was beginning to realise that Saria was no everyday warrior. The snake suddenly whipped into motion. This time, however, it used its tail. It was so fast it managed to knock Saria's sword from her hand. The sword flew across the icy cavern. She checked, but she had no more arrows left. She was now defenceless. The snake plunged head first at tremendous pace. Saria could do nothing; instead she just closed her eyes and waited. She smiled as she awaited death. She could be moments away from seeing Flick again. Suddenly the wind stopped the breeze, and the noise from the snake vanished. She wondered if she was dead, but nothing felt different. She opened an eye. The snake was inches from her face, but it was no longer alive. It was completely encased in ice. Saria stepped back and looked around confused. Nearby at the cavern entrance EggWiff stood resting on his staff.

"Welcome back!"

EggWiff nodded as he was collecting himself. It was a shock to awaken and then have to cast a spell so quickly.

"Will it last?" Saria searched for her sword as she spoke.

"Long enough," he called back. Hail had appeared beside him.

"Shouldn't we leave – before it defrosts or something?" Hail was clearly a little scared.

"No, we wait."

Saria walked over to them. She was wiping off the melting slush from her sword and then placed it back into her sheath.

"Is this where she is?" Saria let her eyes wander the cavern, but there was no indication this was the place.

Laughter echoed out through the icy cavern. The ice on the lake began to sizzle and melt, until what was left was the huge cold lake. The laughter faded, and everything went back to being still.

The snake remained frozen as the cavern's beauty turned into an eerie moment of tension.

"That was anticlimactic," Saria muttered. She continued to stay on guard. That laughter must have come from somewhere.

The lake sprayed up without warning. The three travellers stepped back so the water didn't get to them. It shot up and continued to swirl, until the water spread out and held its place in mid-air. The water morphed its form. Its liquid shape formed little rain droplets and then continued to flow like two waterfalls either side of what appeared to be a forming face. The water began to show two liquid eyes, a perfectly formed nose, and the outline of well-defined lips.

Although this process only took a few seconds, it was very impressive.

Once she was fully formed, the Water Spirit gave a smile. EggWiff took this as his cue. He stepped forward, rested on his staff, and bowed to the great Spirit.

"We seek your guidance and wisdom, Water Spirit." EggWiff stayed kneeling but raised his head.

"Please, my name is Wispar. What guidance do you seek?" As she spoke, Wispar sprayed droplets of water. She clearly didn't seem too upset about the snake.

"We have many enemies at the moment, and we fear if we don't keep Cupido Sacra safe, then all of Sahihriar may be in danger."

Wispar's smile faded. It had been many years since she had heard someone speak of the mystical jewel.

"If you have come for my guidance, then this is it. Stay well away from Cupido Sacra. It only leads to pain and destruction."

"Look, we can't. If Gathnok gets hold of it . . ." Saria stepped forward. She didn't mind respect, but she hadn't climbed a mountain to be told the obvious.

"Gathnok! You know of him?" Wispar smiled once more. How interesting it all suddenly was.

"I do." EggWiff continued to stare up with his blue eyes. That's when Wispar could see it.

"By the Elders! Are you Marvie?"

EggWiff flinched at the sound of his old name. That was a part of himself he had left behind long ago. Wispar had heard of EggWiff before – many, many years ago. Before EggWiff could respond, the spell which had trapped the snake clearly became broken as the snake suddenly began to slither once again. However, it simply slid off behind Wispar and coiled up. It knew it had been defeated.

"If you wish to find the jewel, it lies within the Nether

Realm. In order to reach it, you must go and see my brother Forlax at Magmount. He has power over the portal to that realm. But be careful! My brother isn't as generous as I am." Wispar bowed her head slightly, and her face fell into the lake with a thundering splash. The snake, which was coiled behind it, slowly sunk deep down under the surface. Then the lake froze over, leaving the cavern as they had found it. EggWiff wondered which Spirits would hold the power over the portals to what realms. At the time of the great change, the Spirits were given the power to control the portals to the five different realms. Some thought it was to tease the grounded Spirits and remind them of the places they would never see. Others, however, were aware of the power of the Spirits, and in Sahihriar there were none better suited to protect these portals.

"May not be as generous, but I bet they don't come with a large killing snake!" Hail exclaimed. It was funny how his comments became bolder once the danger had gone.

"Magmount will be a few days' walk from here. We must move quickly." EggWiff turned and began to walk out of the cavern. It hadn't escaped him that Wispar was scared at the thought of Gathnok gaining control of the jewel. And if an Elemental Spirit was afraid, then so should they all be.

"Criminals always think themselves better"

Chapter Ten

"You must let me through." Gathnok's shadowed body leered in front of the great guardian of fire.

The great Spirit roared as he let out heat from his body. He looked just like his sister Wispar. However, his body was a fiery orange and red. His body flickered and waved as if it was entirely made of flame. He had red eyes with orange swirls. The Spirit was floating at the centre of MagMount. A lake of molten lava surrounded him. Gathnok stood on a raised ledge which poked out from the inside walls of MagMount into its hollow centre.

"It's because of that jewel we were all put in danger, Gathnok." The Fire Spirit sprayed tiny orange sparks as he spoke.

"That was a long time ago, Forlax. Only you have the power to conjure the portal I need."

"We Spirits protect the elements and the balance of

Sahihriar. You know I cannot allow you to get Cupido Sacra back. It possesses too much power for one mortal being to wield." Forlax hovered. His voice was deep and booming. It echoed amongst the mountain walls.

"I need it to save Lainla. She's dying. The Spirit of Magic itself is dying!"

"And a new spirit will rise in her place. The jewel could not save her last time. Now is to be no different." Forlax took some small pleasure in seeing his former friend so desperate.

"It grows in power; it'll be enough to save her. You can have it back afterwards. Forlax, it's Lainla" Gathnok was getting desperate and increasingly frustrated.

"I loved Lainla also, but I cannot risk the world for your heart."

"So you've become another one of the Elders' tools?" Gathnok yelled.

"Leave now. I shall not let you through."

"I shall not leave until we are done, old friend." Gathnok knelt down and was frantically searching for something he could do, a way to conjure the portal himself.

"We are friends no more!" With this, Forlax's body flickered like a candle in the wind.

The whole of MagMount shook as the lava began to rise. Gathnok's shadowed body shook as he hoped the rock wouldn't collapse into the lava lake beneath him. He managed to look up just in time to see Forlax send a wave of scorching hot air towards him. The pulse of air hit and instantly sent Gathnok's shadowed body through the mountain wall and out the other end. Gathnok tried to catch hold of something, but he couldn't as his body began to hurtle itself down the jagged side of MagMount. He felt his body being flipped and tossed by gravity, and yet all he could do was think about how he failed Lainla – again.

He landed with a thud. His magic was drained. He felt only pain coursing through his body. He tried to get up but couldn't, as he was now paralysed. Instead, he sat silently and thought of Lainla. He was comforted by only one thing. Soon they will be together again, in death.

Gathnok laid at the foot of MagMount as time continued to pass. The pain continued as he could feel every scratch, cut, and bruise on his body. His eyes felt heavy. He felt his very life force slipping away. He was about to close his eyes for the last time when a blinding light flashed over him. He thought it could be the end, but this was strange. The light was split into two. One was to his right and the other to his left. As his eyes adjusted, he saw that the light was coming from two beings smothered in light – one of which was slightly grey and the other slightly blue. They were hovering above the ground over him. He tried to speak, but he simply couldn't move. He switched his glance between them as he began to wonder what they were going to do and why they were here.

Suddenly his body felt different, lighter almost. It was as if he were coursing with a new sensation. His body felt warm and began to glow as it changed from being shadowed and started to show flashes of his old human form. The pain began to fade as he felt his power coming back. Gathnok's mind was racing. Only one other thing had the power to heal, other than Cupido Sacra, and that was the great Elders themselves. His mind flung a thousand questions around in his head. What were the Elders doing on Sahihriar? And why were they healing him? Surely he posed a greater threat with Cupido Sacra back? However, if they were back and healing him, that meant they could also heal Lainla.

He willed himself to speak with all his might, but he was still being healed and struggled to form a sound. There was one final flash of light, and with it the Elders had gone, but Gathnok had been completely healed. As soon as he could, Gathnok screamed.

"Wait!" he yelled, but it was too late, as the Elders had vanished. Gathnok was left desperate and alone with only his questions in his head for company.

* * *

<u>Five Years Ago</u>

"Come on! You call yourselves warriors?" Saria was standing before the Amazons in training.

The new potentials were young and were experiencing the hardships of training. The Amazon warrior Saria was one of the elite. Amazons worshipped her skill and natural ability. She was making them train hard, as she had to ensure the townsfolk kept their respect for her. Saria's class always took place in the great forest courtyard at the centre of the Amazon settlements. It's said that at one time all the Amazons lived together in a great city on the northern parts of Sahihriar. However, many years ago when the "Great Change" occurred, the Amazons disbanded and decided to create settlements all over Sahihriar. Saria's class was renowned because of her great teaching ability. She found the praise rather strange; she wasn't doing anything particularly special. She just followed the Amazon code. That's all it took – discipline and control.

The only real concern she had was training in the open. This meant she had to make contact with all the Surthan breeds around. She felt disgusted by them; they were weak and pathetic. The Surthan breeds were used for chores and meaningless tasks. This gave the Amazons more time to train and fight.

The forest was warm, and Saria enjoyed the feel of the sun on her face. The heat and light gave her tactical awareness. She was, however, getting seriously frustrated with her trainees. All they needed to do was memorize a ten-part fighting sequence, but they couldn't manage to do it. The trouble was their youth; the thought of being a warrior was still fun. They had no idea how wrong they were. She decided she needed to show them the reality in life.

She called over to one of the Surthan dwarfs nearby. The slim pale dwarf was carting around some wood for the new outpost. He glanced over at the call of his name. His body looked bruised, and his eyes looked tired and aged. Everyone stopped and looked at Saria, as very few Amazons spoke to Surthan breeds.

"Don't make me call you again." Saria's voice was stern and cold.

The thin dwarf looked frightened, but also calm at the same time. He promptly dropped his cart and walked over to Saria. The class stopped practising and looked on with interest. Even some of the fellow Amazons stopped and looked on.

"This is a being. Although a Surthan breed, he still exists. He thinks, he feels, he laughs, he has wants and he has needs." Saria stopped and looked at the attention she held over her class.

Then without warning, she drew her blade and sliced at the dwarf's neck. His head landed with a thud, as his body slumped to the floor. Many of the young Amazons gasped, as it was the first death they had seen.

"Gone! All of that taken away in an instant. All it takes is one false move, one off thought, and you're just a memory. Sahihriar doesn't care if you die. Life doesn't care. It's always down to you."

The lesson ended there, by ending an innocent life.

* * *

<u>*A Sacred Past*</u>

The city of Correlani was bustling with many magical folk. Gathnok was completely overwhelmed. He had never seen this many magical folk before. He looked around as small faeries flew by, elves bustled alongside them, and Gathnok even saw a few caged Mithworks, which are bird-like creatures and said to be very rare. The noise and bustle of the city made it hard to hear and concentrate. Gathnok was worried. It would be the perfect place for Darkmagi to lurk, as they'd easily be lost in the crowd. He looked at the compass which continued to shimmer and create warmth as they followed the needle precisely. They stayed close together and tried not to communicate with anyone. The less suspicion they aroused, the better. It was often spoken about in the outer villages how dangerous and corrupt the city could be. Villagers would only go there to trade and would stay in the main square.

"Do you think we're close?" Wispar said. She kept Kip close as she didn't like the feel of the city.

"I'm not sure. The compass feels warm though." Gathnok was beginning to learn the different intensities of heat.

"We should move quickly and find the star before nightfall. They'll struggle to find us in the dark," Lainla said, as they crept through the city.

It was actually a rather impressive sight, seeing these tall and powerful warriors walking through the city. Although they didn't look very distinct, there was a sense of power about them.

"It wants us to go here."

They walked down a side alley which led them off the main market square. The city was built out of new stone and looked clean in comparison. Stone buildings and walls were scattered like some giant maze, with small alleyways in between. The alleyway led them out into a small street that seemed to be full of shops. This street was less busy, which made them relax slightly.

221

Asemai looked up at the old store signs. She could make out one for clothes, another for weapons, and she thought she could see a food store. Her stomach grew excited as they hadn't eaten well since the Amazon city.

"Can we get some food? I mean later," Asemai said.

"It might be wise to stock up on rations," Euthan suggested.

"After we get the star, if there is time," Gathnok said, still following the compass.

They followed the street, noticing that the stone was beginning to become dirtier, and soon a sign hung above them.

OLD CORRELANI: NOT FOR OUTER CITY FOLK.

"Well, we don't normally get a warning, so that's rather nice," Wispar said with a smile.

They went under the sign, and, sure enough, the walls looked old and worn, not as bad as the ruins outside the tomb but not far off it. The street seemed dirtier, and the buildings looked smaller and more cramped. If the Darkmagi would be anywhere, it would be here. The shimmering compass soon lead them around the street corner. It was just starting to show signs of getting darker, as some of the fires had been lit in the streets, smothering it with an orange glow. The compass led them right in front of an ancient building. It had an old wooden chipped door and a window to the left. The top floor had one large bay window at the top. Unlike a lot of the other buildings, the lights were out and it looked very much shut.

"So we wait?" Kip said, looking up at the larger Spirits.

"Do we have time?" Forlax was once again the speaker of truth without subtlety

"Well we can't just break in," Asemai replied abruptly. Everyone looked nervous. "Right?"

"I don't like it either, Asemai, but we don't have time. This might be the easiest way," Gathnok said.

"He's right," Lainla said.

Neither of them liked the idea of it, but if they could get the star without involving anyone else it might be easier.

"I'm not about to steal." Asemai looked at Gathnok with the same distrusting look as before.

"Neither will I," Euthan added.

"Okay, what if we go in, get the star, but promise to wait until the owner returns? We can't risk the Darkmagi getting hold of it first. They won't play by the rules."

"We don't want to hurt anyone." Wispar gave Asemai a reassuring smile.

"We won't steal it?" Asemai confirmed.

"I promise," Gathnok said.

He was a little annoyed, but she had a point. They were not pretty criminals, and just because they had the power to take it didn't mean they had the right too. Asemai nodded her agreement. Although the lock was metal, it was Euthan who stepped forward to take care of the locked door. He held out his hand to touch the wood. As it was a natural material, it shuddered slightly, and the old hinged fitting soon came from the door, leaving it free to pry open. Asemai looked wide-eyed at Gathnok.

"Err, we'll fix that," he said, hoping he wasn't about to have a whirlwind thrown at his face.

"Hmm!" Although beautiful, Asemai could also be rather intimidating.

Gathnok went in first, and the compass glowed brighter and felt warmer than it had before. This was clearly the place. It was a small room which was the floor of a shop. The counter looked old, and the walls had wooden shelves with old pieces of different metals on them. Over by the corner were an old *stove and a table with a hammer on it. Looking around, they all came to the same conclusion.*

"They're still blacksmiths?" Lainla was the only one to voice this conclusion.

"Must have stayed in the family."

The room had a small wooden staircase in the opposite corner that lead to the top floor. The compass needle pointed directly at it.

"It's upstairs," Gathnok said.

They all went to go up the stairs.

"Hey, wouldn't it be funny if the guy was just asleep?" Kip said with a grin.

The Spirits all stopped. Not one had considered that the inhabitant and keeper of the star might actually be upstairs asleep.

"Well, I guess it'll save time waiting for them," Gathnok said with a cheeky grin. Lainla smiled at his banter, but Asemai and Euthan did not seem amused. Forlax didn't like the constant looks the two of them shared.

They crept upstairs, and the old wooden floor boards creaked. Gathnok was the first one up as the shimmering compass showed them the way. It revealed a smaller upstairs room which seemed pretty bare. There was a bed next to the side wall which to his relief was empty. There was a small cabinet by the bedside and a larger one on the opposite wall. The compass pointed directly at it.

"It's up here!" He went over to the small wooden cabinet, which seemed far too unimpressive to hold the magic of a cosmic star. He opened the double doors, and sure enough, inside was a small sphere. He took it out and placed it in his hands, even though it had a large piece of string which made it into a necklace. It didn't glow, shimmer, or sparkle. Instead it seemed more like a shiny rock. Gathnok looked over at the others.

"*Thank the Elders for that compass, because we would never have found that,*" Wispar said with a disappointed look.

"*It does seem rather unremarkable,*" Forlax noted.

"*Most remarkable things usually do,*" Lainla said with a smile.

"*So what now?*"

"*We wait, right?*" Asemai said rather firmly.

"*Yes, we wait,*" Gathnok reassured her.

Forlax and Lainla sat on the bed, and the others stood, except for Kip who knelt down against the wall. He was really tired, and the moment he relaxed, he felt himself begin to drift to sleep. They had barely gotten comfortable when they heard mumblings from downstairs as the wooden door had been pushed open.

"*Hello!*" a voice called. It was a male voice and sounded mature. A small glow appeared from downstairs.

"*What do we do?*" Wispar whispered.

"*Erm, try not to look menacing,*" Gathnok replied, flustered

"*Try not to look . . . oh, never mind!*" Asemai was baffled by Gathnok sometimes.

Soon they all heard the creak of the floorboards of the stairs as the glow ascended. The voice called out once more before appearing, cowardly, at the top of the stairs.

The creature peered around to see the six warriors now standing in an oval formation. He also noticed a small imp fast asleep slouched on the floor. The being appeared to be a gnome. He was a small creature with long pointy ears. He had a small flat nose and rough skin. His hair was a dark midnight blue, and his eyes were almost black. He looked dirty and tired.

"*Who are you? What do you want?*" he snarled, as he glared at each of them. He had learnt not to take chances in Correlani.

"We wish you no harm. We need to explain something, and there isn't much time," Gathnok said.

"Why?" The gnome put down his large satchel and continued to glare at the intruders.

"We need to take your necklace, the cosmic star." Gathnok held out the necklace.

"The cosmic what? That's just a pile of junk," the gnome snorted.

The Spirits looked at each other. He'd maybe be more willing to part with junk, but they couldn't deceive him. Asemai smiled and stepped forward.

"It's not junk. It's extremely powerful, and we need it to complete out quest." She tried to sound comforting and friendly. She wasn't used to being in such a position.

"What quest?" the gnome asked curiously.

"To save Sahihriar," Asemai said awkwardly. It was a lot to take in.

To their surprise, the gnome began to laugh, and a smile formed over his face.

"So you want to take something I care nothing about to save the entire planet?"

"Yeah, I guess!" Gathnok was confused as to why the gnome wasn't more angry.

"And that's it. You don't want my store or to hurt me?" asked the gnome.

"No of course not," Asemai said, rather concerned.

"Then by all means take it," the gnome said.

"You understand it's very powerful, right?" Asemai wanted to be certain he knew what he was giving up.

"My dear, I have no interest in power. If I did, then I would not be a blacksmith, now would I?" The gnome stood to one side to allow them to pass and leave.

"How good are you? As a blacksmith, I mean?" Gathnok asked.

"I don't think that's relevant," said Lainla with a smile. They had been given what they wanted. Why was he wasting time?

"The best in Sahihriar. Why?"

Gathnok threw the gnome the necklace, which he caught with ease. "We have a small request."

The gnome, who was apparently named Sombre, agreed to turn the necklace into a new jewel. It turned out he wasn't much interested in the hows and whys and claimed little interest in his heritage. Sombre had often fought off burglars and murderers who seemed to lurk in the streets of old Correlani at night, so he figured he couldn't do much wrong in befriending six elite warriors. Besides, he enjoyed a challenge, and work had been slow. Darkmagi were something Sombre cared about, as he heard many tales of the suffering they had caused throughout Sahihriar whilst trading in the market. Due to the sense of urgency, he offered to work through the night. Besides, he didn't want to wake the small imp. He invited what were now his guests to rest in the small upstairs until morning, when he would be finished.

"That was pretty easy," Lainla said, as she rested against the wall by Gathnok.

"Do you think we can trust him?" Gathnok replied.

"Gnomes are known for their generosity and kindness," Euthan interrupted, as he was learning next to Lainla.

"Well we've been lucky so far." Gathnok couldn't continue as a yawn interrupted him.

Lainla smiled. "I agree," she said, as she felt the heaviness of her eyes. Gathnok was always amazed at how beautiful she was.

Smiling at the comfort of her beauty, Gathnok found himself slowly falling fast asleep. After both Gathnok and Lainla were asleep, Asemai turned to Euthan as she was sitting on the other side to him.

"You awake?" she whispered.

"Hardly," he replied. Euthan was exhausted, and with everyone else asleep, the room had a stillness that would make it easy for him to drift away to sleep.

"Do you think we're doing the right thing?" Asemai whispered, careful not to be too loud.

"I wouldn't be here if I didn't, Mai. Why? What's troubling you?" Euthan had known Asemai since she was a little girl and had sworn to protect her after the Darkmagi took her brother.

"I don't know. Death made it sound like the other prophecy could be true, and if that's the case, then when Cupido Sacra is awakened, Gathnok will have all the power."

"But if our prophecy is right, then we'll save Sahihriar," Euthan whispered back, trying to reassure her.

"But he's just a boy." Asemai looked over at Gathnok.

"That's why we'll make sure he does the right thing. We're spirits now. We won't let him destroy anything." Euthan squeezed her hand comfortingly and closed his eyes.

"Euthan?"

"Hmm?" He was barely awake.

"I hope you're right." She tilted her head to the other side and tried to push her worry from her mind, before also drifting off to sleep.

Gathnok woke up and yawned. He regretted moving as he felt the stiffness of his neck from sleeping against the wall. He looked round to see everyone else was still asleep. It was surreal, as the room looked so much brighter with sunlight shining in. He smiled as he looked at the peaceful Lainla. She managed to achieve a graceful beauty even whilst sitting against a wall. Gathnok hadn't even noticed, but as he got up, he saw something glistening on the floor. He got up and leaned over, as he couldn't believe what he held. It was almost a perfect copy of Cupido Sacra, the one from the tomb. It was smooth and clear but weighed slightly more. Sombre had kept his word *and worked through the night. He carefully picked it up and placed it in the pocket that wasn't occupied by the shimmering compass. He stretched properly, and his movements began to stir the others.*

"Is it morning?" Asemai moaned as she got up.

"Where's Sombre?" Euthan asked.

"I don't know, but he left this." Gathnok took out Cupido Sacra for them all to see. Kip was the only one still asleep.

"It's just like the original." Lainla brushed her hair behind her ears as she glared at the jewel.

"So I guess we get moving?" Forlax said. "Find the Ancients before the Darkmagi do?"

Wispar went over and began to nudge Kip, who seemed not to have moved during the night. It took him a moment, but he was soon on his feet and standing with the others.

"Yes, the compass should lead us." Gathnok took out the compass and was surprised. He had felt the warmth when he had woken up and assumed it would be shimmering. However, he assumed it was because Cupido Sacra was nearby. Now they had it, the compass should have stopped.

"What's wrong?" Wispar said, as they could see his look of worry.

"The compass should have stopped when I picked up Cupido Sacra. Unless . . ."

"Unless . . ."

"It's not shimmering because of the jewel!" Gathnok's eyes widened as he leapt to the stairs and began to run down them. The others followed.

They were all quickly at the bottom, and the sight made them gasp. Sombre was being held up by some form of magic with a Darkmage holding a sword to his throat. Another ten Darkmagi stood behind them as they were all huddled in the small blacksmith's shop.

"Release him!" Gathnok demanded.

"When we have Cupido Sacra," the evil voice bellowed from the hooded shell.

Gathnok looked at Sombre, whose small gnome face was ridden with fear. His cheeks streamed silent tears as his eyes pleaded for help.

"We won't let you win," Gathnok said as he tried to think of a way out of this.

"Your powers aren't fast enough to prevent his death, Spirit."

They were right. Gathnok's mind raced. He had Cupido Sacra, and it was the only thing that could save Sahihriar. But who was he to sacrifice another life? Sombre wasn't part of this. It wasn't his fault. Gathnok looked over at Lainla, who just gave a sympathetic expression. She could understand his turmoil.

"Then he'll die." Gathnok almost choked on the words as he stared into Sombre's eyes. He wanted a way to show he was sorry.

"What? We can't..." Asemai glared at Gathnok.

"We don't have a choice!" he yelled back at her, before turning to the Darkmage.

"I'm sorry," he said to Sombre. "Let's do this."

Gathnok braced himself for battle whilst the others did the same – except for Asemai and Euthan. He noticed, but didn't have time to argue about it. Forlax immediately conjured up a flame of fire between them. The important thing was not to be touched by the Darkmagi. Wispar had summoned a spurt of water to go through the fire wall and take out the Darkmage that was holding Sombre at sword point. She was too late. The immediate signs of flames triggered the Darkmage to plunge the sword through, causing the gnome to scream out for a moment before his body slumped to the floor. Gathnok looked away and held back his pain. The blacksmith's shop was too small, and they didn't have time to fight them. They needed to run and gather their thoughts.

"Push the wall back," Gathnok shouted to Forlax.

He nodded as the flame wall grew larger and moved gradually towards them.

"We need to run!" Gathnok was now looking at Euthan, as he knew they needed an exit and soon.

Euthan turned to the small wall behind him which had no back door. Fortunately he could make one. Darkmagi began to try to climb through the fire wall, as they had magic to protect them. As they did so, Wispar would throw a powerful jet of water at them forcing them back. However, this wasn't going to work for long. Euthan quickly placed his hand on the wall, and soon the stones began to shake and shot out the back of the wall, as if they were shot with a canon. Soon there was a gap large enough for them to get through. They began to huddle out, with Wispar and Forlax still fighting them back. They were the last ones through.

"We need to slow them down!" Gathnok said.

The other Spirits understood, as each of them began using their abilities on the old building behind them. The stones quickly crumbled over the hole, water poured into the building as forceful winds whirled round inside. Forlax's flames burnt as it was carried in the air like some fiery tornado. Soon the building collapsed under the distress. They didn't even wait but quickly began to run for the nearest exit out of old Correlani. The building wouldn't stop the Darkmagi for long, as only Gathnok's touch could do so. So they ran in the hope that they had given themselves enough of a lead. For the race was now on to find the Ancients first and restore magic to Sahihriar.

* * *

EggWiff, Saria and Hail were now walking towards MagMount where Wispar had told them to go see her brother, the Fire Spirit Forlax. EggWiff had managed to remain silent since he had turned back. He wondered what WiffEgg might have said or what he really knew about what was going on. However, that was not the only reason for him being quiet. His actual thoughts were occupied by something else. He was trying to think of a way they could convince Forlax to let them through and go to the Nether Realm. It was Gathnok who taught him all about the Elemental Spirits, when he was teaching him in the Fifth Realm. However, he never would fully explain their origin, but called them "old friends". If this was true, then they may already be too late.

Saria and Hail were walking side by side but were not speaking to one another. They were both lost in thought. Hail was thinking about Essence. He kept trying to stop himself, but he couldn't help it. It was his faith and passion. It had been the very reason for his being for so long; how can you have faith, when all it does is cause you pain?

Saria stopped and looked around. The sun was setting making an orange stream of light, whilst the first moon of Sahihriar was now visible.

"EggWiff, we should stop here for the night." Since the Farewell, Saria had more confidence speaking to EggWiff.

EggWiff turned to look at her. His face was smothered in a disgusted look. "We cannot stop. Do you have any idea what could happen if Gathnok obtains the jewel?"

"Actually no, but if we're not awake enough to stop it, then it doesn't matter. Just for a few hours?"

"We walk on!" EggWiff's tone wasn't as harsh but still showed little sign of compassion.

"Hail, what do you want?" Saria asked.

"Huh, what did you just call me?" EggWiff shouted as he spun round. He couldn't believe Saria dared insult him.

"I didn't. I was speaking to Hail."

EggWiff stopped as Saria pointed to the Holy Master. For two days they had been travelling together, and he hadn't even once wondered what his name was.

"You didn't even know that, did you?" Saria looked appalled at him.

"He is the enemy. He killed Trickle!" EggWiff stood forward to confront the Amazon dwarf – which was funny, as the size difference was laughable.

"No, Morbid did. I was there. You weren't!"

"You have a habit of being there when people are killed, don't you?"

Saria's eyes narrowed in pure distaste. She leaned in, standing on tiptoe and whispered with strong intensity.

"If we survive this, and you're still angry, we'll do this. But for now there are bigger and more important things going on."

"Nothing was more important than Trickle's life."

"Really, I wonder if she'd agree with that. With this…" Saria backed away. She knew EggWiff was a good man. What had happened to Flick was entirely her fault, and she would live with that for the rest of her life, but what had happened to Trickle wasn't EggWiff's fault.

They had stopped in a forest path lined with trees. The Elemental Mountains were all surrounded by forest, which gradually changed depending on the element that was closest. It was so nice walking from the Iciliks Mountain to MagMount, because with every step it grew warmer and warmer. They had stopped about midway between the two, so the temperature was just right. Saria liked the warmth of a forest, as it reminded her of her old Amazon settlements.

Just when EggWiff was about to respond, they heard a giggle come from the nearby trees. The group stopped and looked around. EggWiff's heart stopped, as the giggle reminded him of Trickle. They all peered out as three women walked from the bushes onto the path.

The women looked identical. They were slim, yet curvy. They had beautiful round faces, big pouting lips, and hair that bounced around their faces to just below the shoulder. The only things that set them apart were the colours they wore. They each had different hair colours that were the same as their eye make-up, lipstick, clothes, and a jewel which hung round their neck.

The one on the left had adopted the colour red. The shimmering red ruby that she wore highlighted this colour well. The middle woman had the colour green and wore a sparkling emerald around her neck. The last mysterious women, on the far right, wore the colour blue, and she wore a deep, rich blue sapphire.

"Look, Sister, the criminals are acting savage," the ruby triplet said with a sly smile.

"Only one of them is criminal, Sister." The emerald triplet stopped and looked at EggWiff.

"Then only he would carry the burden of his crime." The sapphire triplet was the last to speak.

Once finished, they began to walk towards them in unison. Their femininity made them alluring. Saria flinched, but Hail waved his stump-like hands to stop her. She looked at him sideways.

"That's Ruby, Emerald, and Sapphire. They are the imperial elite guards. Saria, they are deadly." Hail was whispering but didn't dare take his eye off the three women.

"Hail, where has your army gone?" Ruby spoke first.

"Or is your army attempting to steal more Essence from yet another storage facility?" Emerald continued.

"It would be a shame if we have to kill even more of your pigs," Sapphire concluded. It seems that taking turns was a pattern with the triplets. It was very unnerving, as they managed to speak on cue and with such fluidity.

EggWiff and Saria glanced over at Hail. He just looked away ashamed.

"We have no conflict with you." EggWiff stood forward to greet the women.

"That is good…"

"… as we have no conflict with you either…"

"Simply show us the Essence, and we'll be on our way."

The three women stood and waited.

Saria glanced over at EggWiff. She actually hadn't thought about the consequences of abandoning the punishment, which was funny really, as she used to preach its importance to the group. EggWiff glanced over at Saria. So far his crime had been so random he hadn't expected any consequence of forgetting the Essence; in fact it wasn't up to him.

"I no longer have it." EggWiff felt tense. He felt his fingers glide over and around his staff.

"You willingly defy your punishment?"

"Break the laws of Sahihriar?"

"Criminals always think themselves better."

The three sisters always wore a smile, as if they were in on some joke that the others weren't privy to.

Saria stepped forward and confronted Emerald. The look on Hail's face said it all, for only he had seen the power of these three women.

"You don't understand. It was stolen. It wasn't his fault." Saria was blurting out her words fast. She wasn't frightened though. She had killed more than three opponents at once before. Besides they didn't look like much!

Emerald looked down at Saria. The triplet's beauty was clear.

"Like we…"

". . . haven't heard it…"

"… all before!"

With this, the three guards each drew a long sword and adjusted their stance ready for a fight. Instantly Saria had done the same. At the same time, EggWiff had twirled his staff into the air and caught it ready for a fight. Both Saria and EggWiff spun left as Hail moved in safely behind them. They were ready for the fight to begin.

Saria's sword danced left and right as Ruby and Emerald attacked her from either side. She ducked and swung with lightening reflexes to avoid the steel blades. Sapphire had moved towards Hail, but EggWiff had swung his staff to intervene.

"Stay back!" he called, as Hail watched on nervously.

EggWiff's jaw was suddenly met by the backhand of Sapphire. As he swung low, she first struck upwards knocking him back. Hail didn't have time to think. He quickly pushed EggWiff to the side, so that Sapphire's blade plunged through his arm and not his heart. EggWiff let out a cry of pain. Saria was getting tired. She had managed to get a couple of punches in, but the sheer speed and strength of the two guards was unlike anything she had seen before. She heard EggWiff scream. Fearing the worst, she instinctively looked back. She saw EggWiff cradle his arm as Sapphire stood over him. Sapphire had her sword ready and was about to strike, this time on target. Saria stepped forward and went to help him but was stopped as she felt Emerald's blade slice through her gut. She looked down to see the blood seeping through her green Amazon clothes.

* * *

Morbid was concentrating hard, as it was crucial he performed the ritual correctly. As Death, his powers had tripled, and he knew he was powerful enough to conjure a new being. He just hoped he wouldn't mess it up. Without a guide, finding Cupido Sacra could take twice as long. He had the energy rising out from the very ground of Sahihriar, and he was managing to channel it into a ball of almost static energy in front of him. The static energy would occasionally spark or glow. Morbid, however, needed to stay alert. Channelling such potent energy through him was dangerous, even though he was Death.

Morbid was in the clearing where he had summoned his father Death. He chose the site because it was now very familiar and also lingered with his energy from his former spell. Morbid was kneeling close to the ground. As the night drew in, he looked like a small crouched shadow as his cloak hid his white bones in the night. Due to its intensity, Morbid began to feel his bones shake as they rattled together in their sockets. Morbid didn't mind this too much, as he didn't feel physical pain. Yet he could see why not many people tried channelling magic through Sahihriar. He dug his thin skeleton fingers into the dirt beneath him and tried to hold on. His body began to jerk violently as he felt a pulse of energy shoot up through and hurtle towards the ball of static energy. It swirled and glowed and on collision made a huge wave that sent Morbid hurtling back across the floor of the clearing.

However, his hands didn't go with him. They were left stuck firmly in the ground. He stayed lying on the dirt as his soul ached from the spell. Now detached from his hands, he knew he'd struggle to get back up anyway, so instead he waited. After a few moments lost in thought, he was rather surprised to see someone standing over him. It was a small imp being. He had long brown shaggy hair that covered his eyes. Two small glowing eyes could be seen peering through. He wore a grey rag that was draped over him. The imp beamed a huge smile. He held up Morbid's two hands so that he could see them.

"Hey, don't worry, Father. I've got your hands."

"Father? Who are you?"

"I'm Message, the nether guide. You did just conjure me, right?" Message handed Morbid his hands and helped re-attach them. "Better, Father?"

Morbid looked up and was about to correct him, but he had such a childlike innocence. Besides he wasn't going to get distracted by him. It didn't matter what he called him, as long as he helped him get the jewel.

"Can you take me to the jewel?" Morbid was now on his feet.

"Sure. Although I have to warn you, many powerful things hold an interest in the jewel."

"I am Death. I am absolute. I am nothing."

"Even Death has cause for fear sometimes." Message looked up and then stretched out.

"I can handle my own. Where do we start?" Morbid stood with his reaper in hand and his cloak billowing. He was truly frightful. However, the childlike Message had no fear.

"We must go to the Elemental Mountains – more specifically to MagMount – to go see the Fire Spirit Forlax. Only he has control over the portal to the Nether Realm."

"And is that where Cupido Sacra is?" Morbid began to scan his mind for the MagMount mountain.

"Uh-huh." Message wasn't really listening. He knew all of this. It was so odd to have so much knowledge about a world he had never belonged to. So far, he liked being alive.

He looked round and noticed the blackened sky, the two moons, and the faint sign of Forgward in the sky. "Night-time! Night-time! Oh we should sleep then."

"I need little sleep and we don't have time," Morbid exclaimed.

"You summoned me to guide you to the jewel. I can do that, but I need rest, Father." Message had decided that where he stood would be a good enough spot to rest.

"Two hours at the most. I did not realize you would need rest once summoned." Morbid sat down also. He did not need the rest, but he'd watch over Message as he slept.

Message closed his orange eyes and began to drift off to sleep. "Father, thank you!"

Morbid felt a twinge of pain every time Message used the term "father", but he didn't want to make it an issue. He was sure his powers as Death would stretch to ignoring one word.

"For what?"

"For letting me feel." With this, Message lowered his head and let himself sleep for the first time.

* * *

Gathnok ran by her side. Lainla was lying with her hand over her wound. Her fairy wings no longer glowed blue and seemed lifeless in comparison. She struggled to do anything other than sit and wince in pain. He crawled over to her and instantly began to stroke her hair.

"Lainla, they're here; they have come to Sahihriar."

Lainla managed to open her eyes wearily and smiled at the comfort his voice provided.

"Lainla, the Elders are here." Gathnok was smiling, as the knowledge of having the Elders here meant she had a hope of being cured without the need of Cupido Sacra.

Lainla was too weak to speak, but her mind buzzed. The Elders were on Sahihriar. They'd make sure the plan was carried out – that Gathnok would use the jewel, and EggWiff will help him. She felt relieved; it was no longer her job to carry the burden of the secret mission, the reason why they had all come together. The Elders could end everything they had started.

The relief washed over her. She felt herself slipping away. She managed a weak smile at the man she loved before closing her eyes. In her final moments of life, she looked back to a time when she was happy, back to when she was living in the fifth realm and when she was loved. Holding onto that thought, Lainla finally passed on – again.

Gathnok, however, didn't even have time to notice. His look of sheer despair after she had closed her eyes quickly vanished. He let go of her hair and sat back suddenly. For Lainla had begun to appear above her body, in a ghostly transparent form. She felt her mind come hurtling back as she opened her eyes. She felt as though she was being torn from her body. She knew she was dead. She had been through it before, so she was more aware of what it felt like. But why hadn't she moved on? Was this part of the Elders' plan?

"What is this?" Lainla stared at Gathnok. He now seemed so unreachable.

Gathnok had been alive for many years – more than he often liked to admit – but he had never seen a being like this. Of course, he knew why it had happened.

"Morbid! He isn't collecting the souls of the fallen." He looked up at her. "You're trapped here." Gathnok looked on at her. He realised that he had gone about this all wrong. All he needed was to keep Morbid distracted, and then he'd never have to lose her. Nor would he need the Cupido Sacra.

"Plans Change"

Chapter Eleven

It was now night-time; the sky was clouded, and the land looked grey and cold. However, from the horizon there suddenly appeared a great light.

"Message, what is that?" Morbid stared head on, although it was too bright for Message, who covered his eyes and squinted.

"I do not know, Father. They are beyond my knowledge."

Morbid prepared his reaper. Eventually they could see that there were two bright lights that were coming towards him. Morbid was troubled. Clearly these entities were alive, yet he could not sense a soul.

They eventually stopped a few meters away from them. They could now see two bright beings smothered in light. They were almost identical apart from the taint of blue and grey. Message stopped. He looked confused. He stepped back with awe.

"You know who we are?" The grey Elder spoke.

"Elders, how have you been?" Message thought polite conversation couldn't hurt.

Morbid sighed and relaxed. "I have nothing to say to you."

"This wasn't the plan, Morbid." The blue Elder glided forward.

"Plans change."

"This one doesn't. You need to carry on leading them towards the jewel. You must get EggWiff ready."

"Or I could take the stone and destroy it."

"You know the consequences of that. You will all suffer." The grey Elder also floated forward.

The argument was getting faster, and as much as Message knew, he didn't have a clue what they were talking about.

"As I recall, it's only you Elders who would lose out."

"Your father understood the importance..."

"My father is dead because of that wizard. Don't expect me to help him."

"Your father, yourself, and Lainla all have a role to play." The blue Elder seemed sterner with these words.

"Well, they're both dead. The only way I can guarantee my revenge on everything is to make sure that jewel is lost forever."

"You can't!"

"Stop me then. Interfere with Death. See how long your precious balance survives then." Morbid had leaned in close to the lights. He knew they could do nothing.

The Elders knew it too. Death was a natural part of life. He was as pure as Sahihriar itself. They would give anything to be able to fling him back into another realm, keep him from the jewel. But that would break every balance. That's why they waited and recruited his father. He understood the importance of the plan all too well. Now it was failing.

Morbid didn't wait for a reply. Instead, he brushed

through the lights as if they were nothing. Message stood stunned. He couldn't believe anyone could treat the Elders like that, let alone his father.

They walked on a bit, not bothering to look back, but eventually it grew dimmer, so Message guessed they were gone. Morbid was walking faster.

"So, you know the Elders then." Message felt uncomfortable.

"It's not important; just make sure I get to where I need to be."

"Of course." Message's mind wandered. He found it strange how Death himself was grieving for a loss. "So you wish to stop all of this? Maybe save your father?" Message knew precisely what was going on.

"It's no concern of yours."

"Yeah, I just don't see why you don't use your powers to travel back in time and stop it all."

Morbid was so stupid he couldn't believe his stupidity. He had the powers of Death now. Why didn't he just go back and stop EggWiff from killing his father?

"Although, I guess you wouldn't want to go back and just stop EggWiff from killing your father. That would be stupid!" Message said

"Oh yes, of course!" Now Morbid really was convinced his head was hollow. He waited in the hope Message would inadvertently advise him further.

"It makes much more sense to go back to the beginning and stop Lainla from ever being killed in the first place. Then none of this would have happened." Message continued to walk as if the conversation was casual and not the huge revelation it was for Morbid.

"Well that is a plan!" Morbid said, realising how that could solve all of his problems.

"It is? You are clever, Father!" Although Morbid couldn't see, Message was smiling at himself.

* * *

Lainla floated and waited. She knew now that she needed to keep Morbid away from Cupido Sacra at all cost. Morbid didn't even know that the jewel had been locked, and it could only be awakened by using the key. That was something only she and Gathnok knew. Even so, she couldn't do it herself. It was all made so much more difficult by Morbid gaining the powers of Death. If Marvie hadn't killed him, then Morbid would be very little threat.

However, she needed to make sure Marvie would prevent Morbid from destroying the jewel. To do so, she needed to use one of Gathnok's former minions. She closed her eyes and focused her mind. She hadn't made this mind connection before; she was new to her ghostly ways and wasn't sure it would work.

Lainla placed herself in the black void of his mind. It was actually pitch black, which was suitable, as the darkness even hid her ghostly figure. She waited, as the Holy Master pig appeared in the darkened space.

"G– Gathnok?" Hail knew this place all too well. However, he had long assumed he would never be forced to return.

"No. My name is Lainla. I have come to show you something." Lainla's voice came from the darkened surroundings. She didn't want to frighten the pig.

"No, take me back now. My friends need me." Hail last saw Saria being stabbed by Emerald's blade.

"This is important…"

"Send me back!" Hail was now yelling.

"I have something to tell you."

"I'm done doing what Gathnok wants." Hail was relieved

that it wasn't Gathnok he was dealing with, but he was still angry.

"This affects you as much as it affects me."

"Take me back!" Hail would have tried to run, but after he ran for ten minutes the first time this happened, he knew too well it was useless.

"Morbid plans to destroy the jewel."

"Well, that isn't my problem." Hail's eyes peered as Lainla's warming voice continued mysteriously from the shadows.

"It is your problem, Hail. Cupido Sacra holds the key to magic. If it is destroyed, then the Elders and magic will be lost." Lainla tried to sound convincing, but Gathnok might have destroyed all the trust left in him.

"Then go, stop him, and leave me be!" Hail was so annoyed he was hardly listening. He wanted nothing more than to go and help EggWiff and Saria.

"I cannot do it alone. You must convince EggWiff to stop Morbid before he destroys Cupido Sacra."

Hail hated Gathnok. He stole his army, his faith, and his life from him. He had been his puppet, and he wasn't going to let it happen anymore. He was outraged that Gathnok would send someone to tempt him. His mind wondered why it was so important that EggWiff should stop Morbid. What was Gathnok planning? Without his normal fear, Hail thought he'd better make the most of the situation, so he began to try to get the most from Lainla.

"Or convince EggWiff to stop him so Gathnok can get his jewel back."

Lainla didn't blame Hail for his disbelief. If only Morbid and Death were still around, then she wouldn't be carrying out this mission herself.

"That jewel contains the essence of magic itself. If it's

245

not used properly, then Sahihriar won't be given the magic it needs, and without that, it will perish."

"Why should I believe that?" Hail was tired. He just wanted to go back.

"Because of this."

Hail spun as the voice came to his ear. He turned and saw the ghostly figure standing behind him. Hail jolted as his eyes widened, and his mind surged with pain as he cried out in the void. He held his pink skin tight as he felt his head might split into two. Suddenly his mind flashed with images as he began to have a vision.

* * *

Hail saw a green jewel being held by two beings he couldn't fully see. The jewel began to show swirls of mystic green light inside. That light, however, began to grow brighter and brighter. His mind flashed again as he began to see Sahihriar. It was as if he was watching it from flying on a Mithwork. He watched as the still earth slowly began to tremble and then quake. As Sahihriar moved, small waves of green energy began to bleed from the gaps. The magical green mist rose and swirled in the air, like trees that shot up from the ground. Hail was witnessing magic being pulled from Sahihriar. The green jets didn't just swirl upright. They were so powerful that everything around began to get hurtled in – the ground, the trees, fields, and villages. Still the ground shook, and Hail could see more and more jets of magical energy. He saw Amazon settlements destroyed in moments. Even the Elemental Mountains were destroyed. He could hear the screams of everyone, as all they could do was struggle. Hail saw the destruction of Sahihriar and struggled to believe what he saw. However, in amongst all the pain and chaos there was something else. Five different coloured lights could be seen swirling up from the ground and up into the sky. Their sense of purity and power was overwhelming. Hail

struggled to believe what he was witnessing, the destruction of
Sahihriar and the birth of the Elders.

* * *

Saria felt the blood, but only for a second as she regained
focus. She ducked down low and rolled to avoid the swing
of Ruby's and Emerald's blades. Her side hurt, but it wasn't
the first time she had been wounded in battle. Meanwhile,
EggWiff closed his eyes as he awaited the final plunge. Hail
suddenly shot back to reality. He barely had time to register
what was going on around him. Just as Sapphire was about
to make the final plunge into EggWiff's chest, there came
a piercing screeching from above. Sapphire allowed herself
to look up, and although it was only for a moment, it was
enough. EggWiff kicked her away whilst still cradling his
wounded arm. Sapphire stumbled back onto the floor as her
blade was flung onto the grass. Hail, still disoriented from
his encounter with Lainla, began to help EggWiff back to
his feet. They both looked up to see what made the sound.
A Mithwork was flying above them in a circle. Its feathers
fluttered as some fell to the ground. Suddenly the Mithwork
bent its head low and swept in down towards the ground.
Within moments it was hovering above the ground and using
its claws to attack Sapphire. Sapphire swung her arms and
kicked at the beast. Emerald and Ruby were instantly alerted
to Sapphire's pain. Emerald took out her blade and with
Ruby began to run towards Sapphire, completely ignoring
Saria. She got to her feet and winced again as she felt her
side. She watched as the giant bird-like creature continued
to attack Sapphire with its claws. Just before Emerald and
Ruby could make it to their sister's aid, a thin swirling disc
came spinning from the forest edge. The wooden disc shot
through the air in a blur as it quickly collided with the back
of Emerald's and then Ruby's legs. Both of the guards were

forced forwards as they buckled over and hit the ground hard. Saria watched intently. She noticed the Mithwork's eyes glance over into the nearby bushes. The circular disc spun back and flew towards the bushes where it had come from. The bird flew up and hovered in front of Sapphire a little higher. Then it let out a loud squawk, before kicking Sapphire hard in the chest. As the bird did this, it flipped itself over in the air. The dazed Sapphire felt the kick's full force and went flying back, falling onto her two sisters. The bird didn't wait and shot straight up into the air.

The three guards looked up from the ground to see EggWiff now standing tall. He smiled before pointing his staff and yelling, "Timeless!" Green waves of energy shot out and encased the three women in a liquid-like cage. They struggled for a while, before the spell stilled them.

EggWiff sat clutching his wounded arm. Hail stood next to him. He had barely managed to take in everything that he had just seen as the images of his vision still plagued his mind. Saria smiled and went to take a step forward. With her first step, she felt slightly light-headed. She found herself holding her head. She looked down to see that her wound still oozed with blood. She touched it and saw the blood on her fingers. EggWiff and Hail watched as she fell to the floor.

"Is she okay?"

EggWiff and Hail looked over to see a boy, who was nearing manhood, watching them. He had black hair that was rather long; it stopped just over the eye. He was slim in build and had green eyes. Although tall, he was still shorter than EggWiff. He wore garments of blue, which loosely fitted his body. On his waist he wore a brown belt, which held a curved wooden object. On his back he had his sword wrapped around him.

Hail stepped forward suspiciously. "Who are you?"

"The warrior who just save your lives…" The mysterious being stopped and looked at EggWiff. His whole face changed as his mouth fell open.

EggWiff and Hail looked at each other, puzzled. The warrior stepped forward and peered into EggWiff's eyes.

"Marvie?"

EggWiff stepped back in surprise.

"Who?" Hail responded.

"Marvie!" The warrior repeated, still fascinated by EggWiff.

"No, EggWiff," Hail replied again. He looked at EggWiff confused. Why would someone call him Marvie?

"EggWiff? But that is not your name." The warrior was surveying him as if he were in a cage for amusement.

"I . . . I…" EggWiff's mind raced. Who was this being that knew him from so long ago? And what was he doing here now?

EggWiff's mind throbbed, as all he could do was look at the warrior. There was something familiar in his mannerisms, but he was sure he hadn't met this being before. Just as he was about to think of something to say, a way of explaining, the familiar sensation flooded his body. He felt his mind slip away as the green mist surrounded him.

"Oh, Elders!" The smell hit Hail's nostrils as he instantly covered them. It was stronger than last time as he was standing much closer.

The warrior who was standing by caught the smell and also reacted badly. "What of Sahihriar is that?" The warrior's eyes began to water, as he had never smelt anything so foul.

"That's WiffEgg." Hail gestured to the now hunched and relaxed EggWiff.

"I thought it was EggWiff?" the warrior replied.

"Yeah, this is the other him. It's complicated." Hail walked away as the mist began to clear.

The warrior looked at him confused. "You know that this is Marvie, right?"

"No, it's EggWiff. Don't you listen?"

"Never mind. Is he okay?" the warrior said.

"Bloomin' heck! Not another new person? Saria, do you just audition for them or something?" EggWiff looked round for the only person he remembered from the new group. He noticed that the pig was still around. Suddenly he felt a twinge of pain on his arm. "Ouch! Jeez, I'm bleeding! Why am I always getting hurt with you people?"

The warrior looked disappointed and saddened and stepped back from EggWiff.

"Maybe you're not him." He had been so sure. He'd seen images before from his father. Also Fecki wouldn't have sent him if she wasn't sure.

EggWiff's eye caught the collapsed Saria on the ground. He looked at her and noticed the puddle of blood. "Is she…"

"No, she's just injured. But we need to get moving." Hail knelt down beside her and gestured to the three frozen sisters, still trapped by his spell.

EggWiff turned to look at them and jumped back. "Jeez! Who are they?" His new surroundings distracted him from the pain in his arm.

"You just fought them," the warrior said. He was beginning to think this EggWiff was a bit simple.

"I did that?" EggWiff turned to Hail in shock.

"Yeah, look we'll explain everything. Can you help lift her?"

"Sure." EggWiff bent down low. His body felt giddy, as he hadn't had a drink in a long time.

"Perhaps I can help. Emae!" The warrior called out over

to the nearby bushes. They began to rustle and blow as the Mithwork bird reappeared from behind the covering of the forest and flew out into the clearing.

EggWiff stumbled back. He wasn't expecting to see a giant bird. Hail looked at it in awe. As the Holy Master, he had been lucky enough to ride on some of the most elegant and swift giant Mithworks in Sahihriar, but this bird surpassed them all. It was smaller and had rich orange and red feathers that shimmered in the light. Its wings were perfectly symmetrical. Across the bird's neck was a brown satchel. The bird's eye swirled an orange glow. The warrior walked over and patted the neck of the great bird. Then he turned to the others.

"My name is Minso. I am a warrior from the Fifth Realm. And this creature is Emae."

"I'm Hail, and this is EggWiff." Hail had his majestic tone back when formally introducing himself.

"Place your friend on Emae." Minso was beginning to realise that this Marvie had changed vastly from the person he used to be.

EggWiff picked up the small Amazon. He held her so that her weight was on his other arm and the bloody wound was covered and had pressure on it. He stumbled over and placed Saria over the body of Emae. The bird didn't even flutter as Minso stood by her. Once she was on the bird, EggWiff stopped and held his arm. The wound still bled slightly.

"You alright?" Hail said as he stared at the wizard.

"I will be when I get a blinkin' drink!"

Minso looked at the wizard. He was convinced it was Marvie, but something must have happened to him. Although many of the beings in the Fifth Realm believed him dead, Minso refused to believe it, and now this wizard before him looked so like him but behaved so differently.

Minso reached into the satchel that hung from Emae and pulled out a small bottle of gin.

"Here take this." EggWiff's eyes lit up with glee as he took the bottle and smiled his thanks.

"There's a clearing not far from here. We can rest there for tonight and should be safe."

"Why are you helping us?" Hail, although distracted from his vision, was aware that Minso had helped them fight the sisters, and if it weren't for him, they'd all no doubt be dead. But he was no stranger to Gathnok's trickery.

"Let's just get to the clearing and I shall explain." Minso wanted nothing more than to steal EggWiff and bring him back to the Fifth Realm. The Freeyers had healers. He had searched for years for the wizard, and here he stood before him. Minso had never prepared to be disappointed.

Emae hovered above the trees with Saria still unconscious laid on the bird's back. Minso led as Hail and EggWiff followed. Hail was thinking of his vision. He wanted to tell the others and ask what it meant, but couldn't. He wasn't going to have the discussion with WiffEgg, and Saria was injured. He thought he'd better wait. EggWiff in his merry state giddily swayed happily along. The gin had eased his pounding head, and the alcohol relaxed any serious worry he may have had. After a good half-hour of walking through the forest and feeling the heat as they approached closer to MagMount, Minso walked out into another small clearing.

They set up the blankets that Hail had been carrying on his back. The pig was rather relieved when he noticed Minso had his own from the satchel. They spread them out, whilst EggWiff sat happily by himself. He was rather relieved he could sit down, as he hoped the forest would stop spinning. Once they had placed Saria down and wrapped a torn piece of cloth round her waist to stop the blood, both Hail and Minso sat down.

"As I said, my name is Minso. I'm known as a Freeyer in the Fifth Realm. We are warriors who fight to free the Fifth Realm from the evil creatures that took over. We fight to return it to how it was."

Hail gave a blank expression. "I'm afraid I only know about Essence. Don't know much about your realm."

"The myth says that long ago my realm was a paradise, a haven for my forefathers. That's because a great healer ruled it. He ensured that the evil was held at bay by using a great mystic jewel known as Cupido Sacra. What is it?" Minso noticed the drastic change in Hail's face.

"What was this healer's name?" Hail stared deep into the brown eyes of the warrior.

"Gathnok. Why?"

Hail stood up and glanced over at EggWiff, who had managed to nod off on his blanket.

"I think there's some stuff you should know, Minso."

Hail sat down and began to tell Minso everything that he knew.

* * *

Gathnok sat hidden amongst the shadows. He watched the youngish-looking warrior aid Hail. He smirked as the former pig master now worked with the enemy. Since Lainla came back, he had lost track of Marvie's position. His mind wandered to how good it was to hold her again. He had to stay focused if he was to keep her on Sahihriar. As long as Morbid was distracted, then it should be alright. His only problem was making sure Marvie didn't seek out Cupido Sacra. Gathnok couldn't allow that power to go to an enemy, especially if it could be used to steal Lainla's spirit. Gathnok stopped as he sensed the intense feeling he'd sensed only a few times before. He turned to see the two Elder Spirits standing behind him. Gathnok quickly turned his shadowy head to check on Marvie and the others to see if they had been alerted by the Elders' presence.

"Don't trouble yourself. Only you can see us."

Gathnok's caution kicked in. "Why are you here, Elders? You wish to take her from me again?"

"Such a simple question, yet one you rarely use." The blue and grey Elders were rather eerie as they stood smothered by light.

"You took her from me before, so it's reasonable to think you'd do it again." Gathnok was curious. Clearly the Elders wished something from him.

"The simple question of why! So simple, yet you seem to accept so much of recent events."

Gathnok stood and said nothing. He guessed it was time to listen.

"Instead of worrying about her departure, you should instead ponder on her return."

"What do you mean? There's a reason she came back?" Gathnok let his mind wander. He had been too occupied, but the Elders raised an interesting point. Why did Lainla come back as a spirit? And what interest did the Elders have?

"There is a reason for everything. Maybe it's time you learnt of those reasons." The Elders vanished.

Gathnok felt a chill as he was reminded of those words before he was banished many years ago. But surely the Elders plan hadn't been working for all this time? Gathnok was left with nothing but questions, but he suspected that Lainla knew the answers.

* * *

"You sure I can do this?" Morbid asked his little guide.

"Yeah, Death can travel between times; it's just not something that's advised." Message was sitting in front of the skeleton, holding his skeleton hands.

"But if we can stop what happened, then none of this would be like this. Sahihriar would remain peaceful and safe, and my father would still be Death."

"He sure would," Message replied with a childish grin. "Right now, concentrate on the time and place you want to be. Reach out to the soul of that time and focus. See the soul in your mind and draw it near. Make it visible, and take yourself to it, understand?"

"Okay."

Morbid did as he was told. He focused solely on the soul he wanted. He thought about that soul and drew it out. It was relatively easy, as the soul had been calling to him for the last day or so. But he didn't want it in its current form. He wanted to go back. He looked back and concentrated. He began to lose sound and sight of his surroundings, but he was still aware of Message's hand on his. He saw the tall house on the hill in his mind. He saw the different rooms as his mind raced towards the soul. He stopped as he could see it. He could see her clearly in the room. He could see her long blonde hair, her beautiful soft skin, and gorgeous big lips. She was tidying up one of the rooms and humming a tune. Morbid could hear it in his mind growing louder and louder.

"Father!"

Morbid snapped back into reality. Suddenly the world around him had focus and a place again. He looked down to his side to see Message standing beside him, his orange eyes glowing out at him from the darkness.

"You did it! We're here."

Morbid nodded. They were both standing outside the grand home on the mountain. It seemed like a nice day. They surveyed it.

"The house is protected from the Elders; they say that no one with a trace of evil in their soul can enter." Message walked up to the door and turned to Morbid. "However, I'm a creation and you're dead. Neither of us needs to worry."

Morbid nodded, and they opened the door to walk through. However, neither bothered to close it behind them. They both silently crept through the house. Soon they could both hear the humming as they peered through the small crack in the door. Message was in awe as he first laid eyes upon the beauty of Lainla.

"So do we wait here so we can stop whoever ends up killing her?" Message was whispering.

"That's the plan." Morbid was trying to whisper, but when he didn't have neck muscles or air it was difficult.

They waited a while. Neither minded: watching Lainla was almost enchanting, as she moved so softly. Her smile and warmth was intoxicating. Her humming was soft and was heavenly to listen to. After a while Morbid and Message were beginning to get confused.

"Are you sure this is the right time?" Message whispered.

"I am certain."

"So where's the killer?"

"Maybe our presence here warned him off. If that is the case, all we have to do is wait."

Message suddenly felt very uncomfortable. He hadn't been living long, but from all that he knew, he knew he loved it. He liked being able to touch, to breathe, and to smell. But most of all he loved his new father. He liked having someone to talk to, to exist with. Message knew the longer they waited, the less time he had to enjoy all of these things. He watched Lainla and then looked at Morbid. He couldn't do it. He couldn't sit and let the world he knew fall through his fingers.

"I'm sorry, Father." Message whispered, before jumping up.

"No, Message!" Morbid was too late in realising what was going on.

Message had jumped up and taken the reaper from Morbid's hands. He had flung open the door. Lainla spun round and gasped. That's all she had time to do as Message closed his eyes and swung the pointed edge of the reaper into the chest of Lainla. The force was so strong it flung her onto the floor. Message stood back and dropped the reaper onto the floor. He stared in horror as the beautiful women lay clutching her wound. Morbid's ears pricked up as he sensed another soul very close by, a soul he was very familiar with. They looked at each other as they heard the screams of Gathnok calling out Lainla's name. She began to whimper as the pain grew inside of her. Message was shaking as shock took over. They saw the green light come from just outside one of the other doors leading into the room. Morbid ran over to Message and threw his cloak over the imp so Gathnok wouldn't see. Message only managed to catch a glimpse of the great warrior before vanishing with Morbid.

* * *

"Where have you been?" Lainla was used to floating, but not like this. She was trying to distract her own guilt over going behind Gathnok's back.

"I have been watching Marvie and the others. They seem weak. Now would be a good time to manipulate them." Gathnok walked in and stood staring at his ghostly wife. He loved her still, even now.

"You did what?" Lainla glared at him.

"Morbid can't take you if he is distracted." Gathnok was speaking softly but was also looking for signs of what the Elders said were true.

"Gathnok, look at me! I am already gone. I was meant to be gone years ago." She floated on close to him. "I can't even hold you." She let her transparent hand touch his shadowed cheek.

They had both become so lost from the people they used to be.

"I won't lose you again, unless there's more to all of this . . ." Gathnok stood looking at the woman he loved.

Lainla sighed as she heard those words. She had known Gathnok for many years, and she knew by the tone in his voice that he already knew she was holding back on him. She loved Gathnok with all she had, but she couldn't carry on like this. She couldn't keep being held onto for the sake of her love. She wasn't going to be selfish; there were bigger things at stake. She floated back away from him and stared into his shadow face.

"Gathnok, there's something you must know – the reason why I came back, the reason why you're here. I have to tell you the truth about all of this."

"What are you talking about?" Gathnok stared in disbelief; the Elders hadn't lied.

"I have a hidden mission."

"A hidden mission? To do what?"

"To ensure the destruction of Sahihriar." Lainla floated with her head low. She couldn't even look at him.

Gathnok stopped and stared at her. "Why would you want that?" The Lainla Gathnok knew and loved could never intentionally cause harm. He struggled to believe that she was serious.

"A lot happened whilst you were gone. Things got more

complicated," Lainla replied. She was trying to find the right words to make him understand, for him to see it was the only way.

"Then explain it."

"Remember the prophecy that the Darkmagi spoke? They were right."

"No, we were right. We stopped them. The five warriors stopped them," Gathnok said, lost in his confusion.

"We both were right. The prophecy was translated badly. We were meant to save Sahihriar and now we're meant to destroy it." Lainla tried to seem calm as she spoke.

"How do you know this?"

"Death, Morbid's father, once stumbled through time to find that everything had been lost. Not just Sahihriar, but all the other planets and stars – all of it destroyed as if it never was."

"That's impossible! The Elders gave birth to the stars thousands of years ago."

"Only because the Elders were created to begin with. They exist outside of time and space from us. Death travelled through reality and time in order to find the cause. Apparently, it was at this time – this place, when the prisoners stop you from finding Cupido Sacra." Lainla found it hard to say the right thing in the right order. Her thoughts were so jumbled and she still was adjusting to spirit-hood.

"But they haven't stopped me! They won't! I won't let them!"

"Because Death came back and altered this world. He started by telling the Elders, who decided to bring me back as a Spirit of Magic. It was also Death who convinced you to send the Amazon to decrease their numbers."

Gathnok thought about it. It was Death who convinced

him to implement these changes. But it still didn't make sense.

"Well, it worked then. They have not stopped me. I am free to use the jewel, but I shall not abuse it to cause the destruction you speak of. We can fight the prophecy. You mustn't worry yourself." Gathnok raised his arm to bring comfort to Lainla.

Lainla floated back in distress. "No, you don't understand! Cupido Sacra has grown too powerful. Once awakened, it will destroy magic but give birth to the Elders in the process. This would mean keeping the Universe and our past intact."

"So if Morbid gets the jewel…?"

"Then he shall destroy it, thus destroying magic and the Elders along with it."

"And if we get it?"

"Then we use it to give birth to magic and the Elders, but Sahihriar will be destroyed."

Gathnok may have been on a path of darkness lately, but this was something beyond his comprehension.

"It's a big loss, but so many more future and past lives will survive because of it. Our love will be able to have lived because of it."

Lainla was now smiling comfortingly. She could see he was reluctant still. "It would have been okay if Morbid hadn't inherited the powers of Death. Now he's trying to destroy Cupido Sacra, which would mean the Elders never existed, and so neither did any of this."

"I think I understand. I just can't see how it can work." Gathnok couldn't yet see how it made everything fit together, and he also trusted Lainla's word beyond his own thoughts.

"We can. We just need to get to Cupido Sacra before Morbid, awaken the jewel, and then use it."

Gathnok almost laughed. "You make it sound so simple." He looked up at Lainla as he became serious once more. "They won't help us, and without the key we can't awaken Cupido Sacra."

"We must convince them to work with us," Lainla suggested. She knew this would be a challenge.

"They won't work with me, and I cannot work with them. The Amazon will pay for what she did to you." Gathnok might accept the truth about Cupido Sacra, but he wasn't willing to forgive Marvie and his friends.

"Stop blaming her, Gathnok. This isn't anyone's fault but our own. We've been so selfish with our love, and by creating that jewel we've made this path." Lainla stared at Gathnok. It was time they both faced up to reality.

"But..."

"No more buts, Gathnok. So many people have been hurt because of us. People we used to care about. We have a chance to fix it before it's too late."

"I cannot just forgive them." Gathnok was looking at the pain on Lainla's face as it challenged the anger he felt within.

"I'm not asking you to. Please, please, don't turn our love into something I hate." Lainla's ghostly face formed tears.

There was silence for a little while. Gathnok in his shadowy form stood and thought about everything. He knew that stopping Morbid was right, and he also knew he needed the key. He was so lost in the hurt on Lainla's face that he began to realise she was right. Their love had destroyed too much.

"Looks like we're going to see Marvie."

Lainla smiled at Gathnok. She was suddenly reminded of why she had loved him so much.

"The Honest Truth"

Chapter Twelve

A Sacred Past

They were walking pretty fast with Gathnok leading and the shimmering compass guiding them. He felt the weight of the jewel safely in his pocket as they all continued to look back. They knew the Darkmagi wouldn't be far behind them, so they were all on high alert. Gathnok hadn't said much to the others, and Asemai had yet to speak to anyone. Her upset over the death of Sombre was clear as the words from Death continued to linger in her mind. Kip was walking rather slower than the others, which forced Wispar to turn around.

"Kip, come on! We have to keep moving." Wispar turned and grabbed his hand.

"I… I don't want to . . ." Kip said, as he pulled his hand away.

The others continued to walk on, as their conversation had gone unnoticed.

"What? Why?" Wispar slowed down and made him walk by her side.

"Once we stop the Darkmagi, then I'll be alone again." Kip hung his head low as he spoke.

"What? Is that what you think?" Wispar said, as she suddenly realised his worry.

"Well, sure! The only reason I'm here is so you don't have time to find me somewhere." Kip shrugged as he shuffled his feet.

Wispar stopped and knelt down next to Kip and took both his hands into hers.

"I want you to listen to me, Kip. I know I'm not your family, but I promise you that I will never give you away. I'm here to stay."

"You mean it?" Kip said sheepishly.

"You bet." Wispar smiled and gave the Imp a hug. "Now we'd better catch up before we get into trouble."

They walked on and found that the group had stopped.

"It's beginning to get brighter. We can't be too far now," Gathnok called back.

"Yes, the great mountains are near here. It would be a good hiding place for the Ancients to be," Euthan said, as he surveyed the land.

"We just need to cross that lake." Kip pointed as the needle pointed directly over a vast and sprawling lake.

"Can we go around it?" Lainla asked, although none of them could see a way around.

"No time," Gathnok said, peering back once more.

"Then how do we get through it?" Asemai spoke rather bitterly.

"Wispar?" Gathnok turned to look at her.

"Whoa! That's a lot of water, Gathnok," Wispar replied, as she realised what he was asking.

"You can totally do it though," Kip said smiling up at her.

"Erm . . . sure . . . I mean, there's no way we can go around it?" Wispar asked hopefully.

"I'm sorry, but there's no time," Gathnok said, as they continued to walk towards the lake's edge.

"I'll help you. I'll make a wind tunnel to help keep the water back." Asemai smiled at Wispar.

"Okay, we better hurry."

They walked right down to the edge of the vast lake. Little pools of waves hit the edge, and the water looked murky.

"Let's hope I can do this," Wispar said, as she forced a smile to the others.

"Just do your best," Kip said, as he held on to his caretaker's hands.

Wispar took a deep breath and concentrated on the water before her. Conjuring water and controlling it felt slightly different, so she had to make sure she got the energy right. Soon enough, the water began to peel slowly backwards and divide into two, making a narrow pathway for them. At first Asemai began with a gentle breeze, but as she moved ahead, she made it go stronger. Wispar felt the release of pressure, as she only had to keep the side and back walls of the lake from closing in on them. They all began to walk through the lake, and they could feel their feet begin gradually sinking down into the soft mud beneath them.

"Ugh, great!" Lainla said, as she walked through the mud.

They walked quickly but steadily as Wispar and Asemai pushed the water further back. Sprays of water still splashed back on them as if they were walking in very faint rain. They pushed on, as they all thought it was surreal walking surrounded by water. They couldn't see their magic, so it was as if an invisible shell was protecting them as they walked through.

"What was that?" Forlax said, as he peered into the water.

"What was what?" Lainla replied.

"I thought I saw someone in the water," Forlax said, as he continued to survey the watery wall.

Lainla peered in but couldn't see anything. The others hadn't noticed the discussion as they continued to move forward. They moved about another meter before Lainla stopped suddenly.

"Stopping isn't a good idea," Wispar called, as she felt the heavy strain of keeping so much water at bay.

Asemai too began to struggle, and they were only half way across the lake.

"I saw something – like someone swimming in the water," Lainla said, as she stood back away from the water.

"A Darkmage?" Gathnok called.

"I don't know," Lainla said.

The group stopped moving forward, as they suddenly felt very trapped. They were surrounded by water which Wispar couldn't control. If they were to be attacked now and lose control of their powers, they'd all drown. They all began peer into the murky waters around them. Gathnok got a fright as he began to see dark figures begin to swim closer to the water wall. It did look as if someone was swimming inside the lake. However, their speed and fluidity meant that they couldn't have been Darkmagi.

"What are they?" Lainla asked.

More and more of these silhouettes appeared, and they seemed to grow bigger as they swam towards the lake wall.

"They're closing in. Stay close!" Euthan yelled, as each of them huddled in.

They watched as it all went still. Wispar began to wince. Holding the water in one place was tough, especially as Asemai could only help push the water forward. They all jumped as suddenly a large being dived through the lake wall only inches away from them. It soon disappeared into the other side and was only visible for a moment.

"What was that?" Gathnok asked.

"I don't know. It looked like it had scales," Euthan replied, as he had been the closest.

Wispar was feeling weak and needed all her energy on the task, and as a result Kip was standing on his own. Another being shot through. This time it was closer, and Forlax had to move his arm or else the fish like creature would have caught him.

"They're trying to get us!" he cried.

None of them had dreamt that they would be disturbing someone's home. Water creatures were unheard of in Sahihriar. However, it was too late to do anything, as all they could do was continue to gradually move further towards them.

"Should we fight them?" Forlax yelled, as small sprays of water still rained down on them.

"No, they're just trying to defend themselves. The sooner we get out the safer we'll be."

Both Asemai and Wispar continued to move gradually as the group faced the water. The beings stopped appearing, and they had moved a fair distance and weren't far from the other side. They all hoped they had maybe scared off their attackers, when suddenly from the left wall a large creature emerged and shot across the exposed tunnel. Wispar's heart stopped as she felt Kip's hand touch her arm as he cried out. They all turned to see Kip being pulled into the other side.

"Kip!" Wispar called.

"No, wait! If you lose concentration, we're all dead," Gathnok yelled, as they surveyed the lake wall.

"Find him! Find him!" Wispar pleaded, as she struggled even further to hold the water.

"I can't see him!" Gathnok, Lainla, Euthan, and Forlax all looked in.

"He must be there. Use your powers!" Wispar cried.

"We can't! Wispar, we have to move forward," Forlax replied.

"I won't leave him!" Wispar shouted, as she stood her ground.

"We can't fight them, and if we don't, we'll all die. Please, move forward. You can do this." Forlax held his sister's arm as he pleaded with her.

"Not without him!" she screamed.

"Wispar, listen to me. What would he want us to do?" Forlax said, looking at the anguish on his sister's face.

The others looked on as the pain on Wispar's face was only too clear. Tears began to stream down her face as she forced her legs to move forward. She realised in that moment that Kip was gone. She had failed him. Wispar's grief seemed to make her powers stronger. The water seemed to push back much quicker as they took more and more steps. Soon, and before another attack, they had walked up the muddy bank of the lake and were out the other side. Asemai held onto Euthan's arms, as she too was very weak from using so much power. The others looked back at the lake. What once had seemed so beautiful was now the grave of Kip. It was a chilling thought. Although saddened, Gathnok didn't have time to dwell on what had just occurred. He needed to keep focus, and the Darkmagi wouldn't be far behind still. He looked down at the compass which pointed to the tall tips of the great mountains.

Wispar practically crawled out on the bank as she sobbed uncontrollably. Although weak, she managed to hobble over towards Gathnok looking distraught with grief. She screamed as she approached him.

"You made us go in there! I didn't want to go. Why would you make us go?" Wispar was trying to pound his chest, but she was too weak from loss.

"He was going to stay with me. He was going to…" Wispar's words were lost, and she collapsed at Gathnok's feet as she buried her sobs in her hands. *The others looked on with sympathy and sorrow.*

"We must keep moving," Gathnok demanded, although rather uncomfortably.

"Can't she have a moment?" Asemai seemed annoyed.

"We don't have time." Gathnok tried to sound sincere. He was sad about Kip, but they'd all be dead if the Darkmagi found them.

"We'll make time! It's not up to you to always decide what to do!" Asemai shouted back. She went over and put a comforting hand on Wispar's back.

"Saban put me in charge. The Heart leads the Spirits!" Gathnok raised his voice in reply.

"How do we even know he was telling the truth? How do we know any of this is right?" Asemai snapped back.

The other Spirits were now standing behind Asemai whilst Lainla stood by Gathnok's side.

"I didn't ask for this!" Gathnok yelled. He was so angry that they would think he relished his authority.

"Neither did we. Death warned us, and he must have done so with reason!"

"Yeah, because Death is clearly a trustworthy guy!" Gathnok said with obvious sarcasm.

"He helped us didn't he?" Forlax had now joined in.

Gathnok looked at them and could see that they were all on the same side. Kip's death had clearly been the last straw in their loyalty.

"We're so close now," Lainla said, trying to convince them to stay.

"Well, you would be on his side," Euthan muttered.

"I believe in what he's doing," Lainla replied, trying to brush off the implication.

"Please! It's clear how you feel," Asemai said.

Gathnok looked at Lainla who looked back at him. Both

of them had sensed a connection since they had first met, but they didn't imagine they had been that obvious. Lainla quickly stared over at Forlax who was staring at them with a stern face.

"It's clear how you both feel, Li," he said, as his eyes revealed his pain.

Lainla could hardly look at her childhood friend, as she knew the pain she must have caused him.

"Why don't you give us Cupido Sacra and let us find out what's really going on?" Asemai asked, as she held out her hand.

"The jewel was meant for me," Gathnok said, as he took a step back.

"And you're sure you're ready for all that power?" Asemai said with a questioning look.

"I don't have a choice," he replied.

"We're giving you a choice," Asemai continued.

"I won't let you keep me from this quest," Gathnok replied. He wasn't just thinking about himself. He believed Saban and had to fight to keep Sahihriar safe for Marvie.

"We have all the power here. Don't make us use it, Gathnok."

The Spirits were now all standing and looked rather intimidating as they confronted him and Lainla. Gathnok suddenly felt a rush of fear and worry. He knew he would easily lose in a battle against the other Spirits. Just as this feeling swept over him, he felt a strange surge of energy go through him. It was a feeling he hadn't felt before. The shimmering compass began to glow and got so warm that it almost burnt his hand. He was confused as to what it was doing, as were the other Spirits as they took a step back confused. Soon the compass flashed a bright blinding light that caused Gathnok to shield his eyes. After the moment passed, Gathnok took his arms away from his face and looked at the Spirits. They were all lying on *the floor completely unconscious. He looked to his side to see Lainla standing next to him beaming a smile.*

"How . . . ?" Gathnok asked curiously.

"No idea, but let's just keep moving. I don't like this place."

Gathnok nodded back as for a moment he allowed himself to be lost in her eyes.

"Bye, Kip," she said softly, as she took one last look at the lake.

Gathnok nodded as they began to head for the great mountains. They left the Spirits lying on the ground, completely helpless with the Darkmagi not far behind them.

* * *

Hail sat and told Minso everything – well, as much as he could. Saria had filled him in on what she could, claiming it was for his own protection in case Gathnok tried to trick him again. He explained how he was the ruler of the holy pigs, how he served under Gathnok, about the four prisoners and the fate of Flick and Trickle, and how the drunken fool asleep beside him was the long lost legend, Marvie. Minso sat and listened. He had come from the Fifth Realm to find Marvie again. He swore to bring back peace to his home. He struggled to believe it. Marvie couldn't help the Fifth Realm, because he was too busy fighting to save Sahihriar and all the realms. Hail had just finished explaining why the triplets were attacking them, when Saria began to awake. Both Hail and Minso ran over to her side.

"How are you feeling?" Hail said.

Saria opened her eyes to see Hail's big snout in her face. She tried to hide her look of disgust and quickly managed to smile back. She looked over to her other side to see the black-haired warrior.

"Who are you?" Saria tilted her head back. Her warrior

instincts didn't like strangers so close, especially seeing as she was weak.

"Relax Saria, he's Minso. He helped us when we were attacked. You were hurt."

"I'm aware of what happened, Hail." Saria didn't mean to sound so bitter, but her side was still sore, and she didn't like the fact someone else was around who could slow them down.

Hail stood back and was given a harsh reminder that he was just their prisoner, not their friend.

"You don't need to thank me," Minso said smugly.

"I wasn't going to. We would have managed on our own." Saria held her side as she sat up against the tree. Amazons were known for healing fast, but the wound was still severe and hurt more than Saria would ever admit.

"Next time I'll leave you to die then," Minso said with an infuriating smile. Minso couldn't help be reminded of Fecki when talking to the dwarf. Saria quickly disliked him.

"Good, that's when I would thank you." She smiled back mockingly.

The night had drawn in fully now, and the stars and the moons were out in the sky. It was a little warm for the night, but that's only because they could now see MagMount and feel its heat.

"Umm, Saria, there's something I need to talk to you about." Hail knelt down beside her. He was nervous. How would she react when he told her of his vision?

Saria was about to respond, when a foul smell caught her air. Both Hail and Minso immediately covered their nostrils. It was the smell of stale egg that Saria was becoming worryingly used to.

"WiffEgg?" Saria was asking Hail.

"Actually, you missed him. This should be EggWiff back," Minso said.

Saria gave him a puzzled look. Why was he acting like he'd been part of the group the whole time? "Oh, that's something then."

Minso and Hail stood up and turned to see if EggWiff had slept through the transformation. They were rather taken back when they found he was standing right behind them.

Minso looked at him in awe. "You are Marvie, aren't you?"

"Not for a long time, not anymore." EggWiff stood forward and looked at Saria. "Will you be well?"

"Should be," she nodded back. The fact he showed concern was a good sign of progress between them. However, she was sure neither of them had forgotten the confrontation they had earlier that night.

With Saria's health confirmed, EggWiff stood back and turned to Minso. "How should I know you?"

"My father helped you in the Fifth Realm during the time of darkness." Minso was standing tall and proud.

"You're Jago's boy?" EggWiff said, seeing the likeness more clearly.

"Yeah!" Minso didn't expect EggWiff to remember his father.

EggWiff put a hand on his shoulder. "He was a good man. You should be proud."

Minso nodded with a smile. "I am, thank you."

It was strange how this was the Marvie he was expecting to find – not some drunken criminal running from his deranged uncle.

"Interesting! I remember Jago as a young boy."

All four of them swung round to see who had spoken. Gathnok stood in his shadowy form in the middle of the clearing. Lainla, the Spirit of Magic floated next to him in her ghostly transparent form.

EggWiff twirled his staff. Hail moved in behind him. Saria winced as she struggled to get up, but couldn't. Minso, who caught on fast, quickly drew his sword in one hand and held his wooden disc in another.

Lainla floated towards them with a comforting smile. "We haven't come to harm you."

"We've come to tell you…" Gathnok began.

"Tell us what?" EggWiff held onto his staff and didn't let his eye move from Gathnok's.

"The honest truth about all of this, about why all of this has happened, and what needs to happen next." Lainla was speaking softly. She was now floating by Gathnok. One was smothered in darkness, the other transparent to the world.

"It's a trick!" Hail called out.

"All you need to do is listen. Please, Marvie."

There was something in the way Gathnok sounded. His said his name with sincerity. It was something EggWiff hadn't heard in many, many years.

EggWiff lowered his staff slowly and rested upon it. Truth is, his arm still hurt, and it was easier to do this than hold it raised in anticipation.

"Very well. We shall listen."

"Time is a precious and delicate thing. Its very fabric is ever lasting. With every decision we make, we alter that fabric and therefore the consequences for all of Sahihriar."

"Actions have consequences. We get it." Saria was in no mood for a lecture.

"You said you'd listen." Gathnok was slightly enraged by the little Amazon. Truth is, he still wouldn't mind ending her life, regardless of the cost.

Lainla waited for it to go silent before continuing. "This isn't the first time-line we have all existed within. There was another time, when things turned out very differently to how they have turned out now."

EggWiff was puzzled, and he was about to interrupt but then thought it better to listen for now.

"In this other time, four prisoners, known as Trickle, Flick, Morbid, and EggWiff, were sentenced to community service – a meaningless chore to spread the word of Essence. However, what they didn't know is that Gathnok, a being enraged by despair and grief, had returned to Sahihriar and had planned to use the mystic jewel Cupido Sacra to wreak revenge and bring back his lost love."

"Meaning you?" EggWiff prompted.

"Yes, meaning me. In his moment of darkness, the shadowed being decided to take over and control the son of death, the person you know as Morbid."

Minso stood listening. He was overcome with emotion. Standing before him was the myth, the ultimate healer Gathnok. He had been real for all this time. And he said he had known his father. He never dreamt he'd be here, and now all he could think about was Fecki and the other Freeyer warriors. They'll never believe him.

"But none of this is any different. All of this happened." EggWiff held onto his staff again. He couldn't be sure if they were wasting his time or not.

"Well, this is where it changes, Marvie." A tingle went through EggWiff as Gathnok said his name again.

"Saria was never assigned to distract the travellers, and because of it they were able to realise what had happened to Morbid and help him. In doing so, they managed to trick the shadowed being and stop him from using Cupido Sacra. The jewel was never used."

"And what about Trickle and Flick?" EggWiff held his breath.

"They were never killed." Lainla smiled at the comforting thought.

Hearing that, or just thinking that there might have been another time, another world where Flick wasn't dead caused Saria to form a tear.

"I'm confused. Why tell us of this time? Why taunt us with this existence when you know it's already ruined." EggWiff gestured at Gathnok.

"Because of what happened next," Gathnok replied.

"Once the jewel was taken and Gathnok had been banished, everyone thought Sahihriar was safe. However the day the jewel was taken was the beginning of the end."

"The end of what?" Minso couldn't help but ask. Everyone gave him a disgruntled look.

Lainla stopped and glanced at Gathnok. He too turned his shadowy head towards her. "The end of everything. That day was the last ever day of anything. Sahihriar, the other realms, the stars and other planets – all of it just vanished with only emptiness forever."

EggWiff took a step forward. He was struggling to believe such a baffling story. "Then how do you know any of this? If emptiness took over, how can anyone possibly know?"

"Death. Death has the ability to shift through time. One day he looked into the future and saw the emptiness, saw the nothing. He felt it. He knew that by not using Cupido Sacra, something so awful must have happened."

"Which was?" EggWiff was less stern with his words. He was more curious to see where all of this was going.

"He believed that Cupido Sacra held the ultimate power, and once activated, it triggered the destruction of Sahihriar and the realms, but in doing so, it gave birth to the great Elders."

"Don't be absurd. The Elders already exist. They have been worshipped for years!" Hail laughed at the notion.

"The Elders exist beyond time and space. To us they may appear as though they've always been, but they must have been created at some point. There was a prophecy told to us many years ago – that five warriors would either destroy or save Sahihriar. We already saved it once. Now it's our time to destroy it."

"Which will help create it…" Gathnok was pleading with his former apprentice.

"So Death came back, and that's what changed everything?"

"Not exactly. Death came back and spoke to the Elders. He convinced them to turn my soul into the Spirit of Magic. Once awakened, he told me everything. He explained that he chose me because of my connection to Gathnok and that he made me a spirit so I could work closely with him and search for Cupido Sacra without suspicion. He then spoke to his son Morbid and informed him of what was going on. He performed a spell so that Gathnok's hold would have no effect over him, but he made sure he committed his crime and was in place to join with you all."

Gathnok took over the explanation. "Death then appeared to me claiming he was willing to help. He encouraged me to manipulate Morbid but also convinced me to hire you to distract them further and kill the elf, which I did."

"And getting Morbid to kill Trickle." EggWiff's lip curled with anger.

"Yes, who had known he was working under his own free will. You see Death believed that with Trickle and Flick dead and you kidnapped, then nothing would stop me from gaining control, using Cupido Sacra, and thus creating the existence of everything."

"What went wrong then?" Minso asked. He was fascinated by all of this.

"I fell for Flick . . ."

"I killed Death . . ."

"And I lost my faith . . ."

Minso looked at his new companions. "Oh . . ."

"Those and other things. Morbid was never meant to get the powers of Death, and now he threatens to destroy Cupido Sacra and with it the existence of everything."

"But surely he knows what that would do?" Saria asked.

"Yes, but since EggWiff killed his father he no longer cares. Either way, to him his world is destroyed, but at least this way, he destroys the only thing he has ever known – Death itself." Gathnok's shadowy form was less frightening now, even to Hail.

"But there's still one thing that doesn't make any sense," EggWiff said.

"Really, just the one? That means you're doing way better than me." Saria noticed Hail smile.

"Which is?"

"Why bother with us to begin with? Why didn't you and Death just get the jewel and end it on your own?" EggWiff couldn't believe any of this. Was he to believe Flick and Trickle died so Sahihriar could be destroyed?

"Long ago, when your uncle and I went to the Fifth Realm, Gathnok began using the jewel, and so it grew in power. Fortunately he was strong enough to handle it."

"But learning of its power, I knew I needed to protect it. So I placed a protection spell. If the jewel was ever taken from me or lost, then it would lie dormant, building in power until it was reawakened by the key."

"So where's the key?" Saria asked.

"I knew it had to be something I would guard with my

life. Something so important to me I would never lose it. So I chose you." Gathnok stared straight at EggWiff.

Before EggWiff could respond, Minso had decided to butt in again. "So let me just get this straight. If Morbid gets the jewel, he'll destroy it, and this means magic and the Elders are destroyed. But if EggWiff gets the jewel, he'll use it to give birth to the Elders and magic, which will destroy Sahihriar in the process."

"To be brief, yes."

"Okay, just making sure." Minso was beginning to understand how this was far bigger than his own mission.

"How can I be the key though? I have no idea how to awaken Cupido Sacra."

"Actually you do. It's buried deep within you. I gave you this information before, but I'll help explain all that later," Gathnok looked around, "in private."

EggWiff went and stood back with the others. "So we listened, but we still have no reason to believe any of this!"

All four looked at the two beings with disbelieving expressions. They weren't so easily convinced.

"Think about it. What was Death doing in the tower? Why was I brought back as Spirit of Magic? Why would Gathnok send Saria and the pigs when he could have taken you at any time? It all fits, Marvie."

EggWiff couldn't help but believe her. Despite everything, he had always believed Lainla to be a being of goodness and truth.

"I believe them."

The whole group looked at Hail.

"Back in the forest, when you were fighting. Lainla came to me in my mind. She . . . she showed me something, a vision." Hail looked up at the others. He was nervous and scared. He could still hear the screaming, still see the terror on the beings' faces before being swept up in the green jets. Gathnok's shadowy head turned and looked at Lainla.

"A vision of what?" Saria placed a hand on Hail's pink skin. She could see he was distressed.

"Of what will happen if Cupido Sacra is used. It destroys everything."

Hail's head remained low as he refused look anyone in the eye.

"So how do you know it created the Elders?" EggWiff asked with less sympathy.

Hail looked up and showed everyone his tear-ridden face. "Because I felt it. It was no trick – no trick at all."

"Marvie, either way Sahihriar is destroyed. At least our way Sahihriar has a chance of ever being, and worlds beyond this one can still be born. You knew us once as two good beings. We want to do what's right." Lainla pleaded with him with her eyes.

He turned and looked at the three others. Hail and Saria looked disgusted. Minso looked vacant.

"Very well, you may travel with us – for now."

"EggWiff, you can't be serious!" Saria yelled. How dare he agree to such a thing?

"How can we not? What if what they say is true? What if by ignoring this, Morbid destroys everything?" EggWiff spoke rather calmly. He wasn't close to being convinced that Gathnok and Lainla were sincere, but there was something about it all that made sense, an annoying twinge of familiarity that he couldn't put his finger on.

"They have hardly been honest so far. He is the enemy. We should be attacking him!" Saria replied sternly.

"Try it, Amazon!" Gathnok sneered back. He would like nothing more than for her to give him an excuse to attack.

Both Lainla and EggWiff held up their hands in protest, forcing Saria and Gathnok to stop.

"Trick or not, Saria, we cannot allow for them to escape and risk them finding Cupido Sacra first. You can travel with us for now, but be warned, my magic has grown since you last taught me. Try anything, and I vow with everything I have to defeat you."

EggWiff glared into the empty void of Gathnok's blackened face. He didn't trust Gathnok for a second and would be poised at any moment for some sign of attack. Yet somehow he still couldn't shake the feeling that he was making the right choice.

"Even Death Should Fear Sometimes"

Chapter Thirteen

"I think he tried to hex me!" Message looked up at Morbid "You're mad, aren't you?" Message lowered his head so more of his fringe covered his face.

"Why would I be mad? You simply killed Lainla, continuing this time-line which was the whole reason we went back." Morbid didn't really do sarcasm well. Without facial expression, it didn't really work, but it was the only thing he could do to distract his frustration.

"Yeah, it was a silly thing to do!" Message said shamefully. "We could always go back and try it again?" It was a poor attempt at redemption.

"No, because clearly our actions simply exist within the time-line we acknowledge, and if things changed, then it would place us in a mind-set that would appear to be the norm, so we wouldn't know of it," Morbid finished.

Message stopped. "I have all the knowledge of all of Sahihriar, and even I didn't understand a word of that!"

"We've wasted a lot of time." Morbid looked down at Message.

"Okay, I understand. One quick nap and then we'll…" The small imp was the constant optimist.

"No more time." Morbid placed his white hand on the imp's shoulder. Message literally blinked and then felt an intense heat wash over him. He opened his eyes and looked around. They were in a large mountain with a lake of lava beneath them. They stood on a small piece of rock that stuck out from the inside of the mountain walls. Behind them was a crumpled hole leading to the outside.

Message turned and looked at Morbid. "That was awesome! Let's do it again." Message was very excited.

"Not just yet. I assure you, we'll no doubt be doing it again."

Suddenly, jets of fire swirled up from the lake majestically into the air. Morbid noticed Message's mouth stood open in awe. Message caught Morbid looking at him.

"Forlax – he takes a while, but he'll be with us in a moment." Message smiled back and then went back to watching the fire form into Forlax the Fire Spirit.

After a while, the fire jets stopped and a large flame flickered into shape. Forlax once again appeared floating above the lake. He peered at Morbid and Message.

"Well, it's been a while since I saw you."

Message jumped as Forlax's speech sprayed sparks.

"I am not the Death you know of. I am his son, formally known as Morbid." His father once told Morbid to have great respect for the Elemental Spirits.

"Yes, I am aware who you are. I met your father once a long time ago. Why have you come here, Death?"

"My companion and I wish to travel to the Nether Realm." Morbid stood tall and spoke clearly.

Message flinched at the word companion. He hoped he was something more to his creator.

"Very well." Forlax's flamed body swirled and shot out more jets of fire. This time they began to form and circle beneath the ledge. It spun faster and faster until it formed a vortex.

"That was easy."

"You're Death. Only angels have the same level of rights as you. Oh, and the Elders, of course. But, yes, all spirits must do as you wish. Seriously, did you just skip the Grim Reaping classes?"

Although Message's comment was meant as a joke, Morbid couldn't help but feel some form of sadness. He didn't know as much as he should, but that's because his father was taken from him. That's why he would seek his revenge despite the cost.

"I cannot stop you from going, but I know of your reasons, Death. Be careful." Forlax was staring at Morbid. Although bound to the lake, his duty, and the elements, Forlax once had much more freedom and knew all too well the capabilities of the mystical jewel.

"I can handle my own."

"Even Death should fear sometimes." Forlax nodded as Morbid looked over at Message. Message just gave a cheeky shrug and jumped into the portal. Morbid had dismissed the words from Message, but since repeated by Forlax they couldn't help linger in his mind. He too then jumped into the portal, into the nether realm.

"Message, you do know where you're going, right?" Morbid walked next to his little guide.

The portal had opened out into a large vast sandy desert. That's all the Nether Realm really was though. It consisted of large patches of stark land, sometimes just grass, sometimes sand, and sometimes just lakes of water. Very few beings lived in the Nether Realm, as the isolation and stillness were said to slowly drive beings insane.

"It's why you conjured me, Father. You shouldn't worry so much. It can't be good for you… Okay, never mind."

"This is strange."

"Yeah, I know. Death in a Desert. I'm sure that's a song!" Message began to chuckle.

"I meant it's strange I can't sense any other souls here, not even Gathnok's."

"Yeah, well, he and Forlax hardly get on, but that is just a long and messy story. So we're the only beings in the nether realm?"

"Yes, it's why I cannot transport us to the dwell of Cupido Sacra."

"I know. Your powers work by being drawn to the souls around you." Message was walking along the desert. Things were strange between them now.

They walked for a while in silence. With every step they were getting closer to Cupido Sacra, so Morbid could end it all.

* * *

The group sat in the clearing. Saria and Hail sat talking. They couldn't believe EggWiff agreed to join them. Minso was busy feeding Emae. He occasionally looked over at Gathnok and Lainla who were sitting next to one another. He was so keen to go and talk to the great warrior. But even he could see there was bigger stuff going on. EggWiff got up and walked over to Gathnok. To his surprise, when Gathnok looked up he could see some shadowy detail of his face. Maybe it was because he was back close with Lainla.

"I need to know about the key now!" EggWiff stood

tall and proud. He had never feared Gathnok, but he didn't trust him either.

Gathnok stood up. He was just as tall as EggWiff. It was almost as though Gathnok was EggWiff's shadowy reflection. "Let's go and talk."

Lainla watched as they walked off. She was actually really proud of Gathnok. She had no way of knowing how he would have taken the news, but he was loyal to what was right – something she had long forgotten. She got up and then floated over to Saria and Hail. Both of them gave her an off glance as they pretending not to notice her coming over. Hail actually thought she looked scary floating in a ghostly figure in the darkened forest.

"May we have a moment alone, please?"

Hail gave Saria a concerned look, before nodding and leaving the two alone.

"About what happened…" Saria began.

"No, please, I understand what you did. Saria, we've known each other for a while now, and I used to think of you as a friend. I don't blame you for what you did." Lainla smiled at the Amazon.

"Lainla, I stabbed you through with my sword. You can't forgive me for that. I was upset and angry, and when I saw what you meant to him, I just…"

"You did what you were trained to do. After what you had to do with Flick…"

"Lainla, I barely knew Flick. It's no excuse."

She knelt in close to Saria's side. "He cared about you, and you cared about him. It's enough."

Saria understood she wasn't just talking about her and Flick. She paused for a while before looking at her.

"Is this just another trick, Lainla? Because honestly, I'm just tired. I'm so tired of all of this."

"I wish it was. I really wish it was."

"As an Amazon, I somewhat understand that he did what he had to. And because of recent events I also know what it's like to lose someone." Saria then lowered her voice and went into a harsh whisper. "But I will never trust or like him for as long as we both exist."

Saria lent back and held her side.

"I can accept that. Now get some rest," Lainla smiled. She was so relieved she had made peace with Saria. She was perhaps her only friend. Lainla only hoped that Marvie would come to understand things in time.

* * *

Gathnok and EggWiff walked along the forest. Neither of them had said a word.

"I didn't kill Lainla. Deep down you must know that. She must even know that." EggWiff had stopped walking.

"So she tells me." Gathnok was almost hidden amongst the shadows.

"Then why can't you believe that?"

"I know what I know!"

"What? So you just stick with the first explanation you can think of?" EggWiff now stopped and confronted his uncle.

"You're the only person who could have gotten so close without warning."

"Gathnok, we both know that there are many powerful beings that could have done this."

Gathnok stood and stared at EggWiff. He knew that he was right, but it was easier to blame EggWiff. For so many years he built up so much anger towards his nephew. That wasn't going to go away so easily. EggWiff could see the resolution in his shadowy face. He could sense his anger. EggWiff sighed and was too tired to argue.

"Evidently you shall always believe what you wish. But

I know I did not kill Lainla, and I know that others have suffered for that belief."

"Someone always suffers with belief. It's the way of Sahihriar." Gathnok glared into his powerful nephew's eyes.

"So what happens now? You've yet to explain how I'm the key." EggWiff sat down at this point. He figured they were far enough away from the others.

"You still don't sound like you believe." Gathnok knew full well that it wasn't even an hour ago when he was doubting every word of the same story.

"Forgive me if your word means very little right now. Kidnapping someone tends to cause distrust from some people." EggWiff scowled at Gathnok. Who was he to turn up now and act like some saviour to everything?

"Why do you think I took the time to kidnap you? Without you I couldn't ever get Cupido Sacra back."

"And so Lainla tells you a story, and suddenly you're Gathnok again. Don't be a fool!" Once upon a time EggWiff would fear saying these words to his mentor; now he enjoyed them.

"I'm simply trying to do what's right. Believe it or not, that's all I've ever done."

"Actions speak louder than belief. Yours show nothing but destruction. Why not get them to help?" EggWiff asked.

"Get whom to help?"

"The Elders. If this risks their existence and the creation of everything, why aren't they stopping Morbid?" As much as he was trying to be irritating, it was also a valid point.

"You know as well as I do that by their own rules they cannot directly interfere."

"Yet somehow they managed to interfere when banishing you to another realm. How did you escape by the way?"

EggWiff was rather curious about this, and this was an excellent means of finding out.

"It isn't relevant. We must stay focused."

"Gathnok, you have come here asking me to trust you. That trust must be earned."

There was a moment's pause whilst Gathnok resisted his urge to attack. Instead he remembered what was at stake.

"You're right. The Elders did banish me. They sent me to the Second Realm. I thought it would be filled with chaos and torment, but instead it was filled with peace and tranquillity. It was my grief that made me insane first, made me question and forget." Gathnok turned and looked at EggWiff. "But it was my will for vengeance that made me survive. My mind, heart, and soul had been completely blackened, and I was almost savage. I was the only thing that was dark and evil in the Second Realm, so soon enough that shadow took over me." Gathnok stopped and hoped that would be enough.

"That doesn't explain how you escaped."

"I didn't escape. I was set free. Once the Elders believed the shadow had swallowed all signs of Gathnok, they sent me to Sahihriar to be free. They justify it as 'punishment' and not interference. After being on Sahihriar for long enough, I began to meet people, people who helped me gain some sense identity – enough to remember her, which was all I needed. I learnt to turn others into shadows such as myself by using my anger and hatred. That's how I managed to create my army and followers."

"So you then had enough to come after me, it would seem." Although the story was sad, EggWiff didn't feel sympathy for Gathnok.

A silence fell between the two. EggWiff realized that Gathnok had upheld his side. The least he could do was listen to Gathnok in return.

"So this key . . ." EggWiff suddenly asked.

"At some point in time and place, you gave yourself the knowledge of how to awaken Cupido Sacra. It seems that you did this in order to protect the time-line and create the opportunity in case we fail."

"If what you say is true, then we are destined to fail." EggWiff was determined to find the flaw in Gathnok's trickery. His sudden shift of compassion was suspicious to say the least.

"We decide our own fate. But in case we do fail, you must go back and give yourself the knowledge you possess now."

"You expect me to leave now? Leave my friends, when Morbid is moments away from getting Cupido Sacra? I shall not leave them with you as their protection."

"But I'm offering you the one thing you want most in this world. You could go back. You could go and save Trickle."

EggWiff eyes widened. Gathnok was right. This was the thing he wanted most in the world, and he wasn't about to let the opportunity pass him by.

* * *

Morbid had been walking for a while with Message through the desert of the Nether Realm. He was beginning to wonder why he could not see the temple entrance yet. He knew Cupido Sacra was close, because he could feel it. Message was happily walking; he seemed perfectly content to walk for so long.

"Message, are you sure you know which way you're…"

"Father, you're so silly. You keep asking me that!" Message replied with a little giggle.

"I'm not seeing the entrance, and I know the jewel

is nearby." Morbid didn't seem to mind as waves of sand whirled up inside his hooded cloak and around his head.

Message sighed and shook his head. He knew Morbid was new to his role as Death, but seriously, it slightly concerned him how little he knew of his own powers. Message looked at Morbid and smiled. He suddenly grabbed hold of Morbid's reaper and threw it across the desert. It landed in the ground with its blade partly dug in. Morbid didn't say anything and just turned to look at Message. Message stayed looking at the reaper confidently as if he was waiting for something to happen. A few moments passed.

"Umm, maybe it's broken?" Message thought aloud.

"Maybe that was just pointless!" Morbid replied. He didn't have time to waste. The sooner the jewel was destroyed, the sooner everything could disappear, and he wouldn't have to carry the burden of his inheritance any more.

Morbid took a few steps forward to retrieve the reaper, when suddenly the ground began to quake. Morbid stumbled back as he instinctively went over to aid Message, who was looking rather smug at his own brilliance. The ground erupted and broke off as the spot where the reaper had hit was slowly rising. After a while it was clear that a building was opening up from below. It was made of old stone and had four large pillars at the front. An entrance was set in behind the pillars. The roof was sloped at an angle, coming up from the ground and slanting to the top. The reaper was stuck in the centre of the stone building's roof. Message began to cough as waves of sand swirled into the air as it flowed down from the erupting temple.

"Ta da!" Message said, after much spluttering.

"The jewel cannot be inside there. It's far too small."

Message took Morbid's cloak and pulled him around and closer to the temple. He took him between the two middle pillars, which revealed that the dwell entrance did not lead into a small shelter but instead was the top of steps that led down under the ground.

"Oh . . ."

"Yeah, that's just the entrance to the dwell. You'll find your jewel down there!" Message looked a bit saddened by this.

"And my reaper?" Morbid gestured to the still suspended reaper at the tip of the building.

"Oh, you get that back once you've done the test."

"The what?"

"The test – to prove you're worthy to enter the dwell" Message looked up at Morbid "I forgot to tell you about the test, didn't I?"

Morbid nodded.

"Well, in my defence, you're meant to be Death the all-powerful. I figured you'd know about the test."

A blinding flash of light shot out from the temple. Both Morbid and Message instantly knew who it was.

"You're really willing to destroy it all, aren't you?" The grey Elder stood to the side of the reaper. This time it was alone.

"It would be easier for everyone if I did. Just because you value your existence…"

"It's because we value all existence. You have no idea what you're destroying!" The light glowed a darker grey, which showed its anger.

"Then stop me!"

The Elder just hovered and didn't say anything. It was Message who spoke next.

"They can't. They're bound by their own rules never to intervene directly." Message enjoyed having the knowledge of the world around him. To him knowledge was the only real power.

"No, we can't directly intervene, but we can influence the rules."

"You're going to change the test?"

"The test is what it will always be. In order to enter the dwell, you must have an empty heart."

Morbid looked at Message.

"I am Death now. The only person I cared for is gone. My heart will always be empty." Morbid was tired of this banter. He walked right under them and between the pillars. He took a step between the open door way and placed a foot on the first step.

The second he did so, his body was whirled back by the wind that flung him back from inside the temple. He hit the ground with a thud, his arm severed from the socket.

"You sure about that?"

Morbid could see the Elder from where he lay.

"Why did that not work?" Morbid looked over at Message.

"Because of me. It didn't work because of me." Message head hung low in shame. He had long since figured out that the Elder was out to stop them.

"You care for him now, almost like a son. You may be Death, but your heart is far from empty."

Morbid reached over and picked up his arm, although he didn't take his eyes from Message.

"In order to destroy everything, you have to destroy the only thing left that matters to you!"

Morbid stood up and glared at Message.

"However, try doing this without the powers of Death. We feel it's only fair this way." The Elder laughed; the change in power was pleasing.

"You cannot take my powers. That would be intervening. You care too much for your precious balance."

"The one you threaten to destroy?" With this, the Elder

shone a dark rich grey and waved its hands towards Morbid. Grey shots of energy seeped through the Elder's fingertips and whirled around Morbid. Morbid felt a surge of energy swirl through him as the power was intense. He knew he was losing his powers. His cloak disappeared from around him, and the reaper dissolved away from beside the Elder. Morbid crouched on the ground as he adjusted to his loss of power. "Your powers are temporarily stripped. Pass the test, and they shall return."

Morbid was furious. He couldn't comprehend how the Elder was able to do what it had done, but he decided to let himself be defenceless for as short a time as possible. His head turned eerily and stared at Message.

"Father!" Message backed away, as for the first time Morbid was truly terrifying to him.

"I must do what has to be done." Morbid began to walk slowly towards Message. Suddenly the surroundings seemed bleak.

"But why? I mean, if all isn't lost, then why bother? There's still time to make it right." Message began to walk backwards.

"My father is dead. The only way to prevent anyone from going through the pain I feel is to stop it for everyone." Morbid didn't have a plan. His reaper was now gone, and he had no means to dispose of Message. But he'd find one.

"But everyone feels pain. It's how it is. You summoned me to lead you here with all the knowledge of Sahihriar so you could come this far, but with that knowledge, I know that there's so much more than your pain."

"And with all the knowledge you possess, can you tell me for sure that it's better to go on with pain in the world than to end all suffering entirely?"

Message thought. He knew that his only chance of survival was to convince Morbid out of his plan.

Message looked up with his orange eyes through the huge fringe of hair. "I can't . . ."

"Then die!"

Morbid lunged forward and held out his arms to grab Message. Instinctively, Message ran and dived under his arms and rolled out of his way.

"Just because I cannot use magic doesn't mean I won't find a way into that temple. I created you, and I will end you." Morbid struggled slightly to see his Message in so much distress.

"You really have this much conviction in your belief?" Message prepared himself for another attack.

Morbid began to pace towards the small imp being. His determination would be his answer. Morbid was inches from Message and was about to take hold, when Message, without flinching, stood tall and stared into Morbid's hollow eyes.

"Then do what you must do!"

Morbid stopped suddenly.

"Do what must be done! If I cannot argue against your belief, who am I to condemn it? You gave me this life. I cannot choose when it is taken away."

Morbid looked at Message, who was originally nothing more than a guide. Now he had grown into something more, the closest thing to having a son he would ever know.

"Do it quickly, Father."

Message closed his orange eyes and looked at the world around him for the final time. He held on to the hope that his father knew what was best, as all children sometimes do.

* * *

"So you understand the ritual to bring you back?" Gathnok didn't like the thought of EggWiff messing with the time-line, but it was important he go back to give himself that information to awaken the jewel.

"I understand, but if I am successful, then this will all be different, and I shall have no need for it."

"You still don't understand it all, do you?" Gathnok tried not to sound patronizing. EggWiff just gave him a curious look in reply. "This spell will give you knowledge that you may not have meant to possess. Think about your dreams and your visions. Deep down you have always known all of this. It's what led you here."

Gathnok watched as EggWiff sat and contemplated what he said. It was true that his visions and dreams did warn of Morbid's betrayal and the presence of Gathnok. EggWiff disliked the feeling that maybe even with the knowledge of the future, he was powerless to save Trickle. Seeing EggWiff was lost in his thoughts, Gathnok decided to continue.

"This spell requires great use of magic. You shall be weakened when – I mean if – you return."

EggWiff said nothing and simply gave Gathnok an unhappy look.

"There are some rules though. The first time you jump through, make sure you give yourself the knowledge at that moment, as it's the strongest you will feel in the other time."

"I understand." EggWiff was only half listening. He wanted nothing more than to get going so he could fix things – fix Trickle.

Gathnok could see his disinterest. His shadowy form moved swiftly in the night forest and got right up close to EggWiff. "This is serious. Whatever you do, you have to make absolutely sure your past self doesn't see your future self."

EggWiff was desperate to ask why, but he felt it would only further delay his visit to the past.

"You can begin when ready. And if this is some form of trickery, I will find a way to vanquish you." EggWiff spoke rather calmly, but that only added a sense of realism to his words.

From what EggWiff could make out, it appeared that Gathnok nodded. After a while, EggWiff heard the chanting words of Gathnok. He tried his best not to listen to them; they were similar to the words of the spell that would be needed to bring him back, and he didn't want to get confused.

Soon the forest flickered as the energy of the spell formed into a swirling flame-red vortex which appeared to lead into more darkness. EggWiff contemplated doing a protection spell in case this was all a lie, but truth be told, he didn't really care either way. He'd lost everything he had loved.

Without much hesitation, EggWiff left the leaf-strewn ground and stepped inside the vortex. He couldn't help but close his eyes.

EggWiff opened his eyes. It was as if he hadn't been transported to anywhere, or at least he felt like it – if it wasn't for the fact that he could no longer hear the forest noises and he could hear faint cackling and yelling. EggWiff allowed his vision to return and gain focus. As it did so, he was shocked by what he saw.

Laying a few meters away from him was the body of his much younger self, clearly passed out. He noticed that he was surrounded by an arched tunnel made of dirt and earth. He peered to his left and saw that a hole was punctured through. EggWiff looked back and saw the portal out of the Fifth Realm. Although in shock, he didn't have the time to dwell on everything. He went and knelt down by himself. He poked his body lightly with his staff to ensure he was fully passed out. Gathnok's words of warning ran through his mind, but surely it wouldn't matter if he was unconscious?

Seizing the moment, EggWiff began to chant the words which would supposedly give him the knowledge to awaken Cupido Sacra. He was only a few words in, however, when a ball of fire came hurtling through the tunnel wall. Instinctively, EggWiff waved his staff through the ball and shouted "Dispel". The ball of flame instantly popped like a bubble and vanished into nothing. Looking up, EggWiff could see the dragon through the hole. He knew he couldn't continue with this interruption. He stopped kneeling and turned so he was fully facing the dragon.

He knew he didn't have enough time to fight a dragon, even if it were a baby dragon. Instead he used some of the mind links he had used when working with Trickle. He closed his eyes and reached out with his thoughts. He had to be careful he wouldn't connect with his own younger mind, as he was sure (what with his luck) that it would have dire consequences. However, almost instantly he connected with the dragon and confused it to the point it went away.

Taking a deep breath, he turned once more and looked at himself. It wasn't until now that a haunting realisation came over him. All his life he had wondered how he got out of this tunnel, and furthermore, why he had come out of it cursed. The spell to give him his knowledge is what triggered his curse, his differing personalities. His mind spun as it all seemed to fall into place. The knowledge was so well hidden and powerful that his mind created two people to share the burden.

His hands began to tremble as he felt sick to his stomach. For most of his later life, EggWiff had wished nothing more than to be normal. He cried himself to sleep night after night wishing he had the power to take away his curse. How could he bring himself to bring all that future pain onto himself? However, everything so far had supported Gathnok's theory, and if he did this right, then he would have Trickle back soon and she could help him again. She'd make it all right again.

He stood over himself and let the words wash over himself. He closed his eyes and tried not to think of how much pain and anguish he was bringing on himself. He had to think of how it all happens for a reason, how he'd meet Trickle, and it would be worth it - that someone so unique and special would make up for years of pain in only a few weeks. With each word spoken, he could feel the energy seeping down through as he felt a little weaker. Fortunately, the spell was over soon. EggWiff couldn't stop his eyes from filling with tears as his stomach felt like it was doing somersaults. He forced himself to keep his emotion at bay. Instead he bent down and held EggWiff's wrists in his hands. Crouching down, he began to shuffle backwards and in doing so dragged his younger self a long way towards the exit portal. Once by the portal, he managed to prop his younger self up. He winced in pain as the wound in his arm bled through and made itself felt.

"Good luck, Marvie." EggWiff whispered it, knowing too well he couldn't hear himself. With a big effort he managed to push the body through the portal, which closed up rather suddenly behind him.

With the first part of his mission through, he could go and do what he was supposed to do – go and save Trickle and make sure she'd be waiting when he went back. Calming his nerves, EggWiff stepped through the red portal once more, both excited and terrified at seeing his lost friend again.

* * *

Gathnok watched as EggWiff stepped through the portal. He could only pray that whatever changes to the time-line he would make, they'd be for the better. He walked back towards the clearing and saw the others all sitting. Lainla, in her ghostly form, was floating a little way away from Saria, Hail, and Minso. They all managed to look up as they noticed the shadows moving and figured it was him. Saria and Minso instantly clutched their weapon, whilst Hail just tensed up. So far they had made no move to harm them, but they weren't going to take the risk.

"Where's Marvie?" Minso asked abruptly.

"He's busy." Gathnok didn't bother to acknowledge Minso. He was unimportant to him. Instead he went straight over to Lainla.

"Busy being dead?" Saria asked.

"He'll be back soon enough."

"Saria, I know this is difficult, but if we're to stop Morbid, then trusting us has to start now!" Lainla was slightly frustrated by Gathnok's lack of tact in the situation. She also hoped he hadn't just killed EggWiff. She continued to smile at Saria but couldn't help but lean in and whisper in Gathnok's ear, "Tell me he's still alive."

"Of course."

Lainla forced her smile even wider.

"So we wait for him to come back?" Hail was directing the question to Lainla.

"No time. Morbid is seriously close to getting hold of Cupido Sacra. We must head for Magmount. It's the only way we can get through to the Nether Realm in time."

"So you just want us to leave EggWiff?" Saria asked.

"Now is not the time to pretend you care, Amazon."

"It's no pretence. You can't show up here and expect to separate us. We've lost too many people." Saria was stern yet determined.

"With the powers of Death, the temple's traps shall not

hold him back." Gathnok's black face remained transfixed on the little warrior.

"I don't care. We still have a way to go to get to the top of Magmount."

"Surely more reason for us to leave now?" Lainla understood Saria's determination, but she also agreed that they did not have time to spare.

"One hour, we shall wait an hour. If he's not back by then, I will assume you killed him, and we go our separate ways."

All her warrior instinct was aware that both Gathnok and Lainla had managed to divide the group, but she was determined not to let herself be fooled again. Plus, she wanted the time to heal some more, although she made sure that those thoughts didn't show.

Lainla looked over at Gathnok, who had broken his gaze, and looked away with frustration. Lainla was aware that they needed EggWiff, as he was the key. She only hoped he had successfully completed his mission and would be back in time.

"Okay, have your hour." Lainla attempted a smile, as she didn't want to cause further rift between her and Saria. She instead turned and went to calm Gathnok down.

Saria's wound still hurt, so she went back and knelt by the tree. Minso and Hail walked over to join her.

"Think he's still alive?" Hail asked.

Saria looked over at Gathnok and let her hate wash through her. "He had better be!"

* * *

Sapphire, Emerald, and Ruby sat on their dragon beasts and watched as their army jumped from the ledge of Magmount into the portal to the Nether Realm.

"We thank you again, Forlax. You may have just saved us all."

The great Fire Spirit nodded his head. He couldn't believe that the jewel he once loved and knew so well would now cause so much pain and destruction. Truth is, none of them knew what was right any more. It all came down to belief.

"We shall return shortly. Once we have taken care of EggWiff, we shall do as you ask and protect the jewel."

"That jewel wields too much power! Don't be fooled by its temptation." Forlax could almost laugh at the lack of understanding this generation had.

"We shall do what is right. You have our word."

The army of a hundred, which had been kindly provided by the Supreme Court judge, had all jumped through the portal.

Once again the triplets spoke in turn before leaving.

"We…"

"… shall…"

"… win!"

The warriors jumped through the portal to stop Morbid and in their eyes save Sahihriar.

* * *

EggWiff stepped out of the portal and almost walked straight into a tree. He had no idea where he would step out into, but he hoped he had already met Trickle. It was night time where he was, and he was surrounded by a forest. He slowly stepped forward towards what looked like the boundary of the forest. He ducked down, as he knew he couldn't afford to mess it up. He peered out through to a clearing and could see an orange glow in the distance. He saw himself and, more importantly, Trickle sitting on a log not too far from him. Looking round, he saw a shadow pile which he knew to be Flick. He couldn't see Morbid, but he guessed where he was. Being careful not to get too close, EggWiff began to step out of the forest into the edge of the clearing. He remained hidden but was now close enough to make out what they were saying. He caught himself asking Trickle about having everything he wanted. If only he could go and tell himself that all he needed was right in front of him. He sat through the rest of their frustrating conversation and waited for him to leave. Eventually he did. Seeing his chance to go and tell Trickle everything, he decided to take it. He walked round out of the shadow and made sure he didn't bump into his earlier self.

Although his heart pounded as he approached Trickle, he kept thinking of everything to say – how to avoid being taken, how to stay clear of Morbid. EggWiff walked in to the wave of light the fire had produced.

"Jeez, EggWiff, you scared me," Trickle said, as she turned her head in surprise.

EggWiff stopped dead in his tracks. Here she was alive and well, so innocent about everything that was to follow. His eyes widened as all he could do was stare. She looked more beautiful than he could remember.

"You okay, sweetie? What's wrong?" Trickle asked.

He could hardly breathe. How could he do this? He wanted nothing more than for Trickle to be alive and well, but this wasn't right. Deep down, he knew that Trickle would gladly sacrifice her life to give birth to potentially millions more beings. It wasn't his choice or his right to change the world because of her. She wasn't that selfish, and he had no right to be that selfish in her name. It wasn't until he stared at her one final time that he knew all of this. He stopped his staring and broke into a smile.

"Nothing is wrong at all, little one." Saying that again made a tear roll down his cheek as he spoke. "It's important that you know. You are one of the greatest females I have ever met both inside and out." EggWiff smiled, knowing the comfort these words would give her.

As Trickle smiled, EggWiff turned away. He wanted that to be his lasting memory of her.

As he walked away and back into shadow, he had a thought. Morbid was right now asleep against a tree. He hadn't received the powers of Death yet. He was vulnerable and close. EggWiff went and hid in the shadows for a little while. He had to make sure everyone was asleep.

Once he was sure they were, EggWiff walked out and crept along to where Morbid was leaning against the tree. If he ended it now, Trickle and Flick could still be alive, and then they could be more open to, in time, helping Gathnok and Lainla use the jewel. EggWiff walked right up to him. He was careful but also knew that skeletons were heavy sleepers. It would take something rather strong to wake him up. EggWiff stumbled back as a strange sensation came over him. He raised his staff in the hope he could finish Morbid before the moment was lost. EggWiff felt his mind lost again as the green smoke appeared. The only comfort to him this time was that he understood why.

"Ouch! My arm!" EggWiff spluttered loudly as he came to. He immediately noticed the skeleton in front of him! "Whoa!" Remembering Saria's recap of events, he knew that he didn't want to be near Morbid. He swung round and went to run, but in his drunken state he stumbled and knocked into Morbid. With fear fuelling him, the confused EggWiff ran off. He thought he heard a thud, but he didn't dare look back. Instead he just ran. Once in the forest, he figured he could run and hide for long enough until he could go find Saria. However whilst running he wasn't even aware he had stepped back into a red vortex, as the red wave surrounded him and pushed him forward sending him back to his own time. His mission in the past was now complete.

* * *

Morbid turned and faced the Elder. "It is done. Now return my powers!" He stood tall and awaited for the Elder to comply. Now Message was gone, he truly had nothing.

"Or maybe it's more fun this way?" The grey Elder was

displaying more emotion in its voice than an Elder should. The slight sound of vengeful joy in its tone echoed from the top of the temple as the Elder vanished, leaving Morbid weak and defenceless to face the perils of the temple ahead.

"What have you done?"

Chapter Fourteen

A Sacred Past

Wispar opened her eyes and immediately wished she hadn't. She saw standing over them a few dozen Darkmagi. The last thing she remembered was Gathnok and the shimmering compass. The others began to stir awake. Although Wispar knew she should be frightened, she just wasn't. She didn't seem to care, not now Kip was gone. The Darkmagi stood watching over them. They had no weapons this time, and they didn't seem like they were ready to attack. It was Forlax who got to his feet and spoke first.

"He's no longer with us."

"So we can see." The Darkmage still seemed menacing and cold.

"We don't believe one person should hold so much power, not when the prophecy is so questionable." Asemai spoke this time, and she was curious to see how they would respond.

The Darkmage bellowed a shrill laugh. "So now you believe that he's the one to destroy us all."

"We're not sure what we believe, but we won't allow that to happen," Euthan said.

It was all happening so fast. None of them believed Gathnok was evil, and the Darkmagi had been so ruthless. But Gathnok was about to gain all the magic from the Ancients, which seemed dangerous in anyone's hands, let alone someone so young.

"So you tried to stop him?" the voice from darkness asked.

"He stopped us though, and now he's heading for the Ancients. We may be too late to stop any of this," Asemai said as she peered over at the great mountains.

The Darkmage laughed once more; this time it was a loud bellow.

"Why is that funny?" Forlax asked.

"We've been stealing magic all over Sahihriar. Did you really think there was only a handful of us?"

"I don't understand," Wispar added. "Why would there being more make any difference?"

"Because, child, most of us are already with the Ancients." With this, the Darkmage laughed some more as the Spirits looked at one another. Gathnok and Lainla didn't know it, but they were already too late and heading right towards a trap.

* * *

Gathnok and Lainla began to climb the rocky mountains. There was a small old path carved into the mountains which led them up and around towards the steep peak. These ledges were small, however, and were tricky to navigate. Luckily for them, they had the compass. Lainla had been quiet since they left the others. She simply stayed behind Gathnok as the compass lead the way.

"We must be close," Gathnok said, as he almost seemed excited.

"Great!" Lainla attempted a smile, but her voice couldn't hide her worry.

Gathnok stopped and faced her. "What's wrong?" He couldn't cope if she turned on him too.

"It doesn't feel right without him here." Lainla looked so sad.

"Forlax?"

Lainla took Gathnok's hand when she saw the hurt on his face and forced him to look into her eyes. "They weren't wrong what they said. I've felt this . . . this connection since we met. I didn't always want to, and I don't understand it all but I can't . . ."

"It's okay. I understand. I feel it too," Gathnok said with a reassuring smile.

"I just wish we didn't need to hurt him," Lainla said weakly.

"Someone always gets hurt with love," Gathnok replied.

Lainla gave a smile at his words, and suddenly she felt reassured. She did love him. He had so much passion and energy for his quest, not just to save Sahihriar but to help his family. She believed wholeheartedly the goodness in him, and if he were to receive the Ancients' power, then she'd help him control it. She leaned in with her head as her stomach fluttered. She closed her eyes and tilted her head slightly. Gathnok's heart pounded as he moved his hand to gently touch her cheek. Soon their lips were embracing as they fell into a soft, lingering kiss that sent a tingle down Lainla's spine. After a while he pulled away and held his head close to hers.

"We should keep moving," he said softly.

"Yes, we should."

They pulled away from each other's hold and began climbing the mountain. The sun was high in the sky, and the heat was making the climb difficult. But soon the Ancients would imbue the jewel with their magic and everything would be okay again.

"Not so fast, Spirit!"

Gathnok and Lainla watched as three pigs with large spears turned from the mountainside on the path ahead.

"Not you again!" Gathnok wiped the sweat from his brow as he sighed with annoyance.

"I said we'd seek our revenge," the pig snorted, as it glared into their eyes.

Even though they had weapons, it was hard to take the pigs seriously. They were so small and stumpy.

"We won't allow you to go any further, not until you repay your debt," the pig replied, trying to seem as menacing as possible.

"I think you'll recall we did well in defeating you last time," Gathnok said smugly.

"No, I recall you not doing much of anything. It was your friends who held the real power." The pig snorted as it laughed.

Gathnok and Lainla looked at each other. The path they were on was high up on the mountain's edge. The path was also narrow and could just comfortably fit Gathnok and Lainla side by side. It was not the place to have a battle.

"I'm still a spirit. Trust me, you don't wish to do this." Gathnok stared back into the pig's eyes. Truth is, he was bluffing. He'd already lost one jewel, and he hadn't come this far to lose another. He held it tight in his pocket as he hoped the threat of his magic would be enough.

"You lie, Spirit. There's no power in you." The pig nodded its head.

Just as it did so, the two pigs on either side raised their spears and pointed them towards Gathnok and Lainla. They lowered their heads and began to charge at them. They were a little taken aback, but Gathnok managed to step to one side before the spear plunged through him. Lainla, who had proven her warrior skills, stepped to one side and grabbed the spear as it went suddenly past her head. She was about to kick out but

*forgot the weakness in her leg and in a moment lost balance.
The pig snorted as it used this opportunity to swing its weight
on a spear that acted like a lever, pushing Lainla back as she
fell back. She stumbled to hold her weight as she went off the
mountainside.*

*"Lainla!" Gathnok called, as he watched her disappear
from the side of the mountain. Gathnok felt a sudden wave of
anger. It was intense and unlike the energy he had felt before.
The heat of the sun still scorched him, but that wasn't it. This
heat, passion, and anger were coming from within. He felt his
body surge as he grabbed the spear that was being waved at
him. With strength of a thousand men, he easily snapped the
thick wooden spear in two. He turned and instantly kicked out
at the pig who stood by the mountain's edge. Although it was
small and heavy, the pig didn't just fall back, but the force of his
powerful kick sent the pig hurtling through the air and way off
into the distance as it fell. His strength was phenomenal. The
other pig tried to lunge at him, but with his newfound power
it was worthless as Gathnok simply took hold of the pig's body,
raised it up high above his head, and turned to face the third
pig with vengeful hate in his eyes.*

*"So, I was mistaken." The pig trembled as he watched its
fellow pig struggle in Gathnok's grasp. "I beg of you, let us
go. We'll disturb you no more." The pig's eyes were wide with
fear.*

*Gathnok looked at it with disgust as rage and hatred fuelled
his soul. They had taken Lainla and they had ruined Kip's life.
They needed to be punished. He let out a loud cry, and in a
sudden fit of rage he threw the pig down the mountain's edge.
They both could hear the shrill squealing as it fell. Gathnok
breathed heavily as he felt the rage flow through him.*

"Go!" He spoke through gritted teeth.

*The pig trembled as it walked past Gathnok and didn't take
its eyes away from him. Just before it was about to disappear*

behind the winding mountainside, the pig stopped and stared with fear and conviction on its face.

"There is true darkness in your soul, Spirit – true, true darkness." With these words the pig turned and ran away.

Gathnok let the words linger in his mind before sighing as he felt his energy calm slightly. He couldn't believe that Lainla was gone, and he collapsed on the floor as tears swelled in his eyes. He had now lost everything, all for a destiny he didn't ask for. He only had her for a moment, and he couldn't stand to think he'd never look into her eyes...

"What are you so sad about?" Lainla smiled as she turned the corner.

She was struggling with her balance but was up on two feet and slowly walking towards him. Gathnok beamed the biggest smile Sahihriar had ever seen and leapt to her side.

"How?" he asked, baffled by her amazing return.

"I fell onto the lower ledge – almost went right over." She gave a quick smile but winced as her back was in agony.

"I don't know what I would have done if you had." Gathnok kissed her head gently.

"Well, you turned that pig from pink to white with fear, so it must have been something." Lainla was joking as she hadn't witnessed the darkness of Gathnok's actions.

"Yeah." In truth, Gathnok had scared even himself in that moment.

He was brought back to earth by the feeling of warmth in his pocket.

"Can you make it?" he said, indicating the path ahead.

"I got this far, didn't I?" She smiled, but she also held onto his arm as they both continued to climb towards the Ancients.

* * *

"Did you mean what you said about having a team already up there?" Wispar asked, as they travelled with the Darkmagi.

"Yes. It's likely that they are already dead," he said without emotion.

"I hope for your sake that isn't true. If anything has happened to Lainla..." Forlax yelled.

"Then you'd better hope we catch up fast."

The group continued to travel up the mountain, as they hoped that they would be in time to stop a slaughter.

"Watch out!" Euthan swept a protective arm over Asemai and pulled her close to the mountain's edge.

Squealing, a pig fell right past them from above as it continued towards the bottom of the mountain.

"Well, that was strange!"

Asemai was cut off as another pig squealed its way past them. There was a moment's silence as they took in the odd occurrence.

"Why is it raining pigs?" Forlax asked.

"I don't know, but I bet Gathnok has something to do with it."

"Which means they might still be alive," Forlax said hopefully, as he vowed to save Lainla.

"It means nothing. We must continue." The Darkmage was not amused by their banter.

They continued to walk further up the mountain, when they heard some sort of snorting sound. The Darkmage who lead at the front raised his arm and signalled them to stop. They could not yet see what made the sound. They stood for a moment in the heat as the wind gave no breeze. They were anticipating perhaps a small army of pigs but were all surprised when they only saw one, with tears streaming from its face. The pig looked up and saw them all. Its eyes looked so lost, and it looked pale with fright.

"He holds true darkness." *The pig spoke through sobs.*

The front Darkmage stepped forward as Wispar guessed what he might do.

"Stop!" *she yelled, as she looked at the frightened pig. The Darkmage turned its hooded head to look at her.* "Let him go. He's not a threat," *Wispar urged, as she refused to let more people suffer. She still hated pigs, but even Kip wouldn't want a life wasted.*

The Darkmage stopped and took a step back, allowing the pig to walk past freely. As it did so, Asemai just felt confirmed in what she already knew. Gathnok showed signs of evil.

* * *

Gathnok smiled as he felt the compass became intensely warm in his hand. He knew that he was moments from the Ancients as the compass needle began to move slightly and focused in on their exact location. They were also a fair bit up the mountain. He had noticed before that the mountain seemed to have a great ledge on its side, with part of the mountain hollowed out making what would seem like a large platform above. He figured that was the place, and if he was right, they'd be turning onto it very soon. He held back his hand as Lainla gave it a reassuring squeeze, and he felt in his pocket for the dormant jewel. Cupido Sacra was resting weightily where he left it. He clutched it inside his pocket and held the compass in the other hand before turning the corner.

They turned onto to what was a large stone platform made from the expanded ledge of the mountain and the hollowed-out space of the mountainside. However, Gathnok and Lainla were shocked at what they saw. Sitting on what looked like stone carved stools were the eight Ancients, dressed in their white robes. They were old in appearance and looked frail, much as Saban did back in the cabin. Their seats were placed in a circle so that they could all face one another like some sacred council.

The Ancients, however, were not alone. Standing behind them in a larger circle were Darkmagi in their deeply coloured robes. The Ancients didn't move or even acknowledge Gathnok was there. Neither did the Darkmagi.

"Welcome, Gathnok." One of them spoke as he stepped into the centre.

"Release them," he said, staring at the Ancients.

They were not moving, because they were old and didn't need to move. They held great magic, but only Gathnok had the power to truly defeat them.

"Give us Cupido Sacra and then we shall have no need to kill them." He waved his hand at the Ancients.

Gathnok took a step forward. "We could all just walk away, and then no one would need to die." It was his final attempt to stop them. He didn't want to have to fight.

"With magic left in Sahihriar, you'd be able to fulfil the prophecy. You'll destroy Sahihriar with that jewel."

"The prophecy said that we'd also stop the destruction of Sahihriar. We can't both be right." Gathnok took another step closer as he spoke.

"It's not a risk we are willing to take."

"So I see." Gathnok took one step closer and was now standing close to the sitting Ancients with only a few meters between them. There was a slightly larger gap between him and the Darkmage. Lainla watched on and hoped that whatever Gathnok was planning would work.

"The jewel" The Darkmage put out his hand and held it there.

Gathnok looked around. He was surrounded by Darkmagi who could kill all the Spirits in seconds. Three of them had begun to move in around them; they were close to the cliff edge. Lainla moved back and began to lose balance and found herself kneeling down. Gathnok knew there were too many to fight, and he couldn't risk Lainla. He noticed the Darkmage's hands were exposed and couldn't help feel this was some kind of taunt. Feeling his heart pounding in his chest, he took a couple of steps forward and took out Cupido Sacra from his pocket. He got inches away from handing it over before he stopped and glared into the mask.

He leaned in and whispered with bitter intensity.
"You took my sister!"

He immediately turned and threw the jewel towards one of the Ancients. He waited with bated breath as one eye watched Cupido Sacra soar through the sky, whilst his left arm instinctively shot out and touched the bare flesh of the Darkmage's face. The other Darkmagi responded immediately and stepped forward, each ready to drain the magic from the Ancients. Luckily, the Ancient seemed ready somehow and caught the jewel in a sudden grasp. As soon as he did so, the other Ancients held out their arms which almost completed the circle, leaving Gathnok inside. The Darkmagi ran and touched the Ancients, but as they did so, they were flung back as they each began to glow a pure white, not too dissimilar to the way the shimmering compass did. Gathnok felt a surge of power as they continued to glow brighter and brighter. The Darkmagi were unable to break the powerful spell. Gathnok sat down low as the beacon of light shot up from the mountain's edge. Lainla just looked on in awe. Soon they shone so bright that Gathnok could see them begin to almost dissolve in front of him. It was like what happened to the Darkmagi once they had been touched, but this seemed more gentle and natural, as if they were somehow changing form.

Soon one of the Ancients seemed nothing more than a pure light dancing in the air, before it suddenly swept down and into Cupido Sacra. The jewel began to glow and haze with a taint of green, and it slowly elevated itself from the ground. Soon another Ancient had taken himself into the jewel, which continued to hover in the circle as it filled with more light and power. The scene was magnificent, as Gathnok was surrounded by pure and total energy, and vapours of light danced around him before being swept into the jewel. He managed to stand up. The light was no longer blinding as the Darkmagi looked on. Cupido Sacra was floating at shoulder height as the last of the Ancients went inside. Now it glistened with a green glow, and Gathnok could feel its power just from being near it.

"Stop!" a Darkmage called, before Gathnok could take hold of the jewel. "Think about what you're doing. You'd be killing hundreds of beings."

"At least you're not innocent." Gathnok looked at Lainla, who gave an admiring smile.

Taking one last look at the figures that haunted him, he reached out his hand and took hold of the awakened jewel. As soon as he did so, Gathnok felt power like he couldn't imagine. It was beyond anything he had felt as a spirit. It was overwhelming and intense, and it felt as if his body was breaking apart and his soul was in control, as though he was not limited any more. He cried out. The power was too much, but the magic held him on. It glowed slightly, and then suddenly a large green pulse of light shone, almost like a ring of light, emerged from the jewel. It spread further, and as soon as it touched the Darkmagi, each one vanished, like shadows when exposed to light. The pulse travelled, however, and continued to spread across the mountain, hitting the Darkmagi who were close to the mountain's ledge.

"He did it!" Euthan announced, in shock at the disappearance of the Darkmagi.

"What? What does this mean? It's over?" Forlax asked the others.

"Not yet, it's not," Asemai replied, more determined to stop Gathnok now he had so much power.

They continued to climb as the pulse spread across Sahihriar, destroying every Darkmage it touched and, as it did so, releasing their energy back into the planet, keeping it safe once more.

"You did it," Lainla said, as she ran over to Gathnok.

He was kneeling on the ground and seemed out of breathe, but he was alive and was holding Cupido Sacra in his hands. She bent down and looked at him. He had shown so much bravery and risked everything for his belief. She kissed him and helped him to his feet, where he embraced her. They stood standing in each other's arms as Gathnok sighed with relief. He had held the weight of Sahihriar on his shoulders for too long, and now finally it was over. Now he could relax and begin to build a new and normal life.

"Well done!" Asemai said, as the other three stood behind her. They had just appeared round the corner and onto the mountain's ledge. Gathnok and Lainla immediately let go of each other and faced them.

"I did it! We stopped them," Gathnok said with a smile, yet there was something so distant in their eyes.

"We know. Now all you have to do is destroy Cupido Sacra," Asemai said, and she stepped forward.

"We can't destroy it. It holds too much power . . ." Gathnok began.

"We don't know what that would do," Lainla added. "Look, we've done what we came to do. Let's just all go home."

"How can we trust that he won't fulfil the prophecy with so much power? Why won't you give it up?" Wispar looked at him curiously.

"Because that's not how it's meant to be," he replied. "Cupido Sacra is safe in my hands."

"Only for now I fear," Asemai said, with almost a sadness on her face.

"Please, please don't do this. I'm just so done," Gathnok said, as he forced the tears back from his eyes.

"We can't allow one person to hold so much, not with knowing what could be . . ." Asemai nodded and braced herself for battle, as did the others behind her.

Gathnok wasn't that worried. He felt the power of Cupido Sacra and knew it could defeat them. He was just so saddened by the fact they couldn't see the good in him. They didn't trust him enough to make sure he'd do the right thing.

Gathnok felt a sudden gust of wind build up towards him, and he could see the small wind force shoot towards him and

Lainla. He immediately focused, and instantly Cupido Sacra shone and revealed a light green shield that appeared in front of both him and Lainla. The wind hit it, but the barrier remained strong. Soon all of the Spirits were using everything they had against the shield. Water, fire, stones from the mountain's walls all pounded the green shield, which seemed weakened by the full force of the Spirits. Gathnok screamed as he held the barrier in place. He tried to stay grounded, but he felt the magic pushing him back as the barrier was weakened and his feet struggled against the force. Gathnok suddenly felt weak. It was too much power too soon, and he let go of his control over the barrier. He knelt down weak as Lainla still stood by his side. The Spirits stopped their full-on attack and watched the weakened Gathnok .

"It's not too late," Wispar said.

"Destiny says otherwise," Gathnok replied.

Flames flickered towards only Gathnok, but he was quick to wave the jewel and create a small barrier which blocked the attack. He was hit by rocks which began to pelt at him, but they too were quickly blocked, although Gathnok could feel himself getting weaker. Forlax was getting mad and was tired of using magic. He was soon sprinting towards Gathnok with fury in his eye. If magic wouldn't defeat him, then maybe his hands would. He was moments from him before Lainla stood in front of him and stared Forlax in the eye.

"Leave him be." She spoke with confidence.

"Stand aside. You still choose to protect him. After everything?" Forlax yelled.

"I choose to protect Sahihriar. That is what he has done." Lainla couldn't understand why they couldn't see the good in Gathnok.

"After everything, I find I don't know who you are," Forlax said.

Lainla was hit with a punch of emotion. She grew up with

319

Forlax. They had shared a childhood. For him to say that meant they had truly lost one another.

"I could say the same." Lainla's lip trembled as the tears formed.

Suddenly a shot of water hurtled past her and hit Gathnok with tremendous force. He wasn't expecting it and went flying across the large stone ledge and tumbled across the rocky surface. Lainla gasped as she ran to him. He still held Cupido Sacra, but he was weak. His magic felt drained, and so did his body. He didn't even have the energy to get up.

"I'm sorry it came to this." Asemai genuinely looked sincere in her words as Lainla and Gathnok watched the Spirits raise their hands for their final blow. Both of them shut their eyes and held on to one another. Even with Cupido Sacra, they weren't powerful enough to stop them.

The Spirits were moments from unleashing their fury, when suddenly a small light shone across the ledge, and they all turned to see what had occurred. Each of them was stunned by what they saw. Standing on the ledge were two beings completely smothered in a white glow. No features could be distinguished, and they gently glided above the ground. They weren't completely white, as each one had a tainted glow. The one on the right had a taint of purple, whilst the one on the left had a taint of orange. Not knowing how they knew, each of the Spirits stopped immediately and knelt on one knee. They were in the presence of gods. They were in the presence of the Elders.

"You must stop this, Spirits." The soft purple Elder spoke. Its voice was soft and gave no indication of gender or emotion. However, it was warming and comforting.

"We were merely trying to help Sahihriar, to stop the prophecy," Asemai said, still knelt down with her head facing low.

"We know. However, prophecies will always come to pass no matter how hard we try. It's what separates them from

stories. *In your betrayal, you turned against your calling as spirits and risked the safety of Sahihriar."*

"*We were trying to protect it,*" Forlax said in a slightly harsher tone than he should have used.

"*Your fate has been decided. We recognise your loyalty as spirits, but your freedom is a liability we cannot allow for. You will continue as spirits, but you will be rooted to Sahihriar, stripped of your freedom.*" The orange tainted Elder also spoke without distinction.

"*I don't understand!*" Wispar said, daring to stare at both of them.

"*It isn't for you to understand.*"

With these words, the Elder waved its arm in front of the Spirits as they each vanished with the Elder to begin their punishment. Gathnok and Lainla stood up despite being left with the purple Elder. They were both worried they too would be punished.

"*Well done, child. You have saved magic and kept Sahihriar safe.*" The purple Elder spoke with a hint of emotion, almost pride.

"*So we were right. The other prophecy isn't true?*" Lainla asked.

"*I wouldn't worry about prophecy. Just worry about him.*"

The Elder waved its arm, and suddenly baby Marvie appeared in his cot in front of Gathnok. He beamed a smile of joy and shrieked his name before carefully scooping him up into his arms. He closed his eyes as he thanked Saban for keeping his promise.

"*We shall take you three to the Fifth Realm. There you can watch over the realm and live in peace. Cupido Sacra shall remain with the Heart that can wield it.*"

Gathnok held Marvie and looked at Lainla. He had saved Sahihriar and managed to find something he had lost, a family.

Staring into each other's eyes, they felt a strange sensation as the Elder waved them to the other realm before too disappearing.

The mountains were empty, and Sahihriar continued to turn. The sun and moons continued to rise and fall as there was no longer anything to threaten the balance of this land. Their quest had finally ended.

* * *

Saban stood in the white space next to Death as both of them knew what had just occurred in Sahihriar.

"Interesting, isn't it, that he doesn't know?" Saban said casually to Death.

"What? That he was destined to save Sahihriar?" Death replied.

"No, that he is still destined to destroy it, and you must make sure it happens."

* * *

Morbid walked down the steps. The walls were damp and moist, and the stones were covered in sand. The steps only led down into darkness, as the only light was that of the entrance. Morbid wasn't sure what was in store for him in the tomb, but he was sure it would be full of traps. He had no real remorse for killing the imp, as it was his place to do so; after, all it was he that had summoned him. Besides, once he destroyed the jewel, then all of Sahihriar and everything else would be destroyed. And then only then could Death be a thing of the past.

As he walked carefully down, he tried his best not to trip on the sand. If he were to fall now, then he may not be able to reassemble himself, especially without his powers. He couldn't get over how the Elder was able to interfere like that. It went against the balance and every sacred belief of Sahihriar. However, what he was about to do meant that rules would probably no longer apply.

* * *

They stood around waiting for EggWiff to reappear. The sun would be rising soon, and they knew they'd have to leave. They were all aware they were embarking on something larger than themselves, but it was enough they had each found a larger cause that was worth fighting for.

Emae had fallen asleep and was slumped on the floor. Minso was sat propped up against her and had also fallen asleep. He hadn't meant to, but he had recently achieved his lifelong mission, discovered a lost legend to his people, and had been told he'd never see the people he loved again. It was understandable he'd be exhausted. Gathnok and Lainla remained chatting to one another. Saria, whose pain had decreased somewhat, was staring at Gathnok in case he would try something. Hail did very little. He would normally have prayed, but since losing his faith he had no reason to try. Instead he sat and let his mind wander on the vision. Although still so painful, he was desperately trying to make some sense of it, refusing to believe it was now a vision of the future he was fighting for.

"Arggghh!" EggWiff had popped out of the bushes in a speeding flash as he sprinted. His drunkenness and lack of pace made him buckle, and he tripped. EggWiff skidded and landed at the feet in front of the others. "Ouch, that hurt! I think I need a drink!"

Minso woke up in the commotion. Saria sat up and walked over. Her movement didn't give much pain, which was a relief. She went over to EggWiff as the others watched.

"Morbid is back there. I saw him and ran," EggWiff panted, still lying flat on the ground.

"What? You just saw Morbid?" Minso was looking at this mad imitation of the Marvie he knew.

"Yep! However, I don't think he followed." EggWiff was stumbling all over the place. His voice also constantly changed in tone and volume.

"Should we panic?" Minso said, immediately holding up his wooden disc.

"No!" Gathnok stepped forward. "He's just confused after his mission. However, he's just proven it was a success." Gathnok's shadowy form showed no indication he was pleased. It seemed he struggled to let go of his evil persona.

"You okay, WiffEgg?" Hail asked, helping him up.

"My name is EggWiff, and who are you to call me a liar? Huh? Huh?" EggWiff started getting very loud towards Gathnok.

"EggWiff, calm down!" Saria placed out her arm to stop the drunken wizard from lunging at Gathnok and Lainla.

"What are you doing? They are the evil ones, remember! He had me in a cage." EggWiff was confused. Why were they now with the enemy?

"It's changed now. We're here to help." Lainla tried a comforting smile.

"And who are you?" EggWiff stared at the ghost.

"Oh that's right. We've never met. I'm Lainla, Spirit of Magic."

"Well, I suggest a change in job!"

Lainla gave him a confused look.

"Well, from what I can gather, Death has gone off on one, and magic is just confusing!" EggWiff was using Saria's weight to support himself upright.

Lainla couldn't help but smile. As much as she hated to admit it, there was a lot of truth in what EggWiff was saying.

"Look, we need to go to Magmount. We have to stop Morbid before it's too late." Minso began to pat Emae to gently wake her up whilst he made sure his satchel was properly secured. Minso showed little patience for the drunken EggWiff.

"You think you can manage that EggWiff?" Saria asked.

"No, I'm not going!"

"What?"

"I'm tired of this. All I ever do is get into stupid situations. I've been fighting odd things, I've been in a cage. I've had shadows after me, and now you want me to go fight Death. No!" EggWiff had sat himself down at this point and was examining his empty bottle rather disappointedly.

The others stood watching him, wondering how they would do this when the key refused to come.

* * *

Sapphire, Emerald, and Ruby flew on their small dragons, closely followed by the army of a hundred. These warriors were kitted out for a battle, all with the customary silver armour, shields, and swords. The sisters stopped when they saw the raised temple entrance. They halted the dragons and turned them back so they were facing the army. Sapphire raised her arm, and the army stopped dead in its track.

The triplets then flew over the great army and called out their instructions.

"You're to stay where you are . . ."

". . . and to guard the temple entrance . . ."

"No one is to get through!"

Some of the greatest warriors of Sahihriar were in the army of a hundred, and the triplets had been in charge of them for years and knew of their loyalty. They swung down by the entrance of the temple and dismounted from the dragons. They left the three dragons to guard the entrance for further security as they each walked round behind the temple entrance.

"We should be paid a high price for this, Sisters." Sapphire didn't like the desert. The heat and dryness made it difficult to perform as a warrior.

"Indeed, how is your wound?" Ruby noted that the bird's claw marks were still visible and cut into Sapphire's arm.

"Better. I think being frozen by his spell may have helped." Sapphire didn't like to think that any criminals were helpful.

"I still don't see why we don't just go get the jewel now. With its power, we'd easily be able to fend of those bands of freaks." Emerald was stretching as she spoke.

It was now evident that the triplets speaking in unison only happened when they were addressing other people.

"Because that is not what we were ordered to do. The council told us to kill EggWiff, Morbid, Trickle, and Flick." Sapphire had held out the parchment which had their names written on it.

"Yes, but only the wizard remains," Ruby replied.

"That doesn't change our mission. We shall retrieve Cupido Sacra once the criminal has been dealt with. Understood?" Sapphire gave a glare towards Emerald.

"Yes, of course!" Emerald replied with a hint of annoyance. She couldn't help being drawn to the power of the jewel.

* * *

"EggWiff, we don't have time!" Saria was still standing by him.

"Then go without me. I'll just go and get a drink!" EggWiff got up and prepared to leave.

"You cannot leave. We need you. You're the…"

Hail coughed loudly to interrupt Saria. The drunken wizard was already unwilling to travel with them. He didn't need the pressure of knowing his importance. Understanding his point, Saria turned back round to EggWiff.

"Look, I swear you can get some drink once you have come with us. You don't even need to fight Morbid." Saria was actually surprised by her patience. Not too long ago she would have killed him for his selfishness and moved on.

"You promise I can get some drink?"

"Saria we have to leave now!" Gathnok's frustration over further delay was clear.

"Oh, shut up! Go stand by a flame or something." EggWiff smiled at his own joke.

Hail couldn't help but give a small chuckle. It was nice to see someone stand up to the man who caused him so much fear.

"Yes, I promise." Saria tried to smile but she wasn't in the habit of doing it.

"Okay, let's go!"

They all began to stand up and ready themselves for the long steep climb up MagMount. The Iciliks Mountain was much smaller, so this would be a harder climb. Also, with every step the heat would become more unbearable.

"I shall go straight to the top with Lainla. We shall start to convince Forlax to let us through." Gathnok's voice was very demanding.

"No, we don't separate from now on. We all must stick together."

"We don't have the time!" Gathnok's face darkened as it was clear his frustration was increasing.

"Well, we have what you need." Minso had now joined in to help Saria. "So it looks like you have little choice."

Although new to the group, Minso was beginning to understand things a little more clearly. He liked the strength the Amazon showed, and despite his dislike of EggWiff's condition, his loyalty was to him.

"Very well, but that means you can't fly off on your bird either."

Gathnok was aware this was a lame retort, but he struggled with his helplessness. He so loved being by Lainla's side, and the comfort he got just from looking at her was enough, but at the same time they were fighting for something much larger now, and their lack of understanding grew tiresome.

Minso didn't care to get into an argument with Gathnok and merely nodded his agreement. Saria looked over at him and appreciated his help. Truth is, Saria was just getting tired of all of this. Gathnok and Lainla walked up front. Minso and Saria walked almost side by side with Emae flying closely above them. Hail and EggWiff trailed behind as Hail helped support the light-footed EggWiff.

* * *

Meanwhile, up high on MagMount the great Fire Spirit Forlax was enjoying watching over Sahihriar. It was his job to ensure that every lit flame would light a spark and then create fire. If not, then the sacred balance would be heavily damaged. He and his brother and sisters must all work peacefully together to ensure the stability of the world. Forlax often thought how clever the Elders were to conduct such a fitting punishment, yet he was revolted by the fact Gathnok and Lainla went free. Something made Forlax pause. Gathnok! Just as he was thinking of his former friend, his fiery mind swirled and burnt a scorching blue flame. Forlax could sense that Gathnok had returned and was climbing to the peak. Forlax laughed at the notion; surely he must know that even without using his powers Forlax was powerful enough to sense him coming. However, the fact he dared try enraged Forlax as the molten lake began to boil and rise. Forlax wasn't going to allow himself to be disturbed any further – least of all to allow him Cupido Sacra back. Although no one could hear it, Forlax laughed to himself as he put in place Magmount's greatest defence to finally rid himself of Gathnok.

* * *

Morbid was walking down the steps. He wondered if it were some form of a trick as the steps didn't seem to end. He could sense the power of Cupido Sacra nearby, but he knew it would be protected by magic and traps, possibly created by Gathnok. Eventually the steps became larger and fewer, and soon Morbid found himself at a small stone door. He allowed his small skeleton fingers to brush against the door to see if there was a handle or some way of opening it. The door, however, quickly sprang into life and slowly began to rise upwards, creating an eerie sound. Small pockets of sands spilt out from the doorway as the door slid open. Morbid stopped still. When it came to traps, there were always two ways it could go. One would be a trap to stop you entering the room, which meant the room was likely to be safer. On the other hand, if it's easy to get into the room, it's likely to be impossible to get out. Realizing he had little or no choice, Morbid walked into the room.

His first thought was that the ground seemed solid and not likely to fall away from under him. He looked around. Instead of being in a large room, he seemed to be in a dimly lit tunnel, although this wasn't going downwards, and after a couple strides he seemed to be at a crossroads. Looking around, he realized that all the corridors looked the same – identical, in fact. Morbid sighed. It appeared he was in a labyrinth. With the powers of Death, the maze would have been no challenge, but as Morbid he was as helpless as any mortal. He began to walk down one of the corridors. He then would turn, turn, and then turn again. He forced his mind to remember his steps, as he didn't want to lose the entrance he had just come in by. Coming to a dead end, he turned and began to retrace his steps. It didn't take long for Morbid to realise he was lost in the labyrinth. He began to feel a sense of isolation, as no sounds could be heard. The corridors were lit with small flames hanging from the wall, which must have been kept lit by magic. Morbid continued to look around in sheer frustration. With every second, he was wasting more time. He knew Gathnok and EggWiff would be after Cupido Sacra by now. He wanted to kick the walls. He wanted to use his powers but couldn't. Instead he knelt down. He needed to out-think the labyrinth, and he was sure there would be a way. He allowed himself to get lost in thought to find a solution to his problem.

* * *

The grey Elder was worried. It knew that by binding Morbid's powers it had broken every sacred rule of Sahihriar. However, the being believed that these were desperate times. If they were to ensure their creation, then Morbid must be stopped and Gathnok must use Cupido Sacra. How could the rules apply when nearly all hope was lost? The Elder wasn't going to allow Morbid to win nor to lose the chance for an infinite number of lives to exist once Sahihriar was gone.

The god-like being was sitting in the First Realm. It was a realm full of dark and mysterious creatures. It was often noted as being the mirrored realm to the Second Realm, as they were the complete opposites of each other. The Elder was sitting waiting. It could sense that the other Elder was following it. However, they were equal in power, and so all it needed to do was keep hiding long enough for Gathnok to win. The grey Elder sighed as it sat in the blackened ogre's cave; the being could sense its company.

"What have you done?"

"What must be done," the grey Elder replied, not even bothering to look back.

"I understand why you may wish to stop Morbid…"

"It has nothing to do with that." This time the grey Elder did look back. The Elder wasn't being clouded by feelings of the past. Stopping Morbid was the right thing to do despite the rules.

"Then why do it? We're not supposed to directly intervene." The blue Elder reached out to place a hand on the grey Elder's shoulder in comfort. However, the grey Elder knew it was bound to be lectured on the rules of interference. It didn't wait for the blue Elder to continue, but instead the grey Elder shimmered away. At least it could perhaps buy some time until Morbid could be stopped.

The blue Elder that remained wouldn't allow emotion to control it. Overpowering its emotions, the being used its powers to sense where the other Elder was hiding. It was annoyed to find it was no longer in the First Realm, which meant an actual search was needed. The Elder shimmered away to follow and get some real answers.

* * *

Lainla, Gathnok, EggWiff, Hail, Saria, and Minso had been travelling for some time. They were only one third of the way up Magmount, and the intense heat made it difficult for them to walk. Lainla and Gathnok remained in the lead, as the heat didn't affect either of them. The others, however, were sweating. Hail was trying to remember how cold he had been in the Iciliks Mountain, hoping he could convince his body to be that cold again. A pig's skin wasn't very thick. EggWiff was in the middle. He was absolutely exhausted as

331

his mind throbbed and the heat made him tired. He was trying to focus on how long it would be till he had a drink. He still wasn't sure about travelling with the shadow. The ghost unnerved him. The only person he really felt okay with was the Amazon, but he still missed the old group.

"You should be more patient with them." Lainla didn't want to provoke Gathnok, but she was hoping to get rid of more of the evil within him.

"We don't have time for their odd ways."

"It wasn't even a day ago you were out to kill them. You must understand their distrust." Lainla went to place a comforting hand on his arm, but it just waved through.

Gathnok attempted a smile. Since being reunited with Lainla, the shadows in his face had slightly more definition; although not close to being clear, some of his features could be seen.

"A day ago I didn't know about the full situation."

Lainla stopped and turned to Gathnok. "That wasn't my fault. You still blame me for that?"

Gathnok stopped and turned. "You were back. You were here the whole time and did nothing. Too busy being Death's pawn."

The rest of the group stopped upon hearing Gathnok shout.

"I couldn't come find you. I was busy making sure that this lot didn't stop you from using Cupido Sacra!"

"Or you didn't want to come find me." Gathnok stared into Lainla's face. If Sahihriar was to be destroyed soon, it would be better if they were honest.

Lainla stopped and glared. Her ghostly features looked furious. "You selfish man, I didn't ask to die. I was happy with you, and you know that. I also didn't ask to be brought back. Don't stand there and act like any of this is easy for me."

"Don't…"

"Shut up! You've said enough. If you can stand there and believe I like any of this, then you just ruined a beautiful memory of a time that couldn't be touched."

Gathnok was going to argue, but he could see the pain on Lainla's face. Even though a ghost, Lainla was still able to cry, and she did. She floated away towards the back of the group. Gathnok watched, before continuing to walk in the intense heat. Lainla was now walking by Saria. This made Saria uneasy. She could see Lainla was upset, but she wasn't sure she was ready to comfort her. There was something about stabbing someone and killing them which seemed to damage a friendship.

"You alright?" Minso was looking at the upset ghost.

"I shall be. Thank you." Lainla smiled at Minso and then glanced at the silent Saria. She didn't blame her for her lack of compassion.

"I cannot go any further! I need to rest." Hail was talking more to himself than anyone in particular. He had learnt he wasn't important enough to be listened to.

"Do you wish us to stop?"

Hail almost stopped with shock, as Gathnok for the first time had shown him some sense of compassion.

"Don't talk to me. Not after what you did." Hail's snout crinkled in disgust.

"What great pain did I cause to you?"

Hail stopped and glared at him, causing the rest of the group to stop again.

"This is bloomin' gonna hurt my legs soon!" EggWiff muttered.

"You invaded my mind. You took the unholy steps to make me do your bidding." Hail walked in close and peered into his eyes. "You took my faith."

"Faith doesn't come in objects and armies. If you had real faith, then nothing I could do would change it."

"You took the Essence."

"And what was the Essence? What did it really do? Faith can only come from you. Don't blame me if you're not strong enough." Gathnok turned to walk back.

Hail stopped and let his words wash over him. He refused to believe what he said and was filled with anger and rage. Suddenly he couldn't hold back any longer. Hail found himself lunging towards to Gathnok in rage. Gathnok turned and saw the pink figure lunging towards him and managed to shift his shadowy form out of the way. Hail landed with a thud on the mountain ledge. Gathnok was about to hold out his blackened hand, when a loud cry could be heard from Magmount's peak. Gathnok immediately recognized it to be Forlax.

"What was that?"

Saria and Minso immediately took out their weapons. Gathnok and Lainla shared a look of worry. They understood all too well Forlax's fury. EggWiff in his drunken form kept looking at the mountain peak, scared of what was to come. Hail didn't even get up and instead looked around. Minso was about to suggest going to take a look on Emae, but was interrupted by the sound of quiet rumblings. Soon it got louder as the ground beneath them began to shake. They each looked up and soon they could see it – hundreds of giant molten boulders, most of them twice the size of Saria, were rolling fast down the slope. They had only a moment to respond. Minso didn't even react first. It was Emae who flew down, and Minso leapt on top of the bird. Saria looked at the frightened EggWiff. If he were the key, then his safety was vital. Instinctively she rolled towards him. She managed to slice one smaller boulder with her sword before the other stronger ones appeared moments after. EggWiff just clung onto his staff and closed his eyes. He didn't remember saying words, but he felt a wave of energy go through him. Saria opened her eyes and saw they were both protected by a magical barrier. They were soon surrounded by the molten boulders as they came from both sides, smashed into the barrier at the front, and then rolled over the top. Gathnok in his shadow state managed to weave in amongst the boulders with ease. Lainla in her ghostly form gasped as a huge boulder came towards her. She felt strange as she remembered that she wouldn't be hit; instead they all went through her as if she was air. They were all protected in some way from the burning crashing rocks, except for Hail. He had no magic's to protect him and instead could just lie on the ground, as the rocks continued to bury him.

* * *

Morbid had walked around for about an hour and was very lost and very confused. He knew there must be some way out, but he'd never find it without any powers. The corridors taunted him by showing a gap above them. He had tried to climb them, but the stone walls were too damp, and finding a grip was impossible. If only there was some way to get over the walls, he thought. He made one final attempt as he leapt onto the wall. His thin white fingers had nothing to grip as his whole body slid and fell. Although unable to show any emotion, he was very frustrated. He was so close to Cupido Sacra, and he had very little time left. If he could get over the wall, then he'd be high enough to see his way through the labyrinth. Morbid stopped as something in his hollow head clicked into place. He didn't need to go over the walls, just be able to see what was on top of them. He knew already that his body couldn't manage it, but there was no reason why his head couldn't. Morbid stood back and looked up at the wall. He only had one shot at getting this right, and he hadn't come this far to ruin it. Slowly and carefully he raised his arms and took off his skeleton head from his neck. With his head firmly in his own grip, he swung his arms a few times for practice. On the third swing he timed it well and let go, flinging his own head up into the air. The head landed with a thud on top of the thin labyrinth walls. Morbid knew the chances of landing upright were slim, so he accepted the fact his view was from sideways. This didn't matter. For now he could see the entire shape of the labyrinth and the way he had to go.

Although detached, his body and mind were still linked by his spirit which continued through his skeleton frame. His body didn't move as well as usual, but it did move, which meant that Morbid was able to tell himself which way to move. After falling over twice and a mishap with one of the flaming torches, he found that his body had made its way to the wall in front of him. Morbid took one more look and tried to work out the next few turnings. Hoping he had memorized it correctly, Morbid began quickly opening and closing his jaw. His head tilted, moved, and slid off, being caught by his own hands. He knew that it was a lengthy process and all of it was a reminder of how frustrating it was to be powerless. But at the same time, at least Morbid knew he had found a way to solve the labyrinth.

* * *

Minso touched down on the mountain's walkway. The avalanche had lasted a good few minutes as Minso hovered above helpless to watch. Gathnok and Lainla appeared from the rocks below, and it seemed they were both unharmed. They looked at Minso, who nodded as a sign of his safety. They didn't wait long before EggWiff and Saria erupted from the boulders.

"I must deserve a drink for that."

"Yeah, I reckon you do!" Saria held out her hand to help the wizard step out from the enclosed huddle of boulders.

"You two okay?" Minso asked. He couldn't help but have a surprised look on his face.

"Yeah, it turns out WiffEgg knows some magic of his own," Saria said with a level of seriousness as she brushed small crumbs of rubble from her warrior garments.

Everyone stared at EggWiff with surprise.

"I wasn't actually kidding about that drink." EggWiff hoped with so much attention that someone would actually listen. His sober head was beginning to get on his nerves.

"Where's Hail?" Saria was looking around and was now ignoring EggWiff.

The group stared blankly at her.

"I bet he didn't have time to get up. Lainla, go look below." Gathnok's voice was soft and not demanding.

"Of course." Lainla immediately swung down, and her transparent body dived through the rocks. It only took a few seconds before she saw pinkish skin trapped under the pile. She then floated back up. "He's down there and doesn't appear to be moving." Lainla looked at Gathnok. It wasn't that she had forgotten the harsh words that were spoken, but for many years she had stood by Gathnok's side in many a dire situation.

"I'll get him out." Saria stepped forward to start lifting boulders when she stopped and felt a twinge of pain as she looked down at her side.

"You're bleeding." Lainla looked at her friend concerned.

"I'm fine," Saria said, although she no longer tried to lift anything. She stood inspecting her wound. She must have stretched it when rolling to EggWiff. She knew it would be fine soon.

"Ugh! Fine! Everyone move out of the way!" EggWiff

started waving his arms to clear some space. "Seeing as I can do magic, I shall free the pig!"

"Yes, and your magic is wonderful, but maybe we should allow someone with more experience…" Lainla looked at EggWiff. Even as a ghost she was still beautiful.

Gathnok knew she was referring to him. He didn't mind, but it had been a while since he had performed such specific controlled magic. Many centuries ago he even had the help of Cupido Sacra when performing such spells. But they didn't have time to debate Gathnok's ability. They watched as he prepared himself. EggWiff was a bit disheartened that he wasn't allowed to do more magic, but he watched the bizarre shadow being. They stood back whilst Gathnok waved his arms over the rocks beneath him. He felt energy, potent and pure energy, travel through him. Pure energy comes from Sahihriar and is the essence of magic itself. Evil magic comes from the soul. It's not pure and therefore never as powerful. They waited until soon the boulders began to float up. They were suspended in air, like bubbles floating up around them. Gathnok stood focused but showed no strain. His body, however, was changing. The shadows seemed to get lighter as more features could be seen. Soon they could see Hail down in a small hole created by the boulders. Minso immediately jumped down and dragged the unconscious Hail out. Gathnok had moved the boulders down the mountain.

"Is he okay?" EggWiff was leaning over Hail whilst Minso checked to see if he was still breathing.

"He's still breathing, but I don't know for how much longer." Minso looked concerned. He had no medical skills.

"We need a healer!" Saria would normally turn to herself or EggWiff, as they seemed to most have the most power in the group.

"We do . . ." Once again Lainla had to turn to Gathnok.

"You're a healer?" EggWiff looked wide-eyed and impressed.

"Are you?" Saria didn't know this.

"He was one of the most renowned and powerful healers of all time." Lainla gave a small smile of pride.

"The shadow guy who trapped me in a cage is a nice healer! This is why I don't like being sober."

"Well, do something!" Saria gestured quickly at the bruised Hail before them.

Gathnok didn't waste much time and soon crouched down. He placed his hands on Hail's rounded belly and let the energy channel through them. It had been a while since he had done healing by touch. He used to just use Cupido Sacra.

"Is it working?" Lainla whispered.

"Patience!" Gathnok was too busy concentrating. He had never healed a pig before and was finding it difficult. After a few more seconds Gathnok got up. "I have done all I can. The rest is up to him."

"He's still not awake," Saria said, confused. She still wasn't' sure about trusting Gathnok.

"I've done all I can."

"How the heck are we meant to carry his tubby body up this mountain in this heat?" Although he was moaning, EggWiff had a valid point.

"He can ride on Emae. She'll keep him safe." Minso nodded to Emae, which made her swoop down on command. He patted her as she landed, whilst Saria and EggWiff helped move Hail onto Emae.

"We have to keep moving. We have little time." Gathnok walked on without looking at the others. Lainla went to float beside him, but remembering the harsh words they had said earlier, she decided to float a little way behind. Emae squawked before flying a little way above them with the wounded Hail. Minso, Saria, and EggWiff followed on.

* * *

Morbid turned what he hoped to be the final corner of the labyrinth. He had detached his head a total of six times, and by now his joints were beginning to feel loose. He turned to see at last a different corridor leading out of the maze. The corridor was lined with the same stone walls, but they weren't damp or lit by flame. Instead there was a faint green glow. Not only did this dimly light the way, it was also a sign that he was getting near to Cupido Sacra. Even though he was sure more traps would follow, Morbid began taking the first few steps along the corridor to face what was next.

"Let That Live In the Past"

Chapter Fifteen

A Sacred Past

Gathnok peered out across the land. He looked out among the purity and good that filled the Fifth Realm. The love he felt deep within was his amazing powerful source – that and the ancient mystical jewel known as Cupido Sacra. The jewel let out a shimmering green glow that stood at the tip of his staff. Gathnok now wore a long white cloak, the sign of his status amongst the inhabitants of the Fifth Realm. The jewel fuelled itself on love and pure love alone. Only the most spirited and most empowered soul could have wielded the stone. With his power he was the angel of the Fifth Realm, banishing evil and defeating black foes that might dare to challenge him.

Not only had he become renowned as a great warrior, but he was also known as one of the best tutors in magic history, with only the ever-mighty Elders as competition. Gathnok had trained many apprentices, each becoming a powerful sorcerer. His latest was a young impressionable wizard named Marvie. Gathnok sensed great potential within his apprentice and was enjoying the training sessions they had shared. He often thought about his struggle to keep Marvie safe all those years ago. Gathnok had aged somewhat, yet his appearance was striking, and he often struck fear into the hearts of the evil creatures in the Fifth Realm. He had discovered over time that it was his ability to love that was his greatest gift. Gathnok's love for the world was equal with the love of his soul partner. Lainla had stood by his side for all these years and everyday had grown more beautiful. The higher beings had never known such love as these two shared. It was pure and indefinable. Their souls were truly entwined with destiny and with one another.

The realm had been filled with light and love for many years. Gathnok loved his work and the good he was doing, as he was blessed by the greatest love of them all. This is the way it was and how it was meant to be, until the day of darkness came – a day that no one had foreseen. Even the higher beings themselves were blinded by what was soon to come.

Gathnok left that morning. He knew her smell and every inch and detail of her beauty from mind alone. Her long blonde hair and her hazel eyes made for an enchanting woman. Their home was on the highest point of the Fifth Realm. It looked over the entire land. As guardian he had to have full sight at all times. The house was a magically blessed palace, which was guarded by the higher beings. No one with the slightest of evil in his or her soul could cross the barrier. His life was perfect.

After battling two dragons and healing a wounded tribe of fairies, Gathnok returned home to have his forgotten nightmares return in reality. He climbed the mountain with uncertainty. For some reason he couldn't shake the feeling that something was wrong. Something felt different. However, the jewel didn't warn him of anything. His front door was left ajar. He stepped into his palace. The day was dawning and the air was humid. His kingdom was peaceful for another day. As soon as he had crossed the magical threshhold of the barrier, the jewel began

342

to glow brightly, warning Gathnok something was wrong. The world stopped, and he stopped. He stared transfixed at the jewel as if it wasn't real. He could handle anything. His power was immense, but the only place he wouldn't accept danger was at his home. Without hesitation he ran throughout the corridors. The rooms were cold and masked within shadow, but he didn't care about anything as his legs pounded the different floored surfaces, each step bringing more fear into him than ever before. The closer he got, the brighter Cupido Sacra shone. As he screamed out her name, the walls echoed with it as he prayed with everything he had for her to call back, wishing for her to be safe. The walls were empty and black. The house was blank and didn't feel like his anymore. He slowed as he came in front of a door. He sensed presences inside. His beloved was one, but he could sense another, but this creature was new and dark. He listened softly to hear a soft whimpering from inside the room. The room he was in was dark with Cupido Sacra emitting a small green glow. With the bottom of his staff he kicked the door open slowly and became poised, ready for battle.

Once the door was opened, he saw a shadowed figure standing over his beloved huddled on the floor. Only for a brief second could Gathnok manage to see orange glowing eyes staring at him from the shadows. Gathnok had the hex ready as he managed to curse him before the figure dispelled and was gone from sight. Gathnok didn't care that that's all he had time to do. He just wanted her to be safe. He ran to his loved one's side and bent over her. Now Cupido Sacra dimmed lower, but its small green glow filled the room, allowing him to see her face. Her face was pale and cold. Her eyes were empty and lost. Her lips were dried, and her hair lay flat. Gathnok could still see her beauty and forever would. He peered down to see her blood-stained chest soaking her clothes. He tried to smile at the weakened Lainla and scooped her up into his arms. The wound didn't look that bad, and Cupido Sacra could heal anything.

He carried her into one of the spare rooms and laid her gently on the bed. She winced in pain but was now looking into his eyes. She loved him just as much now as she ever had.

He peered into her eyes, as she did his. Her body was rising up and down gently, a sign she was still alive. She smiled slowly as she raised her hand to caress his soft cheek. He held it in her

hand in his and kissed it slowly as silent tears flowed from his eyes.

"I'll heal you. Hold on!" His voice was quivering, as the sheer horror in what he was seeing took away all basic thoughts. He knelt down and picked up his staff and held it over her body. He wiped a tear away before using his energy to combine with the jewel to heal her wounds. Yet the jewel didn't respond. The bright mystical green glow that usually emitted from the jewel had faded.

"What? I don't understand. It's not working." Gathnok's entire world began to crash down as the realisation that he might lose Lainla became a stark, chilling reality.

She tried to smile, but instead a splutter of her lips formed a spill of blood from the side of her mouth. "It's okay." She spoke softly.

"Hush, don't speak. It will work." He tried again yet the jewel remained dormant. "Why don't you work!" Gathnok screamed, and he threw his staff across the room as the tears of anguish continued to flow. He was powerless to help the one person he'd sacrifice anything for. He didn't want to cry. He didn't want to show his fear. His heart was pounding. He held so tightly onto her hand, vowing to never let go. As long as she was staring back at him, then he could hold on. "You're going to be all right. Just hold on! I'm here now."

She managed a feeble smile. A single tear formed in her right eye.

"I'm so tired," Lainla said weakly. It was as if she didn't know what was happening.

Gathnok began to stroke her hair softly and kissed her cheek.

"Sleep then my love. You sleep, and I'll see you soon."

Lainla managed to let her fingers brush his cheek and smiled at the thought. Her face then creased in pain as the bleeding wound in her chest stood still, and her gaze became *still and transfixed as he felt the grip of her hand loosen. She was lost from the world, forever sleeping.*

Gathnok sat in the darkened room in shock. He refused to let go of her hand as he could barely breathe. He shuffled forward and sat looking at her beautiful face. The jewel was mighty, but it didn't have the power to raise the dead. He knew she was lost and that for some reason Cupido Sacra and the Elders had betrayed him.

As the days went on, the Fifth Realm was thrown into turmoil. Evil and dark creatures turned the realm from a heaven to a hell. They had made it their own. He didn't fight because he didn't care, because she was gone. One thing began to dominate his thoughts and took over the good he felt. He would have his revenge. He knew who had killed her, and he was going to make sure that all they felt for eternity was pain and sorrow. His plan was perfected, and he knew this wasn't going to be a simple kill but a horrific torture. Cupido Sacra was going to ensure that – until destiny intervened.

* * *

"Give it back! Take me back!" Gathnok's voice soared throughout the light.

The great Elders existed outside of time and space. Only those of importance or those summoned could be called before them.

"You have turned from your calling. You have created destruction for the Fifth Realm. Your heart is unworthy of such power" The voices all spoke at once. It was impossible to tell how many there were. They were shrouded by the light above Gathnok.

"She is gone! How can I fight now? How can I be anything? You won't bring her back to me. I need Cupido Sacra so I can exact my revenge." Gathnok's voice was bloodthirsty, pain and

anger surged through his veins, and his respect for the Elders was gone. His respect for everything was gone.

"We cannot allow further bloodshed. We shall send you to the Realm of Innocence, and there you will once again feel no pain or grief. You are bound to that realm until all anger within your heart is vanquished." *The voices began to mutter amongst one another.*

The Temple of Light existed within a realm of its own. The Elders controlled all five realms and the common world as it is known. Legend believes that there are five Elders, one for each realm. The realms are known as numbers. Only the Elders can give the names, and only the Elders can speak those names. In the Temple of Light the Elders were indistinguishable.

"Why didn't you protect us?" *Gathnok squinted as he spoke to nothing but light. He was ignoring his sentence.*

"Magic is a powerful thing – something so in tune with the planet's life force that it's unstable, unpredictable, uncontrollable." *The voices were soft and showed no emotion.*

"Are you saying that her death was simply an accident?" *Gathnok knew these words would be the last he said as he slowly felt himself being pushed further away from the light into a portal to another realm.*

"There is a reason for everything. Remember this."

Gathnok felt a hand pressing him back, although he saw nothing. He began to kick and scream, and he knew his magic was gone. Powerless to struggle, he screamed out for his loved one until his voice was just an echo in the temple.

* * *

"I wish they'd hurry up and get here. I want to fight." Emerald was getting annoyed, waiting around in the tent that had been put up for them to wait in.

"You always want to fight." Ruby was enjoying the rest.

She cared very little what was going on. She was used to big battles, and this one didn't frighten her.

"I still don't see why we don't get the jewel now," Emerald muttered.

"Because we need to make sure EggWiff pays. Then we'll make sure Cupido Sacra is safe." Sapphire was tired of explaining this to Emerald. She was lying on one of the blankets, trying to make the most of the recovery time she had.

"But if we had the power of Cupido whatever, we could easily take out the wizard."

"We don't need power; we have enough. We have our mission. We've never needed anything else."

Ruby stayed silent. She was often witness to an argument between Sapphire and Emerald.

"We've never had an opportunity like this."

"Emerald, you heard Forlax. That jewel could destroy all of Sahihriar."

"Well, I wouldn't be foolish enough to use it that way . . ."

Sapphire flung back the blanket that was wrapped over her and marched up to Emerald. She grabbed Emerald by both her arms and moved her face in close.

"We are not here for that jewel. We will not be using that jewel, and our only priority is the wizard. Do you understand?" Emerald continued to glare into her sister's eye.

"Understood!"

Sapphire was not about to let Emerald ruin what they were about. Too many beings were corrupted by power and evil. The triplets worked for the courts to fight for justice. As the one born first, she knew it was her job to keep Emerald in check. She was determined to stop EggWiff and all who helped him. Sahihriar was not going to be destroyed.

* * *

They continued to walk up the mountain. The heat was still unbearable, but they all knew they had to continue. Saria was worried about Hail, who still rested on top of Emae. She hoped Gathnok had done enough. However, if they didn't stop Morbid, then it wouldn't really matter what happened, as they would never exist in the first place. Emae screeched and swooped down low by Minso.

"Hey, he's waking up!"

They stopped and all went over to Emae, where Hail had begun to oink faintly as his eyes opened.

"What abomination?" Hail's voice was raspy and dry.

"You were wounded in the avalanche. Gathnok healed you the best he could," Saria said, as she looked into Hail's eyes.

"And it worked. I thought you were dead."

Hail didn't know what was worse, the fact his entire body ached or the fact WiffEgg was still with them.

"Why?" Hail asked.

"There was an avalanche. You didn't get to safety in time," Minso said, he continued to pat Emae as a reward for her obedience.

Hail's snout creased as he turned his head in disagreement. His eyes began to water as he looked in discomfort. "No, I mean why? Why did you let *him* help me?"

"He saved your life, Hail." Lainla was somewhat angry at his lack of gratitude.

Hail spluttered a small saddened laugh. "Not much left to save."

Saria could see the sadness in his eyes. Hail was a being who was driven by his faith, a faith that was manipulated by Gathnok.

"We should keep moving."

EggWiff, Minso, and Saria all wondered if Gathnok could feel the intense heat. Maybe he wouldn't be so eager to keep moving. They went back to walking as Hail seemed too upset and weak to walk himself, so he continued to lie on the back of Emae. Minso made a point to walk on up to the front beside Gathnok.

"Are you okay?" Minso asked, as he was slightly nervous. Marvie was well known in the Fifth Realm, but Gathnok was legendary.

"You seem to be the only person here who cares." Gathnok didn't even turn his head to look at him.

"You haven't done anything to me, but you did a lot for the Fifth Realm . . . until you left." Minso wasn't sure how far he should push the matter. His heart was racing. He was talking to Gathnok himself.

Gathnok was surprised by the young warrior's reasoning. He noticed the sly comment about him leaving, but the Elders were to blame for that. He just wished Lainla would accept the effort he was making to redeem himself.

"Finally!" Saria spoke from behind.

Gathnok and Minso turned to see a green mist surrounding them, followed by the gross stench. Gathnok struggled to see through the heat and green fog. He heard a loud yell from EggWiff, who suddenly appeared out from the mist. His eyes looked angry as he lunged forward.

"Marvie, don't!"

Minso's plea was too late as EggWiff waved his staff and knocked Gathnok in the face, hitting him hard. Using the bottom of the staff he swung it across and buckled Gathnok's legs. His shadowy form fell on the floor. EggWiff pointed his staff at Gathnok's throat.

"Did you know?" EggWiff was furious.

"That the spell was the beginning of your curse? Yes, we both did." Gathnok tilted his head towards Lainla.

EggWiff looked back at the ghostly Lainla, who looked on concerned.

"Wait! His illness is because of you?" Saria asked confused.

"The spell you performed caused your mind to separate, but it is not my fault." Gathnok flung the staff to one side and got back on his feet. "You're all so quick to blame me, when I have actually done very little. It was Morbid who killed Trickle, and it was you who killed Flick," he said, pointing at Saria. "Both were working on your own free will. All I ever did was try and take you so that I could use your magic to awaken Cupido Sacra."

"That much magic would have killed me, and you know it." EggWiff glared into his eyes.

"Yes, and at that point I didn't care. But no one's death is on my hands!"

Saria was annoyed at his attempt to justify himself. "Your army killed Hail's people!"

"But he is still alive, is he not? It was he who sent his army after mine. I didn't want any battle between our people. All I am guilty of is trying to get back a love that was stolen from me."

"But you hurt people by doing so, my love." Lainla stared at him. She hated that her death had caused so much.

"Those who are hurting often cause hurt. But none of that matters now."

"Why? Because you have her back?" Saria asked, stunned by his selfishness.

"No, because this is more important. I have put aside years of hate, grief, and anger because of what is going on right now. What Morbid is trying to do is way beyond anything I feel. Instead of realising that, you're all intent on clinging on to your problems. If the Elders aren't created, then there will be nothing for ever. We don't have time to be fighting about things that just don't matter anymore. Sahihriar will be destroyed when we awaken Cupido Sacra, but if we don't get to it before Morbid can destroy it, then we have lost everything."

Gathnok was shouting and staring at them all. He had to make them understand, and screaming was the only way he understood.

They all stood and stared at him. There was nothing but silence. They all stopped and took in the words of Gathnok. A horrible feeling grew in their stomachs. They weren't just going for another battle. The end was coming soon, and all of their problems didn't matter. Stopping Morbid was the only thing that was important.

"We don't have time. Morbid has most likely found the temple, and with the ability of Death, the temple's traps won't stop him at all. For all we know, he may already have Cupido Sacra."

Gathnok was interrupted by a blinding light from behind him as an Elder appeared.

"No he doesn't." The grey Elder shone out brightly from the mountain top.

EggWiff stepped back and bowed. Gathnok got up and stood by EggWiff.

"What do you mean?" Gathnok asked curiously. He never had much respect for the Elders.

"I bound his powers of Death. He's as weak as Morbid." The Elder spoke with no emotion.

"That's great, right?" Minso said. From what he could gather, this was good news.

"You couldn't have. The Elders aren't allowed to intervene. It threatens… "

". . . the balance, but this Elder prefers to fight for the right to have a balance."

"Surely you shall be punished?" EggWiff looked at the Elder through the glare of his glasses.

"Not if I keep moving." The Elder shimmered and glowed a little. "I must go. Good luck."

With this, the Elder nodded its head a little before disappearing from the mountainside. Gathnok continued to stare as if distracted. Lainla and EggWiff stood by his side.

"What is it?" Lainla asked.

"This is bigger than all of us." Gathnok looked at EggWiff. If an Elder was breaking the rules, then it confirmed the importance of getting Cupido Sacra back.

* * *

Morbid walked along the corridor with anticipation and concern. Although everything seemed okay, he couldn't afford to waste any more time than necessary. It wasn't long, however, until the corridor came to a small open room which seemed empty. Morbid looked in and surveyed it. The room seemed pointless, as he could clearly see the corridor continued straight ahead across from him. Morbid could see the empty room, and there was little he could do until he was in the room. He contemplated running through, but that was possibly what Gathnok had anticipated. Being dead, his only fear was wasting time, so he decided to steadily walk through. He began to take the first few steps into the room. The floor was lined with stone as were the walls, and the ceiling too was covered in the same stone. It was a box room, and Morbid knew it would be there for some purpose. It wasn't until Morbid had reached the middle of the room and felt his skeleton foot step against a slightly raised stone that he realised the purpose. He pushed on it with his weight. He knew he had triggered something dangerous.

* * *

The four Elders were sitting in their blessed realm as they discussed the missing Elder. They were in a room which was filled with light and existed outside of time and space. It was untouched by anything of the real world. This place was truly sacred.

"He's broken the rules," the orange Elder began.

"He knows of our laws and the reasons behind them," continued the green Elder.

"He must undo what he has done, or else we risk being destroyed either way," the purple Elder finished.

"You all must understand his reasons," the blue Elder spoke with reason.

"We do, but he cannot undo his actions in his past life by changing his actions as an Elder." The orange Elder seemed angrier at the grey Elder's actions.

"None of us asked for this burden, but it's something we must do." The purple Elder was calming yet firm.

"I understand. I shall get him to undo his spell . . . before it ruins everything." The blue Elder nodded to his companions.

"Agreed!" The Elder sensed the realms and continued the hunt for his companion. It understood why the grey Elder was so adamant about stopping Morbid, but it had to somehow make it understand the consequences of its actions.

* * *

They were nearing the peak of Magmount, and they could all feel it in the heat. Saria was thinking about the Elder that had appeared. Up until then she had no reason to believe Gathnok and was waiting for his attack, but if an Elder was trying to stop Morbid, then it must be true. This meant that no matter what happened, Sahihriar would be destroyed. She began to think of the Amazons and all the different settlements. All of her friends and everyone she knew would be gone. Her mind wandered a little as she thought about all the people who would be willing to sacrifice their life and planet if it meant others could someday be created. She struggled to think of many, as practically everyone she knew was an Amazon, and they simply followed orders. One thought lingered in her mind: maybe it was better Flick had died when he did. At least he was saved from this madness.

"How are you?"

Saria's mind snapped back to reality as she noticed EggWiff was walking beside her.

"You seemed a little lost in your own thoughts," EggWiff continued.

Saria wondered if EggWiff had forgotten that the last time they properly spoke they were arguing in the forest, or maybe EggWiff took on board Gathnok's speech and was trying to make peace. She was too tired to care either way.

"I just don't understand," Saria said with very little emotion. She was just tired, and her wound wasn't making the walk any easier.

"Well, the Elders exist out of time and space. However, their creation, their birth so to speak, must have happened at some point. Cupido Sacra has been growing in power so, to my understanding, when I awaken the jewel, it will unleash such potent magic that it will destroy Sahihriar but also create the magic that gives birth to the five Elders."

"But . . ."

"But because the Elders exist outside time and space, it means that they can create Sahihriar in the first place – ironically, from its destruction, allowing all the other planets and stars to continue and give hope for new worlds and life." EggWiff finished his impressive explanation.

"No, I understood all that." Saria wasn't even sure if she

did understand it all, but she was accepting the fact she was going to go along with it anyway. But that's not what she meant when she said she didn't understand.

"So what don't you understand?"

"I stood in Gathnok's tower and swore to you I'd help you kill him. I, you, and Hail all agreed we'd get revenge for what he did. But there he is not two feet from us, and we're just walking with him like it's nothing."

EggWiff couldn't blame the Amazon. Less than an hour ago he was trying to cause Gathnok pain.

"It's difficult, I know. But you must try to understand the bigger picture now."

The heat was causing Saria to sweat, and Amazons were meant to be used to the heat. Her side still ached, and she was frustrated it hadn't healed properly. Her mind flashed to Trickle falling into the Black Sea, Flick falling onto the sand, and the army of the pigs all scattered and dead. She couldn't just wash all that feeling and pain away. She couldn't put aside her training and all she thought to be right just because there was a "bigger picture". Why should she have to obey to the bigger picture? She just wanted it to end, and in that heated moment the only way she could see that happening was to kill Gathnok.

"I know. Thanks." Saria weakly smiled at EggWiff and then began to walk off towards Gathnok.

EggWiff's eyebrows creased as he continued to watch Saria. There was something about the look she had that made EggWiff rather concerned. He noticed as Saria's hand reached up beyond her back towards the handle of her sword. She drew it quickly, which created a small sound. Immediately Gathnok and Minso turned. Saria raised her sword and quickly decided to strike. The sword, however, stopped inches from the shadowy Gathnok as Saria turned to see EggWiff and his staff stopping her.

"You defend him now?" Saria looked hurt more than anything.

"Stop this!" EggWiff's blue eyes were the only plea he could find.

Saria turned round and swung her sword all around her to attack EggWiff from the other side. He was too fast as his staff was there to block it. She kicked out with her small dwarf legs and buckled his knee. In the moment of distraction, Saria punched out, causing EggWiff to fall to his knees. The others watched as it all seemed to happen so quickly. With all the heat, EggWiff was weakened and on his knees. Saria raised her sword. She would wound him if it meant getting to Gathnok. Gathnok was watching everything. His mind finally caught up with him. He couldn't allow the key to be injured.

"Stop!"

Saria stopped with her sword raised and looked at Gathnok.

"If you wish to kill me, then do so." Gathnok stepped forward and held out his arms.

"Gathnok!" Lainla cried out.

Gathnok held up his hand to Lainla's interference. "If killing me is what it takes for you to believe, if it's enough to get EggWiff to Cupido Sacra, then so be it. I'll make that sacrifice. So please, end it." Gathnok was now standing right in front of Saria and was being deadly serious.

* * *

Morbid immediately heard stone moving from above. He looked up to see that some of the stone slabs had moved up into the ceiling. At first there was nothing as Morbid braced himself for the trickery of what was to come. Soon small spurts of sand began pouring in from all sides of the room. Morbid watched as the sand began to increase and poured out much faster and harder. Sand was pouring in from the ceiling and from all sides of the room. As it fell, it glistened in a green glow. Morbid tried to walk out, but sand had already quickly swallowed his skeleton legs. The sand was coming in so fast that all he could do was watch. The room was buried in sand, trapping him in the room. He knew he had to think fast if he was going to find a way to dig himself free.

* * *

Saria stared in Gathnok's blackened face. Why was he sacrificing himself? It must have been some clever mind trick. But then, what if she did do it? They could still use EggWiff to awaken Cupido Sacra. Her mind raced. She wanted to do it, but something was holding her back. If all of Sahihriar was to be destroyed, then it wouldn't matter that much. Gathnok was no fool. He must have understood that as an Amazon she was more than willing to kill him. She pulled back her sword ready to strike. But then something stopped her. This was very similar to the position Flick and she were in before he died. She killed Flick on the basis of her belief, and she was about to do the same thing. Why couldn't she learn that death solved nothing? Saria dropped her sword and knelt down covering her face. She didn't want to cry in front of them, but she just couldn't help it. Soon everything was to be destroyed, and for the first time in her life Saria felt powerless.

EggWiff stood up and watched as the Amazon did her best to disguise her pain. He admired what Gathnok did. Lainla was beaming at Gathnok. She was beginning to see her husband more and more. Minso couldn't help feel but sorry for Saria as he went over and stood by her side as she knelt.

EggWiff was the first to speak. "We must all make an

agreement now. All of us have suffered. All of us are in pain. Now, however, we must agree to let that live in the past. We must agree to unite and do what must be done to stop Morbid, regardless of how we feel. Anyone who cannot agree to this should stay behind now."

EggWiff peered out amongst the group. Gathnok's shadowy head nodded his agreement. Lainla too smiled and nodded, providing a tingle of warmth down EggWiff's spine. Hail was sitting up on Emae, as he was slowly beginning to feel better. Hail lingered for a while as his eyes darted between Gathnok and EggWiff. Eventually Hail also nodded. Minso gave a small confident wink to show he agreed. Saria raised her head slowly after she quickly wiped her eyes. She stood up and looked at EggWiff.

"For Flick?" EggWiff prompted.

"No, for me," Saria nodded, whilst letting herself gaze into EggWiff's reassuring eyes.

* * *

The room had filled up with sand at a very fast rate. Morbid was surrounded by it from head to toe. If he were alive, he would have suffocated but since he was a skeleton, he was completely safe. He just seemed to be trapped in the sand. Morbid admired Gathnok's thoughts behind the traps. The simplicity and yet the danger of the traps were very cunning. Not much of a match for Death, but very inconvenient for Morbid. The loose sand would be easy to dig out of even though it was packed in rather tight. However, whilst Morbid stood suspended by the sand, he noticed that the sand began to darken and get harder. It wasn't long before he realised that water was seeping in to harden the sand. Morbid felt a twinge of annoyance as he watched this happen around him.

He was smart enough though. He made sure he stood

completely still as the sand swept over him. This was because the sand had filled the room so fast that it had formed all around him without pouring inside his skeleton body or head. Morbid prayed it was enough as he began to gradually move his head only millimetres from side to side. This would have been easier if the sand wasn't toughened by the moisture, but slowly as he moved sand began to shift through his open eye sockets and into his head, clearing a small way. He also began to move his rib bones left and right, and again a small amount of sand began to shuffle through. He was frustrated that this trap would also be so time-consuming, but at least he hadn't been wounded and could still reach Cupido Sacra. He began to use his body as a funnel for the sand, which allowed him to very slowly push himself forward through the sand only inches at a time.

* * *

Gathnok held up his arm, signalling the other five to stop.

"Is this it?" Lainla was slightly nervous about seeing Forlax. They shared a complicated history.

"Just around this corner. Is everyone ready?" Gathnok knew first-hand how powerful and stubborn Forlax was. "And remember! Protect EggWiff at all costs."

Emae swooped down low and perched on the narrowing edge.

"Sure you can walk?" Minso asked, as he reached his hand out to help Hail off from Emae.

"I shall be fine. My thanks go to you!" Hail nodded, as he continued to speak with a weakened yet majestic voice.

"Just remember the plan and keep safe," Lainla prompted the others.

All six of them began to walk and turned the corner. They were all preparing to deal with Forlax. If he wasn't going to open the portal to the Nether Realm willingly, then they would have to make him. They were clinging on to the notion that soon they would be out of the heat and able to prepare for the forthcoming final battle. Just before they turned the corner, Lainla caught Gathnok's shadowy face staring at her. As much as it pained him to admit it, he knew how hard it would be for Lainla to see Forlax again.

"Let's go!" Lainla tried to smile comfortingly. She wasn't going to let her passion ruin any more lives.

Gathnok and Lainla then turned the corner ready to face their former friend for the last time.

* * *

Morbid's arm and head shot out of the sand. The wet sand had formed an outer wall that he was able to push against to get his body and legs out. He had to be careful, as he couldn't afford to lose one of his legs in the sand. As he stumbled out into the corridor, sand poured out of his hollow head and body. These traps were wasting valuable time and giving the others plenty of chances to catch up. He knew that was why the Elders took his powers. He just wished he knew how much further he had to go. Letting his anger fuel him, he got to his feet and tipped the last few grains of sand from his head. Walking down the same stone corridors, he approached the green glow. He was now determined to keep going until Cupido Sacra was gone, and the Elders gone with it.

"I Don't Have Time for This"

Chapter Sixteen

They all turned the corner and walked into the large hole that Forlax had created earlier. The large opening was scorching, and they all felt a further wave of heat. Saria wasn't sure if she could handle more heat. They looked up to see Forlax wasn't sleeping in the lava lake but was fully formed in his fiery figure.

"Welcome back! I see you brought company." The sparks Forlax sprayed when talking forced the group to step back a little.

"We seek passage to the Nether Realm." EggWiff stepped forward and knelt to show respect.

Forlax bellowed, which made the lava lake boil and larger sparks flicker out.

"Marvie, I cannot blame you for your ignorance. As a relative of Gathnok you were doomed from the start."

Forlax's flame-like head flickered a smile. Minso now understood why Magmount was so hot. No one had explained to him that Forlax was a giant flame.

"If you do not grant us passage to the Nether Realm, we are all doomed." Lainla floated from behind Gathnok. Forlax's flame grew a little shorter, as even within his flame-like features it was clear he was shocked. "Hello, Forlax."

Forlax stared at Lainla, lingering over the beauty of his former friend. "I cannot allow Gathnok to have control over Cupido Sacra. Not after the consequences last time."

"I don't want it for myself. Death is seeking to destroy the jewel which threatens everything. As a spirit of the elements you're sworn to help us."

"Just like you swore to lead us?" Forlax turned and looked at Lainla.

Lainla stood in silence. If many years ago someone had said she'd be looking at these two people, one as a shadow and one as a giant flame, she would have laughed.

The truth is that Forlax was delighted in the frustration he was causing his former companion.

"Forlax, please. You know what is at stake. We must stop Morbid." Lainla tried to plead with him. Long ago they had been close. She prayed that all of that wasn't lost and the stubbornness she once knew in this being wasn't as strong.

"You cannot stop Death. You of all beings should know this, Li."

Gathnok couldn't help but give a sideways glance, as he kept being harshly reminded of the past these two shared.

"Forlax, you're an Elemental Sprit, a big ball of flame! You of all people should know it can happen."

During this banter EggWiff, Hail, Minso, and Saria stood by the gaping hole in Magmount's wall.

"Do you know what's going on here?" a baffled Hail whispered.

"Something about Forlax liking Lainla but now being annoyed with Gathnok."

"Oh, right." Hail thought it better to keep his mind

off things that didn't concern him. He put it down to still feeling weak.

"Forlax, everything is dependent on us getting to the Nether Realm now." Gathnok was furious with him. How could he allow the past to mess with the present?

"There was a time when I followed you without question. Now I follow no one, and I say no." Forlax's flame mouth flickered into a smile.

"Then I am sorry, as we have no other choice but to make you."

Everyone then knew that this was the signal as they all moved into place.

* * *

Morbid followed the green glow which seemed to be coming from somewhere. If he were alive, he would have felt rather afraid at being completely surrounded by damp and smelly stone brick. The tunnel had begun to descend, so he was carefully trying to make sure he didn't slip on the steps. He had been held up enough, and the green glow of Cupido Sacra just taunted him. Soon he could see that the light was turning a corner as the tunnel suddenly went to the right. He took the last few steps and walked to the corner. Somehow his senses were more in tune with danger, as he knew a further trap was likely to be just round the corner. He didn't have time for precaution and instead turned the corner and stopped as he looked into the corridor. It took Morbid a second to register what he was seeing. There, standing a few meters from him, was himself.

"Interesting!" Morbid surveyed what appeared to be himself.

"Isn't it?" the second Morbid replied.

"I assume you're not here to help." Morbid took stance as he wondered what the reason was behind this trick.

"I'm the final test."

"Trust in Gathnok to be so deep. So how do I get past you?" Morbid was running low on patience.

"Simple. You cannot."

"I don't have time for this." Morbid walked on to brush past his other self.

As he tried to do this, the fake Morbid held up his white skeleton fingers and pushed Morbid back.

"You cannot get past me." The two Morbids' sockets glared at one another.

"Then we fight."

"What makes you think you can beat yourself?" the mirrored Morbid laughed. For the first time the actual Morbid could see how frightening he could be. Since neither of them had powers or a weapon, both Morbids had to make do with what they had. The actual Morbid clenched his thin skeleton fingers and quickly threw out the first punch. The mirrored Morbid instantly blocked and seemed to be a match in strength and speed. Morbid tried to counter, but it seemed the mirrored Morbid knew what he would do, just as he did. Morbid couldn't give up and was determined to find a weakness in this illusion.

* * *

Forlax watched as the group moved into different positions. "You cannot kill me, Gathnok."

Gathnok peered around the inside of Magmount. They all seemed to be in position. "If there's one thing I have learnt, everything can feel pain."

Gathnok then turned to the large hole that had appeared and began to concentrate all his energy. He then walked over and placed his hand on the wall. The group watched nervously, hoping it would work. Gathnok was already weak from all his magic, and it was a long time since he had channelled so much natural energy. Soon the natural rocky walls began to ooze out shadow from where Gathnok was touching. They all watched as the shadow began to wash over the walls. Gathnok was clearly struggling as his body began to crouch, and his breathing had become heavier.

"You're too weak without your precious jewel." Forlax watched smugly as Gathnok's trick posed little threat.

"Now!" Gathnok held his hand back.

EggWiff then took his shadowy hand, Hail took EggWiff's, Saria held onto Hail's, and Minso took hold of Saria's. Minso then knelt down and let his hand touch the rocky ground. They each began to feel a wave of energy flow through them. Gathnok, being the most powerful magically, had to be at the front. EggWiff needed to be second. Although it was hard for these two, Hail, Saria, and Minso weren't used to feeling the magic of Sahihriar, and each of them felt overwhelmed by the feeling. Lainla stood and stared at Forlax.

"You should have let us through." Lainla's heart wept for the change Forlax had gone through.

Soon the shadow had spread right across the walls and had also begun to cover the entrance to the cavern. As this happened, Forlax's flame began to get smaller and flicker as he felt himself beginning to lose power. The shadow wasn't just blocking out the light, but was also blocking out the oxygen. Still the shadow continued to spread, and as it did so, Forlax began to get smaller as the flame lost its white, red, and orange colours, until it was just a small flicker.

"Stop!"

This was Gathnok's signal to stop spreading the shadow. There seemed to be a tiny hole in the rock wall where light beamed in. The cavern otherwise was smothered in darkness. Forlax was reduced to a very small flickering flame. He couldn't even stay fully formed for long. The lava lake also had changed and was no longer orange, and all the flames had died out on its surface. Forlax tried to speak but couldn't. He was suspended in a constant flickering state.

"We'll stop this once you open the portal. Please!" Lainla's transparent eyes pleaded with the flickering Fire Spirit.

Forlax ached as he couldn't sustain anything. He would have fought back, but his powers were drained as the small amount of oxygen kept his powers at bay. He was aware he had very little choice – a feeling he was used to feeling around Gathnok. He struggled as emotions overcame him. How could he open a portal which could end everything? Once upon a time he was sworn to do good. Now he was allowing his old friend to destroy everything once more. Forlax stopped and focused as he forced himself to stay alight for just a few moments. If this was his final chance, then he wasn't going to waste it.

"I'll always love you." Forlax could barely splutter the words as he let his fire-like eyes look at Lainla. Her ghostly image seemed like a foggy reminder of the real beauty she possessed many years ago.

In return, Lainla managed a smile and tried hard not to show the pain she felt. She had hurt Gathnok too much, and she couldn't risk losing his loyalty in the final hour. Forlax dimmed slightly as he flickered in the hollowed-out Magmount. They all waited as they could see that Forlax had begun to conjure the energy he needed to open the portal. He flickered more as he did this, and soon a portal swirled below the ledge and hovered above the lake of lava below them.

"Thank you, Forlax," Lainla said with a smile. Although he had no choice, she knew how much good was in him. Forlax tried hard to watch as he took in the last few seconds he had to watch the beauty of Lainla.

Lainla ran and jumped down into the portal. She wasn't scared of what was coming, as she was already dead. She only lingered because Morbid had been distracted.

"We must go." Gathnok turned and faced Forlax. "I'm doing the right thing."

Without waiting any longer, Gathnok ran and jumped down into the portal. EggWiff did as they had discussed and followed Gathnok. Minso ran and jumped down into the portal, followed by the screeching Emae.

"You go first, Hail."

Hail's snout morphed into a smile before his tubby body ran and jumped down into the portal. Praying she wasn't betraying her Amazon teachings, Saria made sure her bow was fastened to her back and then ran and leapt down into the portal below. Once they were all gone, the shadows faded, letting the light and oxygen back into the cave. Forlax grew back into a burning, scorching flame. He didn't know what was going to happen in the Nether Realm. He just hoped the right thing would be done by someone.

* * *

Morbid's bones were beginning to feel weak as his arms blocked and threw punches. Maybe he had underestimated Gathnok. He couldn't actually beat himself. This mirrored Morbid was equal to him in every way.

"Neither of us can win!"

Morbid was hoping there was another way. Although his powers were bound, he could still faintly sense souls, and a small handful of strong souls had just come through to the Nether Realm.

"Then we change the rules." The mirrored Morbid suddenly stepped back, and a large dagger materialized in his skeleton hand. Without much pause, the mirrored Morbid thrust his dagger forward. The dagger just stabbed the inside of Morbid's rib-cage. Morbid looked down. The dagger hadn't caused any damage, as he had no body to puncture. When the actual Morbid did nothing, the mirrored Morbid stepped back, almost as if he was in shock.

Seeing the disbelief on his mirrored face, Morbid began to make sense of this final challenge. No matter who was trying to get in, this test was designed to make sure they didn't go any further. The mirrored version was always meant to kill the intruder, possibly when they were tired from fighting. However, Morbid was the exception. He was already dead. This must have been the final trap to ensure that whoever may have survived this far would not make it to Cupido Sacra. The spell was meant to be completed, but the mirrored Morbid could see it hadn't worked. Gathnok's magic hadn't prepared for such a flaw, and because of this the mirrored Morbid felt so much confusion that the spell cancelled out. He took one last look at himself until the spell made him flicker away into the air like smoke from a candle.

Morbid walked on through the damp tunnel towards the beckoning green glow. He had travelled to the Nether Realm, found the dwell of Cupido Sacra, and passed all the tests. Now he could end death and suffering forever.

* * *

Sapphire, Emerald, and Ruby walked out of the tent. Sapphire felt much better since her rest. The sisters had warmed up their bodies as they were preparing for battle. They continued to walk out in front of their small army. Soon EggWiff would be stopped, and they could ensure Cupido Sacra's safety.

"This should be fun," Ruby said with a smile.

"Don't underestimate them." Sapphire was less confident.

"Please, we never lose."

They reached the dragons and patted them by the temple entrance.

"We lost last time. Just make sure he doesn't get a chance to use his magic." Sapphire had a feeling in her stomach which she had never felt before. Something about this day wasn't normal. As the night began to draw in, she had a feeling she needed to say goodbye to the sun.

"We won't. He'll pay, Sister."

Sapphire looked over at Emerald and gave her a smile. They looked over, and on the horizon they saw EggWiff and his friends appear.

"Here . . ."

". . . they . . ."

". . . come!"

They raised their swords ready for the final battle.

"You cannot stop Death"

Chapter Seventeen

Morbid noticed that the dark walls soon began to have a brighter glow of green. Something not far from him must have been emitting some light. He followed the steps which eventually evened out to a level path. They stopped and led through to a great stone corridor with stone tiles lining the floor. The temple looked ancient. In the far distance Morbid could see a rim of green light stuck behind a huge tomb door. He didn't wait but instead sprinted over to the tomb door. The huge stone door was at least twice the size of him. On the door was a picture of a wizard holding a staff. The picture of the staff was engraved into the wall. Morbid knew instantly that the picture was EggWiff and the engraved space was his key to the chamber.

Morbid looked at the locking mechanism. If only the poor fools who built the temple had known the power of Death. Even though his powers were still bound, he hoped he had enough energy to pull off this one last challenge. Morbid placed his skeleton fingers on the tomb door and concentrated. He managed to send a surge of energy which tripped the system. The door rumbled as it slowly rose up high. As it did so, streams of green light shone from behind it. Morbid stepped through to find himself in an enormous underground chamber. The ceiling was as high as the steps he had climbed, but instead of being damp and dark, the chamber was bright and clean. It was lined with stone but also covered in ivy and lush greenery. At the end of the chamber there was a circle of five huge pillars. Each pillar had different coloured flowers growing up them representing the five different Elders. The pillars went straight to the ceiling, which was difficult to see from the floor. Some white stone steps led up to the centre of the circle on which stood a small pedestal and a burning, mystical green jewel – Cupido Sacra.

* * *

EggWiff, Lainla, Gathnok, Saria, Hail, and Minso riding on Emae crossed the desert in a sprint. It wasn't until they could see on the horizon a line of warriors that Emae swooped in low to the ground, and the others stopped so they wouldn't be seen.

"Who are they?" Minso asked.

"The army of a hundred. The ugly triplets command them." Saria was familiar with most armies. She was trained to know as an Amazon.

"They're most likely guarding the tomb." Hail also knew of this army because of the number of times they had stopped his army from attacking Essence storage facilities.

"We'll need to get past them to drop EggWiff at the entrance."

Both Lainla and Gathnok knew everything to do with the jewel, Gathnok because of his history with it, Lainla for the same reason, and being the Spirit of Magic helped.

"Yes, once I'm inside I shall be taken to the jewel immediately. Gathnok and Lainla, how do you plan to navigate through the traps you spoke of?" EggWiff looked concerned.

"A shadow and a ghost should move swiftly enough through the traps unharmed."

"Well, that's fine if you're a ghost and shadow, but we'll not get through." Hail looked concerned. His own army scared him

"Good. We'll need you to hold back the army and give us enough time to awaken the jewel."

"I am no warrior or sorcerer. A former preacher has no place on the battle field." Hail was not about to throw himself into a battle he knew he couldn't win.

"You can ride on Emae. She can fly close enough to drop EggWiff by the entrance. From then on the sight from above could prove useful." Minso patted the bird and tried a reassuring a smile. "We'll hold them back."

Saria nodded. Lainla and Gathnok, like two opposing spirits, walked out into the army. Gathnok's shadowy form weaved amongst the army, hidden by his own darkness. Lainla moved so fast that she was just a trick of light. Both were gradually making their way unseen to the temple entrance. Hail looked nervous about his new-found responsibility. EggWiff seemed less concerned. He looked at the pig. Lately he had come to respect him and no longer deemed him a worthless prisoner.

"Have faith!" EggWiff said. His old face provided much comfort. Hail smiled back before mounting Emae with the help of Minso and Saria. They sat ready before flying off.

"So we'll take fifty each?" Saria was reaching behind her and loading an arrow into her bow.

"I guess." Minso raised his wooden disc ready to throw.

"Minso!" Saria lowered her bow and looked at the warrior.

"It's okay, I'm ready to die for this." However, Minso had no intention of dying and secretly hoped they'd be another way and he could survive. He had promised Fecki he would return, and now more than ever he needed to.

Within moments their first shots were made as they ran towards the army. The army was aware of their position and had turned to face them. Saria fired her arrows with stunning accuracy as she ran, whilst Minso threw his disc every time it was returned. Hail was shakily riding Emae with a stern EggWiff behind him. Many warriors noticed the bird and the odd arrow flung up towards them. However, Emae flew swiftly even under Hail's handling and was too high to be hit.

It seemed like only a breath had passed before Emae swooped down low and hurtled towards the temple entrance. EggWiff was ready, crouched down on Emae, and was ready to take his chance. As the bird swept in and was just low enough, EggWiff leapt off Emae and landed with a thud on the ground. His knee ached as it hit the floor, but as he now had a vast army behind him, he knew he had to take the few steps necessary to be taken to Cupido Sacra. He forced himself up but was soon greeted by the swing of a sword. Luckily, he was low enough to dodge the attack; he rolled and spun round to see his attacker. Emerald, Ruby, and Sapphire stood, each with their weapon ready.

They spoke no words as EggWiff glared into their eyes. Their hatred and determination was painfully clear. The triplets didn't waste much time, as soon they were thrusting their swords and attacking EggWiff. Using his staff, he was able to deflect each of the attacks as he continued to walk back. He knew he only needed to take a few more steps and then he could go and stop Morbid. He felt relieved as he stepped back and felt the ground harden beneath his foot. The triplets slashed with their swords as EggWiff began to fade before them. Unbeknown to EggWiff, as the swords made contact with his staff, the triplets also began to fade with him. They were all being taken to the chamber together.

* * *

EggWiff opened his eyes to find himself in an enormous chamber. The room was filled with green light. He was a little taken back by the sudden transportation, but he was used to suddenly emerging in strange places. He peered round to see Morbid's bare skeleton body walking towards the five great pillars. Although he couldn't see the jewel clearly, he caught glimpses of the bright green glow through Morbid's skeleton frame. It was clear that Morbid was walking towards it, that he was only meters away from Cupido Sacra.

Morbid stopped. He could sense EggWiff in the chamber.

"You killed her!" EggWiff said, holding his staff. He looked majestic and strong.

"I was fighting for a cause, to do what had to be done." Morbid didn't even turn around. He just spoke to the room.

"And that makes it right?"

Morbid turned his head slowly. To see his white face surrounded by bright green light shining in from behind him was very sinister. "Is it not the same cause you are now fighting for?"

"I have not taken a friend's life for that belief – yet." EggWiff raised his staff.

"You wish to fight me, or them?" Morbid tilted his head to the entrance of the chamber.

EggWiff turned to see Sapphire, Emerald, and Ruby

appear at the door to the chamber. EggWiff was alarmed to see them, although it wasn't hard to figure that they had been transported with him.

"Now we can save Sahihriar and get revenge," Emerald said.

"Be a shame if we had missed our chance," Sapphire continued.

"You ready to die?" Ruby finished.

"Listen, if you prevent me from awakening that jewel, then you end all life, all existence forever." EggWiff was pleading for reason, although he knew what he was saying was a hard thing for anyone to believe.

"And in return we must sacrifice Sahihriar?"

"For your belief in something beyond this world?"

"You cannot even offer proof."

"It looks like we've all got our beliefs." Morbid had now turned completely and was walking towards the centre of the chamber.

EggWiff too walked forward, whilst the triplets did the same. Soon they were at a standoff. Only a few meters separated them.

"But you seem to be missing your powers, Morbid. How do you plan to stop us?" EggWiff couldn't help but be smug. Without his powers of Death, Morbid would be an easy opponent.

Morbid didn't say so, but EggWiff was right. Without his powers of Death, destroying them and then the jewel would almost be impossible. He was cursing the Elders for binding him. By doing this, they had gone against everything. His anger, he hoped, would be enough to get him through.

* * *

The grey Elder sat and happily watched the events of day unfold with Morbid so helpless, EggWiff had only worry about the triplets. And even they had no desire to destroy Cupido Sacra, only to take it. It watched as the security of their existence was almost certain. The Elder was well hidden in the Second Realm. It didn't need to be close in order to know what was going on, as it could see all. However, it was this knowledge which also made it know it couldn't hide from its other for long.

"You've been hiding from me." The blue Elder spoke from behind the first.

"You know why, I assume."

"And I wish I didn't. How could you take Death's powers? You tampered with the balance. You threatened everything." The blue light swirled very dark to indicate its anger.

"Death threatens everything. I'm simply ensuring there's a balance to keep. Stop being so blinded by your own light."

"The other Elders agree with me. The battle must be fought on even terms, despite the risk."

"Or maybe you wish to have a different outcome?" The grey Elder knew it was striking a nerve.

"That was another life for all of us. I am merely doing what must be done. Return Death his powers." The Elder turned almost black as it moved its face very close to its companion. The voice was harsh and laced with anger.

The small inn they were in began to tremble as a forceful wind gushed all around it. The beings inside were taken aback, as none of them could see or hear the Elders. Some were flung onto the floor as others began to scream at the strange occurrence.

"Fine! But you have risked us all. I just hope you understand that." The grey Elder didn't shimmer away. Instead it floated up high and gradually became brighter and brighter, knowing there was little more it could do. It went back to the other Elders to watch the coming battle.

The blue Elder also began to take itself back to the other Elders. They had done all they could and now it was up to the beings of Sahihriar to do what was right.

* * *

Morbid stopped and turned and was about to stall for more time. After all, he only needed to reach Cupido Sacra and then he had won. Before his jaw could speak, he felt a strange sensation. He bones rattled, and a force of energy began to seep back into him. He knelt down on one knee and very quickly realised what was happening. EggWiff and the triplets stepped back with caution. Letting out a loud and mighty cry, Morbid stood up and held out his chalky skeleton arms as the dark robe of Death covered him, whilst his weapon of Death formed in his hands. Death's powers were reawakened. He tilted his head up slightly. Morbid was no longer defenceless, and as the look in his opponents faces changed, he prepared for the final fight to begin.

Morbid swung first, causing EggWiff's instincts to counter. Morbid swung his reaper at EggWiff's head. He ducked down and swept under it. He immediately had to hold up his staff. Sapphire's sword swung at him. He was getting too old, and his reflexes weren't as good as they once were. He had mostly relied on magic, but he had no time to perform a spell. Morbid twisted his cloak as it billowed, and he deflected the swords. They were all moving swifter than the wind as they intertwined amongst one another.

EggWiff's staff swiped low as it knocked Ruby to the floor. Morbid went to swing the reaper down onto her, but she rolled and was quickly assisted by her sisters. It was soon apparent to EggWiff that he could not fight four on one, especially when three of them were fighting together. If help didn't arrive soon, he could see himself losing.

* * *

Outside in the open space of the Nether Realm, Saria and Minso found themselves surrounded by the army. They continued to go at them. Luckily, Saria and Minso were easily skilled enough to stay one step ahead. The advantage to their being so many was that many of them had to wait until they saw an opportunity to attack. Saria and Minso were good at fighting even though the army's skills were some of the best in Sahihriar. The only problem was that Saria and Minso would quickly get tired, as every time they knocked a warrior down, another would take his place.

Hail was riding up on Emae far above them. Sometimes he'd call out useful phrases to alert them to a sideways attack or an attack from behind. He was frantic with worry, but he rather liked the fact he was helping from a safe distance. He was doing the Elders' work and that gave him a sense of purpose. In a funny way, the Essence did lead him to his destiny. He took some sense of pleasure in that. He watched as Saria and Minso forced back warrior after warrior.

Emae, however, had glided too close to the entrance of the temple, where one of the triplets' dragons had spotted them. It roared and let out a tiny fireball at Emae. The bird was quick to notice and swooped up higher to compensate. Hail held on tight as he noticed the near miss. He was relieved as the fireball spun off into the sky. He smiled as he looked down at the two warriors who were a little distance away. They were still surrounded by the army. Hail could see a sword about to strike Minso's back.

"Minso, look behind you!"

Minso turned and managed to dodge the attack and slice the warrior through his armour. He looked up to nod his thanks, only to see that one of the small dragons had flown in from behind Emae. It didn't screech and let out a silent, small, but lethal fireball.

Minso was too distracted by further attacks to call out or warn him. The fireball made contact with the back of Emae. Neither bird nor Hail saw it coming as they were thrown out of their flight. Emae twisted in pain, which flung Hail down into the mass of the army. Emae screeched, as her wings didn't flap properly and she was forced down. The army swamped the spots where they fell.

"Saria, I can't get to them!" Minso screamed through the sound of clashing weapons. He was doing all he could to push them back, but there were too many. "Emae won't last long!"

"Neither can I! Hail!" Saria called out for him, but no response came. With that many warriors around them, both Saria and Minso knew that Hail and Emae were lost.

"Minso, we need to protect the entrance. It's too late for them."

Both Saria and Minso had fought their way rather close to the entrance. If they went back to confirm what they already knew, then they might never reach the tomb.

* * *

Gathnok and Lainla reached the chamber rather quickly. They could hear the clashing of the weapons halfway down the steps. Gathnok stood and saw the chamber that he had seen only once before many, many years ago. Lainla instantly found the pedestal and hovered over to it. Although a ghost, she was still a spirit and would do her best to protect the essence of magic. It was her duty.

Gathnok saw EggWiff struggling against the constant attacks and immediately leapt into action. He ran up, and without losing stride he leapt in the air, and using his two legs he kicked Morbid in his exposed rib cage. This sent Morbid hurtling back to hit the wall with a thud. His bones began to become disjointed, but he was prepared. He used his magic to fly them back into their sockets. With his reaper in hand, he prepared to fight Gathnok.

EggWiff immediately felt the difference. Now he could focus on the three sisters. They didn't seem too distracted by Gathnok's interference. They each took a turn in lunging at him, but he was fast enough to respond. Sapphire hit high mostly, so naturally he'd duck low, but the other sisters had learnt to go low at the same time. Thankfully, his ivory staff was long enough to block two sword attacks at once.

Morbid stood high and tilted his head slightly. There was something sinister in this small gesture. Gathnok stood ready. He didn't have a weapon, but he didn't need one. He had years of warrior experience behind him.

"You thought you were so frightening in that forest."

"You were very convincing. Who knew you were simply playing along?" Gathnok once wanted the power of the jewel for his own selfish vendetta. Now he just wanted to do what he could to make things better.

"I did what I had to, to ensure that Sahihriar wasn't the only world. My father saw what happened and what was meant to happen. You risked it all."

"And now you oppose those teachings." Gathnok was stalling. He knew they'd fight soon, but the more they talked, the less energy would have to be used by both of them.

"Why make way for future worlds that will only be full of more pain and death?"

"Because it's not our decision to make." Gathnok was tired of talking. Morbid was too far lost in grief for his father to be reasoned with.

He moved forward and tried to grab the reaper. Morbid

was ready and twisted the reaper, forcing Gathnok to let go. It was followed by a kick in his shadowy stomach.

Lainla watched as she saw EggWiff fighting the three sisters and to see Gathnok fight Morbid. Although she was aware it wasn't what she should be focusing on, she couldn't help but feel a small sense of happiness to see the two family members fighting side by side once more.

EggWiff was busy fighting Sapphire, Emerald, and Ruby. He knew he had to do something fast, as three on one were still difficult odds. They were relentless and terribly strong. Their thirst to win was intense. Over on the other side, Gathnok and Morbid continued to fight at such a speed no mortal eyes could keep up.

Lainla could see EggWiff needed some assistance. There was a move she had taught EggWiff long ago. Gathnok was too conventional to teach Marvie less "traditional" moves in combat. She called out his name, which caused him to look over. Even the sisters caught a glance. Lainla held up two fingers and then pointed. At first EggWiff didn't have a clue what she was doing. It wasn't until he was back fighting for his life that he remembered. Lainla smiled as she saw the twinkle in his eye. "Two-point" was a move he had been taught, which got two foes at one time. He had to remember the timing and the sequence right. If he were wrong, then it could give an opening to the stronger and faster sisters.

He saw his chance and took it. He rolled to the side as fast and as fluid as his tall old body could allow. Two of the sisters immediately moved forward to attack. In that moment Emerald was standing directly in front of Sapphire. EggWiff spun round on his heel a full ninety degrees. Seizing the moment, he struck the pointed edge of his staff through the chest of Emerald. Her eyes widened with shock as it plunged deeper and cut the stomach of Sapphire. They didn't scream. They didn't have to. Ruby, who saw it all in a flash, was stuck dead in her tracks. EggWiff removed the staff and stepped back as the two bodies slumped the floor. Both were now dead. Ruby stared at her dead sisters, her eyes filled with water, but the tears remained on her eye lids. Her face turned to one of pure fury.

"I will kill you now!" Ruby raised her sword. She was determined to save Sahihriar – even if she had to do it on her own.

EggWiff just smiled. "Please try." His confidence had returned. With only one sister left, he could now make use of his real power – his magic.

* * *

Saria and Minso found themselves into the mouth of the entrance. They weren't going to go onto the stairs, but once they were under the shelter of the temple entrance, it meant the dragons' balls of fire couldn't hurt them. However, being angled down on the stairs meant they were now fighting upwards. This meant they were now at a huge disadvantage.

"You'd think they'd be better?" Minso was smiling as he was once again duelling with yet another one of the warrior drones. His arrogance was blatant once more.

"Don't be too smug. We're not out of this yet." Saria's arm was in agony, yet she continued to slice and kick back the drone warriors. She only hoped that soon the jewel would be awakened and it would be over.

"Please, Amazon, I could fight these in my . . ." Minso felt the cold steel cut through his heart. "Fecki . . ." His body became numb, and all he could think about was how he had failed Fecki and the others.

Saria yelled as she avenged him with one motion. She quickly grabbed Minso's arms and dragged him back further down to get some distance between them. She knelt over him and stared into his eyes. She didn't say anything. Instead she stood up to confront the oncoming danger. However, as she turned to get up, Minso grabbed her arm.

"Make sure they finish it." With this, Minso rolled his head and slipped away.

Saria's mind flashed back to Flick as he fell to the floor. At least Minso wasn't killed by her hand. She stood up and looked back down the stairs into the darkness. Whatever was going on below, they were about to be joined by a lot of warriors. She turned and ran down into the darkness with the army following.

* * *

As Gathnok and Morbid continued to fight, so did EggWiff and Ruby. Ruby's anger had fuelled her fighting, and she was now waving her sword. Her speed, strength, and reflexes were astonishing, but it barely compared to fighting against all three. He remained on the defence, allowing Ruby to slightly exhaust herself. He knew he wouldn't get many chances. After a flurry of many attacks, he watched Ruby's chest. Her breath had quickened, and he saw that small moment she took to recover. Seizing this moment, he swung his staff into her ribs. She ducked at the pain. As she did so, he raised his staff high and hit her hard under the chin, forcing her to fly off her feet and land hard on her back.

EggWiff had thought about what spell would be appropriate, but he quickly realised it didn't matter. According to Hail's vision, once the jewel was awakened, they'd all be destroyed. He decided on a simple transportation spell. It would use a lot of energy, but at least it would be one less being's blood on his hands.

He raised his staff, which caused Ruby to grab the end. She clearly thought he wished to kill her in the same manner as her sisters. Instead he nodded his appreciation of a good battle. In a lot of ways he understood their cause.

"Removiera!"

Ruby looked ready to scream as blue energy dripped down from the bottom of the staff and almost drowned her in the energy. Then suddenly it was as if the energy had pushed her down into the floor. She was gone. EggWiff knelt down. His body ached. He had to move faster than he had for years, and he had just performed a potent spell which almost drained him. He only hoped he had enough to awaken the mystical jewel.

He turned to see Morbid still lost in battle with Gathnok. This might be the best chance he had of awakening Cupido Sacra. His legs ached, but he willed himself to start walking silently towards the pedestal. He began to pick up stride as he came closer and closer. Lainla floated behind it, willing him to move quicker.

He was only a few meters away, when the wind howled. He turned to see the reaper of Death flung only a few inches in front of him. The blade landed sharply into the edge of one of the pillars. He turned to see Morbid staring at him and Gathnok kneeling on the ground.

"You killed my father!" Morbid showed no sign of fatigue or injury from his battle with Gathnok.

"And you killed my friend!" EggWiff forced himself to stand up straight but was secretly leaning most of his weight on his staff. He honestly couldn't survive a battle with Morbid.

"Do you think this is what Trickle wanted?" Morbid questioned, knowing his weak spot.

"I know it is. She'd sacrifice her life and few others if it meant those lives could exist and have a chance to be reborn. I'm honouring her memory. You simply defy your father's."

Morbid's head turned as he heard the tomb door begin to quake as it slowly closed. They waited to see what caused this entrapment, and they were answered by Saria rolling through at the last moment. Continuing her roll, she flipped herself up onto her feet as the door closed behind her. She looked back and then looked at the others.

"Thank the Elders for bow and arrows! We're going to have to hurry. That door won't hold them back for long." The intense stand-off had clearly gone completely over Saria's head. "We're still fighting him, aren't we?" Saria suddenly caught on. With this, she withdrew her blood-soaked blade and prepared for one final fight.

"You can't take us all," Gathnok said. He hoped he wasn't wrong.

The door banged heavily. Clearly the army was using extreme force to get through.

"Morbid, just accept that we've won. Whether we destroy Cupido Sacra or use it, Sahihriar is still destroyed." Lainla looked at the skeleton of Death.

"Your father risked everything so this could come to pass. He wanted there to be hope of new worlds, to give birth to the Elders so Sahihriar could be born to begin. Do you really want his existence to mean nothing?" Lainla had now floated towards him as she spoke. Her compassion and sensitivity were still strong, even if she were a ghostly image. "Let us do this. If the jewel doesn't give birth to a new world, you have my word as Spirit of Magic to let you destroy it."

Morbid stopped and thought. He had killed Message for this cause – a fight he did believe in. He was just so tired of the pain. He was still so angry at EggWiff for killing his father, but deep down he knew that couldn't be an excuse. His father hated Gathnok for what he let himself become due to grief, and now Morbid had become just as bad.

EggWiff heard a sound he thought he'd never hear again – the chattering of Morbid's jaw as he cried.

"I just want the pain to stop!"

Lainla floated over and kissed his hollow head. "Bless you, Morbid! Your body may be empty, but your heart is not."

Morbid fell to his knees and continued to chatter. He had wished so many times that he had tears to cry for his pain. The tomb door banged violently again.

"Okay, we need to be awakening quickly!" Saria knew what was behind the door, and she was in no mood to do battle with them again.

"Hail and Minso?" Lainla asked.

Saria turned and looked at her. "They're not coming."

"Jago would be proud." EggWiff smiled at the comforting thought of the two of them at peace as he turned and faced the mystical jewel.

"You remember what to do?" Gathnok had walked up beside EggWiff. They had discussed the spell to awaken the jewel back in the forest.

"Yes, once I've awakened it, you'll then channel your magic through it, triggering Hail's vision."

"Good to know you were listening!" Gathnok and EggWiff walked up the steps and stood either side of the pedestal.

Gathnok looked into the eyes of Lainla for a final time. However, something inside him knew he'd see her again.

"I'll see you soon, my love," Lainla replied, as if she could read what he was thinking.

EggWiff looked down at Saria. She had transformed since he had known her. At first she was a ruthless warrior, but somehow now she was so much more.

"It was an honour, Amazon." With this, EggWiff bowed.

He almost said something to the distraught Morbid, but somehow he lacked the compassion.

"Ready, nephew?"

"Always, uncle!"

The green light illuminated Gathnok's face to show his smile and warmth at EggWiff's response. EggWiff placed his hand onto Cupido Sacra and immediately felt the energy rush through him. He struggled to focus his thoughts as Gathnok had instructed him. He reached into his mind and thought about Trickle and her crazy mind techniques. That process of focus and determination seemed to help him block out some of the overwhelming sense of power. He managed to clear his mind the best he could and began to chant the spell. He was too lost in his own energy to even hear himself speak the words as the light grew brighter and brighter. The energy began to hurt his arm. He yelled as he forced himself to cling on as the words continued over and over. Cupido Sacra glowed brighter than before, almost blinding the watchful audience. Once the jewel dimmed slightly Gathnok knew it had been awakened. Choosing to use its strength at its fullest, he too placed his hand on the top of the jewel and yelled as the awesome sensation of power surged through him, a feeling he never dreamt he would feel again.

Saria and Lainla watched, ignoring the slamming of the tomb door as it began to crumble slightly.

Gathnok and EggWiff yelled as the power grew. EggWiff knew his part was done, but the magic was holding him. Gathnok knew it was his destiny to end what he had started many generations before. He thought back to all the pain and destruction the jewel had caused – the death and sorrow, Trickle, Flick, Hail, Minso, Hail's army, his own army – all of them destroyed. He closed his eyes and saw images of Lainla lying on the floor with her blood-stained chest. The first time he believed he'd lost her, the sorrow within his soul had fuelled the jewel with emptiness and darkness, something the jewel was never meant for.

Suddenly the jewel let out mighty beams of green light. The room shook as Gathnok and EggWiff were hurtled back. Neither of the bodies made it to the wall. EggWiff's body glowed blue before shining upwards. Gathnok's shadowy form twisted and shone a faint orange before also shining upwards. Saria could only blink before she too was awash with light. Her body crumbled and left a faint green blinding light that followed the essence of EggWiff and Gathnok. Despite her importance, it wasn't long before Lainla was hit, and her body glowed a soft purple and headed towards the stars. Morbid was last. His bones fell as a heap, before a small grey light appeared and followed the others up. Each of them had been reborn.

However, the jewel continued to burn, and in doing so, it began the destruction of the Nether Realm. The beams of green light soon spread, destroying everything in their path. The tomb began to crumble as the army of a hundred were gone within moments. Once they broke ground, the lights stopped acting as a powerful beam and instead swirled up high like huge giant jets, just as Hail's vision had foretold. Soon the vast lands of the Nether Realm had been swallowed, and the power of the jets bled through into Sahihriar. It was only moments before the Forest of Lost Souls was destroyed and all four of the Elemental Mountains. Many beings tried spells. Many tried to run. However, nothing worked. Even the screams of the people were swallowed by the jewel.

It wasn't just in Sahihriar either. Soon the jets bled through into the other realms, swallowing their existence too. If anything was linked to magic, then the jewel would destroy it.

From space the jets stretched over Sahihriar like the giant legs of a spider. Soon it was completely wrapped in Cupido Sacra's hold. Then, as if it were effortless, the jets grew tighter, causing the planet to rupture before exploding out into the universe. The destruction sent a shock wave that destroyed the empty and inhabitable moon next to it but left the second one intact. The stars themselves could shudder at such destruction.

And then as if it had never occurred. Everything became still. The only difference was that Sahihriar and everything that was part of it was now totally destroyed. However, the universe continued, and a greater power had been born. This power meant that Sahihriar could be reborn from its destruction, and in many years to follow a new world could be born – all thanks to four unlikely prisoners . . . who all became victims of fate.

* * *

And that is how it was meant to be. The quest was finished, and the Elders had been born. However, that is not how this story ends. Outer space was still for only a moment, and the Elders had barely begun to become aware, when suddenly space began to stir again. The shock wave began to reappear and shrink backwards. The destroyed moon reappeared as the planet fragments came hurtling back into place. Sahihriar was coming back into form as the green stems of Cupido Sacra appeared and disappeared. Time was reversing; which meant someone was changing the time line. Someone was interfering with the quest, and whoever it was had access to great power.

Now the chamber was back, and everyone was standing in it as time resumed. The green light illuminated Gathnok's face to show his smile and warmth at EggWiff's response. EggWiff and Gathnok were moments away from placing their hands onto Cupido Sacra, when suddenly they saw a flash of a white light appear in the centre of the chamber. Saria stepped back and drew her sword. Lainla looked on curiously. EggWiff looked at Gathnok and then back at Morbid, but he was still kneeling. They looked again as it flashed and sparked, and soon a swirling white oval appeared in the centre of the chamber. They looked on anxiously, waiting to see what form of attack or being might present itself. They tensed and watched as four beings emerged from the portal . . .

End of Book I

Lightning Source UK Ltd.
Milton Keynes UK
175846UK00001B/8/P